KENTUCKY
Brides

Three Romances Complicate
a Simple Way of Historic Life

LAURALEE BLISS · IRENE B. BRAND · YVONNE LEHMAN

D0973031

BARBOUR
PUBLISHING

Into the Deep © 2006 by Lauralee Bliss
Where the River Flows © 2006 by Irene B. Brand
Moving the Mountain © 2006 by Yvonne Lehman

ISBN 978-1-59789-850-8

All rights reserved. No part of this publication may be reproduced or transmitted in any form or by any means without written permission of the publisher.

All scripture quotations are taken from the King James Version of the Bible.

This book is a work of fiction. Names, characters, places, and incidents are either products of the author's imagination or used fictitiously. Any similarity to actual people, organizations, and/or events is purely coincidental.

Published by Barbour Publishing, Inc., P.O. Box 719, Uhrichsville, Ohio 44683, www.barbourbooks.com

Our mission is to publish and distribute inspirational products offering exceptional value and biblical encouragement to the masses.

 Member of the
Evangelical Christian
Publishers Association

Printed in the United States of America.

Into the Deep

Dedication

To Tracie who believed in my historical writing.
Thank you for your support.
My heartfelt thanks to park rangers
Vickie Carson and Joy Lyons
of Mammoth Cave National Park
for all their help and insight.
Special thanks to my husband, Steve,
who tirelessly spent days making phone calls
and arranging for a special cave tour and information.

Chapter 1

Kentucky 1843

A bang on the door awoke Jared Edwards with a start. He rubbed the sleep from his eyes and gazed out the window to see the faint rays of a new dawn just beginning to brighten the sky. He struggled to stand, even as a yawn broke across his face. Shuffling to the fireplace, he lit a candle from a banked ember. It was time he got up anyway. The cow needed milking, and he promised Uncle Dwight he would help plow up the fields.

Jared came to the door, still bleary-eyed from sleep, to find the shadowy image of his uncle standing outside. The man's nightshirt hung out of his pants, which he had obviously donned in haste. The silhouette of horses hitched to a wagon stood against the backdrop of the rising sun. Within the wagon were piles of quilts and what appeared to be his aunt Mattie's trunk.

"Something's wrong, Jared."

Instantly, he found himself alert. "What? What's the matter, Uncle?"

The older man was visibly trembling. Jared stepped aside to allow him in. "It's Mattie. Someone came by to tell me she's doing very poorly. She's in a deep sleep and won't wake up."

Jared stared. *How can that be?* They had only left Mattie a short time ago in Dr. Croghan's care.

"We're going to the cave just as soon as you're ready." Uncle Dwight shuffled inside. He sat down heavily at the small table that Jared had pieced together with leftover oak planks. He ran fingers through his brown hair streaked with gray. "Why did I let you talk me into taking her to that terrible place? A cave of all things! Mattie was safe here. She was happy. She had me to take care of her and not some strange doctor." He again ran his fingers through his hair. "I have to get her out of there. She needs to leave that place and come home."

Jared bit his lip as he headed to the back room to put on some clothes. Just yesterday, when he visited his uncle's place, he found Uncle Dwight staring at a small portrait of Aunt Mattie as a young woman. His stubby finger traced every part of her features while his blue eyes filled with tears. Even then, Jared began questioning the decision he had made. But in his opinion, they had no choice. If they didn't do something, Mattie would have surely died.

When Jared heard that Dr. Croghan had built huts inside a nearby cave to help cure those sick with consumption, he had immediately gone to inquire.

Standing there among the curious onlookers, he saw the man with his head held high, his strong voice echoing in the wooded glade.

"Mammoth Cave has given proof of its magical qualities," Dr. Croghan had stated to the awestruck throng massed before him. "As you know, we have found the remains of Indians perfectly preserved within the cave, without a hint of decay. We have found the air to be of a constant temperature and humidity. And in Mammoth Cave, I have built cottages where the invalids may be cured of their pulmonary infections, rheumatism, even diseases of the eye. And I say that it will do far better for them than any medicine an apothecary can dispense."

Raucous applause accompanied the cheers. What the good doctor described was nothing short of a miracle from on high. Jared couldn't wait to tell Uncle Dwight what he had learned.

When he came home that night, he found his dear aunt doubled over in a coughing spell, clutching a lacy handkerchief tinged with bright red blood—the telltale sign of the dreadful disease that had plagued her for several months. He immediately told his uncle the doctor's claims that the cave could cure Aunt Mattie's consumption. "This must be the answer we've been praying for."

"By putting her in some dark cave?" Uncle Dwight frowned, shaking his head, his broad forehead creased in worry.

"How else could Indians from long ago be kept without decay as the doctor said? The air in the cave must have something miraculous in it. We have to try, Uncle. If we don't do something, she'll die."

"But Mattie will be so far away from me. So far away." He looked back at the bedroom door, slightly ajar. The sounds of her hacking cough echoed from within. "Can I visit her there?"

Jared shook his head. "Not from what I hear, not while she's in the cave anyway. It won't be long until she starts feeling better. Then she'll be home."

"Mattie and I haven't been separated since the day we were married. We've always been together, through the good and the bad. Even when the good Lord didn't give us children, at least we had each other."

Jared sighed. "But the only way you can stay together is if she gets well," he continued in earnest. "Please, Uncle. I believe this is the answer."

A look of resignation finally fell over his uncle's weary features. "All right; I will let her go for a short time. Better we are parted now than forever. And you've always had a good head about things, Jared. Better than that brother of mine who takes his family off to some strange place. I'm mighty glad you didn't go with them. I don't know what we would do without you."

❧

Jared hoped that same trust his uncle had laid in him back then, when he agreed to take his aunt Mattie to the cave, still remained today, with this latest news of his aunt's deteriorating health. He feared a worse fate might have befallen them, a fate more dreadful than the consumption itself. He yanked on a pair of broadcloth trousers and shrugged into a shirt and coat. He stomped his feet into a pair of leather boots and lit a lantern with his shaky hand. *What if Aunt Mattie dies?* The mere thought made him shudder. *God, please help her. She can't die. She can't.*

He ventured into the main cabin where his uncle still sat, staring into the fire. "I'm bringing her back here," Dwight barked. "No use talking me out of it. Mattie's coming home with me. No more doctors and no more living in that cave."

Jared said nothing. The sun had barely begun to reveal the tip of its golden head when they stepped outside. A faint mist hung over the rolling Kentucky landscape. A distinct pattern of lantern light glowed in the distance as neighboring families went about their morning chores. Jared and his uncle climbed onto the jockey seat of the wagon. Jared took the reins and ushered the horses to the main road that led toward the cave.

"I don't care what you say," Uncle Dwight continued. "I know you told me to do this. But if she's getting worse, what are we gonna do?"

Jared had no answer. Without a miracle, Mattie would die—whether in the cave or at home. But he prayed it was not the former. Many times Jared had sought the Lord for a miracle that would revive his aunt. Dr. Croghan and his cave seemed God's perfect answer.

The creaking of the wagon along the rutted road provided a sad serenade to the ride, its melancholy tune broken only by an occasional bird singing merrily from an overhanging tree limb. Jared wished for the right words to say to comfort his uncle, but his mind was a blank. Maybe he should tell his uncle to keep praying and trusting in the Lord.

Long ago, Jared explained to his uncle how, after a preacher on horseback shared with him the message of the Savior's love, Jared accepted Christ as his personal Savior. It was the power of Jared's rebirth, experienced here in Kentucky, which kept him home while his father took his siblings and mother and headed for St. Louis. His father had grown weary of trying to make a living in the exhausted Kentucky soil. Uncle Dwight thought his brother foolish to leave, and he told him so. Dwight then begged Jared to stay on and help him keep up the farm. At first, Jared found the prospect of leaving this place for another intriguing. But he also loved Ol' Kentuck. Not only had he been born here physically, but spiritually as well. This land had left its imprint on his heart and soul. And here he stayed to help his aunt and uncle and to live out his own life, by the grace of God.

It was midmorning by the time they reached the Mammoth Hotel, where visitors came to rest, eat a good meal, and take tours of the famous cave nearby. He had not yet stopped the wagon when an attractive woman bounded from the hotel entrance, her face all smiles. She wore a large straw hat tied with a blue ribbon. The white lawn of her dress, peeking out from beneath the dark cloak, shimmered like new-fallen snow in early winter. She was a vision of bright sunshine on a cool, foggy morning.

"Good morning. And how are you this fine day?"

Jared stared, taken aback by the cheery greeting on a somber day like today.

"We are about ready to leave for the first tour of Mammoth Cave this morning," she went on. "Only fifty cents for the short tour. And it is the most popular."

Fifty cents! Who has that kind of money to spend on a hole in the ground? "We aren't here for any tour," Jared stated flatly. "We came to see Dr. Croghan."

She stepped back as if surprised they were not going to be a part of some frolic within the cavern depths. "I'm sorry. The doctor is inside the cave at the moment, caring for the poor invalids."

"One of them is my aunt. We were told she is very ill. Please send for him."

She stood there as if uncertain what she should do. Finally, she whirled, her cloak billowing about her like a dark cloud. A trace of the sweet scent she wore lingered in the air and reminded him of wildflowers amid the tall grass. Jared had to admit that women were not in the forefront of his thoughts these days. He had too much work to do, what with tending to his place and looking after Uncle Dwight's fields. But the brief encounter with this lovely lady—her smile, her charm, her beauty—awakened something within him, something he would have liked to consider further were it not for his concerns over Aunt Mattie and the farm to tend.

Jared turned his sights back to the hotel into which she had disappeared. Built close to the famous hole in the ground, the hotel formed an impressive sight, comprised of many wooden dwellings, some with several floors. No doubt the young woman knew little of a farmer's life. She had grown up wearing fancy frocks and spending her days in large rooms with fine furniture. He lived in his own small two-room cabin that he and his uncle built by the sweat of their brow. The furniture was handmade. The only items of finery were those provided by Aunt Mattie to "spruce up the place and make it more of a home," as she would say. Lace doilies, a tablecloth she had sewn, a quilt on the straw-filled bed, and occasionally, a vase filled with flowers gathered from the meadow. He couldn't imagine the fine lady he'd just seen living in his humble cabin, even walking with him down some path or sharing a wagon ride under the rays of the fading sun. They were far too different, like night was to day.

Jared sat still in the wagon seat, fiddling with the leather reins. Beside him, Uncle Dwight had not uttered a word. While they waited, Jared saw the wide road leading down to the cave's entrance. It beckoned him and the other visitors to come and enter the murky depths. What was it about this cave that tempted people to pay good money to behold? He had to admit there was a strange lure to it. It drew him in a way he did not understand. Maybe it was the excitement of the unknown, of a new place he had never laid eyes on and existing right beneath his feet.

But at that moment, the lure of a hole in the ground paled in comparison to his concern for Aunt Mattie's failing health. A hard lump filled his throat. What would he do if something happened to her? What would his uncle say?

"Uncle, I'm going to see if I can find this Dr. Croghan myself." Jared jumped to the ground.

"Yes, find him, nephew, and bring him here. In fact, if you can manage it, bring Mattie back, too. I want to take her home. I have plenty of quilts, so she'll be snug and warm. Even brought her favorite dress to wear."

Jared nodded. He left the wagon and ventured down the trail that led to the opening of Mammoth Cave, nicknamed the Wonder of Wonders. He remembered the day he and Uncle Dwight left Mattie here. His uncle clung to her, weeping, even as she patted his shoulder. "Now don't you go fussing, Dwight. I'll be fine and dandy." Jared had to admit a cave seemed a strange place to leave a frail woman. The cave breathed like some living thing. A cool gust of wind blew from within, carrying with it a strange, earthy odor. Jared's breath caught, remembering how Aunt Mattie and others like her were led away into the darkness to some huts built inside. But that doctor was confident the cave would cure them. This must be God's answer to Jared's heartfelt plea. Mattie walked in there sick, but she would come out healed of her affliction. Jared believed it. He had to believe it, even now.

Just then he heard a commotion. Several men appeared from the hotel and headed toward the cave entrance, bearing an empty stretcher and several lanterns. Another man lagged behind and stopped short when he saw Jared.

"You aren't supposed to be here unless you're taking a tour."

"I need to find out about my aunt who is in Dr. Croghan's care," Jared said to him. "Do you know where the doctor can be found?"

The man grimaced. "Go back to the hotel, and we will let the doctor know you were inquiring."

"But my uncle wishes to see him. He wants to take my aunt home. Her name is Mattie Edwards."

"We will let the doctor know. Now go on."

When they turned their attention away, Jared hastened for a stout tree, ducking behind it to observe the goings-on. The men with flickering lanterns entered the mouth of the cave. The breeze from within blew out several of the lanterns. He waited, wondering what would happen. He rubbed his arms. His teeth began to chatter. This wasn't from the effects of cold but a growing fear mixed with uncertainty. To him, the cave entrance was like the opening of some gigantic beast, swallowing up the innocent like the huge fish that consumed Jonah. He prayed it had not swallowed up his aunt in death.

For a long time, he waited. Then a new noise erupted from the entrance, startling him. He heard excited voices and then saw the men appear once more, bearing the stretcher. Rubbing his eyes, he stared harder, only to have his stomach lurch. The men carried a white shrouded figure, the face covered by a cloth.

He swallowed hard. His limbs trembled. *Please God, no.* He rushed forward.

"Go back!" they ordered. "You are not to be here!"

"Please, you must tell me who this is. Please, I have to know."

The men paused and looked at each other.

"W—we were told she was very ill," Jared went on, unable to steady his tremulous voice. "Her name is Mattie Edwards. Please tell me if that's her or not."

He saw the glow of recognition in their faces. Then came the nods that confirmed his fear. "Yes. She died this morning. I'm sorry."

Sweat broke out across his brow. He covered his face. What he dreaded most had come to pass.

Aunt Mattie. Dead.

He turned away and stumbled up the path. The tears clouded his vision. How would he ever tell his uncle the terrible news?

Jared gazed upon the ghostlike face of the woman whom he had come to love like a mother. Mattie's final resting place would be the burial ground not far from the Mammoth Hotel. Beside him, loud wails rose from Uncle Dwight. His uncle's grieving began the moment Jared gave the sorrowful news and continued until now, as they looked upon her in a silent state of death. She was dressed in her wedding gown of flowered calico, which Dwight had packed in her trunk. Her hands clasped the few yellow lilies the young lady at the hotel offered. Jared fingered a lone flower from the bouquet given by the woman in the white dress and gazed at its beauty before looking at his aunt one last time.

When the coffin was nailed shut and the burial completed, Uncle Dwight's wails came to an abrupt end. He turned to face Jared. His face grew red. His fists clenched. It began as a mutter within him and then grew to a roar filled with pain.

"You killed her!"

"Uncle?"

"You did it. You're to blame. You killed her just as sure as I'm standing here."

Jared stared in disbelief. "Uncle, please." Tears clouded his eyes. "I loved Aunt Mattie. I would never. . ."

"Y–you made me send her to—to that death cave. You told me I could trust you. You told me that doctor could cure her. Now she's gone! My sweet Mattie is gone forever." He waved his fist, nearly striking him.

"Uncle. . ."

"Get out of my life! I don't ever want to see you again!"

His throat clogged. His stomach rolled into knots. He shook his head, even as Uncle Dwight continued to shout at him. The death knell had sounded, not only for Mattie but also for himself.

He whirled, not knowing what to do. In the distance stood the young woman from the hotel, the one who had given him the flowers. She had witnessed this whole, awful scene unfold in this place of death. Jared caught but a fleeting glimpse of her white dress, so like an angel, before he ran off into the rolling hills.

Chapter 2

1841—two years earlier

Potato soup and corn bread. Corn bread and potato soup. Susanna watched the soup trickle from her spoon into the bowl of cold watery broth that comprised her main meal. A foot kicked her. She peered underneath to see the feet of her younger brother, stretched to her side of the table. "Stop kicking me, Henry."

"I ain't done nothing," he retorted before his foot slammed into her leg once more.

The elbow of her older brother, Luke, jarred her the next moment, upsetting the spoon. Down the front of her calico ran the watery potato broth, staining her only dress that still looked presentable.

"Luke! How could you! Look at my dress."

"It's just an old dress."

"It was an accident," Mother added. "He didn't mean it."

That was her life these days, one accident after another. Couldn't anyone see how miserable this was? How miserable *she* was?

Enough was enough. She fled the table, running to her secret place, a rock-laden area by a babbling brook. Many a day she came to sit here and contemplate, to throw her woes into the brook and wish for better times. She picked up a stone and threw it hard into the water. *Why, God?* she wondered, gazing into the leafy branches of the trees. It was difficult enough that she never had any new clothes to wear like her friend Polly at the neighboring farm. But now she had a stain on the only dress that didn't have a hole in it, and from awful potato soup, at that. How she longed for pretty dresses of silk, a new bonnet, leather shoes without holes. She wanted something better to eat than cold potato soup and dried corn bread for dinner. She wanted a place where she could eat in peace without having to be bumped and kicked by her brothers. Three times a day they crowded around the tiny table for meals. She could imagine a large home with a separate dining room. The long table would keep her seated far away from her brothers. And she would sit there in a gown of lace all by herself and enjoy every morsel of the fine victuals.

Instead, she was poor, homely, hungry Susanna Barnett in a ratty dress. Susanna threw another stone into the water, watching it disappear. If only her troubles would likewise sink beneath such sweet and refreshing water. If only life could be fair and pleasant instead of harsh and difficult. Day after day, her father tried to make a living from the farm. Day after day, he came home groaning about the rocks, his lazy sons, the mule with a sore in its hoof, and how he wanted to go west with the first wagon trains. "There's nothing here," he complained to Mother. "No food. Can't work the ground. We have no future in Kentucky."

Mother refused to even consider leaving. This was her home, she claimed. Grandma lived in Elizabethtown. Grandpappy was buried here. They had their friends and the little church where they went for services every Sunday. And she hated the thought of traveling so far in a wagon with all the dust, the harsh weather, and the strange Indians.

"But everyone is talking about going out West. The land here is too tired." Papa sat down hard on the stool. "I'm too tired."

They were all weary, so weary they could barely rise to greet the new day. Susanna hoped that one day Mother would wake up and agree to go out West. To her it seemed the answer. She had heard of Oregon Territory from neighbors who wanted to follow in the footsteps of a man called Dr. Whitman. He had ventured successfully westward with his wife and now called on others to follow. Once in Oregon Territory, her family could build a large house and raise plenty of food to eat. They would pull out carrots as long as the tines on a pitchfork and potatoes as big as the stones that pitted the Kentucky ground. Game would fill the land in great abundance. A life of paradise in a land of plenty.

Suddenly she heard a terrible sound and horses in distress. She leaped to her feet and whirled about. To her horror, she saw a wagon turned on its side and what appeared to be someone caught underneath, shouting for help. Immediately, Susanna came to the man's side. His face was pinched, his voice scratchy. His red hair reflected the rays of sun. He reached out his hand to her. "Help me, please. My leg is trapped. Get help!"

"I'll get help, sir," she said and raced off to the cabin. "Papa, Papa! There's been an accident. A man is caught under his wagon down the road a piece."

Papa and her brothers wasted no time hightailing it to the wagon and the man caught beneath the jockey seat. In no time, they had the wagon erect. Papa stooped to help the man to a sitting position.

"Oh, my leg," the man groaned, grabbing hold of it. Slowly, he sat back down.

"We'll fetch a doctor," Papa said. "Luke, saddle Honey and go get Doc Hodgens."

"There's no need. I'm a doctor," he managed to say.

"You're a doctor?"

"John Croghan. I—I'm sure you've heard of me. I own the big cave. Mammoth Cave." He then began taking off his shirt and ripping it into strips. "Fetch me some tree limbs, boy," he ordered Luke. "Good stout ones. Not too big but not too small. I don't think my injury is serious. Likely just a sprain, but sometimes you can't tell."

"Don't know if I've heard of that cave," Papa said. "Of course I know there are plenty of caves around."

"I know where one is!" Luke added as he handed the doctor the tree branches and watched him bind the wood to his limb with the strips of cloth. "Do you really own your own cave?"

"Yes, young man, I do. I own the biggest cave in this region—" He finished tying off the makeshift splint with a grunt. He sat back with a sigh. "Largest cave in the world, as a matter of fact."

The questions from Henry and Luke came all at once, like a fleet of arrows loosed upon a target. "Where is it? What does it look like? Where do the passages go? What is there to see?"

"That's enough," Papa said. "Right now we need to get the good doctor somewhere safe. I hope my humble home will do for now."

"Thank you, I'm sure."

Together the brothers and Papa assisted the man to the wagon and guided the horses back to the farm. Susanna followed behind, looking at the man laid out in the back of the wagon with his leg bound by limbs and cloth. Her heart thumped within her. This was no ordinary man who had stumbled upon their farm. It was someone rich and famous who owned a magnificent cave. It seemed too good to be true. Perhaps even an answer to prayer.

When they had settled the doctor in Luke's bed, the boys immediately crowded around, asking him all about the cave he owned. Susanna brought the doctor a tin cup of warm milk as he described a wonder of wonders beneath the surface, a place where nothing ever decayed, a place that God Himself etched out of solid rock with His finger. The boys' eyes grew large. They stood fixed in place, never moving an inch, absorbing every word the man said like dry ground beneath a cloudburst.

"I want to go there," Henry declared.

"I'd like to live in a place like that," Luke added.

Dr. Croghan chuckled, sipping on the milk. "If you're going to live there, you'll still have to grow your food in the outside world. You could build yourselves small cottages inside the cave, I suppose. It's certainly big enough. I once even considered putting a library inside the cave myself. How great it would be to study in such magnificence." He grew quiet then. "But it's very dark in the cave. Black as night. Damp. You can hear the water trickling. But it stays a constant temperature."

"I'd grow my corn outside and bring it in," Luke decided. "And use plenty of lanterns."

"Can't grow crops nowhere around here," Papa said thoughtfully. "In fact, one can hardly grow a kernel of corn in this ground. The ground grows rocks instead. And then the ground looks like it's sinking away in these parts. Kentucky is only for the starving."

"We aren't starving," Mother said, her hands flying to her hips. "And don't you go using it as an excuse to leave either, Hiram. That's all anyone around these parts talks about. Leaving and going elsewhere. Like there isn't anything here worth living for."

"There is, I must say," said the good doctor. "If you could see the cave, you would think differently about Kentucky. I remember when Archie first showed it to me. I was amazed. It's a place of refuge. Maybe even a place of healing. I've been studying the possibility. There are caves in Europe where doctors allow invalids to live in them, and they've had excellent results."

"But a cave won't get us the food we need," Papa added glumly.

Susanna looked at the wooden plank flooring of the cabin beneath the shabby shoes she wore. Could there really be something like a cave existing under their house? It seemed so strange to her, like a story she might have heard told by an old farmer smoking his corncob pipe and telling tall tales to his cronies. A huge cave, big enough to live in. An underground castle with rocky engravings like paintings on the walls. This couldn't be a mere story told by the doctor for their amusement. It must be real.

Several days passed before the doctor proclaimed himself much improved and healthy enough to travel back to his cave where he could finish recuperating. In the meantime, the boys had all but exhausted the man, who told them tales of adventures conducted by his servant, Stephen Bishop, the one who mapped out the cave. When Papa came forward to present the doctor with some crutches he had made, a smile spread across Dr. Croghan's face.

"Now I would like to do something for you all," he announced, sizing up each of them.

"There is no need," Mother said. "We are only doing the Christian thing by helping a neighbor in need."

"But I want to. How would you like to work for me?"

One by one their eyes grew large in astonishment. "Work for you?" Papa repeated. "But we know nothing about caves."

"I could use some help. I own a hotel, you see, near the entrance to the cave. I would like to run tours. And I'd like to have you come live at the hotel and help the visitors who come to the hotel for tours of the cave. Archie does most of the managing of the place, but he could use the help. And we expect quite a few visitors to come with the fine summer weather soon upon us."

Papa looked at Mother. The boys immediately latched onto them, tugging, pleading with them to say yes. Susanna could only stand there dumbfounded.

"We don't know anything about caves...," Papa said once more.

"There isn't much to know, really. You don't need to lead a tour or anything. I have guides who do that. I just need a nice family with smiles on their faces who would greet the visitors and make them feel at ease. You all seem perfect for such work."

Papa exchanged glances with Mother. "I don't know. Me and the missus will have to talk it over."

"Of course. When you come to a decision, you can send word to me by way of the general store in Brownsville. But I do hope you will consider it. There's such great enthusiasm here. I believe it's the very thing I need to make my cave a success."

Watching the man slowly mount the wagon seat and wave good-bye, Papa stood next to Mother. "What do you think, Matilda?"

"I don't think we should abandon the beautiful land and farm the good Lord gave to us," she retorted. "And that's that."

~

1843—Present Day

Susanna glanced about the new land God had seen fit to give them as temporary keepers. There were rolling hills with the beginnings of spring wildflowers abloom, trees, the long muddy road that brought in the carriages, and the wooden buildings strung together that comprised the hotel and residences for the visitors. And, of course, the strange aura emanating from that famous hole of Dr. Croghan's known as Mammoth Cave. Two years had passed since the day of the wagon accident when Dr. Croghan injured himself. Susanna had never felt more content. All her dreams had come true when they accepted the work here and took charge of the tours that left the hotel several times a day to see the famous cave. Mother had said all along that God was looking out for them, and now Susanna believed it with all her heart. Standing in the large bedroom she had all to herself and looking at her rich silk gown, her feet clad in new shoes, she knew God had been good to her family. He had seen their poverty and had brought the wealthy Dr. Croghan to their doorstep in their time of need. Not that she would have wished him or anyone injured for her family's well-being. But God had providentially used the man to set their feet on a path of prosperity—and when they might have starved if they had remained on the farm. All things had surely worked together for good for them that love the Lord, just as Mother had often read from the big black Bible.

Susanna gazed about her room. How she loved this hotel. The fine furniture. Good solid wood floors. A ballroom. A library filled with books. The wonderful food served three times a day that included many kinds of vegetables, real sourdough bread, chicken and pork, cookies and tea cakes. And a huge table at which to dine, where her brothers sat on the opposite end, well away from her. Mammoth Hotel had been a glimpse of heaven—until she met Jared Edwards.

For two years, she had been shielded from life, it seemed. The hardship, the pain, even death. Then death suddenly came calling one dreadful day—and in Dr. Croghan's famous cave, of all places. Now, death overshadowed everything.

Susanna learned of Jared's name from the papers Dr. Croghan had in his possession concerning the treatment of Jared's aunt, Mattie Edwards. The woman's death had opened Susanna's eyes. No one was supposed to die here. This was a miracle cave, after all. A cave God had made, as the good doctor had said. A cave that could heal as well as stir up excitement far and wide. But something had gone terribly wrong.

Susanna was one of the first to learn something was amiss when one of the doctor's assistants came running to the hotel, claiming an invalid had died in the cave that morning. Susanna could hardly believe it. She, like everyone else, thought the cave to be the perfect place for the sick to recover. It was an area wrought out of stone and filled with moisture-laden air, a place vastly different from anything that existed in the outside world. Upon hearing about it, people flocked to the cave in the hopes of finding a cure for their loved ones sickened by the consumption. Now, most tragically, someone had died. And to her dismay, it was the relative of the young man who had pulled up in the wagon with the woman's husband beside him, asking to see the doctor. The young man named Jared Edwards.

When the assistants brought out the woman's body, wrapped in a sheet, the older man broke into terrible wails that sent shivers racing through Susanna. She'd never seen or heard anyone so distraught. During the burial the older man fell to his knees, clawing at the dead woman, pleading with her to wake up and come home. And in the background stood Jared with his head hanging low, twisting his hat in his hands, his lips moving in prayer. The sorrow lay thick and heavy around him. It was an awful sight to see. Moved by it all, Susanna did what she could. She gathered what flowers were growing that early in March, some wild trout lilies, and gave the bouquet to him. He took them, his dark eyes meeting hers, his lips forming the silent words, *Thank you*.

And then, she witnessed the scene that still remained fixed in her mind. Awful accusations spilled forth from the uncle as he blamed Jared for the woman's death. Then, in a booming voice, the uncle ordered Jared out of his life. She watched with a heavy heart as the young man ran off and never looked back.

Susanna decided to follow Jared. She wanted to comfort him, to tell him everything would be all right, to show him that someone cared. However, he was too strong and quick, racing through the woods like a fine steed and disappearing over a rise. She slowed to a walk and finally stopped. Her heart beat rapidly; her breath came fast and furious, but her spirit sank. How could this have happened? The cave was supposed to be a place of hope—the same hope that helped her family out of their poverty. Instead, it had become a place of death for Jared and a place that drove him apart from his uncle. His hope had been dashed upon the very rocks meant to heal.

Slowly she made her way back to the hotel, the cheerfulness that once permeated her life vanquished by what she had witnessed. In front of the hotel, Dr. Croghan was conferring with Papa over what happened. The grim expressions were clearly visible on their faces.

"I want men to stand guard over the premises," Croghan told Papa. "I don't trust that man who lost his wife. He seemed quite distraught."

"I'm sure it will pass, Doctor. Life and death are in the hands of the Lord."

"Even so, I want the hotel and the cave entrance guarded. We are the law in this place, and I will not tolerate lawlessness." Dr. Croghan shook his head and returned to the cave to see after the surviving invalids.

Papa sighed, only to straighten when he caught sight of Susanna. "And where did you run off to, daughter?"

"I was following the young man who lost his aunt in the cave."

"Why? There is nothing more we can do."

"There must be, Papa. The doctor promised the people who came to his cave that they would get better. And that man was. . ." She dared not say how his grief had moved her in ways she didn't think possible.

"The doctor promised nothing of the sort. His prayer was, of course, that the people would get well. Nevertheless, not all have the strength to endure the treatment in the cave. Dr. Croghan made sure the invalids and their families knew this."

Her gaze traveled to the place of distress, that dark hole, recalling the cold air rising up from the entrance in the summer. Many times the blast of air beckoned to her on a hot August day to come inside and cool off. She had never yet yielded to the temptation. Papa and her brothers had toured the inside of the cave and marveled over it. She had never seen it; nor was she certain she wanted to now—after what happened.

"There is nothing we can do," Papa said again. "We have business to attend to. Please make sure the guests are assembled and ready for the next tour."

Susanna looked at her father in alarm. "Don't you think we should cancel the tours for today? Someone just died, Papa. We should be in mourning."

A look of irritation filled his rough face. He adjusted the hat he wore. "Dr. Croghan didn't give us orders to stop the tours. We're getting paid to organize them. So we will go on as if nothing happened." He stepped closer. "And you are not to tell anyone about this either. I don't want the guests fearful. This is our work, daughter. This is how we live. Life goes on. So smile and be cheerful."

When he turned and walked away, a great sadness filled her. No one would even pause to mourn the dead. It was only tours and money, work and duty.

Corn bread and potatoes. Potatoes and corn bread.

She winced. *I am no better. I love this new life as much as anyone. God, please help me trust in Your will and not my own wants and desires. Help me know what is right and good in Your eyes alone.*

Chapter 3

G o away!" A door opened. The muzzle of a gun poked out, gleaming in the sun's rays. "I'm warning you. Not another step."

Jared walked tentatively into the yard. It had been awhile since he had been back. He'd stayed away, in his cabin, thinking and praying about his circumstances, giving them each some time alone. Suddenly he caught sight of his uncle's rifle.

"Uncle Dwight, it's me."

"I know who it is. Don't make me use my gun now. Go away!"

"Please, can we talk? We need to talk about this."

"I have nothing more to say to you. Go away!"

"Uncle, I . . ."

The gun fired. Jared jumped as a bullet whizzed by him and lodged in the wooden fencing behind him. A chill swept over him.

Uncle Dwight, visibly shaken, lowered his weapon. "I didn't mean to do that. It was an accident. Please, just leave me alone."

Jared needed no further urging, not after feeling the breeze of a bullet brush by him. He took to his heels, racing by his uncle's fields, which Jared had started to plow before all this happened. Past the fields, he pressed onward into the woods where spring plants were emerging from the cold ground. He paused to catch his breath, looking to see if his uncle had followed. Through the naked tree branches, he saw the faint curl of smoke rising out of the cabin's chimney. He could see the man's rage as he stood in the doorway of the humble log home, waving his fist and shouting. The hard voice echoed in the glade. "Go away! And never come back!"

Jared sank to the hard ground. How could this have happened? *Why, God?* He scooped some clay from the ground and formed it into a ball. Pitching it against a stout tree, he watched the clod hit, then break apart. Just like his life. He had hardly eaten or slept since that terrible day at Mammoth Cave when they buried his aunt. In fact, this was the first time he had mustered the courage to visit his uncle, hoping the tide of grief had passed and reconciliation might be in his grasp. He had never been more wrong, he realized, as the faint smell of gunpowder reached his nostrils. Nothing had changed. The anger, the hurt, the pain was ever alive, even more so now than before. He had no idea what to do about it, either.

Just then, he heard the rustle of fragile bushes. Footsteps crunched through the downed leaves left from last autumn. Fear rose up in his throat. He began to inch himself away, behind a tree trunk that he prayed would offer him some protection. His heart began to race. He wiped the sweat from his brow.

Uncle Dwight appeared from behind the trees, his boots covered in mud, his face swathed in anger. At least he didn't carry the gun. "What do you want here, Jared?" he sputtered. "You sneaking around my place all the time, up to no good." He rubbed his face.

Jared was thankful to find his uncle talking to him. "I miss you, Uncle. We need each other. The fields need plowing. We need to get the crops planted soon."

"I don't need you no more. I trusted you. I trusted you with my Mattie. You told me to take her to the place and leave her in a pit of stone. And look what happened. She's gone. Gone forever, buried in the cold ground. She went into some cold ground and never came out again." He began to cough.

"Uncle, please believe me. If I had known any of this would happen, I'd never have considered sending her there. I loved her, too. I never would have put her life in danger. I wanted to save her life."

His uncle stood there, rubbing his face. He looked tired, worn out, frail, and fragile, like a dying tree ready to fall if hit by a breath of wind. "You just don't know anything about love, Jared. You don't know what it means to have the love of a good woman—someone to care for and someone who cares about you, standing by your side. You don't know what we had, your aunt and I, and what you stole. Now I want you to go away and leave me alone."

The look on his uncle's face sealed it. Jared could say no more. He took to his feet and walked deeper into the woods, away from his uncle's grief, headed for the road. He paused. Where would he go? He refused to return to his cabin right now. There was nothing for him there. It was a cold and lonely place. Whenever he saw the tablecloth his aunt had made or the flower the young woman had given him at the burial, lying in the Bible all withered, his throat ached. Great sorrow filled him. Why was he blamed for this? His uncle should blame the people who had done this to Mattie, that doctor who had made all those fancy promises and then broke every one of them. The doctor who had sentenced Mattie to death by his impressive words of healing and miracles. Tears clouded his eyes. He had believed in the miracle, and the miracle had failed him.

He walked along, kicking up the ground as he pondered his uncle's words. No, he didn't know the love of a woman. Maybe he needed to. Maybe a woman's love would help him understand his uncle's hurt and help redirect his life. For some reason, he thought of the young and pretty woman at the hotel. He didn't even know her name, but he remembered her very well—the white dress, the small bouquet of spring flowers she had given him for his aunt's burial, the solemn vigil she had kept during the service. He looked often at the flower pressed inside the only book he owned, his Bible. Her fine dress of pure white reminded him of freshly fallen snow and illustrated her rich status. Why would he even consider her as someone who might introduce him to the kind of love his uncle described? How could he think she would so much as give him a second glance? She didn't know any more about him than he knew about her. She was wealthy, without a care in the world. He was only a farmer caught up in a spiral of grief and uncertainty. But he did desperately want to know what it meant to care for someone, to have a marriage like his uncle and his aunt had known, to understand Uncle Dwight and maybe himself.

Jared returned to his cabin and saddled his tar-colored horse. He decided he wanted to take another look. Not at the death cave or the fancy hotel, but at the woman who'd been thoughtful enough to be there for him in the saddest of times. He wanted to know her name. Where she came from. Who she was. Why she cared.

He took off down the dusty road. It was a fair piece to the hotel. Along the way, he passed wagonloads of patrons traveling to and from the cave. He didn't know how he would gain the young lady's attention. Maybe he could just be a shadow among the many visitors, a silent observer as she had been, quiet and thoughtful, perhaps even prayerful. Maybe she would be as attracted to him as he was to her. On the other hand, maybe he was being downright foolish to even think she could fulfill the role of which his uncle spoke.

"Whoa, there! Whoa!"

Jared hadn't even seen the horse and rider barreling toward him. He pulled at the reins to slow his mount, guiding it off the road.

"Hey, you'd better look where yer going! I plum near ran you over."

"Sorry about that."

The rider peered down at him. "You look familiar. You Dwight Edwards's nephew by chance?"

"Yes, I am. Jared Edwards."

"I'm George Higgins. Heard about your aunt. Sorry. Death has struck again, it seems. Some kind of curse in that cave; that's what it is. I just come from there myself."

Jared shielded his eyes from the sun's glare. "What do you mean?"

"I lost my cousin in Croghan's cave. He died the day before yesterday. Now I'm heading over to talk to your uncle. I want to know what we can do about this."

Someone else had died in the cave? Thoughts of the young woman vanished upon hearing this news. While Jared realized he should mourn the man's loss, he wrestled with a sense of relief. Someone else shared in the grief, the confusion, and the pain. Someone else had trusted in this Dr. Croghan and found their loved one taken away. He was not alone.

"Where are you headed?" the man asked. "Not back to that cave?"

"Uh." He panicked. "I, uh." He didn't dare tell him what he was up to. . .how he was seeking the woman who worked there.

"Come on and ride with me to your uncle's."

Jared shook his head. "We're not on speaking terms after my aunt passed away. Uncle Dwight blames me for it. I convinced him to take Mattie there, you see—to let that doctor cure her. Now he hates me for it."

"I'm sorry to hear that. I understand, though. My son Riley don't say much to me neither. Well, we can't let this get to us. We gotta come together and see what can be done. Can't let no rich doctor come up with some kinda no-good idea that takes away our loved ones. I miss my cousin something awful. He and I, we went fishing there in the river all the time. I sure do miss him."

"Did your cousin have the consumption?"

"Yes, and he insisted the doctor could heal him in that fancy cave of his. Said how the air there could do wonders. I tried to talk him out of it. Told him he needed to go somewhere warm, like the Carolinas. But he just sat there, skin and bones he was, and said, 'George, I don't have long to live in this world. If the good Lord gave us this cave as some miracle, then I'd be a fool not to try it.' And I believed him." He paused, his face darkening as if storm clouds had drifted across it. "Now I wonder who's the real fool?"

Jared had been told he was the fool for taking his aunt there. But there must be more to this than what he could see with his own eyes. Surely God could make something good come out of this—maybe by bringing people into his life, people he never would have met otherwise. "So what do you think we should do?"

"I'll tell you one thing. I'm gonna find out what that doctor's gonna do about this."

"Nothing we say or do is going to bring back our loved ones," Jared said.

"You're right about that. But we can do something so's no one else dies. In my mind, he ought to close down that place. Seal that cave up. Keep everyone out of it. It's a death cave now. No more grand Mammoth Cave, no siree. We're gonna put a stop to it somehow. Think your uncle might be willing to help?"

The idea of building a bridge to his uncle's affections, a way to span the chasm that kept them apart, appealed to Jared like no other. With his own family gone, he had no one else. Just the thought of reconciliation made his heart leap. "I'm sure he would. He misses Aunt Mattie. I think he would do anything to make sure no one else suffers like he has."

"That's it, then. I'll see who we can get to go talk to that doctor as soon as possible. And we're gonna make such a noisy fuss, they won't be able to do anything else but close that cave." He tipped his hat. "I'll put in a good word for you to your uncle. Make no mistake."

"Much obliged." He was glad to see someone willing to break through the storminess in his life. Maybe a rainbow was about to appear, a promise of something new, a hope for the future.

❧

Back inside his cabin that night, sleep eluded Jared. He tried to rest, but soon got up and started a fire in the fireplace. He was hungry and decided to make some biscuits. He hadn't been hungry these days and often skipped meals, but tonight he would make biscuits in honor of his aunt. She often told him that a young man should be able to do his own cooking—especially once he got married and the woman was tending to the young'uns—but even before that. He could still envision the gentle form of his aunt in front of the fireplace, showing him how to bake biscuits in the Dutch oven over a bed of glimmering coals. Then came her recipe for apple pandowdy. Corn pone. Flapjacks. Sourdough bread. He ate well on the heels of her tutoring. That is, until the dark day when his appetite vanished into the bowels of the earth along with Mattie.

He set to work making the biscuits and spooning the dough into the Dutch oven. He then opened the cabin door for a breath of air. It was a cold night. He saw something dart by in the air. Then another. Bats. They were frequent visitors with all the caves in the area. He didn't like them. They were too swift and mysterious, nearly invisible. At least he didn't feel the night itself mysterious and without hope. In fact, he felt better tonight than he had in a long time, as if hope had been restored. Jared had prayed all evening that this man named Higgins could get through to Uncle Dwight and make him see that Jared wasn't the enemy. Afterward, Higgins stopped by his place as he was putting up the stock to tell him the meeting with his uncle went well. Uncle Dwight and Higgins got along famously, and in the end, they agreed to confront the doctor at the hotel. Maybe on the heels of this meeting, healing and forgiveness would soon follow. Both Mattie and this fractured relationship with his uncle could finally be laid to rest.

For Jared's part, he told Higgins he would try to help, perhaps by convincing the young woman at the hotel to intervene in their circumstance. She had been there at his aunt's burial. He felt certain she would help. There was something different about her, something unlike the others in that place. For one thing, she cared. She had a semblance of mercy. She must be sympathetic to the agony of death to be there at some stranger's burial. She wouldn't have given him the flowers for his aunt's grave or stood by in silent reverence otherwise. Jared intended to appeal to her merciful heart.

He returned to check on the biscuits. Maybe out of all this, good would come. God would knit him with a woman who would teach him about love and life—such as his aunt Mattie had shown until death snatched her away. Maybe it would make him appreciate life more. Maybe he wouldn't feel so lonely either. He would finally have a purpose.

He turned the biscuits over one by one. They were browning nicely. There were good changes coming, like the deep red of a sunset signaling fair weather. For the first time since his aunt's passing, hope filled his heart.

Chapter 4

A golden glow formed on the distant horizon with the first rays of sun awakening the new dawn. Susanna arose from her bed and stretched her arms. A knock sounded at the door. She answered it to find Martha, bringing linen towels and fresh water in a porcelain pitcher.

"Good morning, Martha," Susanna chirped. For some reason, she felt happy and carefree today. Perhaps it had to do with the delightful dream she'd had of strolling through the woods beyond the hotel and encountering a handsome man on horseback. He had tipped his hat to her like a true gentleman. He asked if she cared to ride with him on his black steed—an offer she hastened to accept. He offered his stout hand to help her astride the animal. They rode fast and furious through the tall grass and into the Kentucky woods filled with flowers all in bloom. Susanna could still feel the wind in her hair and hear her laughter.

"Miss?" Martha asked, her face as rigid as stone with nary a smile to be found.

Susanna sent her a quizzical look before turning to dip her hands in the cold water, splashing it onto her face. She patted her face dry with the towel Martha offered. "I do hope we are having a wonderful breakfast. I'm starving."

"Eggs and ham, miss. Yankee dough cakes. Applesauce."

"How grand." Susanna grew hungry just listening to it all. None of the hateful potato soup and corn bread could be found here except for an occasional corn pudding or fancy potato dish.

She hummed a tune as she began the lengthy task of dressing for the day. There were the long, itchy stockings held up by garters. Drawers separated at the waist. A linen chemise. Several stiff starched petticoats, one on top of the other. A corset, which Martha helped to tie. Then a dress with a tight-fitting bodice fastened with hooks and eyes. The skirt arced in a fashionable style, taking on the shape of a bell from the many petticoats underneath. She sighed in satisfaction at her image in the mirror. Perfect for her man on his black horse, if only he would come. She began to twirl around the room, feeling giddy and a bit lightheaded. *I am a fine lady at last.* How she had dreamed of this while sitting by the brook, dressed in ugly calico stained by Luke's clumsiness. Soon there would be no end to the suitors who would arrive, asking permission to court her.

"Susanna!" Mother said from the doorway. "Please contain yourself. You're a lady, after all."

"But today I will be whisked away by a handsome stranger on a horse darker than even that cave," she said with a giggle.

Mother shook her head. "I don't know where you come up with these ideas of yours. Hurry now. Breakfast is being served. Your brothers are already seated. And we have guests."

Susanna took a brush to her hair and quickly wound it in a knot at the nape of her neck, fastening it into place with combs. Curly ringlets graced each cheek flushed with excitement. "Do you think it will be busy at the cave today now that pleasant weather has come?"

"Every day is busy. Since the tourists now arrive at the hotel by stage, there is never a day it isn't. Everyone is curious. And, yes, I do believe the warmer weather brings more people."

Susanna took one more look at her appearance before following her mother to the dining area. Several guests were seated at the large table along with her family, some of whom she didn't know. She offered a greeting and took a seat.

"The day is already half gone," Luke teased. "Where have you been?"

"I was having a wonderful dream, if it's any of your concern."

"She dreams of riding in a fine carriage," Henry added with a smirk.

Susanna held her head high. "As a matter of fact, I did dream of a noble on his black steed who will carry me away to a grand palace on a hill." She unfolded the napkin across her lap and waited expectantly for breakfast to be served on pewter platters.

The brothers hooted until Papa and Mother glared at them, silencing the rowdiness. "You would do well to remember yourselves," Mother said. "We have guests."

Only then did Susanna pay notice to the three men at the table, dressed in their stiff coats, staring at her family. She recognized Mr. Archibald Miller, who managed the hotel, along with two business associates of Dr. Croghan's, though the doctor himself was not present.

"He is caring for the invalids," Mr. Miller responded when asked of the doctor's whereabouts. He helped himself to a large serving of ham.

"I hear another invalid died during the night," said a man who introduced himself as Mr. Witherspoon.

All the giddiness Susanna felt that morning suddenly disappeared. "Another one died?" she said before clamping her lips shut, remembering her station.

"That makes three," Mr. Miller went on, eating ravenously, as if the news only heightened his appetite. "The doctor isn't certain what to think."

"It appears to me this grand experiment of his is on the brink of failure," said Mr. Witherspoon. "I, for one, feel the cottages inside the cave should be closed immediately."

"Let's not be so hasty," another man ventured—a Mr. Grimes, with thinning hair and spectacles, who some said wanted to take over the hotel from Dr. Croghan so the doctor could concentrate on caring for the invalids. "No one knows how sick they were before they entered the cave. It may be that only a miracle from the Most High could have saved them."

"I'm concerned about this news reaching the tourists," Papa added. "We don't want people fearful of going into the cave. It will decrease business. And we depend on visitors for their money."

"But we are talking about people's lives," said Mr. Witherspoon. "They are worth more than money, are they not?"

Papa flushed. "Of course. I meant nothing to the contrary."

Yes, you did, Papa, Susanna thought. *That's all you think about. I hear you and Luke talking. You're always asking how to bring more tourists to the cave, how to convince them to spend their money on the tours and stay at the hotel.* She looked down at her brown silk brocade dress. But if they did not make the money, how would she buy a new bonnet? A gossamer silk dress with rosettes across the neckline for a grand ball or any of the other fashions she had seen in the *Godey's Lady's Book*? Yet she could not ignore the other side of this issue, which she had witnessed that one day—a day filled with grief that still sprang up in her heart, of the man named Jared who had lost his aunt, and then the chastisement he received as if it were his fault.

"I agree that we do have a business to run," said Mr. Miller. "If we must close the underground cottages to preserve the cave and what it gives the visitors, then so be it. The tours can still proceed."

"And what of the invalids in residence?" asked Mr. Grimes. "Where will they go?"

"They can go elsewhere. There are many places for them to recuperate in the South. But surely we cannot allow this to interfere with what we are doing here."

"And what exactly are we doing?" Susanna piped up. "Besides seeing poor people suffer and die and others grieve while our pockets fill with money?"

Papa put down his fork, aghast. Mother stared and shook her head. "Susanna, hush up! Remember yourself."

Susanna ignored her. "I hear what you gentlemen are saying. But is that all we are here to do? Make money?"

"You see?" Mr. Witherspoon said, pointing his fork at Susanna. "The young lady here knows that a gift of God shouldn't turn us into stone. We must think of other ways to use it for the good of mankind and not simply for greed's sake."

No one answered for a time. The eggs and ham grew quite cold on the plates.

Luke finally stood to his feet. "I will tell you how it has been used for good. The cave helped our family out of a pit of poverty and put our feet on firm ground. And I, for one, don't ever intend to go back to that kind of living again."

Stillness fell over the table before everyone returned their attention to the food. Susanna looked down at her dress, remembering that time of poverty, the rags she had worn, the soup and corn bread that comprised her sustenance. But were her present luxuries worth the uneasiness she felt?

~

"That was utterly delightful! Though I fear my shoes will never be the same."

"Amazing," another remarked, removing the dusty cave costume worn by the visitors to protect their fine garments from the dirt and mud that abounded in the cave. "How wonderful that we can go and see such wonders right beneath our feet. The Gothic Chapel. The Star Chamber. Washington's Dome."

Susanna was used to such exclamations from visitors who came out of the cave as they described the features they had seen. It seemed strange that she had not witnessed such wonders for herself. Her father had seen them. So had her brothers. But she hadn't, nor had her mother. Though women did go on the tours, Mother felt it unseemly for Susanna to venture into such strange and dark places. And now, with the invalids living there the past few months, she had no desire to enter it. Yet the stories still proved intriguing. And hearing them for two years now, she felt as if she knew the cave anyway, despite having never seen the inside of it for herself.

"But I did not like seeing the sickly ones," said the first woman, dabbing her face with a handkerchief. "The guide should have taken us on a different route rather than by the dreary cottages. Most dreadful to be in such a terrible state."

Word soon came that yet another invalid had succumbed to the effects of the treatment. Rumors among the staff grew—wondering what Dr. Croghan would do with the sick, and what might become of the cave now that four invalids had died. At least from what Susanna could observe, the news of the deaths did not seem to stop the curious. They still arrived daily by stage and wagon, their faces expectant, willing to pay the necessary fee for either the short or long tours.

"I looked away," said the friend. "How could I not? The dreadful sight made me so afraid."

"Goodness, Margaret. There is nothing to fear. They are but poor, suffering souls. More dead than alive, I must say. I wonder if anything can be done for them?"

"I think they should leave. There are hardly any of them left. Moreover, the cave is so dark and filled with smoke. How one can live in such a place. . .I don't understand."

Susanna remained preoccupied by the ladies' conversation, even as she tried to help a couple buy tickets for the tour. The ladies soon left to partake of the refreshments served after the tour was completed—hot tea and biscuits with plenty of jam. However, Susanna couldn't help but think of the sickness and the people who seemed to get no better, despite the doctor's best intentions to cure them. It seemed a curse loomed in the deep.

"I say, when does the next tour leave, young lady?"

Susanna shook her head and gazed into the eyes of a gentleman dressed in his fine frock coat and high collar. He leaned on an elaborately carved cane. "In about ten minutes, sir. If you would wait in the front parlor for the guides, they will escort you to the cavern entrance. And there are costumes, as well, to put on if you wish to protect your clothing."

He gave a huff and left, mumbling about her inattentiveness and the sorry state of this hotel's staff.

"Are you dreaming again, sister?"

Susanna glanced about to find Luke standing there, holding several lanterns, and ready to hand them to the guides for the tour. "Luke, did you hear the news? Another invalid died in the cave."

He shrugged. "There is nothing that can be done, Susanna. It's not our affair, after all. We are here to help the visitors." He pulled a watch out of his vest pocket. "Please tell the visitors to gather in the hall so we might proceed. The guides are ready." His eyes narrowed. "And don't concern yourself with things you can't change."

Susanna sighed. How could he be so unfeeling? The one who had died belonged to someone dear, like the young man Jared who had lost his aunt. Could they not pause for just a moment and grieve? Or must they only do the tours without a thought given to the ones who had left this world or for those who endured such loss? Mother and Papa would both reprimand her if they knew her thoughts, saying she dwelled too much on the whole affair. They would tell her that life and death were a part of this world. She must concentrate on her work and not let it affect her. If only she could. Maybe if she hadn't gathered the flowers for that Jared fellow. Maybe if she hadn't witnessed the pain in his eyes or heard the wail and chastisement of the older man who drove Jared out of his life. How does one forget that kind of pain?

Susanna returned to the drawing room to see if there were any others interested in the final tour of the day, when Luke came running back. "Where's Papa?"

"I don't know. What's the matter?"

"There's trouble afoot! Quick, we must find him."

Susanna hastened for the living areas to find Mother mending a blouse. "Mother, Luke says there's trouble. Do you know where Papa can be found?"

"No, I don't. What kind of trouble?"

All at once, she heard shouts from outside. She ran for the window and peered out. Fear gripped her spirit. A party of riders on horseback had descended on the hotel. A brownish cloud arose from the many hooves plodding the dry ground.

"Oh, no!" Mother whispered. "What shall we do?"

Susanna hastened for the door, even as Mother pleaded with her to stay. She came to the part of the hotel and the drawing room where the visitors sat huddled together, their eyes wide with fright. "What is happening?" they asked her at once.

"I don't know. Please stay here inside the hotel until we find out."

She slipped out of the room and through a side entrance to meet a burly man dismounting from his horse. He demanded that Mr. Miller send for Dr. Croghan. Papa was there, as well as Luke, trying in vain to calm the irate man.

"He is in the underground cottages helping the invalids," Mr. Miller told the man. "He should be back presently."

"He's not helping anyone!" another man shouted. "That cave is a place of death. Now you get him right now, or we're going in there after him."

Susanna stared at the man cradling the long barrel of a rifle. She managed to cover her mouth before a startled cry escaped. Upon the order from Mr. Miller, Luke raced down the steep hill toward the mouth of the cave to find Dr. Croghan. Many agonizing moments slipped by as the men stood before the hotel, their faces encased in hostile looks. Luke finally appeared with the doctor, who came running up the hill accompanied by several assistants.

"What seems to be the trouble?" asked Dr. Croghan.

"Plenty of trouble," barked the man with the gun. "You killed my Mattie."

"And my cousin, Charles," said another. "In that cave you think helps the sick. They only die in there."

"What are you going to do about it?" shouted a third man. A fourth nodded his head in agreement. The men began to pace about, their faces filled with wrath.

Dr. Croghan lifted his hands. "Please, gentlemen. Let us remain calm. As you know, when you entrusted your loved ones in my care, there was no promise that they would be made well. Many came here quite ill already and perhaps beyond help. But I did my best, and I am happy to say that some are indeed recovering."

The man with the gun stepped forward. "So you're telling me my Mattie didn't have to come here, that she was going to die anyway in your cave? That there weren't no hope?"

"Sir, I'm terribly sorry for your loss. We have done everything to care for them. But as I said, some did not adapt well to the cave's environment. And it may be that your wife was one of the few."

The man shook with rage, even as Susanna watched a younger man step up to try to calm him down. She sucked in her breath. The young man was Jared Edwards. She was certain of it. Their eyes met for the first time since that terrible day when he buried his aunt in the cemetery not far from the hotel. She saw him step back, his gaze never leaving her. Fear gnawed at her. Why was he looking at her that way?

The man then slipped around the crowd of people. She retreated into the dusk, wishing she had listened to Mother and stayed inside the hotel. He was coming toward her, walking at a brisk step, his face set in determination. Gasping, Susanna hastened for the nearest door and safety.

"Please wait!" he called to her.

Something in his voice made her stop—a pleading she could not ignore.

"I need to talk to you."

She tried to settle her nervous tremors, praying she was not about to face some hostile man wishing revenge. "Please, if you have questions, talk to Dr. Croghan. It's his cave, after all. I have nothing to do with it."

"Yes, you do. You have everything to do with it. You may be the only one who can help me. You did once before when no one else cared. I know you care. I saw it with my own eyes."

She looked at him, curious at the words he spoke. "I don't know what you mean."

"The day my aunt died. The flowers you gave me. The way you stood there, watching, listening." He stepped forward, planting his hands inside the pockets of his pants. "I never thanked you for it."

Susanna stood still, unsure of what to say.

"I can tell you care," he went on. "You're not like the others in this place."

"You're wrong. We all care here, very much. The doctor, my family. . ."

"But I believe you care enough to do what needs to be done."

She didn't like the connotation behind his words. "What is it I'm supposed to do?"

He looked around. "Is there a place we can talk?"

Susanna showed him to a wooden bench, one of many that lined the pathways in the area. In the background, she could still hear the raised voices of the men challenging the doctor and see the glow of lanterns illuminating the twilight. "I fear those men might hurt the doctor and my papa," she said quickly. "Your uncle looks ready to use that gun of his."

"He's very sad," Jared agreed, kicking a foot into the dirt. "All of them are. But they don't want to hurt anyone. They know the cave is dangerous and want something done about it. You've seen it for yourself, I'm sure."

"I've never seen inside it."

He looked up with wide eyes as if surprised by this news. "But you know that people have died in it. That it's not safe."

Susanna didn't know how to respond. She never thought of the cave as dangerous, only dark and mysterious, but a miracle of God's creation just the same. *How can His creation be dangerous?* "It isn't a danger. Dr. Croghan only wishes to help people. Like he said, perhaps some came too sick to be helped by his methods. But that doesn't make the cave dangerous."

He stared, unblinking. "I had hoped you, out of all the people here, would see how this place brings nothing but death. That you would help me convince this doctor to close down Mammoth Cave before others suffer."

She stared, shocked that he would even ask her such a thing. She stood to her feet in haste. "I can't do that!"

"Why not?"

"The cave is God's creation. His world beneath the ground. And I believe He wants us to see it, or He wouldn't have made it."

"But He never meant it to be used by others for evil, did He? Or to have people die in it? His creations are intended for good."

The words struck her with such force, she took a step back. All the breath left her. She gasped. "This is not an evil place, and we are not evil people. I don't know how you can say such things. Good night."

She stumbled away, back to the safety of the hotel, with Jared's words stinging her heart. She sat in a chair, trying to make sense out of all this, when Luke and her father returned, red faced and tremulous.

"Dr. Croghan managed the situation well," Papa said, accepting the cup of tea a servant hastily brought to him. "I think the force we showed also helped, having armed men at our call. We will not be intimated."

"They'll be back, Papa," Luke said. "It's only a matter of time."

Susanna looked down at her shaking hands, thinking of Jared and how he had called them all evil. It made her shudder. If only they had stopped to grieve for those who were lost. Maybe none of this would have happened.

Chapter 5

For days afterward, Jared's words haunted Susanna. She recalled his presence as he sat beside her on the bench—recollected his every detail, even down to the woodsy scent his clothes carried. Most of all, when she thought of Jared, she envisioned his determination to see things made right after the loss he had suffered. At night, she dreamed of the people in the cave with their peaked faces, dressed in white garments, their hands reaching out to her. *Help us! You're the only one who can help us! The doctor has us locked in this cave. It's our prison. Set us free and close this place!*

She awoke from one such dream, her chemise damp, her hair hanging in thin strands around her face. She rose from her bed and looked out the window into the moonlit night. She considered what the poor invalids must be suffering right now inside the damp, murky cave. She thought of going to the cave herself and seeing what was happening. Instead she waited until her heart calmed and her breathing returned to normal, recalling the good things that had happened since coming to this place. They were helping people see the glory of Mammoth Cave. If only she could convince Jared that no one here had evil intentions, and the cave certainly wasn't full of evil, either. It was the men Jared associated with who were evil, madmen ignited by their wrath, their swarthy faces filled with rage, the orange flame of the lanterns reflecting in their angry eyes. They were a danger to all she knew and to her family's very existence.

But she also wanted to understand Jared's point of view. His pain and grief. His mission of justice—or so he felt. His concerns rose above evil intentions. He wanted the cave closed only to save people from the agony he now endured. She couldn't help but be intrigued by his plea, even if she disagreed with his intent.

At breakfast, her brothers and father exchanged loud chatter about the previous evening's encounter. Susanna found her appetite gone; instead she focused on their every word.

"We need to get a constable here to protect us," Luke insisted, slathering butter on his biscuit. "Someone from Brownsville, maybe. The doctor mentioned he knows men from Louisville. Anyone who can come keep the peace." He swallowed down the bread in two gulps.

Susanna looked at him in disgust. *All this concern doesn't seem to have affected your appetite,* she thought.

"I don't trust any of those varmints that came here last night," Luke continued. "They may come back next time and start shooting."

"One had a gun on him, too!" Henry added. "I saw it."

"Well, I don't want Susanna to be involved in the tours any longer," Mother added. "It's too dangerous for a young lady."

Susanna lifted her head at this comment. "Mother?"

"I wish you to stay inside the hotel. We have seen the ruffians and rogues lurking around. It's too dangerous to have you speaking with the visitors or helping with the tours. For all we know, those men might come back again, maybe even disguised as some visitors, and they might try to harm you. They are of an evil sort."

She recalled Jared's concern for good and not evil. "Mother, Jared said they aren't planning anything evil. They are only concerned about more people being hurt by living in the cave."

"Jared!" Luke announced. "Who's Jared?"

Suddenly all eyes were focused on her. She set down her biscuit and dropped her head. A rush of warmth filled her cheeks.

"Susanna's going courtin'," Henry said in glee.

Her cheeks flushed even deeper. "Henry, shush. I am not. I don't even know the man."

"You know him enough to mention his name and his words," Luke added, picking up another biscuit.

"Maybe you should tell us about this young man, Susanna," Papa said, staring at her. "Was he with the men who came the other evening?"

"Yes. His name is Jared Edwards, and he told me they only wanted to make sure no one else dies inside the cave. And he asked me to help."

"Man alive!" Luke cried, throwing the biscuit on his plate. "Help him do what?"

"Help him close the cave, I think."

"What?" Her parents and brothers shook their heads in dismay. "Why would some varmint be asking you to help close down the cave?" Luke demanded.

Susanna flushed, wondering if she should mention the flowers that she had given for the burial of Jared's aunt and how the gesture had somehow stirred them both. Instead she shrugged and said, "I don't know."

Luke sat back in his seat with a *thud*. "Papa, this is worse than we thought. Now they are sending no-good varmints like this Jared to set designs on Susanna and use her against us!"

"You aren't to leave this hotel without a chaperone, Susanna," Mother added, her voice rising.

"Mother, really. He means no harm."

"He certainly does!" Luke shouted. "He wants to put us out of business. And he wants to use you to do his evil work. Don't you care in the least what this man is trying to do?"

Susanna felt frustration rising within her. She came to her feet, throwing her napkin on the table. "None of what you say is true," she said, her voice trembling. "The man just lost his aunt. He wants to see people safe. And you treat him and all the rest of them like common criminals."

"They are criminals if they're trying to close down Dr. Croghan and the cave," Luke returned. "That was no pleasant howdy-do they were offering the other night. Those men were bent on seeing us put down, by violence if necessary."

She felt it again. A jab in the ribs, a poke in the arm, a kick in the shin. Her dear brother, making her life miserable once more. Wasn't working here at the cave supposed to have solved their troubles? Did they really find freedom and life here in this place? For Susanna, she found herself drowning once more in a sea of disappointment, and no one seemed to care. Life here was no different than on the farm long ago, except that she had nicer dresses and bonnets and a long dining table covered with a bounty of good food. Her happiness was only on the outside—nothing on the inside, in her heart where the need was greatest. Never did anything appear so real to her as at that moment.

"Aren't you going to say anything?" Luke pressed, interrupting her contemplation. "Either you agree to stand with us, or you're a traitor."

"Luke!" Mother exclaimed, aghast.

She stared at each of her family members, and they returned her stare. Slowly she sat back down and took up her napkin, yet inside her heart festered like an open wound.

"That's better," Papa said with a smile. "There will be no more talk of this. Dr. Croghan has everything in good order. I will abide by your mother's wishes, Susanna, and have you here helping with the ladies. Henry and Luke can assist Mr. Miller with the guests."

"So now I must stay shut up in the hotel like a prisoner?" Susanna demanded. "What crime have I done? All I did was listen to a grieving soul. Isn't that the Christian thing to do?"

"You're already in league with the likes of this Edwards," Luke snarled. "He's causing you to turn against us. And you of all people, Susanna, sitting there in your fine dress. Where would any of us be unless we had the cave and our work here? Would you rather we be digging up rocks and living in a one-room cabin? Perhaps Mother should find that ratty calico you used to wear to make you see reason rather than listening to the dribble of some hateful farmer who wants to see us all destroyed."

Susanna pressed her lips shut. As much as she wanted to rebuke her brother, nothing she could say or do would change anyone's mind. Her words would only fall on deaf ears, as they seemed to do in recent days. The change had to come from God alone.

After breakfast, Susanna wandered out to the field nearby. There she spent time gathering lilies, the same flowers used in the bouquet she had given to Jared. There was something beautiful about the flowers, with their rich petals arranged to drink deeply of the sun's rays. Pressing a lone flower against her heart, she returned to the hotel and her room where her Bible lay on the table. She pressed the flower between the pages of her Bible near a verse in the Song of Solomon that read, "Set me as a seal upon thine heart, as a seal upon thine arm. . . ."

Is this our covenant and our seal, Jared? she wondered. *This flower? Our tying bind that has brought us together, even if we are worlds apart in what we believe to be true?*

It didn't take long for the rooms of the hotel to close in around Susanna. Her heart yearned for the freedom of the woods and even the gust of cold air from the cave's entrance. Seeing the visitors that still came, even with news of the neighboring folk who were angry with Dr. Croghan, made her yearn to help. They were a curious lot, looking not only for a wonder to behold but to see the place that brought so much attention. Some commented about the night the men appeared. Others asked if the cave would now close. Papa and Mr. Miller vehemently denied that would happen.

None of it mattered to Susanna, who quickly grew bored by her new routine. She wandered about the rooms, her spirit as restless as wildflowers caught in a fierce wind. She felt the petals of her spirit torn asunder by all these goings-on in her life. How dare Luke tell her she was a traitor just because she had given away a bit of her heart to someone in need? Had they all become so callous and unfeeling in this place that they couldn't pity another? Isn't that why Dr Croghan built the cottages inside the cave in the first place? To help? Or had he done it only for his own good fortune and name, forsaking the invalids for selfish gain?

The more Susanna considered this, the more she thought that perhaps she should see for herself what was going on inside the cave. Though Mother had forbidden it, Susanna didn't see any reason why she couldn't look inside. Perhaps it might settle things in her mind. She was desperate for peace in a time that had seen nothing but turmoil and confusion.

While Mother was busy doing some embroidery, Susanna slipped out a side door of the hotel. She caught sight of Martha, who lingered by the door and inquired if Susanna needed anything.

"I'm only going out for a bit of air," Susanna told her. "You needn't tell Mother I've left."

Martha opened her mouth to question her, then nodded. "Jes' be back soon, Miss Susanna. Don't want no fussin' from yer mammy now. She be real mad."

"Just pretend you never saw me." She nodded curtly and hurried outside.

A small group of people milled about in front of the hotel, Luke among them. The last tour of the day had just finished, and as usual, the visitors were full of exclamations over what they had seen. Drawing in a deep breath to summon her courage, Susanna slipped past the group and down the wide path through the grove of trees, heading for the cave's entrance. From afar, she could hear the trickle of water pouring into the mouth of the cave as if heaven itself were giving the place a drink. A breath of cool dampness brushed her face. The cave's interior brought forth an eerie feeling. Pausing on a rise just above the opening, she suddenly realized she had no lantern. Without a means of light, she would not be able to venture far before daylight gave way to total darkness.

Sighing, Susanna retraced her steps up the path. Beyond the hotel lay the cemetery. All at once, she caught sight of a shadowy figure hunched over one of the tombstones. Her heart raced. Drawing closer, she could make out the form of a man, his apparel too worn and disheveled for him to be one of the wealthy and refined hotel patrons.

Despite her apprehension, Susanna stepped forward. Leaves crunched beneath her slippers. "Hello?" Her voice echoed through the narrow valley. Susanna paused, startled by the loudness of her own voice, and glanced around to make certain no one from the hotel was in a position to overhear her. Seeing no one on the hotel grounds, she summoned her courage and called out once more to the man in the cemetery. "Hello?"

He never even turned to look her way but kept his vigil at the grave. A chill swept over her. She should leave and return to the hotel where she belonged, but the sadness surrounding the person made her stay.

At last, he turned toward her, but his face and form remained hidden in the evening shadows. "It's me," he said. "Jared Edwards."

Jared! His voice had echoed in her mind since the night they talked. He had come to visit his aunt's grave and perhaps to nurse his feelings of depression and disillusionment. He stepped forward wearing homespun pants, muddy from the fields, a rumpled shirt, and suspenders. His hat lay low over his head. From where she stood, she could see the shocks of brown hair poking out from beneath the hat. Beard stubble shadowed his chin. He certainly wasn't anything to look at. No appearance of a gentleman. Nothing of outward value. And his inner spirit emanated only sadness.

"Have you thought about what I said the other night?" he asked. "About helping me close the cave?"

"I am sorry about your aunt, but closing down the cave won't bring her back."

She turned and suddenly felt his hand on her arm, grasping it in a firm hold. Screams clogged her throat. She looked toward the hotel. No one was in sight. *Dear God, help me!*

"I won't hurt you," he said, his voice husky. "I only want to make you understand." Just as quickly, he released her and set his hat back on his head. His walnut-colored eyes gazed at her.

"We've had this conversation already, Mr. Edwards. There is nothing else I can say or do. As it is, I'm already suffering for having spoken to you the other night."

"What do you mean?"

She opened her mouth, ready to spill out her own pain, the rebuke of her family, the scorn of her brother Luke. "It's nothing."

He stood silent for a moment. "What's your name?"

She stepped back, startled by the suddenness of the question. "Susanna. Susanna Barnett."

"Susanna." The name rolled off his tongue. She liked the way his deep voice said it, much to her chagrin. "Susanna, I believe this cave is a danger to you, your family, and everyone else. I wouldn't say it if I didn't believe it. How much more grief must come from this place for you to see what I mean? How many more people have to die? But you do nothing."

She bristled. "I'll have you know, Mr. Edwards, that I have done far more to help you than you could possibly realize." If only he could know.

His face softened to a tender expression at these words, as if he had suddenly found a comrade in battle.

"What I mean is, I understand that you are grieving for your aunt's death," she went on. "I believe that we all should bear one another's burdens in times like this, as scripture says."

He blew out a fine breath. "So you do understand. Only God could have given you a heart of mercy." He stepped forward. "In your heart you must want to help."

"Mr. Edwards, I will not help close down the cave, if that's what you mean."

Her forceful rebuke appeared to stagger him. "But you just spoke about bearing one another's burdens?"

"I said only that I understood your loss. That doesn't mean I agree with what you or your uncle wish to do here. I'm sorry."

A shadow of disappointment crossed his face. "I'm sorry, too, Miss Barnett. I can tell you are a fine woman, but this cave has taken possession of you like everyone else. It's made you all prisoners."

She gaped at him. "It most certainly has not. . . ."

He continued. "It's hard to break free from a place like that. But you have to see with your heart instead of your eyes. 'All things are lawful for me, but I will not be brought under the power of any.'" He turned, gazing at the narrow hollow that led to the cave's entrance. "This place has a power unlike anything I've seen. Even I was taken in by it at first. I thought it was a place for the miraculous and surrendered my aunt to its care. But I've seen the end result. Death to everything I know."

"I'm sorry for that, but life still goes on, Jared. It has to. Jesus even said, 'Let the dead bury their dead.' So you need to stop burying your aunt and start living again."

When she caught his gaze, his eyes looked wild, like some wounded animal. He paused, shook his head, turned, and then took off into the woods. Susanna stood for many moments. Though the words had stung, it only made her wonder more about him. If only she could understand him—and he, her. Could that ever be possible?

Chapter 6

He shut his eyes against his inner pain. How could a beautiful woman like that be so unfeeling? Where was the graceful doe he'd witnessed that terrible day, the one who gathered the flowers for his aunt's burial, the one who sympathized with his circumstances? How could she say things that hurt worse than the pain he was already feeling? That cave had made her like a blind guide. They were all blind guides leading the blind in that place. They saw nothing but their power and profit amassed at the expense of the weak and helpless. And he thought Susanna, above all the others, would separate herself from the greedy tyranny as she had that day. She had, after all, borne witness to their grief when no one else cared. But it was not to be. The place had taken hold of her as it had everyone else.

"Hi-yup," he ordered the horse, tugging on the reins. The animal obeyed, pulling the plow between the newly planted corn rows that had yet to embrace the sunshine. He hoped to get the plowing out of the way before his uncle appeared. Uncle Dwight had left on some mysterious errand, so Jared took the time to do what he had promised even before Aunt Mattie went to the cave—to care for his uncle's fields. Some would think him helpful and that he was a good Christian. He didn't see it that way. He worked to occupy his thoughts instead of sitting alone in his cabin, consumed by his troubles, wrestling with Susanna's rebuke. Nearly every night he prayed to God to release him from it all, to ease these burdens, or at least make them more bearable. Instead they hung on him like heavy burdens, pulling him into a pit.

"Whoa," he commanded, pulling back on the reins. He wiped the line of sweat from his brow. Jared tried to make sense out of all this. Were they not sheep in the Lord's pasture? Didn't the sheep hear His voice? As a Christian, wasn't he supposed to hear God's voice? Wasn't it God's voice that had told him to send Aunt Mattie to the cave? The voice that said there might something special in Susanna? Then why wasn't anything turning out right? Why did Aunt Mattie die? Why did Susanna have to be like the others at that cave, leeches that drained money from the living and now the dead? "Why, God?" he said loudly.

The horse nickered and turned its head as if to inquire of Jared's troubles.

"It's nothing," he told the animal. "Pa and Ma should be about ready to leave St. Louis and go out West, and I'm here with nothing." He leaned against the plow. "Maybe I should go, too. Head for St. Louis. Be a part of that new wagon team. Start new. What is here for me, anyway?" He kicked at a clod of hard soil. "Nothing, that's what."

The horse returned his gaze to the field before him and whinnied.

"I get the message. Keep plowing. Keep going. What does the Good Book say? Keep looking forward? No one's fit for the Lord's kingdom if he keeps looking back?" *Am I still fit for Your kingdom, Lord?* he asked in his heart. *Or is the past keeping me back, away from You and from my future?*

Just then, Jared saw a dust cloud rise in the distance. A rider was coming up the road, fast and furious. Jared wiped the sweat away once more and ambled through the field to the road. The rider bore the dusky face of a man of color. "Whoa, yip," the man called to his horse. "I'm lookin' for a Mistuh Jared Edwards."

"Yes, sir, that's me."

The man straightened, a bit surprised. "Did you just call me suh?"

"Why not? We are all God's men. We're created in His image."

He laughed and tipped back his hat. "Not many folks think of us the way you do. They think we's just some kinda animal or sumthin'."

"That's why I refuse to own anyone. If someone wants to work for me, I'll pay them."

"Woo-wee. Now that's sumthin' I shore would like. How much you figger you'd pay fer me helpin' in that there field?" He pointed to the barren field.

"It's not my field. I'm working it for my uncle. But if I did have a field this big and I had a good money crop, I'd hire you. And we would talk a fair price for the labor."

"Then you remember me when you git yerself that there field. Matt's the name." His dark hand clasped Jared's in a firm handshake. "I work at the cave."

Jared stepped back when he heard these words. "You work at the cave? You mean Dr. Croghan's cave?"

"Shore do. Even help guide in the cave. Though Stephen does most of it. He's the big guide there. He knows more about that place than anyone does. Why, he's seen things a person cain't hardly believe."

Despite his opinion of the cave and all the misery it had wrought, Jared couldn't help the curiosity that bubbled up within. "Like what?"

"Oh, let's see. A big rock they call the Giant's Coffin. Ain't nevah seen no giant though. Ha! There's a pit that goes on forever, amen. Ain't no end to it, no suh. Dropped my torch down there once. Just disappeared."

"What?"

"A bottomless pit. Stephen used some wood planks there to cross it when he saw it so's he could get to the other side. He twernt skeered one bit, no suh. Can you imagine falling into a pit like that now? See yer years fly by you, you would."

"I guess so," Jared said slowly, trying to imagine such a sight as a pit that went on forever.

"Oh, and Stephen dun find himself fish without eyes in the river that goes underground there. After a place called Winding Way."

"Fish without eyes? In an underground river?"

"Yep. Guess the good Lawd knows them fish don't need eyes if they live in a cave. What's there to see in all that dark? Cain't see yer hand in front of yer face anyways. I've been there with the lantern snuffed out. Cain't see a thing." He laughed. "Though sometimes I think I can. Just my mind playin' tricks, ya know."

Jared stared in awe and, for the briefest moment, he envisioned the cave not as a place of danger and destruction but one of wonder and intrigue. He considered what else such a place held until he saw the man take out a folded piece of paper from inside his ratty coat.

"Got a letter here for you."

A letter for me? Who would be writing me? He could scarcely believe it as he took the sealed communication. "Uh. . .thank you."

"Shore thing. Gotta go. Don't you forget me now when you git yerself that land, you hear? Name's Matt." The man flicked the reins and the horse took off.

Jared stared down at the letter with his name clearly written on it. He found himself a stump to sit on and slowly broke the seal. He unfolded the thick brown paper.

Dear Mr. Edwards,

I beg you to excuse my rude behavior at the hotel the other day. I hope you will forgive me. I have considered what you said. I want you to know that I am trying to understand. I do hope you will try to understand my life here also, so we might come to a reasonable agreement. I believe this is what the Lord would have us do.

Most respectfully, I am,
Susanna Barnett
Mammoth Cave Hotel
Edmonson County, Kentucky

He reread the note three times but still couldn't quite believe it. He gazed upward. Sunlight streamed through the trees with leaf buds just beginning to burst open on the warm wind of a fine spring day. How thankful he was that Susanna had taken the time to write him and share her thoughts. He was glad to see her thinking and considering his side. Beneath the hard woman there was still the glimmer of the one who had held the bouquet of flowers. On the heels of this, too, he realized his own stubbornness. They'd both been argumentative that day, each seeking to convince the other of their own opinions—and both had remained as stony and hard as the cave they debated. They needed more understanding, more of that Christian love and forbearance, a heart of flesh.

He folded the letter and stowed it away in his pocket before ambling back to the horse and plow. "Now what do I do?" he asked. The animal once more turned its head. These must be answers to his prayer, both the talk by the man named

Matt and now the letter by Susanna Barnett. Was God slowly unveiling his future? If so, what was it exactly? Surely his future could not include someone like Susanna. Proud Susanna in her fine dresses, store-bought bonnets, slippers that had never touched the mud of a field, the sweet scent of flowers that drifted on the wind whenever she came near. These signs must mean something else.

"Let's go," he told the horse. Soon his uncle would return, and there was still a good deal of field left to plow. He wanted to be long gone before Uncle Dwight arrived so as to avoid a confrontation.

He sighed as he drove the plow forward. Uncle Dwight and Susanna. And in between them a bottomless pit, eyeless fish in an underground river, and the darkness that was Mammoth Cave. All parts to some great plan yet to unfold, he was certain.

As twilight began to fall, Jared saw another cloud of dust and heard the rattling of a wagon. He hastened to drive the horse and plow back into his uncle's barn just as Uncle Dwight appeared over the horizon, accompanied by several men on horseback. Many of the men Jared recognized from the confrontation at the hotel, including George Higgins and others. Not all the men held a grievance with Dr. Croghan and the cave. Some were simply angry for anger's sake and wanted a quarrel to give them something to do. Each man dismounted, wearing a hardened face and rugged clothing, stained with the sweat of labor in the fields. Some carried guns. One held stubbornly to his jug of liquor.

Jared stepped back into the barn, wondering why they came armed. Were they thinking of returning to the hotel again tonight? All at once, he envisioned Susanna, clad in her snow-white dress, her eyes wide with terror, pleading for help from the ruffians who had come to terrorize them. Despite his apprehension, Jared hurried out of the barn to find out what was afoot.

Uncle Dwight whirled and aimed his gun. "Who's there?"

"Just me, Uncle."

"Howdy, Jared," Higgins said good-naturedly.

"Git off my land!" Uncle Dwight shouted. "You got no right here."

"Don't be so hard on him, Dwight," Higgins said. "Jared's a good fellar."

"Good for what, I'd like to know," Uncle Dwight muttered, leading the way into the cabin, followed by the men, who all talked at once.

Jared threw aside his fear and entered the cabin on their heels. Despite what his uncle said, he was linked to the cave as much as they were and maybe more so. He would be a part of this whether they wanted him there or not.

"So what do you think?" asked a man named Abe Nichols, who poured out his potent brew into cups for all. When he offered the liquor to Jared, Jared shook his head. The odor made him sick to his stomach.

"We have no choice," Uncle Dwight said. "They ain't gonna budge, even if you think they are, Higgins."

"I'd just as soon give them more time before we do something we might regret," Higgins claimed. "We only talked to that doctor once. We need to keep after him."

"Once is enough in my opinion," Uncle Dwight declared. "Time to show him and all the rest of them highfalutin folk that we mean what we say."

Jared stared from one man to the other as dread filled him. *Lord, what are they planning?*

"Hey, and what happened with that girl you know?" Higgins asked Jared. "You talk to her? She gonna help?"

All eyes focused on Jared. He looked at each face tense with determination, anger, bitterness, revenge. "I don't think she can do anything."

Uncle Dwight slapped the table. "There, you see? They ain't gonna do nuthin', I tell you. We're just wasting time. I say we blow 'em to kingdom come."

Jared stared. Again, he suppressed his fear and asked with as calm a voice as he could muster, "So how do you all plan to deal with this problem?"

"We got ourselves a good plan," said Abe, combing his beard with his fingers. "I got me some good powder."

"We're gonna blow up that no-good cave," Uncle Dwight snarled. "Seal it up good so no one can go in there ever again and no highfalutin doctor can make money on the misery of others."

Blow up the cave? He looked to Higgins. Surely he couldn't agree with such a plan. "What do you say about this, Mr. Higgins?"

Higgins took a swig of the brew in his tin cup before wiping his hand across his mouth. "Well, I still think we ought to try and do some more talking."

"Not only that, but you could end up killing innocent people!" Jared added. Their eyes once again focused on him.

"Ha!" Uncle Dwight cried, standing to his feet, his breathing ragged. "And you talk about us killin', after my Mattie died on account of you."

"Now, Dwight," Higgins began. "You can't blame Jared for that. He was trying to help. He had no idea she was gonna die. None of us knew we'd lose our loved ones in that place."

His uncle settled back in his chair, muttering. Jared gave Higgins what he hoped was a look of gratitude.

"And we ain't gonna kill no one," said Abe. "At least I ain't. I just wanna make sure the cave is sealed up. I'm tired of all the fussing about it and the fancy folk coming here by stage to see it. Not a moment's peace around here."

"But people still live in the cave," Jared protested, ignoring the look of anger painted on Uncle Dwight's face. "You seal it shut, and they could be trapped. How can you bury people alive?"

The men grew quiet then, mulling over his words. Even Uncle Dwight stayed silent.

"Jared is right," Higgins declared. "I think we need to let the talking do the work. We'll meet again with the doctor. Lean on him harder than we have been. I think we did rattle them by showing up like we did the other night. So we'll keep it up, and I believe we're gonna see a change."

Jared exhaled slowly, thankful for Higgins's support that put the scheme of violence to rest—at least for the time being. He touched Susanna's letter in his pocket. He couldn't bear to see terror grip her should some explosion rock her home. There had to be other ways to resolve these differences.

"You got some wisdom in you," Higgins commented to Jared when the meeting concluded. He strode over to his mount and patted the animal before gathering up the reins. "Ought to git my ornery son to listen to you instead of him taking off into the hills like he does. He could learn a heap."

"You don't think anyone's gonna blow up the cave, do you, Mr. Higgins?"

"Not now," he said with a grunt, hoisting himself into the saddle and bringing the animal about. "But it's really up to Dr. Croghan what happens next. And I must say, if he wants to avoid trouble, he'd better come up with a solution to this."

"And what if he doesn't?"

"Don't know, Jared. You heard what was said. Look, I had someone close to me die in that cave. Don't you think that place should be closed up? It buried our kin. It should be buried, too. No one should be able to visit there anymore. It's like holy ground, I guess you could say."

"I don't know, sir. I didn't look at it that way."

"Well, maybe you should. Then maybe you would see why your uncle and the others think the way they do." With a "yah" he galloped off down the road.

A wave of dread came over Jared as he leaned over the fencing. *God, what is happening with everyone?* Here he'd thought Higgins might feel as he did, avoiding violence at all cost and seeking whatever peace could be found in the situation. But if things did not go as planned, Higgins could not be trusted either. *God, please don't let it come to violence,* he prayed.

Chapter 7

Jared must have read Susanna's letter at least a dozen times over the course of the past few days. Meanwhile, the fields lay untended, the eggs still in the chicken coop, and the wood unsplit as he sat on the porch step of his humble cabin and stared at the sheet of paper. Even thoughts of the meeting with his uncle and friends rapidly faded away. Instead he imagined her forming the words with each stroke of the instrument dipped in ink, her blue eyes focused on the sentences she wrote, spilling out her heart. At least, he thought her eyes were blue. He wasn't certain. He hadn't really gotten a good look at her eyes, what with the encounter in the cemetery coming as dusk fell. At least he knew her hair was the color of brown sugar. And she wore fine dresses. The mark of a true lady, rich and proud.

He looked around at his cabin. He once thought this place to be the best thing he had ever built. Now, as he thought of Susanna, it looked small and shabby, unfit for a woman of her means. He wiped his hand across his eyes. Why would he be thinking of Susanna living here of all places? She was used to a castle, the hotel with its fine furniture and fancy folk. He was but a humble farmer. She would never consent to a life like this—and with him of all men.

Yes, his uncle had made good money growing cash crops, and he had taken his fair share of the profits. He had money to his name. But his family always had lived simply. He never once considered deserting this humble cabin for a house of brick or stone, with fine furniture on which to rest easy. As his aunt always said, it was good to have extra money on hand for special needs and not to spend it on foolish pleasantries. One didn't know if the plow might break, a horse would need shod, or someone would happen by who could use a helping hand.

Jared stood to his feet and entered his little cabin to look at the money accrued in the jar. There was plenty to spare—money even to buy Susanna something special. Maybe enough to buy her heart and abandon the hotel life to take up residence with him. That would be grand. But is that what he wanted to do? Buy her understanding and her love?

He pushed away the thought and stuffed some of the money into his pocket. He needed provisions from town anyway. Salt pork. Beans. Tea. Maybe he'd get his uncle some of that horehound candy he fancied. And maybe Susanna might enjoy a few sweets as well. A small token, really. He could sweeten up both her and Uncle Dwight at the same time. Make them see that he wasn't an awful person, that he was someone they both could trust.

Jared saddled one of the two horses he owned, the fine tan mare his father had left him. A journey to Brownsville would be a nice diversion from the myriad of thoughts that swirled in his head these days. Soon he was on his way, deciding to make the most of this pleasant spring day. The air felt warm and soothing on his face. The grass had begun to green up, and a few more flowers began their showy display of color, like the violets and pink columbine. It all reminded him of the work he still needed to do. He should be home planting the fields and not heading to town. But other things drove his heart and spirit at the moment, like a lovely young woman who had taken the time to write him when he needed it most. He wasn't good with words, or he would write back. In his eyes, a gift would say it all.

Presently he saw a stately coach heading toward him on the rough road with horses prancing. The driver lifted his hand to Jared, signaling him to stop. The door of the coach opened, and a gentleman peered out.

"Good morning. I'm Otis Clark. Whom do I have the pleasure of addressing?"

Jared steadied his mount with a firm grip on the reins. "Jared Edwards. What can I do for you?"

"We would like to know where the cave is. Mammoth Cave, that is. Can you direct us?"

He felt the heat crawl into his cheeks at the mere mention of the place. It conjured up memories both good and bad—bad on account of his aunt's passing, good because of Susanna.

"The one owned by a certain doctor," the man continued. "Surely you've heard of it. We came all the way from Philadelphia just to see it."

Jared pondered this. Should he tell them to have a good trip and direct them to the right road? Or should he tell them the cave was dangerous? That it hurt people, and they would do better to return home? If he didn't warn them, wouldn't he be a hypocrite?

He cleared his throat. "Yes, I know of it. But I must warn you; there are strange diseases afoot in that place."

"What?" A woman's face now appeared beside Otis Clark's, the bow of her bonnet tickling the man's face. "Did I hear there is some disease in the cave?"

Jared removed his hat. "Yes, ma'am, a bad disease there. Several have died. Including my own aunt."

"We've only heard from friends what an interesting place the cave is," claimed the gentleman. "There are tours and everything."

"They have tours. But with the disease and all, it's just too dangerous to go there."

The man and woman looked at each other. "And we came all this way," she pouted. "How can this be?"

"Don't fret, my dear. It must be providential that this young man is warning us of the danger." He glanced back once more at Jared. "What disease is it, may I ask?"

"Consumption."

The woman's hand flew to her mouth, aghast. "Oh, no! How dreadful! Otis, please tell the driver to take us away from here. I don't want to be anywhere near that cave. Think of our children!" She went on, even as she settled back in her seat. "This is terrible. How can they be conducting tours when there are people dying inside?"

"Thank you," Otis called out before ordering the driver to turn around.

Jared sat still on his mount, watching the coach slowly turn and proceed back down the road from whence it came. Suddenly his desire to go to Brownsville to buy Susanna a gift had likewise been rerouted. He had just sent back people who would have come to tour the cave and feed money into the purses of Susanna's family and, yes, Susanna herself. Nevertheless, he had no choice. Some things were more important than money—like people's lives. Susanna had to realize it. They all did.

Jared looked down the long road that led to Brownsville and decided to continue. If nothing else, he would still lay in provisions at the store. And maybe a small bit of candy for his uncle to sweeten his sour spirit. But anything for Susanna would have to wait for a long time, he feared. Especially if she discovered how he had chased patrons away from the cave she loved.

Brownsville, nestled beside the Green River, was the only thriving community in these parts. The small, close-knit town served the needs of travelers and farmers alike. There was the general store, a mill, an iron forge, and a hotel boasting fine mineral springs with healing in them, or so the townspeople said. Jared stopped at the general store and anchored his reins to a rail. He hadn't been to town in quite a while. In fact, it may have been before his aunt died. He recalled coming here with Uncle Dwight, seeing friends, talking about the crops. The friends had inquired about Aunt Mattie's health, with a sideways glance toward Jared. Uncle Dwight had said he expected her to do just dandy in the cave and, when spring came, to be as healthy as any of them.

Jared swallowed hard at the thought. Now he came here alone, without his aunt or his uncle. The realization convinced him that he had made the right decision to warn the rich folk about avoiding Mammoth Cave. He would do it again if he must. Perhaps he might even put up announcements around Brownsville and at Bell's Tavern, warning travelers not to go there. Maybe that would force the doctor to close. Even if it made Susanna and others angry, he believed it was the right thing to do.

He took off his hat and climbed the set of stairs to the store, stopping short at the window. A young woman stood at the counter, chatting away with the clerk. He wiped his eyes. She had many fine objects spread out before her. He came to the window for a closer look. A new hat lay on the counter. A brush and comb. Some hairpins. A book. All very expensive items.

Just then, the woman turned and pointed at the cracker barrel. When he saw her face, Jared sucked in his breath. *Susanna Barnett!* He looked once more at the fineries. It was not the sight of the pretty woman that stirred his heart. He only saw frivolous objects—fineries purchased in exchange for the lives of his aunt and others inside a cave. He whirled away, sickened by the sight. How could she do such a thing? Exactly what was she trying to make him understand in that letter of hers? That she needed the cave's money to buy her fancy things? That she cared nothing about where the money came from? That she cared nothing for the misery of others?

"Yes, and thank you, Mr. Hensley," Susanna called back as a young boy helped her carry the items she had purchased to a waiting wagon.

Jared wanted to turn away and never look back, but he couldn't. He could not let this pass. He stood his ground on the porch, his hat low on his head, as the errand boy walked past carrying the goods. Susanna came out of the store next, her face relaxed, a small smile sitting on her lips, her dress sweeping the wooden flooring of the porch.

He took a step forward. "Susanna."

She stepped back in response. "Oh!"

"It's me. Jared Edwards."

"Mr. Edwards! You startled me. Isn't this a surprise? Are you here to visit the general store?"

"In a manner of speaking."

"A fine spring day to shop, isn't it?"

"I suppose fine for a few things." He tipped his hat back. "Like buying heaps of fine goods."

She drew her tiny brocade handbag farther up her arm. "I don't understand what you mean."

"A fine day for spending cave money on a new bonnet. Combs. Ribbons. All the necessities of life."

Her face contorted into a mixture of dismay. "I see. Well, pardon me. I must be going. Good day." She brushed by him.

"And, in that letter you sent to me, you talk of understanding?" he pressed, following her. "Is this what I'm supposed to understand? That you have need for all these fripperies? That I might take these niceties away from you if the cave is closed?"

She whirled. "Really, Mr. Edwards. I don't think it's any of your affair what I do with the money God has given me."

"The money God has given you! You talk about God giving you this? God is a God of mercy, not of wanton pleasure."

"A merciful God understands my plight more than you will ever know. And that's because you don't have any of His mercy in you." She headed for the wagon where the driver stood waiting.

46

"What plight could you have possibly endured in your life?" he went on.

"You don't understand, Mr. Edwards. And you never will, because you are blinded by the very things you want to do away with."

"You're right, I don't. I don't understand how you can take cave money like this and use it for your own selfishness."

Her face reddened. "Nor do I understand how you can judge me without knowing me. And that is what you are doing. Judge not, lest ye be judged." She mounted the wagon with the help of the driver.

"Now you jes' go on outta here," the driver told him. "Go on and leave Miss Barnett alone."

Jared bristled. He couldn't let this go, not while he still had breath. "So please tell me, Miss Barnett. What is this plight of yours that I'm supposed to understand?"

"I would tell you if I thought you would pay me any mind at all. But all you see is your own anger. You're no different from your uncle except you're unarmed."

He thought about it, calming himself enough to take a step back and relax his stance. He did want to know everything about her. She intrigued him, much as he hated to admit it. He had nursed her letter as if it was the dearest thing he had ever received. And she really was a beautiful sight to see. "I'll listen. Come with me to the tavern down the road and tell me everything. I will even buy you a cup of tea."

"No, thank you. To the tea, that is." She paused. "But since you asked, I will tell you. You need to know just who and what you are judging." Slowly she eased herself to the ground, sweeping her dress around the wheel. "Wait for me, Solomon. I won't be long."

"Miss Barnett . . . ," Solomon began in protest.

Jared could hardly believe she had agreed to talk to him. Whatever she wanted to say must burn fierce within her, some knowledge he needed to know. Despite his dismay at her fineries, he couldn't help but be taken in by her dress and bonnet. He would take in all of her, her beauty, her dreams, everything about her, if other things weren't clouding his vision at the moment. Maybe it would all be put to rest this day if he but listened.

～෨

They walked for a time, away from the bustle of the town and curious onlookers. Soon they were heading into a field, enjoying the feel of the sun on their faces and the breeze that carried the scents of springtime. Jared was amazed at the confidence Susanna had to go with him. She showed no fear, just determination. Maybe a bit of trust had already begun to form between them, even if it seemed unbelievable. Were they not opposing forces, ready to do battle to keep their own purposes alive? Or were they trying to come to an understanding, as she said, and was this the beginning of something new in their lives?

"This looks like a fine place to talk," she said when they came upon a small stream. She found a rock to sit upon, where she spread her dress in a perfect fan across the stony surface. "I love to sit and look at a stream. There's something about water that is so soothing. The Green River flows by Mammoth Cave, too. Some of the visitors come by boat to see the cave."

His anger began to rise. She must know how talking about the cave would infuriate him. Yet she spoke about it as if it were a pleasant conversation to be had on a warm, sunny day.

She continued. "When I was little I would sit on a rock and wonder what my life would be like in the future. What plans God might have for me. And I would look down at my dirty calico dress and wonder if that future might mean I could have a pretty dress to wear one day. And food to eat."

He said nothing, though he had to admit his curiosity had been piqued by her choice of words.

"I thought about it a lot when we lived in the little cabin I shared with Papa, Mother, and my two brothers. My room in that cabin was the loft. Drafty in winter, hot in summer. I'm sure you know what I mean, Mr. Edwards."

The truth be known, he had never slept in a loft. He had his own room inside his uncle's large cabin. And, of course, once he built his own place, he slept in a small room adjacent to the main cabin. Now he pondered her words. She had slept in a cabin? When? Wasn't that fancy hotel her home?

"Sometimes I would get so cold in winter, I would shiver and come down to warm myself by the fire. Other times I felt like I would die in the heat. Kentucky summers can be hot, as you know. Once I even took off in the middle of the night to take a dunking in the stream. Mother was angry when she found out. But I didn't care. And it felt wonderful, that cool water on a hot summer's night."

Jared plucked a reed and began to chew on it. Where did she get these stories? From some visitor? Maybe one of the servants working at the cave? Surely it couldn't be a tale of her life.

"And when it would come time for the meals, I would go out to the garden and dig up a potato or two. Papa tried to get a plow through the ground. He had bought the land with all the money he had. But he didn't know until later that he was sold a land full of rocks. It grew nothing for him. What potatoes and other vegetables we grew became our food. Potato soup. Some corn for corn bread. Hardly any money to buy chickens or any of the salt pork at the store. Just potato soup and corn bread. Day after day. Mother made it last as long as she could."

He stopped gnawing on the reed to let the description sink in. He wanted to say something but found his mind blank.

"And then came the accident on the road. I was talking to God by a stream like this one. Luke had just upset my soup over the only dress I had, a ripped calico. I came to the stream to pray when I heard a terrible noise." She glanced up then, her blue eyes luminescent as they reflected the sunlight. "A wagon had overturned, and a man was pinned underneath. It was Dr. Croghan. I ran for Papa and my brothers. We helped him to our cabin, and he stayed for few days. Afterward, as a thank-you, he asked us to come work for him at his hotel. We left the cabin and never looked back." She paused to throw a small stone into the stream. "From then on, I cast all my cares away. I never want to look back. No matter what." She turned to eye him. "I know you think I'm selfish and that I don't care. But I do care. I know what it's like to have nothing at all. And since God has blessed me with a few things of worth, then I will take His blessing and be thankful."

Jared could offer no words in reply. Either she had just told him the most emotional lie to convince him of her opinions, or she had witnessed the trials of life that nearly drove her family to the brink of despair, if not for the intervention of Dr. Croghan.

"You aren't saying anything," she noted, taking off her bonnet. The breeze blew the curly, brown-sugar ringlets that framed her face. "You don't believe me, do you? You think I made this up. You think I'm a spoiled, pampered, rich girl who knows nothing of hardship. But it isn't true. None of it. I've lived it all."

"I believe you."

His reply must have caught her by surprise. She had opened her mouth, poised to offer a further rebuke, but instead smiled. "Then I would say we are definitely on the road to some manner of understanding, Mr. Edwards."

"Jared," he corrected, staring intently at her upturned lips. "Call me Jared. Mr. Edwards is my father."

"And where is your father? Your family? I haven't seen them, have I?"

"I don't know where they are."

Her forehead crinkled in puzzlement "What do you mean? What happened to them?"

He relished the concern in her voice that proved comforting. A genuine concern. Not made up. Not pretend. Just like the day his aunt died. She was a woman who cared. He was convinced of it now more than ever. "I don't really know. They wanted to go out West. They left here when they heard of wagon trains soon to make their way to Oregon Territory. They left last year, headed for St. Louis. I haven't heard from them since. For all I know, they may have already left."

"But why didn't you leave with them? Why did you stay here in Kentucky?"

"I stayed because I was born here. And I met the Lord here through a traveling preacher who came to Kentucky. Besides, I couldn't leave my aunt and uncle alone. Aunt Mattie got sick. Uncle Dwight needed help with the fields. And now look at what's happened." He heard Susanna inhale a swift breath as he broached the topic that had separated them from the beginning.

"It must be hard," she said softly. "I can't imagine losing someone so close to me and then not having family around for comfort. Sometimes I wish I didn't have my brothers, as they tend to be quite bothersome. But never would I want to be separated from any of them for very long."

His heart began to stir with an understanding that gave way to hope—hope that maybe God had begun to open Susanna's eyes. Hope that she was ready to come to his side, even closer than before.

"But I know, too, that God has blessed us and many others with this cave," she went on. "I don't believe the cave is a curse. I believe it's a blessing."

"It can't be both. To you a blessing, to me a curse. We can't both be right, and we can't both be wrong."

They sat in silence together, listening to the water play a melody over the rocks. "Then we must come to a truce," Susanna declared, offering him her hand.

"A truce?" He took her hand in his.

"That while we may disagree, we can still respect and understand each other with God's help."

And maybe even more, he thought silently. He gazed at her hand, tiny and velvety white against his rough skin. He'd never felt anything so soft. He held on to it, savoring the feel of it. He caressed the top of her hand with his thumb.

Her cheeks pinked. Her hand shifted in his. "Jared?" she asked softly.

The feel of her hand. The look of her face. Eyes blue like the feathers of a bluebird. Parted lips so inviting. Dare he even think of kissing her? Dare he consider her in such a fashion, as one he could come to know, to love, and even to marry? He dropped her hand and stared off into the distance. At least he did have some understanding now—an understanding that birthed something new in him. He prayed she might consider him in a new light as well, even beneath the obvious image of a Kentucky farmer in dusty boots.

"Maybe we can meet again?" he wondered, somewhat shyly.

"I'd like that very much."

He sighed. Hope was alive and well. He left Brownsville with an excitement in his heart, ready to face whatever came next.

Chapter 8

She whispered his name in the night shadows when the moon rose full in the sky and bathed the Kentucky landscape in a veil of white. She looked often at her hand, the one he'd held in his, and remembered the way his gaze never left hers. It was as if he searched her heart to see what lay inside, much like those who searched the cave for priceless treasure. Something had drawn them together, even if they were still far apart. They lived in two separate worlds, each with its own manner of thinking. She would not relinquish the cave of prosperity, and he would never let go of his claim that the cave meant death. They seemed to be at an impasse, yet they had come to some manner of agreement.

When had the sun risen in the sky, along with the moon?

"Hello! Is your mind far across the ocean again?" Luke had come up, carrying caving costumes for the visitors. "We are here to conduct business, Susanna, or have you forgotten?"

She took the clothing with a halfhearted gesture. "Do you ever think there is more to life than making money?"

Luke glanced up from his work of examining the lanterns to see if they required lard oil. His eyes narrowed to tiny slits. "What kind of a question is that? Have you been talking to that man Jared again?"

She put the costumes on a chair and smoothed out her dress. "I don't think that is any of your affair."

"Man alive, you have been talking to him! Susanna, how could you? Are you still willing to betray your own family?"

"I am doing nothing of the sort. If anything, you should be happy that I've been talking to him." She lifted her head high in the air.

"How would you expect me to come to that conclusion?"

"Because Jared knows the men who came here. If I can convince him of the cave's value, I believe he will protect us from them."

Luke snorted. "If you think that, then you are quite naive. The man has been trying to win you over by his words. He's using you as a spy for his plans. How can you fall for such deception?"

Susanna stared, unable to believe such an insinuation. "He isn't a spy...," she began, even as doubt crept forth. *He couldn't be. He never asked me questions. He never gave such an appearance.*

Luke picked up the lanterns. "A man is wise in his own opinions until corrected by another. You've seen the wisdom in what we are doing here. You wear it proudly every day. Now you could destroy everything we have earned by talking to that man. I'll have to go to Papa about it."

She felt the heat enter her face. "I've done nothing wrong."

He said no more. She watched him leave, her trepidation building. She could envision the look of anger on Papa's face when he heard the news that she had been conspiring with some so-called enemy, planting seeds of destruction in their work. Causing the good doctor and her family to go to ruin. She might be cast away, perhaps to live with poor relatives in Ohio. Papa would order her to leave everything behind, clothed only in sackcloth as penance.

"I've done nothing wrong," she said again, gathering up the cloaks. *If anything, I'm trying to keep terrible things from happening. Jared and I have already begun to come to an understanding. He knows how I feel. And I'm beginning to learn more about him, too, though I wish I knew more.*

She tried to smile at the visitors while handing out the cloaks to protect their fine garments during the tour, but the expression felt forced. There was no joy in this work. There were only questions, wondering what would become of them all. And now, with Luke looking to expose everything that lay hidden in her heart, she became even more distraught.

For now, she tried to cast it all aside. Jared had asked to meet her again for a short walk by the Green River that afternoon. When the tour left, Susanna primped and went in haste to find him waiting in the reeds. The smile he gave warmed her heart. No, Jared may not be a gentleman clad in fine frocks, but he was a gentleman, nevertheless. They strolled along the riverbank, watching bugs skitter across the river's surface. He picked up her hand as he had once before. She liked his touch. He asked about her dreams for the future.

"I don't really know," she confessed. "I can only take tomorrow as it comes. It's enough for me right now." She dare not tell him her dream of the man on the black horse, or of being swept away to a grand home on a hillside, or anything else. She only wanted to live for this moment.

"I've had people tell me I need to think about the future. About things like. . ." He paused. "I guess I'm living one day at a time, too, and letting tomorrow take care of itself." She felt he wanted to say more, but it stayed buried. Instead she rejoiced in the brief time they had before one of the servants came running to find her. When Jared bid her farewell, appearing saddened that the time had been so short-lived, she only hoped they would meet again soon.

At dinner that night, the family offered her looks of disapproval all around. Susanna panicked, wondering if they somehow knew of her secret walk with Jared earlier that day. They gazed at her as if she had betrayed them. She had never felt so alone. How could she tell them that she held no evil intent in speaking with Jared, that she only wanted peace to come from this situation? That Jared was a kind man through and through who only wanted what was best for everyone?

After dinner, Papa called her into the study. He sat down in his chair and waited expectantly. Not long after, the doors opened, and Dr. Croghan himself ventured in, stiff and stern in his frock coat with gleaming brass buttons and polished boots. Susanna felt weak under the gaze of the man who owned the very place where her family lived and worked. Archibald Miller arrived next, equally dressed in fashionable attire, accompanied by a stern expression to match the prevailing atmosphere. She felt even weaker.

They took seats near Papa. "Miss Barnett." They each greeted her.

"Dr. Croghan," she managed to say. "Mr. Miller."

The men nodded to her father. "I have something to read to you, Susanna," Papa said, withdrawing a letter.

Susanna sucked in her breath. "Who is it from, Papa?" she asked in as controlled a voice as possible. Could it be from Jared? Did he expound on the love she felt certain was there, like that day in the woods when he held her hand and even during the walk this very afternoon? The idea made her shudder, especially if such a letter had found its way into her father's hands.

He unfolded the letter and cleared his throat. " 'We were most disturbed to find all manner of disease being entertained in your cave. We had traveled far from Philadelphia, intent on seeing this wondrous sight about which we had heard told. Bless providence; we were stopped by a farmer named Jared Edwards who told us of the deaths attributed to the cave. We now ask that you warn others and put forth the necessary actions to prevent a terrible calamity from happening.' " Pa folded the letter. All the men stared at her grimly. "We know the man who spoke to these people is the same young man you have been meeting in confidence, Susanna."

Jared? But how. . . ? She straightened. "Yes, Papa, I. . .I have seen him a few times."

"And you saw him the night those men came, did you not?" Dr. Croghan asked. "Some say he even seemed to know you."

"He was very disturbed, of course, over his aunt's passing. I saw him for the first time the day she passed away." She wanted to tell him about the grief she witnessed, the flowers she gave, the wrenching of her heart at the harsh words his uncle had spoken. Then the good things that came from it, the day they sat together by the stream when he held her hand and gazed steadfastly into her eyes. The walk by the river this very afternoon when she sensed a knitting together of their minds and hearts.

Croghan and Papa exchanged glances. "Hiram, I've been told this is the same Edwards that has been having secret meetings inside his cabin," the doctor said, his frustration evident. "I'm told he's raising a following. And now he's spreading lies among the very populace with whom we do business." He turned to acknowledge Susanna, who shrank in her seat under his baneful stare. "What do you know about this young man?"

"I—I know he was upset about the cave. He has called it a death cave in the past. I've tried to convince him otherwise, that the cave has many fine features. But I know he isn't raising a following to do us harm. His uncle is very—"

"You see?" Croghan interrupted. "A death cave! This young man has been conspiring in all manner of deceit concerning my cave. And your own daughter is involved, Hiram!"

"Doctor, please." She began feeling more nervous under his glaring countenance. "We have talked, yes. But don't you agree that in pleasant conversation and sympathizing with others, we can all come to an understanding?"

"An understanding of what?"

"I. . .uh. . ." She paused, suddenly confused.

"An understanding that my cave is dangerous? That it is now called the 'death cave' instead of Mammoth Cave? That it is neither fit for man nor beast and should be closed?" Croghan stood to his feet and began to pace. "No. This can't be allowed to continue. We must put a stop to this. If we don't, I'll have no choice but to close if a ruckus ensues."

"You can't close the cave," Miller protested. "Look at all we've accomplished here."

Susanna saw her father turn pasty white "There must be some other way to resolve this," he said slowly.

"Perhaps a meeting," Miller suggested. "Between all of us."

"I will be forced to close unless this situation is resolved," Croghan said grimly. "Already some are urging me to do so after what's happened with the invalids." He whirled to face Susanna. "Since you know this young man, perhaps it would do us well to have both him and his uncle for dinner. Explain the nature of the cave and what we wish to accomplish here. Offer what we can in the manner of sorrow and understanding, as you have said. But at the same time, avoid other difficulties with regards to the cave and its visitors. Do you think your young man will agree to such an invitation?"

"I—I don't know, sir. I'm sure he will wonder what it is about. He will be suspicious. Even when I was making purchases at Brownsville, he. . ." She halted then, realizing what she had said. She didn't want them to know of that day and the encounter by the stream, how something special had been forged between them. "That is, he was most distressed at the idea of making money from a place where his aunt died so tragically."

"You see?" Croghan complained. "No one believes in what we are doing here. Now we have a disease worse than the consumption spreading throughout Kentucky—the disease of spoken lies. And it will be our undoing unless something is done."

"Then it's settled," Miller decided. "We will have the men here for dinner in the hotel's private dining room. We will make it a lavish affair. And pray that good intentions will resolve this situation." Miller pointed to Susanna. "And she must be the one to invite them since she and the young man know each other."

Papa nodded. "Yes, you will personally deliver the invitation, Susanna, since you and the young man seem to have come to some understanding. And I pray this will be resolved. We must keep the tours going at all costs."

Susanna stared at her father. She had hoped he wanted the meeting to restore peace and forge sympathy for the grief caused by the cave. Only by this could they keep Jared and others from warning visitors not to come here. Instead she saw her father desperate to save his livelihood by any means available. No matter what they said, Jared wouldn't believe it, nor would his uncle. They had been through too much. They would look beyond all this to see the real intent, to keep the cave open despite what they had been through.

"God, help me know what to do in all this," she prayed that night. Now, given the quest of delivering the invitation to Jared and his uncle, she couldn't help but feel anxious. Jared and she had begun to build trust between them. Would this now shatter it all?

On the appointed day of the invitation's delivery, Susanna took extra care in dressing and calmed herself with prayer. Since Matt Bransford knew where Jared lived, having delivered the letter she once wrote to him, she asked Matt to take her there. The pleasant spring day and the birds serenading their ride calmed the nervous fluttering of Susanna's heart. The birds flew from limb to limb along the road, soaring above the difficulties of this life. If God could understand the birds' needs, as scripture said, He must also understand what was about to unfold.

The dampness of her hand made the paper she carried limp. Matt tried to entertain her with stories, but her mind remained consumed by her errand. What would she say when she arrived? How would she confront Jared about the contents of the letter? What would he say in response to it and the invitation? And how would she confront him about what she had learned concerning his conversation with the patrons of the cave?

"Yer awfully quiet, Miss Barnett," Matt observed.

"I'm not sure what to say when I see him," she confessed.

"You mean when you see that young fellar? Why, there ain't no reason to fret. He's a fine fellar. We had ourselves a right good talk. He even said I might work the land one day and git paid for it, iffen I can git away from the cave for a spell. Though I don't think Massah Crawn's gonna let me do that."

Susanna glanced over at the man who stared at the road ahead, urging the horses forward. "You talked to Jared?"

"Yes'm, when I delivered that note from you. Pleased he was to git it, I must say. And he dun called me suh, too. Never had anyone call me suh before. Made me feel right important." He straightened then. "Yes'm, he shore made me feel like I was sumthin'. Don't get that much around here. But he said that the good Lawd made us all. And there ain't no difference in the Lawd's eyes."

Susanna marveled at this. Perhaps there wasn't anything to fear. Jared must possess a bit of a merciful heart to give dignity and honor where honor was due. Maybe all would go well.

"Yes'm, he made my day. I've talked to many a folk in the cave there, but none treat me like that man did. They think I'm just a part of that place, you know. But he knows I got feelings. Yes'm, maybe we can get some things changed around here. We could shore use it."

She liked hearing these descriptions that painted a more appealing picture of Jared than what she had heard of late. She always wanted to know more about him, and it seemed the Lord was opening new doors each day.

The rolling hills surrounding the cave soon gave way to patches of green farmland, where those who tried to make a living off the land had built their homes. She began feeling tense once more as the horses plodded ever nearer to their destination. Matt drove the wagon around a bend in the road and toward a plowed field. "This is the field here where I dun seen the fellar. He ain't there now, though."

Susanna strained to see. "No one is working the fields. Head on up the road a bit."

Matt did so, only to come to a junction in the road. He brought the horses to a standstill. "Well, now, I ain't sure where to go, Miss Barnett. This here's the field, all right. Maybe he lives close by."

"We'll ask at the next cabin we come to. Keep going straight." She tucked the lap robe more firmly around herself to protect her dress from the dust, and retied the bonnet beneath her chin. There was no turning back. Papa, Mr. Miller, Dr. Croghan—everyone was looking to her to accomplish the task. They wanted her to help them keep the cave open. Jared wanted to see it closed. Why did everyone think she could help?

A simple cabin soon appeared in the distance, not unlike the one in which Susanna had grown up. She caught her breath as memories washed over her from several years ago. She would stop here and inquire.

In the yard, a man was splitting wood with an ax. His hat sat low on his head even as Matt drew the wagon to a stop. He looked up for a moment before swiping off his hat. "Susanna?"

Jared! She nearly leapt from the wagon in relief. God had guided their steps to the very place.

"This is a surprise," Jared said, offering his hand to help her down from the wagon.

From what she could tell, he did look surprised and even pleased. She rearranged her skirts, shaking out the many petticoats.

"What are you doing here?" He glanced at Matt sitting in the wagon before ramming the ax into a stump. "I take it this isn't a social call." He went over to a water barrel to refresh himself, offering her the dipper.

"No, thank you. And, of course, this is a social call. Or rather a social call to bring you an invitation." She wasted no time handing him the letter crafted by Mr. Miller. She watched his dark eyes travel over the words, wondering what he was thinking. He then tucked the note into his pocket and picked up the ax. Confusion and curiosity filled her, watching him lift the ax and bring it to bear on a chunk of wood. "Have you nothing to say?"

"I have plenty to say, but since my uncle is also invited, I can't say one way or the other. So I won't keep you. I'm sure there are things waiting for you at the hotel."

Susanna could hear the suspicion in his words. She heaved a sigh, wishing these issues weren't separating them; wishing other feelings could come forth instead. "It doesn't matter whether you succeed in closing the cave down anyway. There may not be people coming to the hotel as it is, what with you warning them to stay away like we all have the fever."

He spun around.

"Yes, those people you talked to sent a letter to my father, angry about the cave. Now my father and Dr. Croghan think you only want to cause harm—that you and your uncle are planning harm against the cave."

His face colored. "I don't want to harm anyone, Susanna. You know that. I felt I needed to warn those people as to what is going on inside the cave." His eyes narrowed. "So is that why we're invited to a dinner? So they can put us in jail? Or banish us from this part of Kentucky?"

"No. They want to talk. That's what you wanted in the first place, wasn't it? To make people understand your point of view?"

Wielding the ax, he swung once more. The tool came down hard on another log. "Talking is a good thing, but my uncle won't take kindly to just fancy words. He's heard all the words. He wants something done."

"But civilized people talk out their differences. And I know Dr. Croghan wants the hard feelings put aside. Isn't that good?"

"I suppose it is," he said once more, returning the ax to the stump. "I should be glad. But I know they might also be planning some trick. Something that will make us all go away and never come back. No one offers people like us fancy victuals without some other idea in mind." He eyed her. "Susanna, I hope if you know what it is, you would tell me."

Her face flushed. "Jared, it's dinner and conversation."

Jared wiped the sweat from his brow and gazed at the woods beyond. "I'll ask my uncle what he thinks, but for sure I will come."

"Good. I'm glad." She hoped she sounded as eager as she felt. She wanted him there, even if they were still at odds with each other. Just to be in his presence at the table where she could listen to him rather than the diatribe of her older brother would be a pleasant diversion.

He stood still, staring at her in a way that made her heart leap. She had accomplished her task, but she could also bask in the knowledge that a bond still existed, even if she was dismayed at him for his actions of late. He was not her man on a black horse. But there were things about Jared Edwards that still interested her, more than any dream or any other man, for that matter. Maybe it was what Matt said on the way to this place. That Jared was caring, sensitive, and wanted to help others. No one should fear him but rather respect him. She hoped to see more of that kind of man in the days ahead.

Chapter 9

S he was a beautiful vision to him. Her hair caught in the wind. Her blue eyes held a measure of expectancy as she extended the invitation to him with fair and unblemished hands. He wished he hadn't been so suspicious during her visit, wishing instead he could have revealed his true heart. He had wanted to tell her that he would run all the way if he could, dashing by horseback over hills and dales, just to dine with her and stare into her eyes. How he wanted to shout what lay hidden within his heart, if not for other things that barred the way. He wanted to cast away all obstacles—the suspicions, the rifts, the cave, his aunt's death—everything, so he might experience love and marriage. Perhaps God had opened the door by allowing this dinner to take place. He would speak what lay on his heart and forget about it. He would drink in Susanna for as long as he dared, and afterward, take her on an evening stroll.

As he rode over to his uncle's place, he hoped he could convince Uncle Dwight to accept the invitation without raising further difficulty or suspicion. He had not heard from the man in quite some time. He would have checked on him sooner if not for the recent memories of the rifle and the harsh words. Easing his hold on the reins, he slowed to a stop. The cabin looked forlorn and still, as if shrouded in a veil of sadness. He slowly approached the place, keeping careful watch, and called out a greeting so as not to be hailed by another bullet. "Hello! Uncle, you here?"

The door slowly opened. Uncle Dwight emerged, a blanket wrapped around him, shivering. Jared dismounted from his horse and stared in disbelief. "Uncle?"

"I'm sick, Jared," he said, interrupted by a hacking cough.

"Let me help you." He assisted the older man inside to a chair, where Uncle Dwight fell down with a grunt. The place was cold. Jared set to work stoking the fire. Then he looked around for something to make up a cup of tea. Finding a few dried herbs on hand, he put water in a pot to hang over the fire.

"Never felt so awful in my life," he confessed. "Wish Mattie were here. How I miss her. Maybe this means I'm going to her soon."

Jared said nothing but waited for the pot to boil. He then began mixing some corn pone in an iron skillet coated with lard. "I'll get you food real soon, Uncle. Then you'll feel better." He did not realize his uncle had been staring at him until he turned to pour water onto the herb mixture, letting it steep.

"How've you been, boy?"

Jared looked up, startled. He couldn't believe the question after all the heartache they had suffered, including his uncle's abandonment. "Doing all right, Uncle," he said softly.

"Need you to help plow the rest of the field there," Dwight added, shifting about in the worn blanket. "Won't have no crop come up lessen it gits plowed some more."

"Be glad to, Uncle." Jared pulled up a chair and sat down at the table. "I've got some news, Uncle. Good news, I think."

His uncle raised his eyebrows. "Ain't been no good news around here since the day your aunt surprised me for my last birthday. Made me that fine shirt, remember? And cooked me the best fixin's I ever had. Turnip greens and her fried chicken. We laughed and. . ." He paused. Tears filled his eyes. "I miss her a heap. If only you could know what love is, boy. You'd understand everything I'm going through."

Jared looked down at his intertwined fingers. How could he tell his uncle that he was trying to understand—but through a woman his uncle would consider an enemy? Instead he changed the subject. "I've been doing some talking, Uncle. With a gal. . .that is, with someone who works at the cave. And it looks like the doctor is ready to listen. They want to talk things out."

A light of hope flickered in his uncle's bloodshot eyes. His crusty lips turned upward into the form of a shaky smile. "They do?"

"That's what Susanna—I mean, Miss Barnett, told me when she brought over the invitation." He pulled out the paper. "The doctor wants us to come to dinner tomorrow night so we can talk."

Uncle Dwight coughed again. "Can't do it. Can't hardly get myself out to do my business. Maybe you can ask Higgins to go."

"The invitation only asks for us. I figured that at least I could go. This is what we've been waiting for, Uncle Dwight. I'm sure of it. A sign that could bring some changes."

"The only change I want to see is that cave sealed shut." He took a long drink of the tea. "Tastes mighty good." He closed his eyes for a moment and swallowed, then leveled his gaze at Jared. "You go to that fancy meal, Jared. Tell 'em what we want. Tell 'em they gotta do what's right for all our sakes." Uncle Dwight leaned over, his bloodshot eyes staring at him. "You tell them we don't want no more of their talk, or they're asking for it. You tell 'em that."

"I'll do what I can, Uncle."

Uncle Dwight sat back. "You do more than that. You can make Mattie proud—proud that she has a nephew she can depend on. Make us both proud of you again. It's up to you. You know that, don't you?"

Little did his uncle realize how Jared had struggled with these very thoughts since the loss of his aunt and his separation from Uncle Dwight. He always wondered if he was doing the right thing, such as when he told those fine people from Philadelphia about the deaths in the cave, or even if he was right in asking for Susanna's understanding. He'd spent many nights thinking and praying. He believed the cave was a danger and that he needed to do what he must to see it closed. He wanted to make Uncle Dwight proud of him.

If only he could reconcile that desire with his feelings for Susanna. How he wished the cave didn't have such a hold on her. Why did she have to believe that a wonder existed beneath the ground and value the cave as some mysterious yet living place that displayed God's creation?

He felt pulled in two different directions by those he thought the most of.

"You'd better get that corn pone 'fore it burns."

Jared hurried to rescue the skillet from the fire. He had other things to rescue, too, like the kinship he once had with his uncle. Here was an open door back into Uncle's Dwight's favor. Yet things could easily tumble out of control like a runaway wagon careening from atop a hillside. He could only pray God remained at the reins to lead him safely through these strange circumstances.

Jared stared down at his only decent set of clothes, the clothes he had worked in to plow his uncle's field that morning. He had no go-to-meeting clothes to wear to a fancy dinner at a hotel. He never thought he would need such attire, being a simple farmer in these parts. But now, heading for this meeting at the Mammoth Cave Hotel, he found himself wishing for a proper suit. A fine shirt. A coat with glistening buttons. Good leather boots. He had cleaned off the mud and taken a rag to his old boots to shine them up as best he could. A bit of grease helped to hold down the wild look of his hair. Even so, he was far from being presentable to men of wealth and power, and especially to the beautiful Susanna in all her finery. There was little he could do about it. He had a task to accomplish. He was going for the sake of his aunt and uncle to see if the impossible might be made possible. And, yes, to see Susanna once again.

Along the way he came upon wagons bearing visitors, all dressed in fine traveling clothes and with an eagerness to see and learn about the cave. He wanted to stop them, to warn them, to keep them away. But now he must think about this dinner. He exhaled a sigh, trying to steady his nerves. He prayed a lot and sang a hymn or two. He wished the traveling minister would come back—the one who led him to the Lord. Or his pa, wherever he was. They would know the words to say to men of power. They would have the wisdom Jared needed.

As he neared the hotel, he saw several men armed with guns, parading about as if expecting some rampage to invade these grounds from the night shadows. As he rode up, one of the men accosted him, demanding to know why he was here. Jared fished inside his pocket for the invitation, wrinkled and dirty.

"You look like a no-good varmint to me," the man growled. "What are you doing sneaking around here?"

"Miss Barnett gave me this invitation." He handed it to the man. "If you don't believe me, send for her."

The man looked as if he would rather hang Jared from the nearest tree. He mumbled something unintelligible, then asked his friend to go find Susanna. Jared waited, still and silent, until he saw her appear in the doorway of the hotel. The sight of her left him weak-kneed. Her smile warmed him all the way to his toes.

"Please come in, Jared. We've been expecting you."

He said no more to the men, who continued to glare at him in suspicion. He entered the hallway of the hotel, illuminated by lard-oil lamps. In the soft glow, Susanna appeared all the more beautiful to him. She wore a dress that dropped slightly off her shoulders, the neckline decorated with flowers similar to the ones she had given to him at his aunt's burial. Again he wished he had better clothes to wear. He would look more like a suitor to her rather than a simple farmer. For now, he forced himself not to dwell on all this but rather on the meeting at hand.

"Your uncle isn't here?" she asked in a soft voice.

"He's ill."

She immediately turned, her concern evident in the way her eyebrows drew together and her red lips parted. "I'm so sorry. I hope it isn't serious."

"I don't think so." He wanted to say more, but the words caught in his throat. Instead he gazed at the fine interior of the hotel—chairs and sofas of wood with the finest carvings he had ever seen and window lights every few steps that made the place seem even larger.

Presently they came upon a huge room and a long dining table. Several men in coats talked boisterously with each other, but turned grim and silent when he and Susanna entered the room. "Dr. Croghan, I'd like to present Mr. Jared Edwards," Susanna said. "Sadly, his uncle is ill and unable to come."

Dr. Croghan stepped forward, impeccably dressed, and much shorter in stature than Jared would have thought. His face portrayed a certain youthfulness with large expressive eyes and a head of thinning red hair. "Pleased to make your acquaintance, Mr. Edwards. I trust your uncle is not too ill?"

"He sends his regrets."

Dr. Croghan acknowledged the other men in the room. "May I also present Archibald Miller, who manages our affairs here at the hotel, and his assistant, Hiram Barnett, Miss Barnett's father."

Jared slowly shook the hand of each man. In turn, they each examined him carefully. Susanna's father gave Jared particular scrutiny.

They all took seats around the table. Jared noted the fine tableware and silver that sparkled in the candlelight. He felt small and insignificant in such a setting. What he could possibly say or do to change these men's minds, he had no idea.

Dinner was served and everyone began to eat. The conversation centered on the activities of the cave, the rise in the number of visitors, the difficulty with supplies, and the need for better roads. Jared wondered as he ate when they would come to the matter at hand. Surely he had not been invited to hear only of their business. Or perhaps they meant for the chatter to unnerve him and make him feel even more insignificant, as if anything he had to say would serve no purpose. At times, he glanced at Susanna, wondering what she was thinking. Her gaze remained fixed on her plate, using her utensil with a delicate air, wiping her lips carefully on a linen napkin. For some reason the mere sight of her gave him confidence. When she flashed him a small smile, he felt even more emboldened.

"I'm sorry to hear of your uncle's ill health, Mr. Edwards," Mr. Barnett said at last.

Jared looked up at the sudden comment directed his way. "Yes, sir. He felt too weak to come to this meeting, but he thanks you for the invitation."

Dr. Croghan sat back in his seat. "No doubt you realize why we have invited you here to dine with us, Mr. Edwards."

"No, sir. Not really."

Croghan raised his eyebrow, casting a glance toward Susanna's father and the others present. He straightened in his chair. "We are concerned about the rumors that some wish ill toward our endeavors here at the cave. That, of course, is not in keeping with the common good or with decent men."

"I know there are people grieved by broken promises, sir. I am one of them." He caught Susanna's eye as she looked at him before averting her attention to the doctor.

"And what promise might that be, young man?"

Jared cleared his throat even as it began to constrict. "That your cave has 'given proof of its magical qualities,' as you once said. It preserved those from long ago. It has good air. And you offered to cure the sick with something far better than any medicine."

Croghan flushed with a color to match his hair. "You remember well. I'm impressed."

"It was with those words that I convinced my uncle to part with the only person he ever truly loved, the woman who had been by his side for years, and place her in your care. But because your words were false, she's now dead. And I've lost my uncle's respect."

The men looked at each other. Mr. Miller whispered to Dr. Croghan. "Surely you are aware of the papers that were signed upon your aunt's admission to the sick cave," Croghan continued. "They stated that I would not be held responsible for the outcome of this experiment. And the sick cave was just that. An experiment."

"Yes, I know." The emotion rose within him so that he could barely contain himself. "But such things really do fall on deaf ears when promises are boldly stated before the crowds. And you, sir, don't have a miracle cave. You know that. Your cave has brought nothing but death and money to fill the pockets of the greedy."

The atmosphere in the room turned rancorous. Faces flushed. "I daresay the young man wishes only to bring threats tonight and not a willingness to talk reason," Mr. Miller uttered in a throaty growl.

"I'm not threatening anyone," Jared countered. "I'm only speaking what's in the heart of my uncle."

"And yours as well," finished the doctor. "We know that for certain."

Jared could not deny the fire that had been sparked here this night. Susanna must see the flame as well. She remained still in her seat, twisting the linen napkin in her hands. But he couldn't worry about her opinion of him at the moment.

Croghan set down his fork and folded his hands. "Mr. Edwards, whether you choose to believe it or not, I do understand. Like you, I once had a farm to tend and a hard life to lead. Of course, other matters led to the path of doctoring and to this business enterprise. But I know how difficult it is to make a living here. And desperation leads to decisions one believes are the right decisions. But you cannot allow your guilt to overshadow the good we are trying to accomplish. Helping the sick and deprived. And offering the cave as a means by which people might seek refuge and enjoy a wondrous sight not made by man."

Jared said nothing. The food he ate turned to stone inside his stomach. Maybe he had allowed his guilt to add kindling to the burning fire. But a life was still gone. A family snuffed out of existence. And a proud doctor who still believed in his wonder of wonders, his hand outstretched to accept money, even when staring grief and disappointment in the face.

The doctor continued. "I had hoped that your uncle might come so we could share more about this. It's obvious that you both are angry over what happened. I do hope you understand my sincerity in that I wish all of this laid to rest as the dearly departed rest. I only had the welfare of the sick in mind. If my words brought forth ideas of some miracle to be found, it was not meant to be." He sighed. "Therefore, I am willing to offer your uncle a small compensation to help in this time of need, a token of sympathy for what you both have endured."

Jared looked up, startled. "You mean money?"

"From my personal coffer, young man."

He could not believe it. Money in exchange for peace, to rid them of the pestilence of his uncle, himself, and the others. "You don't mean it. You can't mean it."

Miller began to cough. Croghan flushed. "Of course I do. It is but a small token; I understand that."

"Sir, I don't think you understand at all." Jared came to his feet. "None of you do. Can your money bring back my aunt? Can it heal the grief? Can it change anything at all?" He threw down his napkin and left, striding down for the hall, the anger burning within him. It had been a trap, as he feared, an evil device, a linen bandage slapped over a festering wound. And Susanna sat there, saying nothing to the contrary.

He heard a soft voice then and whirled to find Susanna behind him. She was beautiful to the eye but, to his dismay, a mere product of this place. He realized that now more than ever.

She came forward tentatively. "I hope we can meet again, Jared."

"No," he said quickly. "This is the end. I don't see how I can come back here after this."

Her face disintegrated into a picture of distress. "I'm sorry for tonight, Jared. I wish it had gone better for you."

He looked at her, trying to believe her words. She seemed sincere, yet he couldn't help but remember her words from the past, words that spoke of her bond to this place no matter the circumstance.

"The doctor is trying to make the best out of a difficult situation," she continued. "He doesn't like to see people angry and hurt. He wants to help. That's all he's ever wanted to do. Help."

"So you agree with him? That his money is the help we need? It doesn't help, Susanna. The love of money is the root of all evil. I thought you were starting to understand that. But I guess you don't."

She bristled. "You know nothing of what I believe, Jared. You only presume to know, as you have done all along. I know I need to see with my heart instead of my eyes. I am trying to listen, to allow my heart to see. I wish you would, too, and not let your guilt blind you to everything."

When she turned and left, a part of his heart disappeared with her. What could buy him his peace? Erase this guilt? Calm his soul? If only he didn't feel so confused and so alone.

Chapter 10

Jared took the long way home that night, over the rolling hills and the sunken ground illuminated by the rising moon. What had he expected from the dinner, after all? Did he really think the doctor would change his mind and close down the place he had put all his time and money into perfecting? Did he presume any of them would change their minds, even though he held out a hope that Susanna might? She would never change. Nothing would change. Her family needed the cave for their livelihood. The doctor needed it for whatever suited him. The more Jared thought about it, the more he realized that closing the cave would never happen. The cave was here to stay, as was the river bend or the dark line of trees that framed the horizon. Something else would have to change. Maybe his way of thinking. Calming his mind with the act of forgiveness. Pursuing other thoughts and dreams—of what, he didn't know. At one time, his thoughts and dreams were turning to Susanna. But after tonight, he knew his hopes of love were as foolish as the idea of shutting up Mammoth Cave. Neither was meant to be.

Jared eased his horse to a stop, allowing the animal to drink its fill from a nearby stream. If he went home and shared the confessions of the evening, he knew what his uncle's reaction would be. Unrestrained anger. And maybe a rifle pointed once more in his direction. He would have to convince Uncle Dwight to release his burden in some other way, to find comfort in knowing Mattie was in a better place, and to forgive as the Lord would want. But his uncle had no relationship with the Lord. He hadn't experienced the forgiveness of Jesus in his heart, nor did he have the faith to believe there was more to life than what one saw in this world. It would be like trying to convince a mule to change its ornery ways. But Jared did serve a God of impossibility—a God strong enough to cut through the pride and open his uncle's eyes. And, yes, a God able to erase his guilt and renew his heart.

Jared ushered the horse back to the main road. He was glad the moon was high, or he likely would have needed to bed down in the woods somewhere until it was light enough to see. He bypassed his uncle's place and headed straight for his small cabin. He thought of Susanna living within the spaciousness of a fine hotel with its fancy furniture and chairs of intricate carvings. How could he ever think she would leave all that for his place in the backwoods? She had embraced the hotel life and the cave to escape such an existence. He had to stop thinking that God had brought Susanna to him for a special reason. He had to cease considering that she might be the one he could know and love like the woman Uncle Dwight said he needed. As Jared had told her, it was over.

Jared put up the horse in the barn and went inside the dark, cold cabin. He managed to light the lantern and find a small hunk of corn pone left from several days ago. After the sumptuous dinner at the hotel, the dry bread tasted flat. He nearly choked on it, what with everything spinning about in his mind. There had to be something more God wanted to do in all this. But what?

He grabbed his Bible and began to read. Comforting words from Psalms flowed into his wondering heart like a soothing brook. He looked at the lone dried flower from his aunt's burial tucked inside the pages of Song of Solomon. He opened his Bible to that book and began to read. The words played like a love song. He could only think of Susanna's strong voice this night.

You know nothing of what I believe, Jared. You only presume to know, as you have done all along. I know I need to see with my heart instead of my eyes. I am trying to listen, to allow my heart to see. I wish you would, too, and not let your guilt blind you to everything.

Yes, he wanted her to see with her heart. But was he doing the same? Wasn't his heart filled with other things right now? Things that got in the way, like the unresolved guilt and pain he needed to overcome? *Lord, please take this all away, somehow,* he prayed. *Help me to see Your purpose and Your wisdom.*

Just then he heard the sound of horses and saw the flicker of lanterns through the darkened window. He stood and came to the doorway to see the ragged face of his uncle, along with Higgins and the man named Abe. Uncle Dwight didn't look well at all. He heaved with every breath, nearly collapsing were it not for Higgins assisting him.

"I told you this was a bad idea, Dwight," Higgins said, supporting the stricken man. "We could have seen your nephew tomorrow. It's late as it is, and you ain't well at all."

"No. I gotta know what happened with that doctor. I had to come."

Jared gulped. He didn't need or want a confrontation right now. He wanted time to think and reason, to come up with a way to present the information so as not to further burden his uncle. Now the men burst into his cabin and sat around the table. Higgins ate the last of the stale corn pone, which he seemed to enjoy. "Got any good liquor here to wash it down with?" he joked.

"I don't drink, Mr. Higgins."

He chuckled. "I figured as much. Should've brought my own. Anyway, your uncle wants to know what happened at the hotel. And I gotta admit, I'm curious, too. Imagine getting to eat fine victuals in a fancy place like that. Whoo-wee. How did you ever get such an invitation?"

"The daughter of one of the hotel managers gave it to me," Jared said, rolling a tree stump into the cabin, the only chair left to him. He took a seat near the table.

"You know her pretty good, huh? You taking a fancy to her by chance?"

Jared panicked for a moment, eyeing his uncle for a reaction. When none came, he nodded. "I like her well enough. But that's all."

"So what happened?" Uncle Dwight pressed before breaking into a hacking cough.

Jared watched him take out a handkerchief, which the man quickly concealed after wiping his mouth. "We, uh. . .we ate dinner."

"What did you get to eat?" Higgins asked, his eyes wide in anticipation.

"For crying out loud, Higgins," Uncle Dwight muttered before coughing once more. "Does that matter?"

Jared looked between the two men, who scowled at one another. "I don't rightly recall what we ate, Mr. Higgins. I only remember what we talked about."

Uncle Dwight leaned forward. "So what was said? Speak up now! Did that doctor agree to close the cave?"

Jared swallowed hard, wondering how to broach the news. He prayed for wisdom. "He. . .uh, he seems to understand what happened, Uncle. He's like any other doctor, wanting to help and hoping he had found the right cure. It just didn't work out that way."

"I knew it! That no-good, confounded varmint. You see, George? He's no good. That highfalutin doctor killed everyone in that place."

"He did offer money, Uncle," Jared piped up then. "He called it compensation."

For a moment the men gazed at him in bewilderment. "Money?" Abe wondered.

"He said it was a small token for all the grief we've been through."

Uncle Dwight began to cough again. "Money!" He pounded his fist on the table. "So he thinks money's gonna cover his hide. That does it. I ain't gonna listen to him no more. He only wants to buy himself out of this mess. It ain't gonna happen while I live and breathe."

"At least he did offer something," Higgins said. "Can't say he didn't. That means he cares."

"I don't care. Money means nothing. Nothing at all. And it sure don't bring back the dead." Uncle Dwight stirred in his chair, his face pinched. Jared stared, wondering if this truly was agonizing for him or if the agony stemmed from something else. "You still got that powder you were talking about, Abe?"

"Yep. Good stuff, too."

"Then I say we do it. No more talking. It's time we git going and do what we should have done in the first place."

Jared stared in disbelief. "You mean you're going to blow up the cave?"

"You're right, that's what I mean. Blow it to kingdom come."

Jared looked back and forth at the men and watched Higgins, who stood to his feet and began searching a cupboard for food. "You can't mean that, Uncle."

"I mean every word. Soon as Abe can git the stuff here."

"But Uncle, there are people still in the cave. Sick people. You can't blow it up."

Again his uncle stirred. "They're as good as dead in there anyway," he muttered.

"We'll get them out somehow," Higgins went on, finding a few store-bought crackers to eat. "Even if I have to go in that place myself. Maybe git myself on one of those highfalutin tours. I'll warn 'em to get out of there."

Jared was beside himself. "You mean you agree with this plan?" He couldn't believe what he was hearing, that the man he had begun to trust would agree to such an act.

"Nothing else is gonna change that doctor's mind unless we show some force. The time has come. We've done all we could."

"But how can we answer destruction for destruction? You can't. It isn't right."

Uncle Dwight stood shakily to his feet. "It ain't up to you no more. We're doing this because of you anyway, because you had some fool notion to think that doctor could help Mattie." He reached for his hat, planting it firmly on his head. "C'mon. I ain't staying one more minute in a cabin of a coward with no backbone to do what's right."

Higgins and Abe followed him out to the awaiting horses, muttering as they went. Jared ran to the doorway, watching them saddle up, realizing the unthinkable might very well happen. No, he didn't like what the cave had done. He had his own suspicions about that doctor. But he couldn't risk harming anyone just because of his feelings. Isn't that why he wanted the cave closed to begin with? To protect and not destroy? And what of Susanna? What if his uncle's anger flamed even further, and he brought his gun to the hotel? He shuddered at the thought of the bullet that had just missed him. He couldn't let this happen, not to Susanna, not while he had the means to do something about it.

As soon as they were out of sight, Jared ran to the corral to saddle his other horse. There was still time, he realized, but it grew short. He must ride fast and furious, even if it took all night.

~⟜

Susanna tossed and turned. Sleep refused to come, no matter how hard she tried to shift her thoughts to pleasant things—a babbling brook, the feel of the wind, strolling in the woods to look at the emerging flowers. All she saw was Jared's face, the pained expression, the pleading in his voice for her to help him. The moon shone bright that evening, casting shadowy images on the wall. She rose out of bed and began to pace. No, she did not like how things had gone this evening. What should she have expected, after all? Her father and the doctor would not heed the wishes of someone like Jared, a man below their means, a man who illustrated what they once were long ago, a man they saw as harboring some manner of evil intent. But there was a stark difference between them. For Susanna's family, their salvation had been Dr. Croghan and his offer of work at the hotel to ease their burden. Jared's salvation was peace and protection, life and not death. While she had spoken of a heart willing to seek him out, it was his heart that seemed the stronger one. He could see past the money—even the money offered by Dr. Croghan—to a better purpose. He could have money, but he wanted something greater. It both puzzled and intrigued her.

Susanna glanced out the window to the ground below. Rays of moonlight cast a veil-like radiance upon the quiet grounds of the hotel. She wondered about the remaining invalids in the doctor's sick cave and what might be happening to them there, even at this moment. Here in the hotel, it was easy to forget they existed. But with Jared an ever-present image in her thoughts, she couldn't forget what was going on. Maybe they should close down that part of the cave. Perhaps by closing down the cottages, it would help solve the problem and satisfy both Jared and his uncle.

She continued to stare out the window, pondering it all, listening to the beat of her own heart, when suddenly she saw the dark outline of a horse and rider approaching the hotel. She straightened. She recalled at once the dream she'd had of a man on a black horse ready to whisk her away. Surely it couldn't be her dream come to life—and when she least expected it. She hurried to put on a petticoat and a dress. For all she knew it could be the men returning, wishing them harm. She should alert Luke and Papa.

Instead Susanna lit a lamp and slowly came down the stairs, careful not to waken anyone. There were supposedly guards, hired by the doctor to patrol the grounds, but for some reason they were absent this night. Likely they were at the kitchen refreshing themselves with victuals left over from the evening fare. She came to the side door and opened it. The single rider remained on his horse, searching every window of the hotel as if looking for something or someone. She drew in a sharp breath, wishing she knew who it was.

Then she heard it. A familiar voice calling her name. "Susanna!"

She shook at the sound of her name uttered from the night. She held the lamp up higher. "Who are you?"

The rider dismounted. He came up swiftly. "Please, I have to talk with you. It's important."

Jared! What could he want at this time of night? She glanced about, half expecting him to have brought the enemy with him.

"There isn't much time."

"I think all has been said that can be said, Jared. I don't know why you came back. You told me you never wanted to see me again."

"Susanna, please. There isn't time. I came here to warn you."

"I know. I've heard your warnings. Obviously, neither of us is willing to change."

"You don't understand." He grabbed her hand, forcing her to the path they had once taken on a night as unpredictable as this.

"Stop it!" she protested. "What are you doing?"

He whirled her around. "Susanna, they're coming to blow up the cave!"

She halted and fell onto the bench. "What?"

"My uncle wants to blow up the cave. He was very angry when he heard about the meeting tonight. He went into a rage. He had his friends there, too, including another man who lost someone in the cave. They're making plans to blow it up."

She trembled. "B—but they can't! There are people inside."

"They talked about warning those still in the cave. But I don't trust my uncle. He even said the people in there are as good as dead. If he gets his hands on Abe's powder, he might just come and do it himself. Not that I think he could right now, as he's pretty sick. But I don't know for certain. I wouldn't put anything past my uncle any longer."

She began to shiver. "This is dreadful. I don't understand what makes men do such things. . .and when poor souls can be hurt."

"Because he's hurt, too. Hurting inside, that is. He isn't a Christian like you and me. He has no one to turn to, no one who can give him comfort. He's trying to find comfort in his anger. And now it's turning into a need for revenge."

"I never thought it would come to this. I know I saw your uncle with his gun, but I didn't think the man would really turn violent." She stared at him, his dark silhouette against the dove white of the moon. "So you don't want to close this place down, too?"

"Susanna, right now what I want isn't important. It's doing the right thing that is. And I won't have people hurt. I'd rather the cave stay open forever than see anything like this happen—or you or anyone else get hurt."

Jared's voice was gentle, sincere, unwavering, and determined, willing to follow the Lord in all he did despite how he felt. He was the rider of her dream, the one sweeping her off her feet, and not by some charm but by so much more. She reached out and cupped his face, feeling the prickle of beard stubble in her hand. Tears of gratitude welled up in her eyes. "Thank you, Jared. Thank you so much for coming here and telling me this. It means so much. . .I can't even begin to say." She drew forward. All at once, his arms swept her into an embrace. Suddenly their lips met. His kiss proved the grandest, the most wondrous sensation she had ever experienced.

He lurched backward as if stunned by what happened. "Susanna, I. . ." He stood quickly. "I—I'd better go before I'm seen."

She watched him hasten for his horse before she went to her father. She had to make sure he'd made his escape before this place swarmed with men and guns that were sure to follow on the heels of his warning. He mounted the animal and dug in his heels, galloping away into the darkness. For a moment, she basked in the memory of his presence, the tingle of his lips, the love welling in her heart, even on an anxious night like this. Then she hurried back into the hotel.

~

"Lord, what am I going to do?" He had stopped in the woods, too exhausted to go any farther. He had taken down his bedroll and wrapped himself in it, hoping to catch a bit of sleep. But all he could do was sit up against a thick tree and think about the kiss. Surely it was a kiss wrought out of gratitude and gratefulness, but he knew it was much more. If it were not for the seriousness of the circumstances at this moment, he would return in the morning and take her away from that place. Maybe he still would. They could join the wagons heading to the West, away from the cave, the greed, the places filled with memories. If only it could happen. If only she would agree. He wrapped the blanket tighter around him and stared into the night that would soon give way to a new dawn. Maybe when all this was over and peace was found at last, he might likewise embrace a new dawn in his life, a light he would welcome beyond measure.

Chapter 11

Jared awoke to the sound of a fist pounding on his cabin door. He had slept away the morning after the all-night ride to and from the hotel to warn Susanna of the impending danger. He'd tried to settle in his bedroll in the woods but couldn't sleep. After the horse had sufficient rest, he decided to pack up and head back to his cabin. He arrived just as dawn began to break.

Now with the banging on the door and the morning sun piercing through the window light, he felt a throbbing pain in his temples. Slowly he came to his feet. Dizzy, his head in a fog, he stumbled to the door.

"You no-good coward," a young man hissed. "How could you do that—and to your own uncle, too? How could you?"

Jared stared at the man about his own age. A fist swung in his direction. He ducked and hastily retreated.

"The law came and took my pa and your uncle away!" he cried. "They said someone named Edwards went last night to the hotel and warned them about the plan to blow up the cave."

Jared tried to register all of this in his fog-riddled mind. The ride to the hotel and the encounter with Susanna seemed in another place and time. Then the recollection came crashing back to him as the angry face stared into his and the balled fist readied to sink another blow. "I—I had to warn them. Who are you?"

"Riley Higgins. My pa is George Higgins, and he wouldn't hurt no one. You know, he liked you a heap. He talked about you. Said you had a good head on your shoulders and that I ought to listen. Well, I'm about ready to knock your head clean off for what you did!" The man stepped inside, throwing a chair out of his path.

Jared fell back to the opposite wall of the cabin. "I had to warn them. Your pa was in on the whole thing. He stood right here and agreed to it. I heard him myself. I had no choice."

"You're a coward," Riley hissed. "And now my pa and your uncle are on their way to Louisville because of that doctor. They'll go to jail for conspiracy. That's what I hear." Riley hurled himself into a chair. "I can't believe this. I can't believe my pa's goin' to jail. What are we gonna do?"

For a moment, Jared had no words. He hadn't really given any thought to the consequences of his actions last night. His only thought was to protect the innocents like Susanna and the people still living in the cave. He didn't want to see any more suffering and death. He rubbed his aching head before going to a pail for some cool water.

"You have to go see that doctor and tell him this was all a mistake. You have to tell him there weren't no conspiracy, that my pa wouldn't hurt nobody."

Jared drank deeply from the dipper before letting it fall to the bottom of the pail with a faint splash. "I can't, Riley. It would be a lie. They were planning to do it. They wouldn't try to find a peaceful way out. They were going to take matters into their own hands and not let God help."

"What's God got to do with it?" He spat out the words.

"Everything. Because He cares."

"He didn't keep my pa from goin' to jail."

"He didn't keep a lot of things from happening. Your pa losing his cousin in the cave. My aunt dying. But He has His reasons. It's not for us to try and figure it out. We're to let Him work, even when we don't know the answers. Sometimes He just wants us to have faith that He's going to work it out, even when we don't understand how He's working."

"My pa said you were religious."

"I'm a Christian. Anyone can be religious, but a Christian is one who believes in Jesus. You ought to believe in Him, too. He'd help you through times like these."

Riley stirred in his seat. "I don't have time to sit here and jaw about religion right now. I gotta git my pa out of jail. I'll go see that doctor myself if I have to. And what are you gonna do? Your uncle's dying, you know. He has the consumption. If you had any sense in you, you'd git him released. Lessen you don't care if he dies in jail. If so, then maybe you belong in jail, too." Riley bolted to his feet and left.

Stunned by the revelation, Jared stood still and silent, his heart beating rapidly. *Uncle Dwight has the consumption? No!* He recalled the look of pallor about his uncle and the handkerchief the man had deftly put away when he thought no one was looking. Did that cloth have on it the telltale stain of blood, the sign of the dreaded disease? He closed his eyes in despair. In his zeal to save Susanna and others, he just might have sentenced his uncle to death in some forsaken jail cell.

Jared began loading up a saddlebag. He had no choice. He had to go back to the hotel, back to the doctor, and beg for mercy, for a way out, for another miracle.

～

The road had become all too familiar to Jared, the one leading him to the hotel and Mammoth Cave, though he had no idea what he would do when he arrived. With his sick uncle imprisoned because of him, he, too, felt sick inside. He felt no confidence in the meeting to come. He knew what would happen when he saw that doctor and the others. He had stared those men in the eyes. Met them face-to-face. They were deadly serious about their business and their cave. They would show no mercy. And another of his relatives would die because of something he had done.

The journey seemed long this time. The burdens of his soul were heavy. Maybe he had purposely slowed the trip so as to avoid what he knew awaited him. He veered off the path to the hotel and headed for the river. He would take time to think and pray. Get his thoughts together. Think of what he wanted to say. And allow the Lord to speak words of encouragement to his beleaguered soul.

The river was low. Not much rain had fallen in recent weeks. Saplings bent over the river as if attempting to draw out the life-giving water. There were few fish to be found. He paused then with the horse's hooves at the water's edge and looked at the meandering river. "God, what am I going to do?" he asked aloud. *I need an answer, but answers aren't coming. I know I have to find that doctor. I know he has no right to release my uncle or the other men after what they were planning to do. But what if Riley's words are true? What if my uncle does have the consumption? If he isn't set free, he will die in jail. How can I live with that?* His head fell to his chest, staring at the reins wrapped around his hand. He couldn't turn back, and he couldn't go forward. He was trapped, his heart caught in a snag.

Just then, a song drifted to his ears. He thought it might be a bird, so sweet and lilting the melody, until he heard words of what sounded like a hymn. He edged from his saddle and guided the horse to a tree where he secured the reins around a trunk. Someone approached, her song carrying on the wind. He waited and looked.

Then he saw her, her dress gathered in one hand, touching the water with her other hand. A hat hid her face from view, but he would know her regardless. Maybe she was his answer. He moved slowly so as not to startle her. She continued her singing, a song of praise it seemed, until he came but a stone's throw away. She then jerked herself upright and whirled around. "Susanna, it's me."

"Oh, Jared!" She hurried toward him, her arms outstretched. She seemed genuinely pleased to see him. He wanted to hold her, too, but the pain of this day kept his arms at his side, even as she embraced him. Her lips touched his cheek.

"I don't know what we would have done without you. You saved us." She released her grip on him and stepped back. She looked beautiful, but with a beauty marred by their circumstances. How he wished none of this had happened, that he and Susanna could go off into the Kentucky hills, get married, and make a home for themselves. They would live far away from caves and death and jail cells and consumption and everything else wrong in this world.

"What's the matter?"

She asked it with such innocence, he could scarcely believe it. Surely she must have heard what happened. He avoided her gaze and looked out over the river once more.

"Jared? What is it?"

"My uncle. Higgins and the others. That doctor had them arrested."

She stood still and silent.

"Higgins's son told me they're gonna be taken all the way to Louisville. That's where the doctor's from. He knows the law there. He's going to have them put in jail."

She continued to remain quiet, in another silent vigil. If only she would say something, anything that would ease the burden in his heart and set them all free.

"All they needed was a warning," Jared went on. "They didn't need to be arrested. They didn't do anything. And now I've found out my uncle has the consumption. I need to find that doctor and tell him. I need to make him understand that my uncle won't survive jail." He kicked at the ground. "But no one here cares about that. You said you've tried to understand. . . ."

"Yes, I have."

"It's hard unless you've lost someone you love and then watch others fall because of it. I don't know why this is happening. I thought I did everything God wanted me to do. I talked my uncle into letting my aunt go to that cave after hearing the doctor speak. I thought it was the right thing to do. Then Aunt Mattie dies. And now I'm in the same place with my uncle. I thought I was doing the right thing by coming to warn you. And now my uncle is going to die because of it."

"You can't blame yourself for any of that, Jared. You've done what is right."

"Then why is this happening, Susanna? Why isn't any good coming from this? Why are people dying?"

"I don't know. God knows what our lives will look like once He's done working on them, as my mother used to tell me. He knows the past, the present, the future. I don't think it was a mistake that your aunt came here. I don't believe in chance. If we really are God's, He has a plan for each of us. And His reasons."

Jared tried to listen, but the emotion of the moment proved too far-reaching. "I have to find Dr. Croghan and tell him to release my uncle. Do you know where he is?"

"Most likely he is in the cave. I haven't seen him this morning."

"If I don't find him, another life is going to be snuffed out. Another life that could have been saved." Jared began heading back to his mount, even as he heard Susanna's footsteps following him in the grass.

"Jared, everyone here is very anxious. There are many men on guard everywhere. The hotel, the cave. If you try to enter the cave to see the doctor, they will arrest you, too."

"Then help get me into the cave, Susanna. Help me find a way to see the doctor. If you come with me, they will let us both in."

She stepped backward. "But. . .I–I've never even been in the cave. How can you ask me to do that?"

He untied the reins. "Maybe you need to see it. Maybe you need to see for yourself what the doctor has done and what lurks in there. Maybe you'll realize then that what I've been saying all along is true."

She bristled. "So you still think that closing down the cave is the answer to everything. You say it's to keep out danger. But I think the doctor said it all correctly. You only want to shut up the guilt in your heart. You don't want to deal with it face-to-face. And if you keep trying to do this, it will only eat you away to nothing."

He dropped the reins. His face flinched from the pain of her words. Yet he refused to yield. "I will go myself if I have to and find that doctor. I'll get those sick people out of there."

"And then what, Jared? Will you blow up the cave instead of your uncle and his friends? Will you finish the job?"

They stared at each other. She whirled and began heading up the trail toward the hotel.

"Where are you going?"

"I'm going to find Stephen Bishop. He's the head guide. I'm going to ask him to help us find Dr. Croghan. Stephen knows everything about the cave. He can get us in there and back safely. Stay here so you aren't seen."

He stared in disbelief. Maybe there was a bond between them, stronger than mere understanding or a simple truce. Maybe it wasn't just a kiss of gratitude they had shared last night. Maybe she really did love him and wanted to see things resolved. The mere thought made him hopeful for the future, even if the present looked bleak.

What am I doing? Perspiration beaded on her face. *Do I really care that much about Jared? Can he really be having this kind of effect on me, the kind that would make me do just about anything for him?* She hurried up the trail, past the men with guns guarding the cave entrance. They nodded at her. She sighed. Something stronger than anxiety or even fear was at work here. At the riverbank she had seen a man in pain. A man desperate to free himself from his burden of guilt. A man who needed answers—the same man who had sought to protect her and who now needed her help. She was seeing more and more how much she had changed. Nothing had been the same since that dreary day when she first gazed on Jared a few weeks ago. Little did she realize what a simple bouquet of early spring lilies would bring her. Now she stood on the verge of descending into a dark and forbidden place that, up to this point, she had only heard spoken of. Could love transform a person in such a way as this? Could love make one attempt to do things only dreamed about before? But there was no choice. She and Jared were connected by God's great plan. And she would see this journey through, even if she wondered what would come of it in the end.

The hotel was a flurry of activity when she arrived. Angry patrons milled about, asking why they were not being allowed to tour the cave. She saw her father and Mr. Miller frantic among the irate guests, trying to explain the circumstances without causing a panic.

Susanna brushed by the milling tourists and walked to the humble shacks built behind the hotel. In one of them she found Stephen Bishop, playing with a little boy on his lap.

"Miss Barnett!" he exclaimed. "Ain't this a surprise? I reckon you know my little Tom here."

She smiled briefly. "Stephen, I need your help. We must find the doctor, and he's in the cave. Can you take us there?"

"Ain't no one allowed in the cave, miss. Not right now anyways."

"It's very important that we find him. A man's life depends on it."

Stephen exchanged looks with his wife before handing the young boy over to her. He grabbed some lanterns, a large metal jug, and a leather pouch. "Someone hurt?" he asked, following her outside.

"Yes, he's hurting very badly and needs the doctor's care. I know you can lead us there. You know everything about the cave."

"Yes'm, I shore do. The cave and I are good friends." Stephen paused to fill up the leather pouch with water from an outside well.

"So the cave isn't really a danger to anyone?"

"There's always danger in anything one does. It's what you do with it that matters. The good Lawd gave us minds to think things out. So long as you keep on thinking and be smart, you can make it through most everything. It's when people stop thinking that they git into trouble." He began heading toward the hotel.

"Not that way," Susanna urged, thinking of her father's reaction if he saw Stephen carrying equipment for a tour. "There's too much commotion right now at the hotel. The guests might think you're leading a tour. Let's take the path through the woods."

He obliged. "Yep, they's all riled up today. I hear someone wants to blow up the cave or some fool thing. At least that's the rumor going around. That's why there's no tours today." He began to chuckle. "Ain't no one can blow up that cave. No siree. That cave was meant to be found and explored."

"You seem confident of that."

"More than most folks, I reckon. Maybe 'cause I've seen more than most folks. Miss Barnett, when you go into the cave, you really are steppin' into another world that ain't like our own. It really is a mammoth of a cave."

Susanna drew in a sharp breath. And now she was about to enter the cave that, to her, had only been mere words spoken by people. Maybe seeing the beauty of the underground world and the good work of the doctor would settle any doubts—so long as it didn't create new ones.

Chapter 12

Susanna had no idea why she'd agreed to do this. Despite her best intentions, doubt gnawed at her with ugly teeth. Fear of the unknown nipped at her heels as she drew closer to the cave's entrance. Stephen headed down the trail, loaded with provisions that included extra lard for the lanterns, food, and water.

"I never go anywhere in the cave without my supplies," he said. "Don't never know what might happen."

Susanna didn't like the connotation behind his words. She hoped this would be an easy venture and that everything would go well between Jared and the doctor so that her own relationship with Jared might prosper. She wanted to see the rift gone and a love between her and Jared take its place. The journey between them had been tenuous at best. Now she was ready to stand on firm ground.

When they came to the cave entrance, Susanna motioned for Stephen to wait while she hurried down to the Green River. Jared was there where she'd left him, pitching stones into the water, looking thoughtful and even a bit lost. "We're ready," she said breathlessly. "I have a guide."

Jared followed her up the wooded path. "You didn't tell the guide why we wanted to see the doctor, did you?"

"I only told Stephen we needed to find Dr. Croghan, that someone was sick. Stephen knows everything about the cave. He's been exploring it for many years now."

Jared said little. No doubt his mind was preoccupied by everything that was happening. She wished the difficulty would draw them closer instead of pushing them apart. After last evening and the kiss they'd shared, she felt certain God had brought them together for a purpose. Though Jared had not been the one she once envisioned in her dreams, even if he did own a horse as dark as midnight, there were things about him that attracted her. He was not pretentious. He held no lofty ambitions. He was straightforward in thought and deed, commanded by God, who flowed like a river in his heart. Isn't that all she really needed? Simplicity. Determination. A fine Christian character. And at this moment, one who needed her as much as she needed him.

"Is that Stephen?" he inquired, acknowledging the rugged black man who stood patiently waiting for them.

Susanna nodded. Before they could say anything else, a party of four men came hurrying down the trail, armed with rifles. She heard Jared inhale a deep breath and look back to the river. His apprehension grew so thick she could almost touch it.

"What's going on here?" one of the men barked. "No one is allowed inside the cave on the orders of Mr. Miller and Mr. Barnett."

"If you please, I am Mr. Barnett's daughter. I asked Stephen to guide us to the doctor in the sick cave. We have need of his skill as soon as possible."

The man tipped his hat at her before giving Jared a look-over. "Who's he?"

She glanced over at Jared to see the concern clearly written in his eyes. "He's the one whose relative is in need of the doctor's care. The doctor knows his family quite well. Stephen agreed to take us there."

The men looked at each other and shrugged. "All right, but be careful."

Breathing a sigh of relief, Susanna offered a smile of encouragement. "Shall we be going then?"

Stephen led the way down the sloping trail to the gaping hole of the cavern's entrance. A cool gust greeted her, along with the steady trickle of water. Just then, she felt a brief touch on her arm and glanced back to see Jared's luminous eyes staring into hers.

"Thank you, Susanna. I thought for a minute this might all be a trap."

The mere notion made anger well up in her heart. "If you think that, then you really don't know me at all. You only see me as this." She pointed to the dark entrance. "Something black and terrible. Maybe we do need to go in there so God can open both our eyes to the truth."

Stephen lit the lanterns. "Each of you needs to carry a lantern," he instructed. "Gets dark in there mighty quick. You won't see nuthin' without them."

The dripping of water and the cool dampness already sent a shiver running through Susanna and a wish that she had donned one of the cave costumes the visitors wore. Maybe her chills were due more to a fear of the unknown than the temperature of this place.

Jared was pointing at some long wooden tubes and what looked like boxes lined against the side of the cave. "What's all that for?" he asked.

"Folks lookin' for saltpeter around 1812 or thereabouts—during the war," Stephen said. "They dun got heaps of it from the cave, I hears. Hauled in the dirt from way back in the cave and brought it here to work it out. Once the war ended, they stopped fetchin' it, and folks came just to see the cave itself. And a fine cave it is, too."

Jared rushed on. "Is there really a bottomless pit in here somewhere, Stephen? And fish without eyes in some underground river?"

Stephen laughed. "So you know things about this place already. Who told you all that?"

"Matt. He said you know everything about it. That you've been to places in the cave no other man has seen."

"Well, if it weren't for the sick folk you got and you needin' to find the massah right quick, we could do a little exploring. But I knows we got important things to do."

Susanna couldn't see Jared's reaction because of the small amount of light generated by the lanterns, but she could sense it. Their entry into this dark place had ignited some strange curiosity within him, like a flame of fire bursting to life in a lantern. She wondered about him, even as she felt her own anxiety increase. To her, this dark, dank, cold place was alive, a breathing monster of sorts, ready to swallow them up if they were not careful. She drew closer to Jared, seeking his warmth and protection, even as he continued to pepper Stephen with questions.

"How far is it to the sick area?" he asked.

"Maybe a mile. Hard to say." He then stopped. "We call this part of the cave the Rotunda."

Jared held up his lantern, the light glinting in his wide eyes. "It must be a big room. I can hear the echo of my voice."

"I'll show you how big." Stephen fumbled with a long stick and the lantern. In one sudden motion, Susanna saw something all aflame fly high into the air before them.

"This is amazing," Jared answered under his breath.

Susanna watched the change in Jared with confusion. The cave had begun to do a work in a way she had never anticipated. Where was the man who despised this place? The one who believed it was dangerous? The one who wanted to see it closed? She dearly wanted to ask him but instead concentrated on the dirty path before her, all the while sensing her own growing displeasure with the passages that seemed to close in around her.

After a time of muted silence, Jared turned. "Susanna? Are you all right?"

She was fumbling with the lantern while trying to keep her dress from dragging in the dirt. She was glad for his concern but less so about his zealousness for this place. "I'm just surprised how eager you are to see the cave."

He didn't seem to hear her as, once again, he hurried up to Stephen's side and asked him about the guide's adventures in the deep. Only when they came to a place Stephen called the Church, where the invalids celebrated services with a minister, did Susanna find a bit of comfort in the dismal surroundings.

Jared ran ahead. The lantern illuminated his excited features as he came before the rocky pulpit. "So this is where the ministers stand to preach," he exclaimed as if trying to envision such a meeting.

"You thinking you might become a minister like that?" Stephen wondered with a chortle.

For an instant there was silence. Susanna could see the question had begun to spin interest within Jared. "A minister," he repeated. "Preaching the light of Christ in a dark place such as this. You've given me something to think about, Stephen. Maybe you were sent from the Lord."

He laughed outright. "Ha! When we see the massah there, you tell him you said that. Tell him that I, Stephen Bishop, was sent from the Lawd." He turned thoughtful. "If only it were true. Then I'd be no one's slave, no sir."

The comment cut Susanna to the quick. She saw Jared abandon the rocky pulpit to approach the guide. "I know," he told Stephen softly. "Men are men. They shouldn't be owned by others, except as slaves of righteousness. But I know, too, that the Bible talks about being a servant. We're all supposed to be servants one to another, Stephen. And I think you are doing something great here. Who else could do the work of discovering what God has created under the ground?"

"Tell that to my missus. My massah gives me free rein to explore my cave, but my wife, she sees my work as fool's work. 'Why you go down there, Stephen?' she says. 'You'll go down there, and one day you ain't nevah coming back. Then what am I gonna do? I'm gonna have to raise Thomas all by my lonesome, and you be some kind of statue down in that hole, turned to stone, you will.'" He sighed. "But it's in my blood. I go where the good Lawd leads. And I keep finding things."

"Please," Jared prodded. "Tell me what else you've found?"

His eyes gleamed. "Just you wait."

They continued on. The rocks shifted and clinked together beneath Susanna's shoes. She felt like she was balancing on some rickety log across a creek, certain she would lose her footing. The lanterns began to flicker as the men suddenly turned right, off the main path.

"Oh no," she moaned in dismay. "Jared! Where are you?"

He didn't answer; he had disappeared up a side passage. Slowly she inched her way along, trying to keep the lantern before her to find the way. This is how it had always been with Jared, trying to follow him amid the dinginess of life to see what awaited them both. It happened after his aunt's burial and continued on even now, chasing him over hills and dales and now through the cave. At this point, tired and quite disheveled, she wasn't certain she wanted to follow him much longer.

When she caught up with them, the men were pointing at the cavern ceiling. Stephen had lit a torch and was showing Jared strange black markings from travelers of the past—etchings written onto the rock's smooth surface for all time. She saw names and dates, a few pictures and other symbols, some recent, others from several years back, and even by a former owner of the cave, all bearing the mark of their presence here.

"I would like to write my name up there," Jared said wistfully. "Maybe one day I'll come back and do it."

"And what will you write?" Susanna asked. "Jared Edwards, 1843? A cave of death?"

He whirled then, the excitement in his eyes suddenly vanishing.

"You told me so yourself."

The lantern shook in his hand. "Susanna. . . ," he began, the doubt evident in his voice.

"I'm only repeating what you once told me. But now I think we should be seeing about your uncle rather than finding places like this. Don't you?"

"We be at the sick cave right soon," Stephen promised.

Jared turned away. Nothing more was said as they retraced their steps back to the main tunnel. Susanna knew her words had buried the eagerness he held for the cave. But wasn't he here to accomplish a purpose? She shivered as the cold began to seep into her. She found nothing exciting about this place, only dreariness that reminded her of a stormy night. The sooner they embraced the sunshine once more, the better she would like it.

All at once, she began to smell the pungent odor of burning fires. Susanna choked and coughed as smoke filled the cavern interiors. The flicker of firelight danced across the steep walls as a stone hut came into view. Stephen stopped one of the attendants to inquire as to Dr. Croghan's whereabouts, while Susanna gazed at the humble structures where the consumption invalids lived. Only a few of them still remained. The first huts were empty. Then she saw a bone-thin figure of a man, his beard long, his clothing dirty. He stood in the doorway of a hut, his cough biting the air. It was an image she might have conjured in a nightmarish dream. Then she saw another invalid, similar in appearance. These were not people. They were ghosts in a way, ravaged by their disease. She bit her lip to keep her emotions at bay and went off to sit on a rock.

Meanwhile, Jared roamed among the huts, talking to a few of the people who still lived in their underground dwelling. Most were unwilling to converse, but he found one man eager to share. She watched from afar as they talked in earnest. Jared nodded, pointing at a wooden hut in the distance, perhaps the very hut where his aunt once lived. She tried to understand the changes in him— from a man once angry over the existence of the cave to one so fascinated that he had nearly forgotten his reason for being here. Moreover, when she examined herself, she saw one who wanted to support the cave with everything in her, only to find herself distressed by the disease and the darkness. She found little glory in a place marred by dripping water and the reality that some strange cave had consumed her life.

Stephen approached her then, taking up her lantern so he could refill it with lard oil. "No one here's seen the massah yet," he said. "He comes by in the afternoon or thereabouts. Seeing as that fellar with you is interested in the bottomless pit and all, I could take you to see it till the doctor comes."

"I'd rather leave this place," she declared. "I've seen enough." It had been more than enough—the darkness, the cold, the blackened names on the ceiling, the sickly ones.

Stephen nodded and left. Jared soon ventured over to where she was keeping a lonely vigil on a stone bench of sorts. "Susanna, I'd like to go with Stephen. I want to see what else this cave has while we wait for the doctor to come. He's going to show me the bottomless pit and the river. It isn't far."

"What happened, Jared?" she chided. "So this isn't such a terrible place, after all? A cave that should be closed forever?"

"I was wrong to say all that without finding out more about this place," he admitted, sitting down beside her. She was thankful for his presence, even if his unusual fascination with the cave confused her. "There is much more here than I ever realized." He paused for a moment. "But I also need to tell you what happened, Susanna. One of the men in the sick cave knew my aunt. He told me things I needed to hear." He picked up a smooth stone from the cavern floor. His dark eyes danced in the firelight. "I think God is telling me it was all right to have my aunt come here. That she didn't die unhappy but happy, even if the cave didn't cure her." He blew out a sigh. "If only I could convince my uncle. Maybe if I could bring him here and have that man tell him what Aunt Mattie said before she went to be with the Lord." He regarded her. "Susanna?"

"I hear you, Jared. I'm glad you talked to the man."

Suddenly his hand gripped hers and held it. "So while we are waiting for the doctor to come, let's go see what else is in the cave. You need to and so do I."

"I don't need to see anything more."

He stared at her for a minute. "This place upsets you that much? Why?"

How could she tell him she'd rather not walk about in darkness, that she preferred the light, the sunshine, the warmth, spring flowers, and a babbling brook at her feet?

"Anyway, I don't want you leaving this place alone. If you want to go back, we will. We can see the doctor at the hotel."

His concern for her felt like a warm wind passing over her heart. But she knew he had a renewed eagerness for exploration. Was it right for her to be so selfish? *What should I do, Lord?* Scripture filled her thoughts. *He has not given me the spirit of fear but of power, of love, of a sound mind.* He had bestowed His power through grace, the firmness of mind, and above all, His love to keep her safe. If Jared wanted to go, she would swallow down her apprehension. "All right. I'll go a little farther."

He leaped to his feet as though her words were like horehound candy to him. He smiled. "I'm glad." He picked up her lantern. "I'll stay with you every step of the way. We won't go very far. Just to the river, and then we'll come back here so I can talk to the doctor and resolve everything."

His voice was persuasive, his hand firmly holding hers, his eyes warm. She was glad she decided to continue on. As it was, she could not leave this place alone, as he'd said; nor could she stay here among the sick. Instead she prayed for the will to endure and for excitement to well up within her as it had in Jared.

Chapter 13

He had been mistaken. Dreadfully mistaken. He wished now that all the words, the actions, the things he had whispered in the night and spoke aloud in the day could be undone. All the words about a dangerous cave, a cave of death, a cave no one should ever see again—he was wrong about it all. Never in his wildest imagination had he expected to find such a place beneath his feet. Yes, he had been grieved, guilt ridden, overwhelmed by his aunt dying in such a place. And, yes, he wanted to see the cave closed. But having begun to experience this place for himself, there was so much more here than he'd ever realized. He could no longer harbor the anger or the guilt. Everything had been confirmed by the sickly man, sitting before one of the wooden huts, thin and dejected but with a willingness to talk. He was the sign Jared desperately needed.

"Shore I remember Mattie," the man had told him when Jared inquired. "So she was yer aunt, eh? A fine lady. Good cook, too. But real sick. She was glad to be here, though. She knew she was a burden to everyone on the outside. Here in the cave, she was one of us. We all understood each other and what we were going through. She said she was glad her husband couldn't see her like this—glad that she was here with us who also had the sickness. And she died like she lived, real peaceful-like."

Jared felt the burdens fall from him upon hearing these words. All the past inhibitions with this place of death faded, as well as the guilt. Aunt Mattie had been glad to be here. She was at peace. Everything was all right. He felt renewed in his spirit and ready for whatever came next.

Now if he could only understand Susanna. Her strange reaction to the cave puzzled him. Out of everyone, she should have the most exuberance for this place. It was her livelihood, after all. The place that brought her fine things and made her who she was. But as this place brought new knowledge to him, it seemed to birth within her fear and uncertainty, reactions neither of them expected.

When the time came to depart, Susanna was on her feet, lantern in hand, ready to follow Stephen and Jared down another tunnel and to another new wonder. He hoped as time passed he could ease her fears, which seemed as cold as the rocky walls. If only she could see this place as he did, like a person awakening to a new dawn, eager to marvel at God's handiwork carved from solid rock. But he also felt the need to protect Susanna. To care for her. To make certain nothing harmed her. He would leave the cave in an instant if he felt she was threatened by it. He knew that now, after seeing her vulnerability in this place.

He would protect her with everything in his power—and beyond.

He walked beside her, his hand holding her arm to steady her gait on the shifting rocks. She murmured how her shoes were not made for this kind of adventure. When he asked again if they should leave, she shook her head. "No, I will do this," she said. The lantern light reflected the determination in her face. If not for the excitement of the surroundings, he might have been inclined to gaze at that pretty face even longer, allowing his heart to absorb its beauty, maybe even succumb to the feel of her lips on his. But now they were on an adventure of the body and the spirit. There would be a time and place for such things again.

"Yonder is the bottomless pit," he heard Stephen say. Susanna stopped in her tracks, holding up her lantern. Scanning the deep pit, they heard a trickling of water far below the wooden bridge where they stood. She sucked in her breath and gripped Jared's hand.

"I can't cross this," she murmured, even as Stephen easily ambled over the makeshift bridge to wait on the other side.

"Susanna, you see how Stephen crossed it safely. I'll go each step with you." *Every step in life together, if you'll have me,* he thought.

"I don't like the idea of some bottomless pit under me." Her voice faltered. She gripped his arm. "Just help me across so I don't need to look down."

He smiled at her willingness to go forward, even if she felt uncertain. She trusted him. How he had prayed for it, especially after he'd endured his uncle's scorn and ridicule when he'd called Jared an untrustworthy fool. With confidence, Jared took her lantern in his hand and, with slow steps, helped her across the bridge.

"This is sure a better bridge than what I first used to cross this here pit," Stephen said with a laugh when they had made it over the chasm. "Why, I only had long tree poles then and had to scoot my way to the other side."

Susanna shuddered at the thought, staring straight ahead, refusing to look back at what they had just traversed. "I can't believe young ladies actually do these tours."

"They do indeed, miss, and they enjoy it, too. So, as I tell them, just enjoy yourself. There ain't nuthin' like it." He began to whoop and cheer as if to settle any remaining fear and uncertainty.

Jared returned Susanna's lantern to her. In its flickering light, he saw her smile at the man's antics. "He is a good guide," she agreed. "No wonder everyone loves him."

Dare I say that I think I'm also falling in love with you, Susanna? Jared thought. Maybe when all this was done, God would show them their future through His unfailing mercy, a mercy that Jared had witnessed time and time again. As scripture said, His faithfulness was new every morning. He would bring to pass His will for their lives. How Jared prayed that God's will also included Susanna.

"Winding Way is up ahead," Stephen announced. "Be careful here. The passage is real narrow, and you need to stoop there some."

Jared took his time maneuvering through the narrow crevice between the rocks. Susanna murmured in dismay as the sharp edges of rock rent her dress and her lantern banged against the stone. He ducked beneath the rock that jutted low from the ceiling, looking back several times to make sure Susanna was still with him. "How did you ever find this passage?" he asked Stephen.

"Twern't easy. I was dun buried up to my chest here." Stephen paused. "I had to dig it out."

"Then how did you know it was even a safe passage to walk through?"

The lantern illuminated the sheepish grin on his dark face. "That twern't easy, neither," he only repeated. "But I done looked at my chest and then at my feet. I saw the dirt there, but the way the rock came down and separated at my feet, I said to myself, this here's a passage. And if it's a passage, I'm gonna find a way to git through so's I can see what's on the other side."

Jared admired the man's tenacity. *If only I could be so determined to conquer life's struggles, to find a passageway even if buried chest deep in trials and tribulations.*

"Jared, I'm caught!" Susanna exclaimed.

He helped her undo the hem of her dress, which had snagged on the jagged rocks. "So is this what you wanted to show me?" she asked. "That I should release my vanity to God by letting it all be wasted in this place?" She showed him her dress, torn and dirty from their ramble in the cave.

He had no words to offer. He only followed Stephen deeper into the darkness. Except for their breathing and the sound of movement, the cave had a distinct stillness he couldn't quite fathom. There were no birdsongs here, no tree limbs swaying in the breeze, no sound of rushing wind, no braying of animals. Only a silence such as he had never before experienced. Oh, he'd experienced the silence of his cabin at times. But there were always noises from an active and living world outside. Here, there was nothing. Nothing, that is, until the sound of trickling water broke the barricade of silence. Stephen pointed out a small cascade falling from above that fed the underground river. To Jared, it played like a soothing melody, interrupting the awful quiet they had come to witness along the journey. He was glad for Susanna's hand on his and patted hers in reassurance. He heard her sigh, even as she slipped a little on the muddy trail. He glanced down to see the front of her dress smeared with mud. She was right. There was no vanity to be had in a place like this.

"This here's the river," Stephen said, shining his lantern. "Look real close and you can see some of the critters that live here."

Jared left Susanna to stare into the water, perfectly still like green glass but for the minute ripples that gave proof of life. White crayfish scurried about in the light of the Stephen's lantern. And something else floated lazily in the waters, oblivious to their presence.

"They ain't scared o' nuthin'," Stephen said with a laugh. "You see why?"

"They have no eyes!" Jared said in glee. "The eyeless fish!"

"Jared?"

A soft voice broke the moment. Susanna sat huddled by a rock, trying to hold her lantern in her trembling hands. "I'm getting cold. Can we leave now?"

"Of course. Stephen, we need to go back. I'm sure the doctor is probably in the sick cave by now."

Stephen obliged. "I was thinking of catching one of these critters for my son. Iffen the lady here wouldn't mind?"

Susanna shook her head and managed a shaky smile. "Of course not." She began to tremble, even as Jared draped his arm around her, hoping to ward off the chill. "G—go and see the fish, Jared. I'm sure you want to."

"I'll see it when Stephen catches one. We'll wait here. It's pretty muddy anyway. A person could slip and fall very easily."

Just then they heard a terrific splash. Jared whirled, even as Susanna cried out. Jared hurried to the river's edge. Stephen was in the river, his arms flailing, the bags he wore pulling him down into the murky depths. "Can't keep my head above," he sputtered.

"Stephen, take off those satchels and give me your hand!"

Jared reached out his hand and managed to clasp the guide's hand, asking God for help. Slowly he dragged the man to the rocky shore where, to his amazement, Susanna was there to help. Together they managed to heave Stephen to safety onto a muddy rock.

"It's my ankle," Stephen murmured. "Fool thing. Foot gave out on me and I fell. I've done walked miles and miles in this place and never had this happen."

Susanna held up the lantern as Jared fumbled with the man's shoe. "I can't tell if it's broken," he said, feeling the anklebones. "Can you walk?"

Jared and Susanna helped him to a standing position. "Don't rightly know if I can make it back to the sickroom," he said, hobbling along. "Hurts something fierce."

"I'll go for help," Jared said decisively. "We didn't come too far. Susanna can stay here with you."

"I want to come, too," Susanna said. "It's too cold and I. . ." She hesitated.

"Take her with you," Stephen assured him. "I'll be fine and dandy. Ain't too far to that there sick cave. You can find it easy enough. Just go back to that River Hall a spell, through Winding Way, and over the bottomless pit. You remember."

Jared looked between the injured man and Susanna, then took Susanna's hand in his. "You're sure you'll be all right, Stephen?"

He began to hoot. "Lookie here. I's stayed by myself in this place longer than anyone. Like I done told the lady here, the cave and I are friends of a sort. You go on. I'll be fine."

Jared nodded, feeling a bit more relieved, if not bewildered, by this sudden urn of events. With Susanna close behind him, they cautiously ventured back hrough the passageway.

"Can we find our way to the sick cave, Jared?" Susanna asked, the concern evident in her voice.

"Of course." Gone was the excitement and adventure of a new and different place. Now he had a mission to fulfill and responsibilities resting squarely on his shoulders—to find help for Stephen and to safeguard Susanna through this rocky maze. When they arrived in River Hall, as Stephen called the room, he breathed easier. Looking about, he saw a passage to his left and continued on, with Susanna following his every step. They would be back in the area for the sick very soon if all went well.

After some time he paused, perplexed. He held up the lantern even higher. They had not yet come to the narrow passage of Winding Way that once hugged them close. Nor did any of this part of the cave look familiar.

"What's the matter?" Susanna asked.

"Just looking to see where we're at," he said, trying to keep his voice as calm as he could muster. But inwardly he began to panic. Nothing looked right. Every corridor seemed the same. Where was the passage Stephen had showed them, the one the man dug out with his bare hands? He wished then he had asked for better directions. But the man had confidence in him, and he'd felt confident, too. . .until now.

"Where are we?" Susanna asked, shivering once more.

"I'm sure we're close to Winding Way and the bottomless pit," Jared answered. He moved tentatively forward until he came to a junction of three passages.

"Which way do we go?" Susanna asked.

He wondered the same thing.

"Don't you remember?" she pressed.

His thoughts became a jumbled mess. Nothing looked right in the lantern light, but he couldn't tell Susanna that. She trusted him, as did Stephen. "We'll keep going." The passage he chose remained wide and long, concerning him that they still had not reached Winding Way. Finally Susanna asked to rest and found a large rock to sit on.

"Jared, do you know where we are?"

"Yes. . . ," he began. Then he said quietly, "No."

She straightened. "What do you mean?"

"Susanna, God knows where we are, but I can't find that narrow passage Stephen showed us. We must have taken a wrong turn."

"You mean we're lost?" Her voice escalated as she stood to her feet. "I thought you knew the way!"

He thought he did, too. He wanted to reassure her that they would find their way out, but uncertainty ruled this dark place. The truth be known, he had no idea how to proceed. "I'm going back," he decided. "The best thing for us to do is find Stephen. Maybe with the two of us helping, we can try to get him back to that sick cave. He can show us the way."

Susanna folded her arms tightly around her. He knew she was distressed and angry with him. He was supposed to watch out for her, to be a help, to find a way through this rocky labyrinth. But he couldn't. Her faith in him was all but shattered. Maybe everything else was, too.

He began heading back through the passage. If only he had the eyes of a coon and could see in this perpetual night.

"Are you sure this is right?" came a muffled voice behind him.

Susanna stood there, her dress limp and mud soaked, her face distraught, the chills overcoming her. He couldn't believe he had let her and Stephen down. He began to pray, asking God for an answer, hoping He would somehow redeem this situation.

"Maybe we didn't come far enough," she said. "As it was, we were talking and all. Sometimes the distance seems a lot shorter when it really isn't."

He set down the lantern and promptly plunked himself on a rock. "I don't know what do," he confessed. He picked up a small stone and tossed it out of frustration. "If we try to go back, we might end up in a worse place. Lord, please help us find a way out of here." He dropped his face into his hands. He struggled to breathe, the anxiety pressing down like a crushing rock on his chest. He should have never asked Susanna to come into this place. He should have left her in safety outside these rocky walls and never involved her in any of his troubles. How could he have ever thought she might be the one for him? Or that he could make their relationship happen somehow, someway. He hadn't trusted God the way he should. He had trusted in his own feelings, his own way of looking at things rather than God's perfect way.

Just then he felt her arm curl around him, her touch like a soothing balm to his dry spirit. Glancing up, he again saw the luminous eyes of Susanna in the lantern light.

"It will be all right."

"I should've never done this to you," he confessed. "Never brought you into this. It wasn't fair. None of it. You need to live your life the way you want."

"Jared."

"It was wrong to put the burden of closing down this cave on you. Foolish really. How could I expect that, after all? This place is what helps you survive."

"It's all right. I'm not upset. A little cold maybe." She glanced around the cave. "We'll get out of here somehow."

"When we do, there are going to be some changes. And one thing's for sure; you won't be seeing me again. I won't burden you any further. It isn't right. You have your own life to live."

She stared back, blinking. He thought he heard a sniff of distress. Could it be? Were those the beginnings of tears? Tears for him, one of the greatest fools in this world? Especially after everything he had done?

"Jared, you can't leave." Her voice quivered. "I—I need you."

The words jarred him more than the horror of their current circumstances. How could that be? He had gotten them lost in this rock-filled place. He had cast his cares on her, not on the Lord. He had entertained misconceptions, judgments, everything a follower of Christ should not do. "You don't need me...," he began. "Look what I've caused you. Grief. Pain. And now we're lost."

"No, I mean, we all need you. My family. Mr. Miller. Yes, even the doctor. Desperately." She exhaled a loud sigh. "We would have been consumed by ourselves, so deep in our own way of making money and living far from the life my family once thought was a curse. But you made me see there is more to life than this. That there is a better treasure to be found, and not just in coins or in what I own. There is treasure in family, in loved ones—yes, even in a place like this. I mean, you once hated this place. But when we came in here, you were like a boy on his adventure, looking at everything Stephen was willing to show you with new eyes. You could look beyond what the cave had done to see a place God had created."

He sat there amazed. He didn't think he had made any difference. But she seemed sincere. And, yes, she had made a difference, too. She had survived life's trials to live a life of blessing. She was willing to risk the anger of her family to help him and his uncle in their time of need. She chose to understand and accept him for who he was rather than try to make him into someone he was not. Maybe God was at work after all.

"Susanna, I love you."

He sucked in his breath. He had said the words! Thankfully she couldn't see his warming face in the dim light of their lanterns. But he knew he did love her. He'd held it in for a long time, perhaps making excuses for it, allowing other things like this cave to get in the way. But now the expression of his heart came forth so naturally, as if the words were meant to be spoken here—of all places—under the earth.

And then came the response, as if whispered out of the solid rock that surrounded them.

"Jared, I love you, too."

Her words came simply as well, out of a pure heart. Love, even in a dark and cold place. Even while they were lost, not knowing when they would be found. Love that could transcend circumstances. He reached out and held her. The kiss was simple but filled with warmth, confirming what was in his heart and hers. He cradled her, hoping to ward off the chills. "It won't be long. We'll be out of here soon."

"I only hope the lanterns don't go out." Her voice was tremulous.

He held her even tighter, trying to reassure her, and prayed like he had never prayed before.

Chapter 14

He loved her, and yes, she loved him. Even when trapped in a pit of darkness and with the lanterns quickly dimming. Even when the fear of the unknown rose higher with each passing moment. Even when she thought no one would find them and they might die in this place. She huddled close to him. Nothing else mattered at this moment. Not her fancy dresses. Not her mother's fashion book. Not money. Not Luke's jibes or wondering what her future held. It had to come to this—with everything else stripped away—caught here in a void of darkness, before understanding could break through.

"I wish I had a blanket for you," Jared said in dismay. "I'm sorry for this."

"It doesn't matter. Nothing matters now. I'm just glad we're together." Tears teased her tired eyes and made them burn. She had never felt so weary, but thankful all the same.

"I wonder how Stephen is," Jared murmured.

"He can take care of himself. He's been in this cave so many times. I'm not sure after all this, though, if I will ever come back here." Her voice heightened with anxiety. She tried to steady it, to be a strong woman able to bear up under any circumstance. But she found her resolve difficult to keep. Maybe even impossible. "I'm scared."

"Just keep holding my hand," Jared told her. "Even if the lanterns go out, keep holding it."

"Jared, if you let go of my hand, I'll die." The tears trickled out despite her effort to keep them at bay. "What if we're never found? No one knows we came this way."

"We'll stay right here. The men guarding the cave entrance knew we were coming in. The people at the sick cave saw us go down the other passage. And there's Stephen. Though I know he can't move much, I wouldn't be surprised if he makes it out on his own. He's courageous, that man."

Susanna wished she could be courageous, too, as the Bible said. *Be bold and courageous. Do not be dismayed, for He is with me wherever I go. Even in a dark and dreary cave,* she thought. *Even when I don't know what will happen.*

To pass the time, Jared shared morsels about his life. His deep voice sounded melodious in the cavern surroundings. He talked about his family—his parents and how eager they were to venture westward, his younger brother and sister who had gone with them, and his determination to stay here in Kentucky even after they had left.

"But then your aunt died and your uncle turned against you. Surely you wanted to leave then, didn't you?"

"I thought about it," he admitted. "But something kept me here. Or Someone."

She smiled a bit.

"When God writes your name in the ground, you have no choice but to stay. Mine was written upon this land long ago. I knew I couldn't leave it. Even when everyone else had left and only my aunt and uncle remained. I was born here. I met the Lord here through a traveling minister. Kentucky is my home."

"My mother taught me about God," Susanna reminisced. "I remember sitting by her side one day. She was teaching me how to sew, and she used it to tell me about God. 'Like our sewing,' she said, 'God is making a wonderful garment out of our lives.' I never forgot it." She became silent then, thinking about that simple time when there was only hard work to be had. There were no fancy dresses. No food aplenty. Just a hot loft to sleep in. Irritating brothers who gave her no peace. Even so, she never felt closer to God than she had then, in those difficult times. It was almost as though, when she left those humble beginnings, she'd left God there, as well. Oh, she thought about Him now and then. She prayed. But when life didn't bring any of the difficulties she had come to know, it was as if she needed Him less, when actually she needed Him more.

"What are you thinking about?" he asked, gently pushing back strands of hair that had fallen in her face.

"How much I really do need God in my life. I trusted Him when we lived in that old cabin. God and I were best friends, the way I used to talk to Him by the stream. And, of course, I would pray that He would help me. But when I moved to the hotel, it was as if God became lost in all the finery. I never really felt as close to God as I did back then on the farm. That is, until I met you."

"I know we always want to escape trials. Trials can hurt. But it's those trials that bring us closer to Him."

"I'm sorry I didn't trust you," she piped up.

He looked at her, startled. "Huh?"

"I knew you were trying to do good here, but I didn't want to see my precious life interrupted. You really did open my eyes when we saw each other at Brownsville. I know God has blessed me with nice things. But I know He doesn't want me to lose sight of what is important either. I need to see Him in everything. And if I do stay at the hotel, I want to be more giving. In fact, I'm going to take half my things and see who needs them more than I." She acknowledged her dress. "Things like dresses don't seem to matter as much as they used to."

"Susanna, it's all right to have some nice things. I only said what I did because I was feeling guilty about my aunt. I thought I had caused her death. You deserve to be dressed like a queen. I only wish I could offer you fine things—and more."

She nestled closer to him, feeling his warmth. "Jared, you have. We can pretend this is our castle with the walls around us. And you are my rider on his black steed."

"And what would my lady wish?"

She giggled. If only she could tell him that she wanted to be with him forever.

Just then, their lights dimmed to a single flame. She froze. Fear washed over her once more. "Oh no, a lantern went out. That means the other will go out, too. Stephen filled both of them at the same time."

"Stay here, Susanna. I'm going to see if anyone can hear us before we do lose our light."

"Jared, you can't leave me here."

He left his lantern by her side. "I will be just a few paces away," he promised. "I have to try."

No! Her gaze remained fixed on the lantern's soft glow. Was it her imagination, or was the light already beginning to fade? Jared called out several times, his voice echoing in the cave's vastness. She watched the flame dim even more. "Jared, it's going out! Jared! Come back!"

Then, pitch-black. Never had she witnessed such darkness. At first, she thought she could see him, so close to her. But when she reached out her hand, he wasn't there. "Jared!"

Silence answered. For an agonizing moment, Susanna felt wholly alone, buried in the bowels of the earth.

Then Jared's voice broke through the oppressive black stillness. "I'm here."

She heard his footsteps and thought how he could wander off, maybe even into another bottomless pit. "Jared!" Suddenly she felt his foot kick against her leg and his hand brush her arm. "Oh, thank you, God!" She began to weep.

"It's all right."

"No, it isn't. Nothing is all right. We have no food or water. Now we have no light. What are we going to do?"

He said nothing for a time. His silence only made matters worse. "God, please help us," she prayed. "You know where we are. Send someone to help us!"

Jared's hand swept back her hair. She felt him kiss the top of her head and then heard soothing words fill her ears. He began singing a hymn. "Rock of Ages." How appropriate for this place. She tried to shift her thoughts to God's holy refuge. A strong tower. A firm foundation. Unmoving. Solid. But anxiety came again, like water spilling over her. Her teeth began to chatter.

"I remember being lost once," Jared suddenly said. "And it changed my life."

She perked up at his words.

"I went fishing to a new fishing hole. Didn't tell my parents where I was going. Suddenly it got dark. I couldn't find my way home. Everything looked the same. I saw the stars, but that was all. I bedded down in some leaves, but I was so cold.

"Then I saw this light. I thought that maybe I was going to heaven. It was like a golden light, bright and beautiful. Then it was shining full in my face. Some stranger had come up, holding a lantern, someone I had never seen before. He asked me what I was doing there all by myself. 'I'm lost,' I said. Then he laughed. I thought it was the strangest thing to hear him laugh like that. I didn't think any of it was funny. I was cold and really hungry. 'C'mon and ride with me,' he said, giving me a hand up. I asked who he was. I didn't recognize his name. I told him where my home was. He said there were a lot of people lost like me, wandering around in the darkness. Unable to see anything before them. All of them, caught in the deep and no one to help them. I didn't know what he meant. I asked where they were."

Jared paused, and Susanna heard him chuckle. "So what did he say?" she urged.

"He said, 'They're all around you. But I have a light for you. A good light. A light to see by.' And he pointed to his saddlebag. He opened it and pulled out a huge Bible. I didn't understand, you see. I never went to church. But he told me all about God right there, told me that Jesus is the Light of the world. I never forgot it."

Susanna sat there, mesmerized by the story. The cave didn't seem so dark anymore. "So he was the traveling minister you talked about?"

"And one of the main reasons I didn't leave Kentucky. This is where I found light in the darkness. How could I leave it? Besides that, my aunt and uncle lived here, too. And my uncle still needs to see the light for himself."

Susanna sighed. The chills left her. She felt warm, as if a fire had been kindled in their midst. Somehow she knew everything would be all right. She had a godly man by her side and a God in heaven watching over her. She could want nothing better in a place like this.

⁓

As time passed, they listened to each other's breathing and the distant trickle of water somewhere deep in the cave. Susanna strained to hear the clamor of footsteps, to see the flicker of lantern light. She remained in Jared's arms for warmth, trying to think of things to ward off the uncertainty. She thought about her desire to meet a fine man one day, and marveled at how God had seen fit to bring Jared into her life. She wondered if there was a future for them. She knew, after today, that life at the hotel would never satisfy her. She needed the presence of God to fulfill her heart's desire. He was worth more than anything. He had given her Jared in a time and place in her life when she might have lost all hope.

She lifted her head to observe the surroundings—a pure black unlike anything she had ever seen. No light penetrated this place. None. Even when she thought she saw the flicker of light, she decided it was her mind playing tricks.

That is, until Jared jumped to his feet.

"Someone's coming!" he said excitedly. "Hello? Hello?"

Susanna stared until her eyes began to hurt, looking at the dim light reflecting off the cavern walls. Then there came a reply.

"Hello!" answered a voice. "Someone there?"

"We're here!" they both said at once.

Matt arrived, bringing with him a contingent of men, each with lanterns. Her father. Luke. And several other men she didn't know.

"Susanna!" Papa cried. "You gave us such a fright."

"How did you know where to look for us?"

"Stephen made it back to the sick cave with that bad leg of his," Matt said. "When he found out you hadn't come back, he figured you might have taken a wrong turn. Easy to do in this place. So he sent someone to the hotel to fetch us, and we came lookin'."

Susanna was never more relieved. She grabbed Jared's hand and squeezed it. "God watched out for us," she murmured.

"And a good thing, too," Luke said. He whirled to the men who had accompanied them. "Arrest that man."

Susanna stared wide-eyed as the men surrounded Jared. "What are you doing?"

"I didn't like him from the beginning," Luke murmured.

"It's for the best until we can straighten this out," Papa added.

"No!" She clung to Jared, even as her father tried gently to pull her away. "You can't do this. He's done nothing wrong!"

"He dragged you into this place and nearly got you killed," Luke hissed. "And we heard how he was coming for the doctor, no doubt to harm him, too."

"That's ridiculous! He was only coming to talk to him. Please." She looked to Jared, hoping he would defend himself. He said nothing. "Jared, tell them." He only stared back with sadness in his eyes. "He wouldn't harm anyone. He's only tried to help."

"By causing an uproar?" Papa said. "By associating with men who want to blow up the cave? By taking you away from us? By causing our very lives to be disrupted? There will be no more of this, Susanna. You are not to speak to this man ever again." He nodded, and at once the guards escorted Jared back through the passage.

Susanna wanted to follow, but her father and Luke kept her back. "You don't know what you're doing! You don't know what the truth is. The only thing you know is your money. But it's poison. It's poisoned you against the truth, to the things that matter in life. And now you want to punish an innocent man." She grabbed for a lantern, intent on following her beloved and the men who held him in their grasp.

"Susanna, you are to stay with us," Papa ordered. "I am your father. And as your father, I know what's best for you."

"Then if you do, you'll let me be with the man I love!"

"You can't love a man like that," Luke said with contempt. "He's nothing."

"No! You're nothing! You know nothing about love. You think because we have come to this place that it's made us better people. That it has solved our problems. But all our problems followed us here. All we have ever thought about is ourselves. Jared lost someone he dearly loved in this place. He has no rich surroundings or nice clothing. But he is content. He has faith in God. All he's ever wanted to do is what's right. And I would rather be with a man like that than be as rich as a king." She lowered her voice. "Papa, I have always listened to you. But I cannot listen to you now. You're wrong about Jared. I only wish I could make you understand."

Papa said no more. Susanna hastened to follow the lanterns that were quickly fading into the deep. She didn't care about the cave's darkness, her feet slipping on the rocks, or the chills. She only wanted Jared with all her heart. Tears filled her eyes, which she swiped away in determination. She would not see him taken away, perhaps even to some Louisville jail like his uncle. Not while there was still breath in her. She would do whatever she must to set him free, like he had done for her.

At last, she caught up with the group as they entered the sick cave. Dr. Croghan had arrived and was talking with several of the men who had led Jared away. Susanna managed to catch a glimpse of Jared's face—worn, tired, but at peace, even with his circumstances. Murmuring a prayer, Susanna came forward and burst through the circle of men.

"Dr. Croghan, I must speak with you."

"Miss Barnett! What are you doing here?"

"Dr. Croghan, you must help us. Please, may Jared and I speak with you in private?"

He stared, first at Jared then at her. "I am a very busy man, Miss Barnett."

"Sir, I would not ask except that this is a matter of life and death."

He paused. "Very well."

Susanna motioned to Jared. They followed the doctor to one of the abandoned wooden huts and sat down. She ignored Jared, who shook his head at her, and, instead concentrated on the task before her. "Dr. Croghan, you and I have known each other for several years now. I was the one who found you that day long ago on the road when you were pinned under the wagon. And you have been so kind to us, helping my family in their time of need. Now I beg you to help another who, at this very moment, is dying of consumption."

Croghan glanced over at Jared. "I'm not certain that I understand."

"Jared's uncle. The one who lost his wife. And the one who has been arrested. I know there were plans being made for some manner of evil with the cave. But you must see how this was all brought about by a man sick with grief and sick in his body. Jared's uncle has the consumption."

"Is this true?" Croghan asked Jared.

"Yes, sir. I didn't know it at first. My uncle hid it pretty well. But he has all the signs. The coughing. The weakness."

"I'm sorry to hear this. But you must realize that there must be consequences for evil actions."

"Sir, no actions took place because Jared warned us," Susanna pleaded.

"Yes, and the men were arrested," Croghan added. "I have tried to be diplomatic, as you well know. But I cannot allow others to commit criminal acts just because they don't like my cave."

"But you can understand where this comes from," Susanna pressed. "Out of a desperation to find healing in a time of grief. You're a gentleman of compassion. You wouldn't have built this place if you weren't. You wouldn't have given your time, your money, everything, to try and help the unfortunate. All I ask is for a bit of mercy for Jared's uncle. That he can die in his own bed and not in a jail cell."

Croghan sighed, even as he looked about the hut where they sat. "I had great dreams for this place," he murmured wistfully. "Like you once said, young man, I thought this cave was a miracle. I thought with the air and humidity that it might offer something to those with pulmonary afflictions. Had I known it would hasten death, I would have never opened the cave to the sick." He paused then, as if in deep thought.

Susanna held her breath, praying, pleading with God that the doctor would have a change of heart.

"I will think about what you said," he finally told her. "I'm sorry this happened. I do blame myself for raising hope when there really was no hope. Hope is what drives a man forward."

"Sir, that is why we can only hope in our Savior Christ," Jared said humbly. "I know now what happens when I place my hope in what I see or feel. But faith is hope in what is unseen, in God Himself."

Croghan slowly came to his feet and offered Jared his hand. "I do thank you for warning us of your uncle's anger. Our conversation at dinner has given me quite a bit to think about. Certainly I do not hold you responsible for any of this. You may go."

"But what about his uncle?" Susanna asked.

Croghan shook his head. "I have no answer. Right now, I must tend to the others that are still here." He left in a flourish, even as Susanna and Jared stood alone in the hut with only the distant chatter of voices interrupting the vastness of the rocky space.

All at once, she felt Jared embrace her in gratefulness. "Thank you, Susanna. I can't believe you did this for me."

"It was nothing."

"What do you mean? It was everything. I had made the decision that if I were to go to Louisville, at least Uncle Dwight wouldn't be alone. That I could be there with him."

"We just have to pray that somehow he will be released, Jared. Despite everything that's happened, Dr. Croghan is a fair man. I believe with all my heart he cares."

"If there's one person I've seen care unlike any other, it's a beautiful woman by the name of Susanna Barnett. I'm sorry I ever doubted you."

She smiled, enjoying the warmth of his arms about her. "Let's just get out of here," she said softly.

Chapter 15

Jared returned to his cabin to find it a cold and lonely place. Without Susanna there beside him, and knowing his uncle remained in a Louisville jail, he found it hard to go on. He tried his best to keep up both his farm and his uncle's in the hope of Uncle Dwight's return. He had not been back to the hotel in a week as the work had piled up. But he thought about the cave and the hotel all the time and especially about the fair one who dwelled there. Not a moment went by that he didn't think of Susanna. No doubt, her father was keeping a close eye on her. Always when they seemed to draw closer, something else would pull them apart. Their relationship had turned into a never-ending tug-of-war.

Jared had just hitched the horse to the plow when he heard a wagon rolling down the road. He shifted his hat back on his head to see the dark form of a familiar man hunched over at the reins. It was Matt Bransford.

"You gotta come to the hotel, Mistuh Jared. Come on now. I'll take you there."

He stared, puzzled. "I've got a heap of work to do here, Matt."

"Yeah, but this is important. You gotta come. Miss Barnett asked me to fetch you specially."

He looked at the fields to plow and the wood that still needed to be split. But the lure of seeing Susanna proved too much of a temptation. Every night when darkness fell, he thought of her and the hours they spent in the cave. While the place had been frightening, it had done a wondrous work in them. The truth be told, he wouldn't mind going back in that cave to do something he had been thinking about doing for a while. A secret surprise for Susanna. Something they would both cherish forever. If he could only make it work.

Jared unhitched the horse and led the animal to the stall. He then climbed onto the wagon seat beside Matt. During the journey to the hotel, he inquired about Stephen. Matt laughed, telling him how the man was already leading tours again. "Nothing can hold that man back from the cave. No siree."

"After all we went through, I wasn't sure if I should ever go back inside," Jared commented.

"Why not? Cain't let no bad things hold you back. Shore there can be things that stop you in your tracks. The good Lawd tells you which way to go. But the cave is there for us. And while some things don't work out, it's still a good place to look around." He continued, "And sometimes it does a body good to git lost. Gotta rely on the Lawd. Then you can deal with the things goin' on inside of yourself. That's happened to me, and I'm real thankful for it."

Jared pondered these words and the great work God had already done in both Susanna and himself. He had seen more than he realized. He had felt anger and doubt turn him to stone like the cave. But now he felt freer than he ever had been before. He trusted the Lord with his past, present, and future, even if his future remained uncertain.

When he arrived, the hotel was fairly buzzing with patrons outfitted in their costumes, ready for an adventure into the deep. This time Jared watched them without the animosity he once felt. He knew what they would see, after all. He wanted to encourage them to go forth into the unknown. To see things like never before. And let God do a work in their hearts in the process.

Matt stopped the wagon in front of the hotel. When he asked where he was to go, Matt nodded toward the front doors. Jared entered the hotel, remembering his journey here not that long ago to speak with the head proprietors of this place. He recalled the raw anxiety he had felt. Just then, he stumbled upon Susanna's brother, Luke, giving an assistant some instructions. When the man left, Luke turned. Their eyes met.

"It's you. Well, it seems my sister is quite taken with you."

"I'm sure you aren't happy about that, are you?" Jared wondered.

Luke shrugged. "Susanna's never been happy, even with everything she had here in the hotel. At first she seemed happy. But something changed in her after she met you."

Jared said nothing. Instead he observed the man about his own age, and considered the responsibilities that fell on his young shoulders. They'd be enough to drive anyone to the ground.

"This place is fine enough, I suppose," Luke commented. "It has most everything one needs. But there are some things I wouldn't mind doing again. I miss them."

Jared could hear it in Luke's voice. An emptiness. The need for something more in life. Maybe even the longing for a friend. "How about we go fishing sometime?"

Luke stared at him. "What did you say?"

"I know some pretty good spots. I'll bet since you came here you haven't really had a chance to do things like fishing."

"No. I don't do anything but this." Luke acknowledged the lanterns he held. "I used to fish a lot back at the old place. We had to find our food or grow it. Here, everything is given to you. Somehow I think I miss it. Farming the land. Going hunting for game. Feeling like I'm accomplishing something."

"If you miss farming, I've got a lot of that to do. I'm working two farms right now. I could use some help."

The idea seemed to spark life within the man. "I never thought I would say it, but plowing up the ground sounds like something I might enjoy right about now."

"We'll talk more," Jared promised when he saw a door open and the graceful Susanna appear. Her smile, with her cheeks all aglow, captivated him like nothing else.

"We're ready," she said. "Please come in, Mr. Edwards."

"Why so formal?" he murmured, following her through the familiar hallway and past the window lights he had seen once before. She said nothing but gestured him into a formal sitting room. Dr. Croghan and Susanna's father were seated inside. And to his disbelief, so were Uncle Dwight and George Higgins.

"Welcome, Mr. Edwards," the doctor said with a smile. "I found these two men wandering about, and they claimed to have made your acquaintance in the past."

Jared hastened to give his uncle a warm embrace. Higgins pounded him on the back. "Am I glad to see you," he told the two men. Then to the doctor, he said, "Thank you so much."

"I have it in confidence from these men that they will cause no further trouble with my cave," Dr. Croghan said. "So it didn't make much sense to keep them under lock and key. So long as they behave themselves."

Higgins offered a wave, his face a wide grin. "We'll be good and harmless as kittens," he promised.

"I'll leave you to reunite," the doctor said, followed by Susanna's father. "But I want you all to know, I've decided to close the sick area of the cave. There will be no more invalids housed there. I thought you would like to know." Dr. Croghan nodded and left.

Jared looked to see the reaction of his uncle to the doctor's announcement. He only found a dejected figure, his chin resting in his hand. When Jared came to him, he glanced up with sadness in his eyes. "It was terrible, Jared," Uncle Dwight confessed. "What would Mattie think if she knew I was locked up in some jail? She'd never forgive me."

Jared knelt before his uncle and took the man's feeble hand in his. "Uncle, I have something important to tell you. I think it might help. I was able to talk to an invalid who knew Aunt Mattie in the cave. He told me how happy she was to be there and the great victuals she cooked for them all. She said the people there were like her, that they all shared in the same illness. And she knew it was better for her to be in that place."

"She said that?"

Jared nodded. "She was happy, Uncle. I know we thought she might get well, but I think deep in her heart, Aunt Mattie knew she wouldn't live. And she didn't want to make you sad by her passing. It was all right for her to be in the cave with others like herself."

"But I wanted her with me."

"Uncle, Aunt Mattie is always here with us. Everything she taught us. Everything she did. But she's in a better place. A place of peace, with no pain and sickness. And she's running and laughing, breathing in the good air God made in heaven, free as a bird."

Uncle Dwight began to weep. "I'm so tired, Jared."

"It will be all right now, Uncle. The Lord is with us. He loves us more than we could know."

"I–I've seen it," his uncle said feebly. "I remember what you once told me about the Lord and all. And He did take care of me."

"He sets the prisoners free, Uncle. He can set us all free if we put our trust in Him." Jared patted his uncle's hand. "You know I'm no preacher or schooled in theology, but I do know if we ask the Lord Jesus to forgive our sins, He'll do just that and come to live in our hearts. Whenever you're ready to pray such a prayer, I'd be honored to help you with the words."

His uncle looked at him through tear-filled eyes. "I'm much obliged, nephew. Let me think on it awhile longer. I'll let you know when the time's right."

Jared could see for the first time a heart of flesh replacing the stony manner of his uncle. He prayed that the words he'd uttered both long ago and at this moment would aid in accomplishing the Lord's work in his uncle's life. He gave his uncle's hand one final pat and came to his feet. He turned to see Susanna gazing at him. Her blue eyes were warm, her lips parted, and she nodded ever so slightly.

"You look tired, too," she murmured. "How about something to eat?"

"I'd rather take a walk, if that's all right." He looked to Higgins, who nodded.

"I'll look after Dwight," Higgins said. "You two go on now."

Jared and Susanna found a side door, and together they walked the path they'd trod during other, more serious meetings. Once again everything had changed, but this time it was for the better. The burdens had been cast aside. He felt freedom from the guilt, the pain, and could enjoy this time with the woman he loved. They strolled along, listening to the birds, looking at the colorful flowers that brought the wooded glade to life. Soon they found themselves heading toward the cave entrance. Streaming from the rocks above, a gentle cascade of water serenaded them.

"I can't believe the doctor is closing the sick cave," Jared said.

"There will still be the tours," Susanna said. "But the cave doesn't seem so dark and foreboding now, does it?"

"Darkness and light are alike to God," Jared said. "I think we saw both in there."

"Sometimes I wish things hadn't happened the way they did," she confessed. "If you had been but a simple suitor on his black horse, it would have been so easy to find myself swept away. Instead we had to struggle until we finally came to an understanding."

"We had to go through it this way," he said, squeezing her hand gently. "Maybe we wouldn't have found out enough about each other to know that we can make it through the hard times as well as the good." He paused then. Yes, he did want to spend the rest of this hard life with Susanna. But she was used to the pleasantries of the hotel. The fine surroundings. She had wanted to flee hardship even though her brother claimed she was never truly content. Would she be content to go back to an existence that reminded her of the past?

"Yes, life can be hard," she agreed. "No matter where one is. I thought having money, a nice dress, even a large dining table, would bring me happiness. But it didn't. There was something missing. In the cave we had nothing, not even light. But in God and each other, I found out I had everything I needed and more."

Jared drew in his breath in anticipation as the door opened before him. He dare not shut that door now, not when God had done a miracle in their midst. He turned then, gripping each of her hands in his. "Susanna, I know my cabin isn't a hotel. My table is small. I could buy you a pretty dress after the harvest is in. There will always be surprises for us from on high. I'm sure of it. So, would you consider marrying me?"

"Would I consider? Jared, how I prayed you would ask me!"

He took her in his arms; their kiss confirming what was in his heart—and hers, too. That love and God's mercy can be found even in the deepest parts of the earth.

Epilogue

S o is this the surprise you once told me about?"

He raised an eyebrow. She'd listened to every word he had spoken, every detail, even going so far as to accept him in marriage. Now it was coming to pass. "There are many surprises from on high, like I said," he told her.

"Many?" Her small hand tugged at his, childlike innocence dancing in her eyes. "What other surprises? Tell me! Oh, you can't leave me like this, Jared."

"You know I will never leave you."

She nodded. "I know. How I know. Even when we were trapped in the cave, even with everything happening to us, you were there. Always."

He sighed. "I wanted to know if this surprise is all right with you. To see if you really would like to have our wedding in the cave. It did change both of us and brought us together. Dr. Croghan has agreed to it. And Stephen said he found a perfect place, too, with some grand columns, he called them. I thought with everything that has happened, the cave would be the perfect place."

She grasped his hand in hers, settling any doubts. He had doubted so many times, but there was no need. Susanna did trust him. And he trusted what God had been showing them both—how a cave, though dark and dreary, can bring forth a wondrous light in people's hearts. And he desperately wanted the light of their wedding to take place there. To make their families and everyone see that this truly was a grand place wrought by God and able to bring about blessings untold.

"It sounds wonderful," she whispered, her warm breath fanning his face.

And their wedding was wonderful indeed, beyond all expectation. The glow of so many oil lanterns, the very lanterns that had been their light in a dark place, bathing the chamber in a soft golden glow. The beauty of Susanna in a new dress, which she had first discovered in the *Godey's Lady's Book*, complete with rose trim that fell gracefully from her shoulders. The moment they exchanged vows of marital love before a minister framed by three columns of rock. The wonder of seeing both Uncle Dwight and Dr. Croghan in the same place beneath the earth, standing side by side as witnesses. All the product of God's hand.

Dr. Croghan offered his hand in congratulations. "I believe we have found a new name for this part of the cave," he said with a smile. "The Bride's Chamber will do nicely."

Everyone laughed. When the ceremony was over, Jared was quick to scoop up a lantern in one hand and Susanna's hand in the other. "Where are we going?" she wondered. "Not another tour!"

"To see my other surprise," he told her. "Remember?"

Her eyes widened to reflect the glow of the lantern. She put on the cloak he gave her and followed him through the passage until they came to the chamber Stephen once showed them on their earlier trip. Jared lit a torch. The light gleamed off the stone that bore the blackened marks and signatures of those who had gone before them. The young and the old, men and women, each with hopes and dreams, each with life stories all their own. And now he was determined to have their story remembered as well.

"Can you see it, Susanna? A surprise from on high." He chuckled. "Or at least high up."

She stared hard and began to laugh. "Jared, it's wonderful!"

Etched out in black on the smooth surface of the rocky ceiling was a large heart and charred words preserved for all time.

Jared and Susanna Edwards
1843
A cave of love

LAURALEE BLISS

Lauralee resides with her family near Charlottesville, Virginia, in the foothills of the Blue Ridge Mountains—a place of inspiration for many of her contemporary and historical novels. Aside from writing, Lauralee enjoys hiking, gardening, roaming yard sales, and traveling. She invites you to visit her Web site at www.lauraleebliss.com.

Where the
River Flows

Prologue

1876

The last sunbeams of the day turned the water into a blaze of gold as Rose Thurston lifted the gingham dress above her knees and dangled her bare feet in the tranquil Ohio River. In the shallow water of a nearby creek, young frogs' efforts to imitate the croaking of their elders produced nothing except weak, throaty rumbles.

Rose closed her eyes and let the peace of her surroundings seep into her soul and heart. Spring on the Ohio River! Could any other place on earth compare to the peace and joy of living on a shanty boat? But how would she know? Rose couldn't remember any other life.

Rose's birthday was the first day of June, and her grandpa always promised that by that time, their home, the *Vagabond*, would have started its summer voyage. Grandpa Harry hadn't broken his word in her eighteen years. Rose endured the six months their shanty boat was moored at Louisville, looking forward to the rest of the year when she would enjoy the isolation and pleasure of cruising Kentucky's rivers. Two more months to wait. As Gramps often told her, the river was in her blood!

Lottie Thurston finished her evening chores and joined her granddaughter on the rear deck of the *Vagabond*. She brushed back her silvery gray hair and lowered her body into her favorite chair, which squeaked under her weight.

Rocking slowly back and forth, Lottie said, "Peaceful, ain't it."

"But I have a feeling it won't stay that way," Rose said, motioning to the steamboat, *River Belle*, edging close to their river home. Several blasts from the boat's whistle bellowed out a distress signal. The paddle wheel slapped the water softly as the boat slowed down and drifted within a few feet of the shanty.

Rose pulled her feet from the water and ran inside. The waves caused by the steamboat swayed the smaller craft, and she held on to a dresser to steady herself as she put on her shoes.

The captain of the *River Belle*, who was well-known to the Thurstons, called from the pilothouse.

"I've got a sick woman for you, Lottie."

Rose had rejoined her grandmother on the deck by the time two deckhands lowered a gangplank to make a bridge to the shanty. A small woman, supported by a man, walked timorously across the narrow walkway. She wore a long, gray linen dress with ribbons interwoven on the skirt of the gown. A tiny hat with a narrow brim was perched on her upswept hairdo. The long cloak she wore didn't hide the fact that she was in the family way.

"When your wife is ready to travel, you can hail another packet boat," the captain called to his unloading passengers.

If the brawny man heard the captain, he didn't reply. He was dressed in a black waistcoat, narrow-legged trousers, and a plaid vest. As soon as they reached the safety of the shanty boat, a tortured groan escaped the woman's lips, and she fainted. Her husband caught her before she reached the floor and swung her into his arms. He turned to Lottie, his deep-set brown eyes desperate.

"Are you the midwife? My name is Edward Moody, and this is Martha, my wife. Please, help us."

The woman roused, and her body stiffened in his arms.

"Quick, bring her inside," Lottie said.

Moody ducked his head to clear the low door of the boat.

Lottie quickly spread a heavy quilt over the narrow bed that she and her husband shared. "Lay her here." To Rose, she said, "Bring everything I need while I undress the woman."

"The baby isn't due for two months, or I wouldn't have brought her along," Moody explained.

Lottie started unbuttoning the woman's dress. By the time Rose returned with the ointments and herbs that Lottie used for pain, she had laid the woman's dress aside and was removing her chemise and corset.

The man looked quickly at Rose. "Isn't she too young to be involved?" he asked. "I can help you."

"Children grow up fast on the frontier, Mr. Moody, but she ain't as young as she looks. Rose knows what to do. Go out on the deck and wait. I'll do the best I can for your wife."

The woman on the bed was conscious when Rose brought a bowl of cool water. "I'm all right, Edward," she muttered softly. "Don't worry about me."

"The pains will come in waves," Lottie told her. "Don't try to fight them. Yell if you want to. You'll have time to get your wind before the next one comes."

Rose moistened a clean cloth and started bathing the patient's face. Martha clamped her lips between her teeth, and Rose realized she must be in a great deal of pain. She admired the woman for her courage—not only to start out on a voyage when she was expecting a child, but also her desire to suppress her pain.

Lottie handed Rose the woman's soiled garments, and Rose exchanged an anxious glance with her grandmother. The clothes were soaked with blood. Lottie worked feverishly trying to stanch the flow of blood spreading over the quilt.

Edward Moody had not heeded Lottie's orders to leave the room, and he hovered over the bed. When he saw the blood, he cried, "Do something. She's bleeding to death. Do something!"

"I'm doing all I can, Mr. Moody," Lottie said wearily.

For hours, Martha Moody endured her agony in silence. Finally she screamed, an animal-like sound that raised the hair on the back of Rose's neck and caused cold chills to skitter down her spine. The woman sat upright in the bed as a spurt of bloody fluid gushed from her body, bearing in its wake the immature body of a baby. Lottie grabbed the child, cut the cord, and quickly cleansed some of the clotted blood from the newborn. She turned him upside down and patted his rear. A weak cry escaped the babe's lips. The mother smiled weakly at the sound and slumped on the bed.

"Forget the child," Edward Moody cried, pushing Lottie aside and kneeling by the bed. He pulled his unconscious wife into his arms. "Save my wife. Save my wife! Martha, don't die," he pleaded.

Still working with the baby, Lottie said, "There isn't anything more I can do for your wife. Nobody can lose that much blood and live. I'm sorry."

Moody released his wife and stomped around the small room like a madman, his head clearing the ceiling by less than an inch. "You're sorry!" he shouted. "Is that all you can say? I should have taken her to a doctor instead of letting some quack work on her."

Confronting the man, Rose said, "Don't talk like that to my grandmother! She can't work miracles. Why don't you put the blame where it belongs? You should have stayed at home with your wife instead of bringing her on a river journey in her condition."

"That will do, Rose," Lottie said firmly. "Mr. Moody is hurting enough without you giving him a tongue-lashing." She handed the baby, now wrapped in a scrap of clean blanket, to Rose. "Take him to the kitchen and try to get some sugar water into him."

Rose heated a few teaspoons of sugar and springwater over the coals in the stove. She didn't remember ever holding such a small baby. He looked more like a skinny puppy than a human. "Poor little tyke," she whispered as she dabbed a cloth in the sugar water and held it to his lips. He was very weak, but she succeeded in squeezing some of the liquid into his mouth.

Feeling a strange sense of bonding with the baby, Rose rocked him until he went to sleep. Holding him on her shoulder, she entered the bedroom. Moody again knelt beside the bed, holding his wife's hand. By the dim light of the oil lamp, Rose saw the naked pain in the man's eyes. He remained there until almost daylight, when with a weary sigh, Martha Moody breathed her last.

"She's gone, Mr. Moody," Lottie said quietly.

He buried his head on his wife's breast, and his body shook with sobs. When he stood, he handed Lottie a bag of coins. "Will you take care of her burial? This is enough to pay for your services and the cost of burying her. I cannot delay any longer. The boat's captain said he would lay over for the night in Louisville. I'll be leaving when he does."

Wearily he moved toward the door. Rose stepped forward and thrust the baby toward him. "Don't forget your son."

He stared at her with blank eyes. Without even looking at the face of his child, he said, "I don't want him—you keep him."

Chapter 1

1886

The weather was typical of an April morning in Kentucky. The greening grass glistened in the morning dew. Cardinals sang cheerfully from the tops of the evergreen trees. Rose Thurston pulled the reins of the sorrel mare and guided her Brewster phaeton into Cave Hill Cemetery. Following the irregular terrain past the gravestones of early Louisville settlers, she stopped the vehicle in a section of more recent graves.

Martin, her sandy-haired son, picked up a bouquet of flowers, jumped out of the carriage, and hurried through the dewy grass, scattering a pair of nesting doves as he ran.

Martin Moody Thurston had been born ten years ago today. As Rose followed him, she wondered what Edward Moody would think if he could see his son now. After Moody's rapid departure, Rose and Lottie had used all of their limited medical expertise to keep the child alive. After it was certain that the boy would live, Lottie gave most of the child's care into Rose's hands. When she turned twenty-one, Rose had legally adopted the boy.

Through the years, Rose had expected Edward Moody to return for his son, but she had heard nothing from him since the day he had rushed from their shanty boat. Although Martin was small for his age, he was an intelligent, good-hearted boy, who had been a blessing to Rose and her grandparents. Always in the back of Rose's mind was the concern that his father might return to take Martin away from her.

"Look, Mama," Martin called, as he laid his flowers at the base of a five-foot, recently installed marble angel. "Isn't this pretty? Wouldn't my mother be proud of it?"

The base of the monument bore the epitaph—

MARTHA, WIFE OF EDWARD MOODY
DIED APRIL 5, 1876

Rose had kept the memory of his mother alive for Martin by bringing him to the cemetery several times a year, and always on his birthday, also the date of his mother's death.

Lottie and Harry had used some of the gold coins Edward Moody had left for Martha Moody's burial, but the small headstone they had erected had deteriorated through the years. The Thurstons had invested the rest of his father's money for Martin, when he came of age, so Rose had replaced the stone at her own expense.

"I'll clip some of the grass from the lot," Rose said, "while you bring the food basket from the carriage." It wasn't often that the weather was pleasant enough for a picnic on Martin's birthday, so this added to their joy of the day.

Martin gave Rose an impulsive hug. "Thank you, Mama, for bringing me here. I love you, but I also love my first mother."

Rose ruffled his crisp, straw-colored hair, which was like his father's. Often during the night his wife died, Rose had watched Edward Moody thread his trembling fingers through his crisp hair. Rose had noticed the same characteristic in her son, marveling that Martin exhibited so many traits of this father he had never seen. She had wondered often about Edward, praying that he had found peace from the loss of his family. As she had watched Martin grow, she was saddened that his father had missed all of those important years.

When Martin returned with the food, Rose said, "I'm about finished. Take the basket over to that big rock. The ground is too wet here."

When she reached the picnic site, Martin had already spread a blanket over the rock outcropping beside a towering cedar tree. Opening the picnic basket, Rose said, "Let's see what Sallie fixed for our picnic."

She lifted out a small plate of fried chicken and handed it to Martin.

"Oh, boy," he said, passing the plate back and forth under his nose, sniffing appreciatively.

Rose unwrapped several slices of wheat bread and put two apples on the blanket between them.

"Let's say a prayer of thanks before we start to eat." She took Martin's hand. "God, we're thankful for such a beautiful day after the storms of this week. I pray for the protection of those who are threatened by flooding. I thank You for Martin and the blessing he's been to me. Help him to have a good birthday. We're also grateful for the food. We pray for protection through this day. We love You. Amen."

"Is this all the food Sallie sent?" Martin asked.

Arching her eyebrows, Rose said, "Well, what else could you want? We've got chicken, fresh bread, and apples."

"I thought she might have put in something sweet."

Reaching inside the basket again, she pulled out a plate of chocolate cake. "Oh, you mean like this."

Martin clapped his hands. "Sallie knows that's my favorite."

After they finished eating, Rose and Martin walked toward the section of the cemetery where Civil War soldiers, both Union and Confederate, were buried. Martin always liked to come here, not only to wander among the headstones but also to play in the pond at the base of the hill. Their walk was shortened when the sun disappeared behind a cloud and a few raindrops fell.

"I think we'd better start for home," Rose said. "I had hoped that the rain was over. If the river rises another foot, a lot of houses will be flooded."

The rain was still light when they reached the covered phaeton, and Rose drove slowly through the narrow lanes of the cemetery. At one spot, she had a slight view of the Ohio River. A week of rain had swollen the river, and many steamboats were tied up in the harbor, waiting until the floodwaters passed. Wharf buildings closest to the river were submerged in the muddy water, and the boats were on a level with the tops of some of the structures.

Martin stood up. "I see the *Vagabond*."

Her grandfather's shanty boat was easily recognized, for Lottie Thurston had painted the name in large red letters across the front of the boat. Rose would have recognized it without the name, for the *Vagabond* had been home to her for most of her life. She knew every nook and cranny of the boat by memory.

"Gramps is probably sitting on the deck catching some fresh catfish for your birthday dinner tonight. He knows how to catch fish in spite of the muddy water."

Grinning, Martin answered, "And I bet Granny is baking a birthday cake for me."

Rose ruffled his thick hair. "She's always trying to put some weight on you."

Martin looked at his bony arms with distaste. "You say my father was a big man."

"Tall, with massive shoulders and strong, sturdy legs. His head almost grazed the ceiling of the *Vagabond*, and the boat shook under his weight when he walked."

A sad expression darkened Martin's eyes, and he said, "Wonder why he didn't want me?"

As she had done numerous times before, Rose tried to justify Edward Moody's actions in giving his child away.

"I've told you how weak and sickly you were. It took Granny and me months to make you well. You would have died if he had taken you with him."

"But why couldn't he wait until I got better?"

"I don't know," Rose said patiently, as if she hadn't answered this question many times.

"And why hasn't he come back for me?"

"I don't know that, either."

"Maybe he died like my mother."

"That's a possibility."

"I know one thing," Martin said, with a stubborn facial expression also reminiscent of his father. "If he ever does come back, I won't have anything to do with him."

"Now if that isn't a gloomy face for a birthday boy to have!" Rose chided him.

A roll of thunder threatened another shower, so Rose lifted the reins and urged the horse toward home.

Rose still couldn't believe she was actually living in an Italian Renaissance Revival home, where she felt like a fish out of water. A shanty boat girl living in a palatial mansion in the heart of downtown Louisville! But when John Boardman, a man whose life she had saved, had died a year ago and left his fortune to her, for Martin's sake she had moved into the Boardman house. She still didn't like going to bed without feeling the flow of the Ohio River beneath her, but surely in time she would get used to being a rich woman.

Boardman had built his home on a two-acre plot. The house fronted on Third Street, but he had provided for servants' quarters, a stable, and a carriage shed in the backyard. In deference to his neighbors, he had camouflaged the utility structures with a hedge of evergreens. Rose drove the phaeton into the carriage house, and Sallie's husband, Isaiah Taylor, came running to help her unhitch the mare.

The Taylors had worked for John Boardman for several years, and Rose more or less inherited them along with the house. She didn't know how she could have handled the change in her social status without them. She considered Sallie and Isaiah among her best friends.

"I feared you wouldn't make it home before the storm," Isaiah said. "I sure figgered you'd get wet, Miss Rose."

She telegraphed a message to Isaiah with her eyes, and he nodded, a big smile spreading across his face. He unhitched the mare from the phaeton.

"Before we go into the house, Martin, you might want to take a look at your birthday present."

"Where is it?" Martin asked.

"Isaiah will show you."

"Right this way, sonny," Isaiah said, leading the mare toward the stalls in the adjoining stable. Martin trotted beside him, and Rose followed. After he put the mare in her stall, Isaiah pointed to an adjoining enclosure.

"Happy birthday!" Isaiah and Rose shouted in unison.

"A pony," Martin whispered in awe.

"You made a good choice, Isaiah," Rose said as she looked at the black pony that moved docilely toward them.

Isaiah gave Martin an ear of corn, and he held it out to the pony. "Here, Tibbets." As the pony nibbled on the corn, Martin turned to Rose. "I've always thought if I ever had a pony, I'd call him Tibbets."

"But why?" Rose asked, laughing. "Where did you ever hear that name?"

He shrugged his shoulders. "It came to me in a dream one time." He hurried to Rose and threw his arms around her waist. "Thank you, Mama."

She knelt and returned his embrace. "Thank you for being my boy," she said. Burying her face in his curls, tears formed in Rose's eyes.

"When can I ride him?"

Rose looked to Isaiah for an answer. Thunder rolled across the roof of the barn, and a lightning bolt flashed over their heads. "Not until this storm is over," he said.

"Remember, Martin," Rose cautioned. "No riding for a few weeks unless Isaiah or I are with you. You understand?"

"Yes, ma'am."

The rain had stopped by the time Rose and Martin started toward the river. Although it was several blocks, Rose preferred to walk. As the river had risen, Harry Thurston had shortened the lines on the *Vagabond*, and when he saw them coming, he lowered a wide board to the bank for them to cross. Rose had no fear of the water, nor did Martin, for the river had been his home for most of his life, too. They walked across the small, bouncy bridge without a glance toward the water.

"Hi, Gramps. Did you know about my pony?"

"A pony for your birthday! How about that? A big house to live in and now a pony. You're gonna get too proud for your old grandpa."

"No!" Martin shouted. Running to Harry, he hugged him so tightly that Harry staggered, and Rose moved quickly to steady her grandfather. His legs were crippled with rheumatism, and Harry had lost the youthful vigor that Rose had always admired.

"Careful," Rose cautioned Martin, as she held her grandfather's arm until he steadied himself.

"I didn't mean to hurt you, Gramps. But I'll never be too rich for you. Why don't you come and live with Mama and me?"

"No, son," Harry said. "I was born in a boat on this river, and I aim to die here."

"What's all this commotion I hear?" Lottie said, appearing behind them in the kitchen door.

"Hi, Granny," Rose said. "Need any help?"

"Nary a bit. Everything's about ready."

"Have you heard any predictions about the water crest?" Rose asked.

"Nothing official," Harry said. "But the rise is less than an inch an hour, so I figure it's tapering off."

"At least this late in the season," Lottie said, "we won't have to worry about the river freezing and the boats breaking apart when the river goes down."

When she had lived with her grandparents, Rose had taken the rise and fall of the river for granted. But now she worried about her grandparents living alone. And she was also concerned about the showboat she had inherited from John Boardman.

She should have known that Harry would sense her concern, for as they moved into the room that served as a joint kitchen and living area, he said, "I checked out the *Silver Queen* today."

"Everything all right?"

"Yep. I went aboard and had a look-see. Best I can tell, the two watchmen have everything under control. They were asking if you're still intendin' to take the showboat out by the first of June."

"Yes, I am, Lord willing. And I hope they will stay with the boat for another two months. Martin will be out of school by then." As they gathered around the small table, she added, "I'm scared to even consider it, but I owe it to Mr. Boardman to carry on the tradition of the *Silver Queen*."

They gathered around the table that was nailed to the floor to keep it steady when the river was rough. Lottie not only had fried catfish, but she had boiled greens picked from a nearby field, mashed potatoes, hominy, baked corn pone, and a two-layer spice cake.

After supper, Harry moved to his rocking chair and said, " 'Pears like I'm the only one who ain't given the birthday boy a present. Lottie fixed the good supper. Rose bought a pony. What do you want from me, sonny?"

"Give me the leather bag my father left behind with money in it," Martin said without hesitation. Rose's shoulders slumped, and she dropped her head. Regardless of what she did, she couldn't rid Martin of the desire to know more about his past. Poor child! The only physical connections to his parents were the grave in Cave Hill Cemetery and the leather bag that his father had once held.

Harry shrugged his shoulders and, with a resigned expression on his face, went to a cupboard in their bedroom. From the top shelf he took down a leather bag.

"All right, Martin—you've asked for it enough times, and today it's yours. But," he added when Martin reached for the bag, "you must leave it here in the shanty until you're a man."

Martin nodded, took the bag, and sat on the floor. Silently, he ran his fingers over the bag and turned it inside out, as if searching for a clue to his parentage. He looked long at the document of deposit in one of Louisville's banks. After Martha Moody's burial expenses had been paid, there were still over a hundred dollars in gold coins left. The money had been deposited in Martin's name, with Harry as trustee, so he would have a little nest egg when he came of age. In light of Rose's inheritance from John Boardman, she would have enough for Martin's education, but noting the expression on his face, she thanked God that Martin had something tangible to remind him of his father.

Rose had just turned to take the dishes off the table when a sudden surge of water caused the shanty to list sideways. Two plates toppled to the floor and shattered into small pieces—the sound as startling as a gunshot. Behind her, Lottie lost her balance and fell to her knees.

"What's going on?" Harry said, as he struggled out of the rocking chair and headed for the door. Something struck the *Vagabond* with a deadening impact.

Harry's rocking chair slid across the floor and collided with the kitchen table, barely missing Martin, who still sat on the floor.

Rose helped her grandmother into a chair. "Hold on, Gramps," she said. "I'll see what's happened." She had just reached the door when the shanty boat lurched again. "Gramps!" she shouted. "We're moving!"

Holding to the wall, Harry moved out on the deck, with Rose behind him. The terror on her grandfather's face stunned Rose.

A barge loaded with coal was moving down the river just a few yards beyond them. "That barge must have broken loose from its moorings," she said. "That's what hit us."

"And hit hard enough to snap our ropes, too."

"What can we do, Gramps?"

"There ain't nothin' we can do except pray. I beached our skiff until the water went down."

Now that the water had almost reached flood level, the Ohio was as smooth as a lake, and there was no danger of the shanty capsizing in turbulent waves. But what could they do? The *Vagabond* was not self-propelled. If the boat would stay close to the bank, it might be possible to catch hold of tree limbs and pull it toward the bank or into a small creek inlet. But it was heading toward the main channel of the Ohio.

Lottie peered out of the kitchen door, with Martin hanging on to her apron. "One blessing is that there's not many boats on the river right now," she said calmly.

During the past sixty years, Lottie had survived many crises on the river, and her calmness encouraged Rose. Her grandmother scanned the western horizon where the sun was setting in a red sky with a few black clouds. "We've got about an hour of daylight left."

Harry dropped to his knees on the deck. "Lord, You saved the disciples when things got out of control on the Sea of Galilee. I believe You have as much control over the Ohio River as You did that little lake. The scripture tells us that 'the Lord is nigh unto all them that call upon him.' Well, Lord, I'm callin' on You now. Send help so's my family won't perish. Don't matter about me and Lottie—we've been yearnin' to go home for a good many years. But Martin and Rose have got their whole lives before them. Save them by Your mercy, O Lord. Amen."

Catching hold of a railing, Harry struggled to his feet.

"I believe in the power of prayer," he said to Rose, who moved cautiously to his side and sat down beside him on a bench.

"Mama," Martin cried from the doorway. "I'm afraid."

Rose motioned to him, and he rushed to her side. She hugged him close. "I'm a little afraid, too, but Gramps prayed. God is in control of our lives. We'll be all right."

They traveled past Goose Island and Rock Island and swung into a large curve, which cut off their view of the city of Louisville. Normally, Rose would have enjoyed the voyage because she was never happier than when she was floating on the river, but her pulse beat erratically, and a tight knot formed in her stomach. Several people on the bank waved to them, and Rose wondered if these people thought they were on a pleasure trip.

"There's a ferry landing down the river a ways," Harry said. "If the owner is on his ferry flat, he might be able to come out and snag the *Vagabond*."

"But will we reach there before dark?" Rose asked, with a worried glance at the darkening western sky.

Harry shook his head. After they passed the mouth of a large creek, the water was swifter, and the *Vagabond* picked up speed. The frail craft listed to the left when they rounded a bend in the river faster than Rose thought was safe. But in the twilight, she saw a bulky shape ahead of them.

"Look, Gramps! There's a steamboat tied up to the left. Granny, bring some pillowcases. If we wave them, the passengers on that boat will know there's somebody aboard. Get some pots, Martin, and start pounding on them."

Harry stood and peered intently forward. "That's the *Mary Ann*, and she's got steam up. Cap Parsons will be on board."

In spite of his twisted limbs, Harry danced a little jig around the deck. When he saw the small stern-wheeler edge away from the bank, he shouted, "They've seen us! Hallelujah! Praise the Lord! 'Bless the Lord, O my soul: and all that is within me, bless His holy name.'"

Rose recognized their friend, Captain Parsons, in the pilothouse. The larger steamboats usually had both a captain and a pilot, but Parsons had his pilot's license, and he steered his boat most of the time.

Half a dozen or more men lined the lower deck of the steamboat. Two of them were coiling ropes. One large man stood out from the rest, not only because of his size, but because he was dressed in a suit and tie. He appeared to be a passenger rather than a deckhand. Two other men leaned outward, holding long hooks on heavy chains.

When the steamboat came closer, Captain Parsons, a tall, lanky river man, guffawed gleefully. "Hey there, Harry!" he shouted, and the sound echoed across the water. "How did an old river rat like you get set adrift on the Ohio?"

"It ain't funny, Cap, and none of my doing, either. Quit your jawin' and hook on to this boat. I don't want to lose my home."

When the steamboat was within ten feet of the *Vagabond*, the men dropped ropes around the posts at each end of the shanty. The two hooks were thrown to the fore and aft decks and snagged the wooden floor. The boat came to a sudden halt, and Rose heard more dishes sliding off the kitchen table. But what did that matter? As long as they were safe, she could replace her grandmother's dishes.

The *Mary Ann* backed slowly toward the shore, pulling the shanty boat behind it. Rose had never felt such relief, such thankfulness to God, than she did when the captain of the steamboat swung the *Vagabond* toward the bank. Two of the crewmen jumped to the deck of the shanty boat and helped Harry secure their home to the steamboat as well as to a large tree along the bank.

Calling from the deck of his boat, Captain Parsons invited, "Come over here so we can talk. I want to find out what happened to you. Any damage to the *Vagabond*?"

Lottie came out of the shanty where she'd gone to inspect it. "Just a few broken dishes," she told Captain Parsons. "We were blessed."

Martin volunteered to help his grandmother set the furniture right in the shanty. Rose followed her grandfather to the deck of the bigger boat. The large, well-dressed man she had noted earlier reached out a hand to help her. She didn't need any help, but she didn't want to be impolite. She placed her hand in his and reached the deck of the packet boat safely. She looked up to thank him and staggered backward. Although ten years had made many changes, Rose knew she wasn't mistaken. Edward Moody had returned at last!

Chapter 2

Rose looked wildly about to be sure Martin hadn't followed her. Harry and Captain Parsons were in a deep discussion of the shanty's chances of survival in such an accident.

Edward Moody removed his hat and took her by the arm. "Ma'am, are you ill? Come and sit down."

He directed her toward a bench that was out of sight of the others, and Rose went gladly, for she didn't know if her legs would hold her erect much longer. Apparently Edward Moody had no idea who she was. In her fashionable clothing, she didn't much resemble the eighteen-year-old who, ten years ago, had been dressed in an ankle-length gingham dress without any bustle or extra petticoats. And, of course, he hadn't paid any attention to her—he had eyes only for his wife. He had no time for Rose or his son.

Rose had often wondered what she would do if she ever saw Edward Moody again. Would she treat him charitably? Would she bawl him out for deserting his son? If he didn't recognize his child, would she tell him who Martin was? Why had he returned to Kentucky? Her mind rioted with questions that had no answer while she prayed for the wisdom to deal with Martin's father.

When he had her settled comfortably, Edward said, "That was a narrow escape. It's little wonder that you are upset. How did you happen to be on the boat?"

"The shanty was tied up at Louisville, and I was on the boat visiting my grandparents. A barge broke loose from its moorings and careened into the *Vagabond*. Gramps had put his skiff on higher ground to get it out of the floodwaters. We didn't have any way to escape." She decided to drop a hint to see if he recalled their previous meeting. "I'm Rose Thurston."

His facial expression didn't change. She couldn't believe that her name and the shanty boat wouldn't tantalize his memory.

"My name is Edward Moody. I bought passage on the *Mary Ann* at Cairo. I have some business in Louisville."

Having a pretty good idea of what his business in Louisville was, Rose's pulse quickened, and anxious thoughts scurried around in her mind. Had he come looking for his son? Or perhaps to find the grave of his wife? Did he remember that this was the anniversary of his wife's death? Would it be possible for her to hide Martin from him?

"Come and get your vittles," a loud command came from the *Mary Ann*'s galley.

Rose stood and thanked Edward for his help. Captain Parsons joined them. "Rose, do you want to eat supper with us?"

"No, thanks. We had just finished our evening meal when the accident happened. I'm going back to the shanty to see if Granny needs any help."

"The water is falling now, and I'm aiming to head upriver in the morning. I told Harry I'd tow him back to his landing."

"Thanks, Captain. It won't be the first time you've towed the *Vagabond* from one port to the other. You've been a good friend to the Thurstons."

Edward reached for Rose's hand, and she placed hers in it. "I enjoyed our brief meeting, Miss Thurston," he said. "I'm a stranger to Louisville. Since I intend to stop over for a few days, I'd like to see you again. Will you give me your address and permission to contact you?"

Rose hesitated momentarily. "I live in the Boardman house on Third Street. Most anyone can tell you where it is."

"Perhaps we can have dinner together some evening."

"Thank you. I would like that."

Rose wasn't sure she would like it, but she intended to keep aware of Edward Moody's activities in Louisville.

Apparently during the excitement of being rescued, none of her family had noticed Rose talking to the stranger, for no questions were asked. Rose helped Lottie clean up the few broken dishes, and they returned the furnishings to their normal positions.

Harry had never learned to read, but he sat in his rocker, holding the Bible until Rose and Lottie finished the work. It was a nightly ritual to read a chapter from the Bible and have prayer before going to bed.

Martin sat on the floor at Harry's feet, and Rose and Lottie drew their chairs close. Harry handed the Bible to Rose. "I've been ponderin' about the many times in the Bible when God delivered His people. And I'm hankerin' to have you read about the time God saved the apostle Paul and his friends during a shipwreck."

"That story is in the last part of the book of Acts, Gramps." Glancing at Martin, whose eyes were already drooping sleepily, Rose added, "I won't read the whole chapter."

"You won't have to," Lottie said. "During our years on the river, I've read them chapters often. We know the apostle Paul was on a boat that even the captain thought would be lost, until Paul received the revelation that God would save them."

"Read the part about the angel coming to speak to Paul, Mama," Martin said.

Putting his hand on Martin's head, Harry said, "That's the part I want to hear, too, sonny. I didn't hear no angel talkin' to me when we were tumblin' down the river, but God must have had a whole legion of angels keepin' the *Vagabond* afloat tonight."

"I'll start where Paul related God's message to his shipmates," Rose said. " 'And now I exhort you to be of good cheer: for there shall be no loss of any man's life among you, but of the ship. For there stood by me this night the angel of God, whose I am, and whom I serve, saying, Fear not, Paul; thou must be brought before Caesar: and lo, God hath given thee all them that sail with thee. Wherefore, sirs, be of good cheer: for I believe God, that it shall be even as it was told me.'"

Easing his body out of the rocker, Harry knelt by his chair. "Lord God, we come to You humbly tonight, knowing that we ain't done nothin' to deserve Your goodness. We also know, God, that even if we had gone down with the *Vagabond*, that wouldn't mean Your hand was agin' us. As long as we've got promise of a home in heaven, nothin' can separate us from Your love. Paul the apostle was a great man, Lord, and I call to mind his words in the book of Romans when he said that nothin' would be able to separate us from the love of God, which is in Christ Jesus our Lord. Amen."

Rose wiped her eyes when her grandfather finished praying. Although he had not had an opportunity to be educated, from listening to Lottie and Rose read the scripture, Harry had a vast knowledge of God's Word. Conscious of their lack of education, he and Lottie had sacrificed to send Rose to a girls' academy. How much she owed these two people who'd taken her in when her parents had died!

Martin and Harry settled for the night in her grandparents' bed, while Lottie put sheets and quilts on the bed Rose had occupied before she had moved into the Boardman house. Rose extinguished all lights except one lamp chained to the kitchen table before she joined her grandmother. Lottie was already in bed. Rose left the door slightly ajar to provide enough light to feel her way around the room to remove her clothes and put on one of Lottie's voluminous nightgowns. She sat on the edge of the bed.

"What's troubling you, honey?" Lottie asked quietly.

"Did you see the man I was talking to on the *Mary Ann*?"

"Not close-up. I didn't heed him in particular."

"It was Edward Moody."

Lottie sat upright in bed, and the springs squeaked and bounced under her weight. "Are you sure?"

"I recognized him at once, but he introduced himself."

"Did he know who you were?"

Rose shook her head; then realizing that Lottie couldn't see in the semi-darkness, she said, "No. I gave him several hints, but apparently the events of ten years ago didn't stay in his mind. I'm afraid of him, Granny."

"Wasn't he from Pittsburgh? Maybe he'll head on upriver and not stop at Louisville."

"No. He's going to stay for a while. He told me he had some business in

Louisville. I know what that business will be."

Rubbing Rose's back with her chubby hand, Lottie asked, "You didn't tell him about the boy?"

"I hadn't decided what to do when the cook announced supper, and that gave me a short reprieve to think about it."

"Now that the water is falling, the steamboats will be movin' out. Harry can find a boat to pull us downriver, and we could stay until Moody leaves."

"I've thought of that, but I shouldn't take Martin out of school. Because he was such a puny baby, Mr. Moody probably thinks the child died, and he might just be looking for his wife's grave. But if he starts asking questions, he'll soon learn about Martin. Besides, I wouldn't feel right not to tell Martin that his father has returned."

"I know. Poor little tyke—all these years he's still so hurt because his father gave him away," Lottie answered, settling down on the mattress.

"Mr. Moody invited me to have dinner with him some evening, and I intend to accept. Perhaps I can find out what he means to do."

Rose lay down beside her grandmother and pulled one of Lottie's quilts over her shoulders. "I hope I can keep Martin and his father separated until we get back to Louisville. I need a little time to prepare for it."

"I'll tell Harry to keep Martin occupied and not let him go over on the *Mary Ann*."

"Yes, do that," Rose agreed, turning over and finally falling into a fretful sleep.

Since life on the river was commonplace to Martin, Harry didn't have any trouble keeping the child busy. He had always enjoyed playing with the Shawnee arrowheads that Harry had collected through the years. When he tired of that, while the *Mary Ann* pushed their home steadily upriver, Lottie asked him to help her cut out quilt blocks.

Harry owned a narrow strip of land a short distance south of the Louisville landing, and the shanty boat was pushed safely into place. Rose stayed out of sight until the *Mary Ann* docked farther upstream. By early afternoon, without seeing any more of Edward Moody, Rose prepared to start home.

A worried look on her face, Lottie said quietly to Rose as they were leaving, "I'll be praying for God's will to be done in this matter."

Rose hugged her grandmother. "And please pray for me to have the grace to accept His will."

"God understands, honey. Remember, He gave up *His* son!"

"I remembered that all night long. I want what is best for Martin. I'm grateful for the few hours I've had to come to terms with this before I have to confront Mr. Moody."

"Don't forget that Martin is old enough to have a say in the matter, too."

"Come on, Mama," Martin called from the bank. "I want to get home to my pony."

Waving good-bye to her grandparents, Rose crossed the gangplank and started toward their house. She took the less-traveled streets because she wasn't yet ready to encounter Edward Moody.

Since Rose and Martin had not yet been home following the near tragedy, Sallie and Isaiah hadn't heard about the Thurstons' narrow escape.

"Praise God," Isaiah said when Rose told him what had happened. "The Lord sure had His hand on you."

While Martin excitedly explained their runaway experience to Isaiah, Rose drew Sallie to one side and quietly told her about the return of Martin's father.

"I don't want Martin to know until I find out what Mr. Moody's intentions are. But is that right? He's anticipated his father's return for years. Should I tell him?"

"Use your own best judgment, Miss Rose. But if you want my advice, I can't see that it will hurt to keep the truth from him a day or two."

"That's what Granny thought, too," Rose said. "Mr. Moody indicated that he might invite me to dinner. If he doesn't do that soon, I'll make it a point to see him."

"The boy is excited about his pony now. That'll keep his mind busy for several days."

"Tell Isaiah that I may want him to keep an eye on Mr. Moody."

After getting directions from Captain Parsons for a suitable hotel, Edward left the waterfront and walked up the bank. The falling water had left several inches of mud on the streets, and his boots were crusted with brown silt when he reached the Galt House recommended to him by Captain Parsons. Although water had surrounded the hotel, the interior had not been flooded. Workers were busily cleaning mud from the Main Street entrance.

When he registered, the clerk asked Edward how many days he expected to stay.

"I'm not sure," he said. "Possibly a week or more."

After learning the times meals were served and asking for bathwater to be delivered to his room, Edward walked up the carpeted circular stairway to the second floor. It had been a long, arduous journey from Colorado to Kentucky.

Was he following a dream? Would he have been wiser to have stayed in Colorado? He had set out ten years ago to make his fortune. He had accomplished that dream, but he had soon found out that wealth did not bring happiness. Six months ago he had broken his leg, and while he was immobile for several weeks, he had come to terms with his mistakes of the past. The loss of his family gnawed constantly at his peace of mind. And his relationship with God had suffered during the years when he slaved to achieve his goal.

For long periods of time, Edward had successfully pushed thoughts of the past into the background. But those times when he couldn't forget, his heart became burdened with guilt because he had left his wife for others to bury.

He had never forgotten the girl on the shanty boat who had accused him of killing his wife by taking her on a long journey when she was with child. The fear that the girl may have been right had caused him hundreds of sleepless nights. He had loved Martha wholeheartedly, and no other woman had been able to take her place in his heart. Regardless of why she had died, he should have stayed long enough to see that she received a decent burial. He had left plenty of money for the woman to see to her burial, but he couldn't forget that it was his responsibility.

When he got to that point, he always justified his actions by reminding himself that if he hadn't arrived in Colorado by the first of May, he would have lost the opportunity to invest in the gold mine. Then he would be disgusted at himself for being so persistent. God had thrown all kinds of roadblocks in his way to keep him from putting his money in an investment that was doomed to failure from the first. But, oh no, he wouldn't listen to God or pay any attention to His signs. Edward Moody always knew best!

And what about their baby? Surely the child had died just as his mother had, but he should have stayed until he knew for sure. Had he been disloyal to Martha by not looking after the child she'd given him at the expense of her own life? Was it too late to make restitution?

If the child still lived, he intended to rescue him from the life of poverty he must have endured because he was an orphan. How could he find out if his child still lived?

In desperation, Edward bowed his head on the small table in his room. *God, I haven't been a faithful believer. I've been too busy following my own star to take time to give You any part of my life. God, I'm not asking for myself now. But if the boy lives, will You help me find him so I can make up for the years he's had to live in poverty?*

It had been days since he had slept in a bed, and Edward needed to rest. He decided to postpone his investigation until the next day. Perhaps by that time, in His graciousness, God would give him an answer. Sleep didn't come easily to him, and he thought of Rose Thurston. Perhaps if he arranged to see her she could help him solve the mystery of what had happened to his wife and child.

~

After a fitful night's sleep, Edward was still without divine direction. He ate a hearty breakfast in the dining room, thinking of yesterday's experiences. With the memory of his wife always in the back of his mind, Edward hadn't been interested in women. In spite of the temptations put in his way in the towns spawned by Colorado's booming mining industry, he had lived a celibate life. So why was his mind preoccupied with the woman he had met the day before? How was she different from other women he had ignored? Perhaps it was her appearance. Her sparkling dark blue eyes reminded him of the ocean's waves. Her bronze-gold hair braided and wrapped around her head looked like a golden crown. Several times he caught himself wondering what her hair would look like hanging loose over her shoulders.

Was it too soon to ask her to have dinner with him? She hadn't discouraged him when he mentioned the possibility. He stopped by the desk when he finished his meal.

"Do you have a messenger service?" he queried the clerk.

"Yes, sir," the man said. He pointed to a desk at one side of the lobby. "You will find paper and pen on that table. You write your message, and we will deliver it anyplace in the city, free of charge."

Edward sat at the table, nervously trying to decide what to say. Grimly, he thought he was as indecisive as a boy. After all, he only wanted to have dinner with the woman. He wasn't asking her to marry him. Deciding that brevity was the best approach, he finally penned:

> *Miss Thurston,*
> *I would like to further our acquaintance. I've checked out the restaurant at the Galt House and find it adequate. If you're available to have dinner with me tonight, name a time convenient for you and give me directions to your home, so I can call for you. I will await your answer through the messenger.*
>
> *Edward Moody*

Edward read the message and frowned. He certainly hadn't been brief, and the message sounded stilted. Perhaps he should give her more time and suggest a later date, but his mission was urgent. He didn't know how long he would be in Louisville, but he knew he wanted to see Rose Thurston again before he left the city.

He hadn't had much experience inviting ladies to dinner. Not knowing any better way to compose the invitation, he blotted the note, sealed it, and marked the envelope with the address Rose had mentioned. He took the letter to the desk clerk.

"Please have the return message brought to my room," he said, as he pressed a gold coin into the man's hand.

Rose was at the paddock watching Martin ride the pony when the messenger found her. She read the message and called Isaiah to stay with Martin while she returned to the house. She had known the messenger boy for years, so she invited him to come into the kitchen with her.

"Sallie, give Russell a piece of cake and some milk while I write a response to this message. Then come to the office for a few minutes, please." She was still poring over the letter five minutes later when Sallie entered the office. Rose read the message to her.

"What should I do? I more or less agreed to have a meal with him, but should I put him off for a day or two?"

"You'll fret about it until you do go, won't you?" Sallie queried, grinning widely.

"You know me too well, Sallie. Yes, I suppose I will."

"Then you might as well go and get it over with."

"That's the way I feel about it. I'll go this evening. But I don't want him to come to this house and see Martin. Will you ask Isaiah if he can drive me to the hotel at six thirty? I'd drive myself, but"—she added with a wry grin—"I suppose that isn't the way a lady should conduct herself."

Laughing, Sallie said, "Oh, you're doing better, Miss Rose. I'll go and feed Russell some more cake while you pen the note."

After Russell had been sent on his way, Rose turned again to Sallie for advice. Sallie had worked for society matrons off and on for years, so she was a good mentor for Rose.

"So what am I going to wear, and how am I going to keep Martin from knowing what I'm doing?"

"Wear that new gown you bought last week from Miss Spencer's boutique. And don't fret about Martin—I'll watch out for him. He thinks it's fun to eat in the kitchen with Isaiah and me. And after supper, Isaiah can teach him to curry his pony."

The rest of the afternoon dragged for Rose. She couldn't settle down to do anything. She walked from one room to the other until she was aggravated with herself. Finally she called to Sallie. "I'm going to walk down to the *Vagabond*. Watch Martin, please."

"Sure enough! But don't stay too long. It may take some time to get dressed."

Rose threw a woolen shawl over her shoulders, for a strong wind blew from the river. Signs of spring were around her, however. A mockingbird, perched on a white picket fence, ran through his entire repertoire of birdcalls. Patches of violets lent a purple hue to many of the yards along Third Street. A cardinal's insistent *cheer, cheer* echoed like a trumpet over her head. By the time she reached the waterfront, Rose's temperament was back to normal.

She found Lottie alone on the shanty, patching one of Harry's shirts.

"I may have made a mistake, Granny," Rose said, sitting on the floor beside her grandmother.

"So?" Lottie said. "Everybody's got a right to make a mistake now and again."

Calmed even more by Lottie's complacent attitude, Rose told her about Edward's invitation and her acceptance. "Should I have refused? Would it have been better to put him off for a few days?"

Lottie laid the shirt aside and, with a work-roughened hand, smoothed

Rose's hair back from her forehead. "Always thinking of others before your own self. You're trying to protect Martin. But do you actually think you can keep Moody from learning about his son? People like to think of Louisville as a city, and I reckon it is, but it's still a small town at heart where anybody's business is common knowledge. All the man has to do is ask a few questions, and he will soon learn that Martin is his boy."

"And Martin will have to be told. I'm not sure if I should come right out and tell Mr. Moody or let him find out on his own. This dinner should give me an opportunity to find out what he's really like before I introduce him to Martin."

"I agree. It won't hurt to let one more day pass before you tell the boy."

Feeling better, Rose hurried back home.

Since there was still some coolness in the spring night air, Rose decided that she would be comfortable in the new dress she had bought the week before. Sallie arranged most of Rose's hair on top of her head, with curly bangs and a long fall of hair to her shoulders. She tied the corset strings and arranged the petticoats and bustle before Rose put on the two-piece dress.

Miss Spencer had told Rose that the garment was really a housedress, but considering the everyday dresses she had worn most of her life, the garment seemed elegant to her. The dress was styled from printed silk and plain satin in shades of blue. The long-sleeved bodice had a lawn collar and cuffs, and it extended over her slender hips. The tie-back skirt, trimmed with pleating and large bows, was floor-length with a modest ruffled train.

Although she felt as if she were bound in fetters, looking in the mirror, she knew that she was in the stylish mode of the day and probably wearing the kind of clothing Edward Moody expected of a woman.

As the crowning touch, Sallie set a velvet hat with ruched silk under the brim, trimmed with a curled ostrich feather on her head. Rose made a face at her image in the mirror.

Sallie chuckled. "Now, Miss Rose, you're beautiful and you know it."

"Beauty shouldn't be skin deep. In deciding whether I'm a fit mother for his son, Mr. Moody should look beyond all of this finery."

Sallie gave Rose a quick hug. "Don't worry. He'll see the real you. You couldn't change your true nature if you tried."

Despite her affluence, Rose hadn't aspired to become a part of Louisville's social life, but she did want Martin to be accepted when he was older. Conscious of this fact, she always exerted an effort to act like a lady-born when she was in public. Fortunately, she had learned how to be ladylike when she attended Miss Bordeaux's Academy.

Edward waited for her in the lobby, and when he saw Isaiah help her from the carriage, he hurried down the steps to the street. She extended her hand, and when Edward touched it briefly with his lips, she wasn't prepared for her reaction to his touch.

Dear God, help me to remember that I'm here on Martin's behalf.

Touching her elbow, Edward directed her toward the dining room. Gaslights were available in the city now, but the Galt House dining room still had enormous crystal chandeliers lit by candles. Edward and Rose were ushered to a secluded alcove, also lit by candles. They ordered the specialty of the day—roast beef, baked potatoes, green beans, and freshly baked bread.

After the waiter left, wanting to find out all she could about Edward, Rose said, "Do you expect to spend a long time in Louisville?"

"I'm not sure. I'm rather footloose at the present. I used to live in Pittsburgh, but I've been in Colorado since 1876. I arrived there a few months before it entered the Union. I suppose you could say I grew up with the state."

"Then you intend to return to Colorado?"

He shrugged his shoulders. "I don't know. I had expected to make Colorado my home, but my plans didn't work out as I had hoped." His eyes were bleak, and for a moment he didn't continue. Rose wondered if he had ever considered his son in his plans.

"Didn't you like Colorado?" Rose persisted.

"It was stimulating to be in on the birth of a state, but Colorado wasn't kind to me at first. I had invested heavily in a gold mine that wasn't any good, and I lost most of the money I'd taken with me. I had to start over again, and I had a rough time of it. With a lot of hard work and determination, I finally achieved my goal."

Again he paused, and sadness filled his eyes. Perhaps his lack of money had kept him from returning to see about his son. Would Martin consider his father's loss of fortune as sufficient reason to justify ten years of neglect?

"But when I found out that success wasn't enough for contentment, I decided to leave." His face brightened, and he said, "Forgive me for talking about my own affairs. I'd rather talk about you."

"You needn't apologize. I asked about your life in Colorado. I haven't traveled like you have, so I don't have much to say. Most of my life has been spent on the waterfront of Louisville, except for the summers when Gramps traveled up and down the Ohio and other Kentucky rivers. Mostly he fishes for a living. He has standing orders for fish in the hotels and restaurants in Louisville. He even catches frogs for some of the more elite restaurants. When he travels in the summer, he stocks the boat with dishes and tin household items. He also has pottery to sell. He's done all kinds of things during his lifetime."

"Forgive me for saying this, but you seem to be a poised, educated woman. How did you manage that if you spent your life on the river?"

"My parents died when I was a child, so my grandparents took me in. Gramps and Granny love the life they lead, but they wanted something better for me. Granny worked six years as a cook and housekeeper at Miss Bordeaux's Academy to pay for my education."

"That was commendable of them."

Noticing the compassion in Edward's eyes, Rose was taken aback. She quickly regained her composure and continued. "I suppose so, but I didn't enjoy those years. I was out of place at Miss Bordeaux's, and most of the girls didn't let me forget that I was the granddaughter of the cook. Miss Bordeaux didn't show favorites, and she wouldn't tolerate any persecution, but she wasn't around all the time. Now that I'm older, I appreciate the sacrifice Granny made for me."

"Her sacrifice doesn't seem to have been in vain. You seem to have done very well for yourself."

"I wouldn't be living where I do now if a good friend of our family hadn't left his estate to me when he died. He and Gramps had been friends since he came from New York when I was just a child."

"He didn't have any family?"

"Not unless he had some in New York. If he did, he didn't talk about them."

"It sounds as if both of us have had similar experiences—having to make our own way in life. I didn't enjoy my struggles in Colorado, either, but I'm glad that I stuck with it. Although I realize now that I've missed some of the more important things in life."

Edward paused in his story. *Is he lost in thoughts of the past, or is he thinking about the future?* Rose wondered.

"Tell me something about Louisville, Miss Thurston."

"If you don't think it's too forward of me, you can call me by my given name as everybody else does. It's Rose."

"It would be my pleasure. Rose is a pretty name."

"My parents were landlubbers, as Gramps said. My mother didn't like traveling on the river, and she married a man who worked on land. I was born the first day of June, and Granny said my mother looked out the window at a white rambler rose on their porch and chose my name. I like it, too."

"I got my name from my father," he said. "Now about Louisville?"

"Gramps is the one to tell you about Louisville, Mr. Moody."

He touched her hand. "Edward."

"Talk to my grandpa, Edward. He came here with his parents after the close of the War of 1812. His parents floated downriver on a flatboat. Louisville has been home to the Thurstons ever since. He has some wild stories of the Indian wars and the War Between the States."

It was dark when they finished dinner, and Edward said, "I'd prefer to see you home. I don't want you going alone in the dark."

"Thank you, but I won't be alone." She checked the watch on the chain around her neck. "My coachman is supposed to pick me up, and I'm sure he'll be waiting. You may walk to the carriage with me. That way you will know I'm well protected."

Edward held the door open for her, and she walked down the steps before him. Isaiah was waiting at the curb, as she knew he would be.

"Mr. Moody, this is Isaiah Taylor. He'll take me home."

Edward looked at her, surprise on his face. It wasn't customary for ladies to even acknowledge the presence of their servants, but this faux pas convinced him even more that Rose Thurston was a unique person who made her own rules for living.

The coachman had his hat brim pulled low on his forehead, and his face was obscure in the dimly lit street. "Good evening, Isaiah," Edward said, and Isaiah lifted his hand in greeting. Edward turned to Rose. "Will I see you again?"

"That depends on how long you stay in Louisville."

"I don't know how long my business will take, or how successful it will be. I will contact you before I leave."

He handed her up into the carriage. "Thank you for dinner."

Rose could feel his intense brown eyes following them as Isaiah pulled away from the curb.

"Does he know anything?" Isaiah asked when they were out of hearing.

"Apparently not, but he's a highly determined, intelligent man; and I have a feeling that when he sets his eye on a goal, he works to get it. I'm worried, Isaiah."

"No use borrowing trouble, Miss Rose."

Chapter 3

Edward enjoyed a better night's sleep than he had had for months. He wakened to the sounds of Louisville starting its day—steamboat whistles, the voices of hotel workers, and a cleaning crew sweeping the streets. His thoughts turned immediately to Rose Thurston. His companions for years had been primarily men, and he'd forgotten how pleasurable it was to sit at a candlelit table across from a beautiful woman and enjoy a leisurely meal.

He shook himself into reality. He had an important reason for coming to Louisville, and he must not let his interest in Rose deter him from his search. He tugged the rope beside his bed, and soon a porter answered his summons. He asked for hot water, and when the man returned, Edward questioned him. "Where can I rent a carriage for the day?"

"There's a barn two blocks down Main Street where you can hire carriages by the day or the week," the porter answered. "Business is down a little now because the high water has slowed the river traffic. I doubt you'll have any trouble renting a carriage."

After he dressed and had breakfast, Edward went to the barn and was soon outfitted with a buggy and a horse. He asked the hostler directions to cemeteries in town and wrote down the names and directions. Cave Hill Cemetery was the farthest away, but apparently the largest cemetery, so he decided to start his search there.

Accustomed to speedy western horses, Edward was disgusted with the old nag that pulled his carriage. But the plodding pace gave Edward plenty of time to survey the city. In addition to the river traffic, several railroad lines crisscrossed the town. Captain Parsons had told him that Louisville had a population of more than 160,000. Before he turned on Broadway, which he would follow to the cemetery, Edward passed through a section of town containing majestic houses of varied types of architecture. He drove along Third Street, wondering which of those homes belonged to Rose Thurston.

Apparently Louisville had not suffered much damage during the Civil War, for the homes looked as if they had been standing for many years. Tulips and daffodils bloomed in the lawns he passed.

Searching for his wife's grave would probably be like looking for a needle in a haystack. Edward had provided enough money for a headstone, but for all he knew, those people on the shanty boat might have kept it for themselves. He squirmed uncomfortably when he considered that Martha might have been buried in a pauper's grave. But his conscience pointed out that it would be his fault if she were. If he had stayed behind to arrange for Martha's burial and to provide for the welfare of his child, he would have been too late to have sunk his money in a worthless mine. God had given him warning signs all along the way, but he had been too stubborn to heed them.

Edward pulled the horse to a stop when he reached the cemetery and paused, wondering which of the many curved, hilly roads he should take. Stone mausoleums and towering marble shafts indicated that Louisville's elite citizens had been buried in this cemetery. He turned toward smaller, less majestic stones—believing that he might find Martha's grave. He judged that the cemetery covered more than a hundred acres, and it would be impossible for him to locate his wife's grave unless he found a caretaker.

After driving for fifteen or twenty minutes, Edward decided to return to town and visit the cemetery office the hostler had mentioned to him. Undoubtedly they would have records of burials. Before turning back, he saw a man working a short distance away. If he was the caretaker, he might be able to provide the information Edward needed. He doubted that the horse would move from the spot if he left it unfettered, but he tied the animal to the trunk of a large elm tree. Edward walked toward the worker, who was kneeling on the ground, smoothing the soil over a grave with a trowel. He had a pail of grass seed beside him. He didn't look up when Edward stopped beside him but continued with his work.

"Mawnin', sir," the man said.

"Good morning," Edward replied. "I'm a stranger here, and I wonder if you might provide some information."

"Happy to oblige if I can, sir." The man's voice sounded familiar, but all of the natives spoke in a similar drawl.

"I'm looking for the grave of Martha Moody. I don't know whether the grave is even marked, or even if she's buried in this cemetery."

"You won't have no trouble findin' that grave." The man looked up briefly and pointed to a burial plot marked by a marble angel, several yards away.

"That looks like a new stone."

"Yes, sir—put up a few weeks ago."

"Thanks for your help," Edward said.

Puzzled, Edward walked quickly toward the grave. Martha had died ten years ago—why was the stone new?

The grave was well tended. The expensive stone had a bouquet of flowers at its base. The petals were turning brown around the edges, so they had been brought a few days ago. Who would have placed the stone? Martha had a sister in Pittsburgh. Had she and her husband located the grave and marked it? He turned, hoping the caretaker could solve the puzzle for him, but the man had disappeared. Where could he have gone so quickly?

Edward knelt by the grave, but he felt no emotion at all. Had the years diminished his love for Martha? He had thought that he would love her forever, but living with a memory for ten years must have stifled any feelings he held for her.

Edward returned to the carriage and stepped into it, but he didn't take up the reins immediately. How could he learn who had been caring for Martha's grave? Who could tell him if his son was alive? He had learned long ago that to solve a puzzle he often had to go back to the beginning.

He vaguely remembered the shanty boat where his wife had died and the two women he had seen. Since residents on shanty boats were nomadic people, it wasn't likely that they would still be living in Louisville, but perhaps the man who owned the shanty that they had rescued might know something to further his search. And Rose Thurston had lived on a shanty boat. Perhaps she could help him. He wished he had asked her last night, but while he talked with Rose, Edward had forgotten his mission in Louisville. He picked up the reins, flicked them several times, and finally the nag moved to his commands. He headed toward the waterfront.

Rose stood in the backyard, leaning on the wooden fence, watching Martin ride Tibbets around the paddock. Although Martin had always been hesitant to try new things, he didn't seem to have any qualms about riding the pony. His friend, Cam Miller, a year older than Martin, had had a pony for several months, and Cam sometimes let Martin ride.

Rose stepped backward out of Martin's hearing when Isaiah loped into the yard. He slid out of the saddle and sauntered toward her.

"You had Mr. Moody figgered out, Miss Rose. I found out from the hostler that Mr. Moody had hired a horse and carriage, and that he had asked about graveyards. The hostler thought he was going to Cave Hill Cemetery. I took a few shortcuts and got there before he did. I was real busy workin' when he came. He asked about the grave, and as soon as I told him where it was, I got out of sight. He seemed mournful about his wife's death, and he sure acted puzzled about that new stone."

"What did he do then?"

"He didn't stay long, but he headed back in the direction of the hotel. I rustled on home."

"Thanks, Isaiah," Rose said, her eyes on Martin.

"You worried, Miss Rose?" Isaiah asked.

She nodded. "Yes, I am. I suppose it shows a lack of faith, but I am worried."

"But the boy is yours, all tight and legal, ain't he?"

"That's true, but I want to do what's best for Martin. Maybe he needs a father now more than he needs a mother."

"It'll come out right, Miss Rose."

"I hope so. Now that you're back to watch Martin, I'm going inside."

"Let me know if you want me to do anything else."

~

After Edward turned in the horse and carriage, he ate a light lunch at the hotel before he started out again. The river had fallen a foot or two during the night, but he still walked through a few inches of mud to reach his destination. A thin filter of smoke rose from a rusty piece of stovepipe on the *Vagabond*'s roof. The proprietor sat on the deck of the boat, dangling a fish line in the murky water.

Edward had heard this man's name when he'd boarded the *Mary Ann* a few nights ago, and he cast around in his mind trying to remember it. "Mr. Thurston," he said tentatively. When the man didn't correct him, he decided he had remembered correctly.

"Come on over, Mr. Moody. Lottie, bring our guest a cup of coffee!" he shouted.

"No, thank you," Edward said. "I dined before I left the hotel." He walked across the gangplank, wondering how Thurston knew his name.

Harry jerked his line, and a large catfish landed beside Edward's feet. Harry removed it from the line, dropped the fish into a tub of water, and put another worm on his hook before he gave any more attention to Edward.

"Sit down, Mr. Moody," he said, motioning to a rocking chair. "What's on your mind?"

"Have you lived in this area very long?"

"I was born on a shanty and have lived on one ever since. In the summer, me and my family travel the rivers, but Louisville is our winter port."

Edward squirmed in his chair. "Then you probably know most of the shanty people in this area."

Harry wiggled his fishing hook. "Why don't you speak what's on your mind, Mr. Moody? What do you want to know?"

Edward still hesitated. Would he be wiser to continue on to Pittsburgh or to return to Colorado without resurrecting the past? Did he really want to know what had happened to his child?

"Ten years ago, my wife died in childbirth on a shanty boat in this area. I went to the cemetery today. There was a new headstone on my wife's grave. I want some information about the people who took care of my wife, and I'm curious why this new stone has been placed on her grave recently. I left money for these details to be seen to then."

"That bag of money wasn't all you left behind, was it, Mr. Moody?" a woman's voice asked.

Edward turned and looked at the woman standing in the doorway. He stood up to acknowledge her presence, and she waved him back into the chair. She held a leather bag, which she handed to him.

"A stone was put on your wife's grave. The money left after we bought the stone was put in a bank, where it's been drawing interest. The receipt is in the bag. We didn't use nary cent of your money for ourselves."

"You. . . You're the one who took care of my wife?" he stuttered. "There was only one grave at the cemetery. Did my son survive?"

"Yes. We saved your money for the boy to have when he became a man, but the child don't need it now."

Edward glanced around the humble shelter these people called home, marveling that they hadn't used any of the money that was rightfully theirs.

"But the new tombstone! You should keep the money to pay for that."

"The marker we put up crumbled away. The new stone was put there a few weeks ago by our granddaughter. We didn't pay for it."

"Where is my son?"

Lottie and Harry exchanged glances. "Our granddaughter has him."

"Wait a minute," Edward said, slowly comprehending. "There was a woman and a boy on this boat yesterday. Was that. . . ?"

Harry nodded.

"But why didn't you tell me?"

"Why should we?" Lottie said. "You abandoned the boy once. We weren't about to tell him who you were until we knew your intentions."

"I returned to Kentucky to discover if my son survived. Does he live on this boat?"

"Not now. He's living with our granddaughter on Third Street. Go to the top of the bank and follow Main Street till you come to Third. Anybody can point out the house to you."

"Is your granddaughter Rose Thurston?" Edward demanded loudly, a shadow of anger flashing across his face. "I had dinner with her last night. If she knew who I was, why didn't she tell me?"

"Maybe she wanted to size you up to see what kind of man you are. I hate to say it, Mr. Moody, but you didn't make much of an impression on us the last time we saw you."

"I had just lost my wife. I was overcome with grief. What did you expect?"

"I'm not judgin' you one way or another, Mr. Moody—just answerin' your questions," Lottie said.

Edward felt betrayed. He had liked Rose more than any other woman he'd known since he had married Martha. She had seemed to enjoy their time together last night. Why had she deceived him?

Edward stood up. "I'll go see her then. She told me she lived in the Boardman house. Does she have the boy with her?"

Harry yanked another catfish out of the water. "Yes, sir. She's been lookin' after him ever since the night you gave your boy to her."

Edward felt his face flushing, whether from anger or embarrassment he didn't know. Without speaking, he dropped the money bag on the rocking chair and walked off the deck of the *Vagabond*. It was obvious that reclaiming his son might prove to be difficult.

He walked rapidly to Third Street, and after a few blocks, he asked an old gentleman who was working in his yard to direct him to Rose Thurston's house. The man pointed across the street to a three-story stone-faced house. He marched toward the house with a determined stride.

Rose saw Edward Moody coming toward her home. She turned from the window and walked into the dining room, where Sallie was working. "Will you answer the door? I want to put this off as long as I can. I'll go upstairs until you let him in."

Pausing on the first step of the back stairway, she inquired, "Is Martin still out in the paddock?"

"Yes. He's gonna grow to that pony if he stays on it much longer."

With a faint smile Rose said, "The new will wear off before long."

She went into her bedroom, tense, but excited, too. She dreaded this meeting. Perhaps she should have told Edward last night, but she had enjoyed his company so much that she didn't want to spoil their time together. She had a feeling that their amicability of the night before was about to cease. She looked in the mirror. She wasn't dressed as stylishly as the previous evening, but she still looked all right in her plain linen dress with only one petticoat, and the hem a few inches from the floor.

When Rose moved to Third Street, she had adopted the dress of the society ladies of the town, more for Martin than herself. She was much more comfortable in the homemade dresses that Lottie had made for her, but she didn't want Martin to be ashamed of her appearance. Only a few neighbors had offered any overtures of friendship, and Rose hadn't asked for any favors. To them, she was still the shanty boat girl. For herself, she didn't mind, but she hoped that time would remove the stigma of the early years of poverty from Martin's life.

"Company, Miss Rose," Sallie called from the entrance hall.

Rose leaned against the doorframe and closed her eyes.

Help me, God. Give me the wisdom to handle this situation.

Edward sat on an upholstered sofa while he waited for Rose. He forced himself to take in his surroundings in an attempt to calm his demeanor. He couldn't help but admire the wide entrance hall that stretched the width of the building. A red carpet covered the floor, and along the walls were massive cabinets, holding marble and porcelain articles that Edward recognized as products of Europe. The wide walnut stairway stretched upward for three stories.

He stood when he heard Rose's steps. His indignation, unsuccessfully calmed by the beautiful furnishings, melted at the sight of Rose Thurston descending the staircase. She was as striking in daylight as she had been in the candlelit dining room the night before. She was of medium height with a trim figure. Her bronze-gold hair swept upward from her slender, graceful neck. When she stopped on the bottom step, he noticed that her dark blue eyes were framed by thick, dark lashes, which hadn't been apparent in the shadowy dining room last night.

But her beauty did not quell his anger for long as he again remembered the girl who had been present when his wife had died. The years had erased any memory of the appearance of the girl who had assisted in the delivery of his child. But he had never forgotten her accusation that *he* was responsible for the death of his wife. The thought of her unjust words had rankled for years. He stepped forward and greeted her with a slight bow.

As Rose stood before Edward, the cold expression in his brown eyes brought a chill, but she spoke as pleasantly as possible, under the circumstances. "What can I do for you this afternoon?"

"I've been to see your grandparents."

Since Isaiah had continued to follow Edward's movements, Rose was aware of his visit to the *Vagabond*. She had expected him to call, for her few encounters with him had convinced her that he was a man of action. She had a feeling that Edward wouldn't delay once he decided on a course to take.

"Please come into the parlor," she said. She strolled toward a room to her left—a long room with two entrances. A walnut fireplace dominated one wall, a mahogany grand piano stood in one corner, and tables of various dark woods were scattered throughout. The room was furnished with beautiful, upholstered matching love seats and chairs. Rose sat down and motioned Edward into a seat opposite hers.

"I suppose you know why I'm here," he said as he sat stiffly on the chair.

"Of course," she said.

Sallie entered with a teapot, cups, and a plate of cookies on a tray. She put it on the table between them. Rose thanked her, and Sallie gave her a reassuring smile before returning to the kitchen.

Rose poured a cup of tea and handed it to Edward, then took a cup for herself. She needed it. She was far more apprehensive than she wanted to be.

"Why didn't you tell me last night that we had met ten years ago?"

"I recognized you immediately on the *Mary Ann*," Rose said. "And when I accepted your invitation to dinner, I hadn't decided whether or not to tell you who I was. But I enjoyed the evening, and I didn't want to spoil it by introducing a subject that might lead to controversy."

"I've wondered for years if my son survived, but the pressure of business kept me in Colorado. I came back to discover what happened to him. I want to thank you for caring for him."

"It has been a pleasure."

"And for looking after my wife's grave. The stone is a fine one. I intend to pay you for it."

142

She shook her head. "No. I did that for Martin."

"Martin?"

"That was as close as I could come to Martha—his mother's name. His full name is Martin Moody Thurston—the name I put on the papers when I adopted him."

"Adopted him?"

"Yes, seven years ago when he was three years old."

"You had no right to adopt him without my permission."

Rose placed her teacup on the table and walked around the room before returning to her seat. The tension in the room had erased the camaraderie they had enjoyed temporarily.

"Do I have to remind you, Mr. Moody," she began, reverting to the formal use of his name, "that I tried to give your child to you when you rushed away from the *Vagabond* ten years ago? I remember your exact words. 'I don't want him—you keep him.'"

Edward lowered his head. "Those words have haunted me for years."

"And," Rose continued relentlessly, "*if* you were so interested in your son, why haven't you contacted him during these years? It hasn't been easy to explain to the child why his father didn't want him."

Last night Rose had seemed so feminine and amenable. Today he saw a determined side of her personality. "Am I going to be allowed to see him?" Edward said.

"As far as I'm concerned you may see him, but don't expect any filial affection. You're a stranger to him."

"So you've turned him against me?"

Trying to control her temper, Rose said, "To the contrary. I've taken him regularly to visit his mother's grave so he would have a sense of being her son. For several years I was able to convince him that you were probably unable to come back to see him. As he's grown older, he's made a few decisions on his own. If he wants to see you, I have no objections."

Rose stood again. "Sallie," she called. Judging by the speed with which Sallie entered the parlor, Rose knew she had listened to every word they had said. "Is Martin still in the paddock?"

"He finished ridin' the pony and is headin' this way now."

"Ask him to come here for a little while, please."

In a few minutes, Martin hurried into the room and threw himself at his mother. "I love Tibbetts, Mama. He's the best birthday present I've ever had."

Rose smoothed his straw-colored hair, and taking a handkerchief from her pocket, she wiped dusty spots from his face. His sparkling blue eyes took in their visitor, and he sidled closer to Rose.

Edward rose to his feet, as if on the strings of a marionette. "Martha's eyes," he mumbled.

"I didn't know we had company," Martin said.

Rose gripped his hand tightly. She couldn't think of an easy way to break the news. "Martin, this is your father, Edward Moody."

Edward held out his hand. "Hello, Martin." He wasn't prepared for the expressive anger spreading over Martin's face or for the vitriolic gleam in his blue eyes.

Martin slapped away the hand that was held out to him. "So you haven't been dead or bad sick as Mama and me thought you might be. You just didn't care anything about me. Well, I don't want to see *you* now." He raced out of the parlor, and his steps sounded on the stairs.

Rose clasped her hands to stop their shaking and mentally cautioned herself to be unconcerned about the hurt, lost look on Edward's face. "As far as I'm concerned," she said quietly, "you have your answer, Mr. Moody."

Chapter 4

Edward started after Martin, but Rose blocked the way. He turned on her as angrily as Martin had defied him. In spite of the trauma of the moment, Rose felt like laughing. *Like father, like son.* For the most part, Martin had been an amiable child and had seldom lost his temper. But she was amazed at how his few childish fits of anger were reminiscent of his father's sullen looks.

"You've turned the boy against me," he accused.

The door of Martin's bedroom slammed. Refusing to take offense at Edward's words, Rose ordered quietly, "Sit down, Mr. Moody." When he sulkily obeyed, she posed, "Do you realize how ridiculous it is for you to appear out of the blue and expect the child to cozy up to you? If not, you don't know much about children."

"I know nothing about children."

"I didn't either until Martin came into my life. In spite of your accusation, I have never tried to usurp the place of Martin's natural parents. I've kept the memory of his mother alive in his heart and, as much as possible, have tried to shield him from the fact that you abandoned him. But he's an intelligent, sensitive boy; and as the years passed and you didn't return, he came to his own conclusions."

Edward seemed to deflate before her eyes. "I know that you are right. If you hadn't taken good care of my son, he no doubt would have died. I do appreciate the care you've given the child, and I hope I can make amends for my churlish behavior."

Rose nodded her acceptance of his thanks.

"But that still doesn't change the fact that he's my son—my heir, and I want him now. I've accumulated a good deal of money in the past few years, and I can give the boy more advantages than you can."

With a smile, Rose glanced around the spacious, well-appointed room. "Oh, I don't know. A year ago, I might have agreed with you, but not now. And I've given him ten years of love and devotion. To you, he's just a possession."

"I do love him."

Rose lifted her eyebrows. "After seeing him for less than five minutes, how can you say that? Love comes slowly."

Without comment on her statement, Edward continued. "And I mean to have your adoption set aside. No judge in the land will deny my rights."

"Edward," Rose said. "I don't want to be your enemy. I believe that we both want what is best for Martin. I love him enough that if he wants to go with you,

145

after he's learned to know you, I'll give him up. But you're a stranger to him. Can't you understand that you have to earn the child's love and trust? What are your plans for him, if you should get custody?"

Shamefaced, Edward admitted, "Actually, I haven't made any. I really thought the child had died, but I had to see for myself."

"Now that you know he is alive, you had better approach this matter realistically. Let's say I agreed to turn Martin over to you. What would you do with a ten-year-old boy? Would you take him away from the only family he's ever known? Aren't you concerned for his happiness at all? Don't you want what's best for him?"

Edward stood and threw his arms wide with uncertainty. He then left the room and walked out of the house without any comment.

Although Rose had exhibited a composed front to Edward, as soon as she heard the door close behind him, she slumped in the chair and buried her face in her hands. Sallie came into the room and knelt beside her mistress.

"Did you hear everything, Sallie?"

"Yes, ma'am. Do you think he can take the boy?"

Rose shook her head. "I don't know. It worries me."

"Now the good Lord helped you and your Granny save that boy from dyin' when he was a baby. He ain't about to let that man take him away from you."

Rose took Sallie's work-hardened hand. "Thanks, my friend. I'll never let him go unless I feel sure that it's to Martin's advantage to be with his father. He doesn't seem like a bad man."

"But a selfish one, I figger," Sallie said.

"I'm not sure of that, either. I truly believe he could be a good father, and Martin is at the age when he needs some male guidance. I've often wondered if I can cope with Martin's needs as he gets older."

"Don't borrow trouble. I'll bring you a fresh cup of tea. That'll make you feel better."

Sighing, Rose said, "No, I need to talk to Martin. And I don't know what to say."

"The Lord Jesus will give you the right words."

With leaden feet, Rose climbed the massive walnut stairway. She expected Martin to be facedown on his bed, but he stood beside the window, watching his father walk away from their home. Rose knelt beside him.

"I don't like him," Martin said stubbornly.

Even after ten years, Rose still didn't know how to deal with Martin's moods. She supposed it took a lifetime to know how to bring up a child. She looked at him closely, but Martin apparently hadn't shed a tear.

"Maybe it's too soon to say that. You only saw him for a few minutes."

"Why'd he have to come back now?"

"He said he came to find out what had happened to you."

Edward had disappeared from sight now, and Martin turned to look Rose full in the face. "Do you believe that?"

Rose hesitated, but remembering the stricken look on Edward's face when Martin had rejected him, she answered slowly, "Yes. Yes, I believe it."

"Well, I don't."

"Don't worry about it now. I'll have Sallie bring up some hot water so you can take a bath. You smell like Tibbets."

A grin brightened his face. "I like *him*."

⁓

The next day, after inquiring from the hotel clerk about Louisville's lawyers, Edward went to the office of Duncan McKee on Jefferson Street. A portly man, probably in his fifties, McKee had an office in the rear wing of his antebellum home.

After McKee greeted Edward and ushered him into a square, high-ceilinged room, he asked, "Are you a stranger to Louisville, Mr. Moody?"

"I recently arrived from Colorado."

"And why do you need my services? Are you planning to settle in our city?"

"That depends," Edward said. He hesitated, hardly knowing what to say. Was he making the right move? He wanted his boy, but on the other hand he hated to cause Rose Thurston any trouble. He was obligated to her for caring for his wife's grave and giving Martin a good home. Besides, the woman interested him—the first time he had looked upon any female with interest since the death of his wife. It was a strange feeling, and he didn't know how to account for it.

Briefly he explained to McKee about the death of his wife, his grief at her death, and why he couldn't take the child with him at that time.

The lawyer lifted his hand. "Just a minute. Is Martin Thurston your son?"

"Yes. I came back to Louisville to find him. Rose Thurston told me she has adopted him. Since I'm the child's father, and I didn't give permission for that adoption, I don't believe it is legal. I want you to represent me in overturning that adoption."

McKee's lips twisted into a cynical smile. "For ten years you haven't made any effort to find out what had happened to your son?"

Martin felt his face getting warm. "I've had a difficult ten years, Mr. McKee. I suppose, as you grow older, you get wiser. I eventually prospered, but I realized that my money was *all* I had. Although I feared my boy had died, I had never forgotten him. For years I didn't have the courage to find out. I know I'm not without blame, but it's never too late to correct past mistakes."

"I'll represent you in this situation, Mr. Moody, and I'll give you the best representation possible. However, it's only fair to warn you that you're facing an uphill battle, probably a losing one."

"What can you tell me about Miss Thurston?"

McKee moved papers around on his desk and picked up a pencil, which he turned in his hands as he spoke. "If you think you can take the child because of Miss Thurston's reputation, you don't have any case. The Thurstons are poor people, and Rose lived most of her life on her grandparents' shanty boat. In summertime, the Thurstons are nomads. They are poor. Harry fishes and does other river-related things to keep his family going. But as far as character, you'll not find a blot against Rose Thurston or her grandparents."

"She has never married?"

"No. As far as I know, she has never been interested in any man. She has devoted her life to rearing *your* son, working hard to provide a good education for him. She did that before she had any money."

"I left some gold coins behind that they could have used, but they spent only enough to pay for my wife's burial. They banked the rest of the money for Martin."

McKee laughed and amusement gleamed in his eyes. "I forgot to mention that the Thurstons are proud people."

Edward's conscience hammered that the honorable decision was to leave Louisville and not interfere in his son's life, but he couldn't accept that. He wanted his son, and he knew that he had another reason now for staying in Louisville. But if he tried to force the custody battle against Rose, what would that do to their personal relationship?

Believing that his child's welfare had to come before his own feelings, he said, "Then you will take my case?"

"Give me a few days to study the legalities while you consider if you're sure you want to involve yourself in a lawsuit."

"Will you tell me how Rose Thurston got her money?"

"Yes, since it isn't any secret. It's a rag-to-riches story and a fairy tale all rolled into one. John Boardman came here from New York soon after the War Between the States ended. He traveled through this area when he was a soldier in the Union army, and he liked the Ohio River system. When the war ended, he moved to Kentucky. He invested his money in the river industry and became prosperous. A few years ago he built the large home where Rose lives."

"It's strange architecture."

McKee nodded agreement. "And not to my liking—I prefer the columned houses of the 1840s, but John was something of an innovator. He didn't pattern himself after others."

"Rose said he left the house to her, but I didn't know a large fortune went with it. What's the connection between Boardman and the Thurstons?"

McKee narrowed his eyes, and Edward thought he had offended him. He hadn't meant to imply that the relationship was improper. He opened his mouth to explain, but McKee continued.

"About eight years ago, John had the *Silver Queen* built. That showboat was his pride and joy, and he spent a few enjoyable summers taking it up and down the Ohio and on Kentucky's smaller rivers. In spite of his love for the river, John had never learned to swim. In fact, he was afraid of the water."

McKee paused, and Edward was conscious of the quietness in the room—only the ticking of a mantel clock could be heard.

"Early one morning, Boardman went fishing in a johnboat. He was out in the middle of the river when the boat sprung a leak. He panicked and called for help, but it was a Sunday morning and no one was working around the wharf. He was twenty or thirty feet from shore, but Rose Thurston heard him calling. Rose learned to swim practically before she could walk. She dived into the water and caught John before he went under for the last time.

"In his fear, he tried to fight Rose. She hit him on the jaw and knocked him out. She didn't have any trouble towing him to safety after that."

McKee was a vivid storyteller, and Edward envisioned the scene—a frightened man hindering the girl who was trying to save him. "I suppose Mr. Boardman was grateful and gave her the house."

"Not right away. I told you the Thurstons are proud people. They wouldn't take anything from John. But he never forgot. He made out a will and left everything he had to Rose. He included a note in the will, which she was to read after his death. He pleaded with her to take his estate; 'If not for yourself, think of the boy.' Although Rose was happy with her life as it was and didn't want to leave the river, she sacrificed her way of life to raise Martin in the manner she suspected was his birthright."

"How do you know all of this?"

"I'm the one who wrote John Boardman's will."

"Then I take it you would side with Rose in this adoption matter."

"Take it any way you want to," McKee said shortly. "If I take your case, I'll give you the best representation possible. I'm just warning you to consider your options before you sue for custody of Martin Thurston. You may lose not only your money, but any chance to reconcile with your son."

"What other way is there?"

A crooked grin curved McKee's mouth. "You're a grown man, Mr. Moody. Give it some thought."

Bewildered by the man's manner, Edward replied slowly, "Thank you—I will."

～

Again, Rose set Isaiah to watch Edward's movements. He reported that Edward had gone to Duncan McKee's office and had spent an hour there. Over the next three days, Edward had hired a carriage and toured Louisville and the surrounding countryside. Each day, he had stopped by the cemetery to spend some time at his wife's grave. One day, Edward had walked to the schoolhouse, stood in the shadow of a building across the street, and watched as Martin left school to go home. He had made no effort to speak to the boy. Another day, he had spent several hours at the waterfront, looking over the Boardman boats, especially the *Silver Queen*.

Rose knew that Edward must have learned about her inheritance, and she thanked God for John Boardman's generosity. If she and Martin were still living on the *Vagabond*, Edward would have a major reason to take the child. It was comforting to know that if it came to a court battle, she had the money to hire a lawyer.

Rose couldn't get Edward Moody out of her mind, and it annoyed her that her preoccupation concerned Edward as a man more than as Martin's father. Lying awake at night, she thought of his generous mouth that displayed straight, white teeth, his deep-timbred voice, and his vivid, intelligent eyes. She considered his powerful, muscular body. In spite of his size, Edward moved quickly and gracefully.

Edward's obvious unhappiness troubled her. Most of the time, his expression was serious and somewhat lonely. There was a sense of isolation about the man that made her feel sorry for him. He must have spent ten lonely years without either his wife or son. But when his rare smile flashed across his face, her pulse raced, and she was hard put to remember what trouble this man could cause her.

⁓

During the days of exploring Louisville and its environs, Edward pondered the lawyer's comment that he was a grown man and that there was another way to get his son besides going to court. Mr. McKee had apparently known Rose Thurston for years, so surely he hadn't steered him in the wrong direction. But had he misunderstood the lawyer's meaning?

After a week of indecision, Martin made one more visit to Cave Hill Cemetery. He knelt by his wife's grave. Rather than praying, he talked to his wife as if she were beside him.

"Martha, when I married you, I thought I would always love you. For the past few years, I've been in love with a memory. Now I can hardly remember what you looked like. I had thought that if our son still lived, he would remind me of you. But, except for his eyes, I see only my features on his face. I feel guilty to even think of taking another wife, but I'm doing it for our son. I can't raise the child alone. Please forgive me for the step I'm about to take."

Once he made the decision, Edward didn't delay. He returned the carriage to the barn. He wrote a note to Rose and asked the hotel clerk to have it delivered. After he received a positive answer from Rose, Edward went to his room and dressed with care. He chose a gray broadcloth suit that he had purchased a few months before he left Denver. His vest was of black silk, and a splash of red in his tie relieved the somber colors.

As he walked toward the Thurston home, he noticed a florist's shop, and believing that this occasion warranted flowers, he stepped inside.

"I'd like to buy a bouquet for a special occasion. What do you have available?"

"We have a recent shipment of rosebuds," the florist said. "I can arrange some mixed rosebuds for a reasonable price."

"Cost isn't an issue. I'll take a dozen roses."

Edward was pleased with the man's arrangements—red, white, and yellow rosebuds arranged in a crystal vase. He inhaled the sweet scents of the flowers as he continued toward the Thurston home. He had watched to be sure that Martin had gone to school this morning. He believed he could deal better with Rose if Martin wasn't there.

~

Rose had been in the parlor picking at the keys of the grand piano when Sallie had entered with Edward's note. She took the message from the envelope and scanned it quickly. Puzzled, she glanced at Sallie. She then read the message aloud. " 'Miss Thurston, I request the pleasure of calling on you at two o'clock this afternoon. Your servant, Edward Moody.' " She asked Sallie, "What do you think this means?"

Sallie's eyes widened. "Nothing good, I'll bet. The hotel messenger is waiting for an answer."

"Well, why not," Rose said. "If he wants me to refuse his request again, that's up to him."

She went into the small room adjacent to the back porch that John Boardman had used for his office. Picking up a pen, she dipped it in the inkwell.

I'll be home this afternoon at two o'clock, she wrote on a note card. She put the card in an envelope and sealed the flap with wax. She took it to the man waiting in the foyer and gave him a coin for his services.

She looked at the Chippendale clock on the mantel in the parlor. She had three hours to wait for her guest. She wasn't hungry, but when noon came, she sat at the small kitchen table to eat a bowl of soup. "Sit down and keep me company, Sallie."

Sallie scolded Rose for her lack of propriety in fraternizing with the servants. Rose replied as she always did. "You can take the girl off the shanty boat, but you can't take the shanty boat out of the girl. I'm trying for Martin's sake, but I'll never enjoy this way of life. Give me a fishing pole and a can of worms, and I can be happy all day sitting on the *Vagabond*'s deck. I'm at loose ends in this house when you do all of the work. That's why I'm trying to learn how to play the piano. I need something to occupy my time."

"You sounded pretty good this morning. I recognized 'Yankee Doodle' and 'Dixie.' "

"I learned to play Gramps's banjo before I was twelve, so I ought to be able to master the piano. We'll see."

"What are you going to wear this afternoon?" Sallie asked.

Rose glanced down at her blue-striped dress with its tight-fitting bodice and pleated skirt, short enough to show the toes of her black kid shoes. "What's wrong with this? It was clean when I put it on this morning."

"You always look good, Miss Rose. I just thought you might want to fix up for Mr. Moody," Sallie added slyly.

Rose glanced at her, wondering at the amused look on Sallie's face. She flipped her hair, which she had tied back with a small scarf when she'd gotten up. "If you have time, you can fix my hair. I wasn't expecting to have company today, so I just brushed it and let it hang loose."

After Sallie finished with her hair, Rose still had an hour to wait. If she were honest with herself, Rose knew she wanted Edward Moody to see her at her best, and not just because of Martin, either. She viewed her appearance in the floor-length mirror at the foot of the steps, seeing her lady of the manor pose, not the shanty boat girl. To quiet her nerves, Rose played on the piano until she heard the door knocker. She swung around on the stool as Sallie walked down the hall. Sallie winked at her, her white teeth gleaming. Soon she ushered Edward into the parlor.

"I'll bring some tea after while, Miss Rose."

With a wide smile and a little bow, she left the room. When they weren't alone, Sallie was careful to act the part of a servant.

"I heard the piano," Edward said. "Were you playing?"

Rose's eyes revealed her amusement. "If you listen very long, you'll know I can't play. But I'm trying to learn. It will be helpful if I have to play the calliope on the showboat this summer."

He handed her the vase of roses.

"How nice of you. Thank you." She set the flowers on a table beside the door. "Sit down," she invited and waited for him to speak.

"Rose," he said. "I'll come to the point. This is difficult for me to say, but I hope you will hear me out."

He looked at her expectantly, but she remained silent.

"I've decided that you and I share a common problem. If we work together, instead of considering ourselves enemies, I think we can avoid any difficulties."

Her eyes narrowed, and she spoke stiffly. "So far I've had no reason to consider you as an enemy. Don't give me one."

Edward blundered on, unaware of the gathering storm clouds in the room.

"Martin needs a mother, and I believe you are a good one. He also needs a father. Since I *am* his father, it seems the ideal solution is for us to marry. When I left Colorado, I thought that my son might be living in poverty. I intended to find him and make his life easier, but money doesn't seem to be any issue in his current situation. I've learned that your benefactor, John Boardman, left you well-off, so it would be understood that we wouldn't be marrying for one another's money."

Rose lifted her hand. "Just a minute. Are you suggesting that a marriage between us would be a partnership just to benefit Martin? A legal arrangement?"

Edward cleared his throat, and he squirmed nervously. "Well, I would expect it to be a marriage in the full meaning of the word. I would live here, or I could buy another house."

Rose stared at him with reproachful eyes. She swallowed hard, seething with anger and humiliation. Her curt voice lashed at him.

"Of all the arrogant men, you take the prize, Mr. Moody. You're forgetting one important person in this arrangement. Martin! He made it plain last week that he doesn't want anything to do with you, and he hasn't changed his mind. Until he does, I will not be a party to force him to do so."

Sallie entered with the well-filled tea tray, but Rose stopped her with a wave of her hand. She backed out of the room.

"As for marriage, Mr. Moody, if you think for a minute that I'd enter into a union such as you've described, you don't know much about women. I've prayed for years to find a man who loves me and whom I could love in return. I believe God will answer that prayer in His time. And when He does, I don't want to be tied up in a marriage of convenience."

Rose's voice faltered, and tears threatened to overflow, which only increased her anger. She didn't want to cry before this man who had hurt her so badly.

"I'm not for sale, and neither is my son. We are not interested in your proposition. Leave my house, and don't ever come back."

Chapter 5

A few minutes later, Rose lay facedown on her bed, shoulders heaving, sobbing loudly, when Sallie found her. "Has he gone?" Rose asked.

"Yes, but he sent his apologies. Said he didn't mean to insult you. Whatever that means."

Rose rolled over on her back and sat cross-legged in the middle of the bed and wiped her eyes on the hem of her dress. She patted the bed beside her, and Sallie sat down. "Did you hear what he said to me?"

"Not much of it. I was in the kitchen fixin' the tea."

"He's made up his mind that if we get married, we could both have Martin. He could move in here, and we'd be one cozy, happy family."

"I figgered that was what he had in mind. He might have an eye on your money, too."

"Supposedly, he has plenty of money."

"But you ain't seen none of that coin, have you? Anything I've seen out of Mr. Moody so far ain't impressed me."

"I feel like taking Martin back to the *Vagabond* and asking Gramps to take off for parts unknown."

Sallie favored her mistress with a hearty laugh. "That don't sound much like the Rose Thurston I know—to give up without a fight."

A sheepish grin came over Rose's face. "I have a feeling I will have to fight, for I'm sure I haven't heard the last of Edward Moody." She slipped off the high bed and started unbuttoning her dress. She put on a plain gingham garment like the ones she had worn most of her life.

"I need to talk to Gramps and Granny. Ask Isaiah to go to the school and walk home with Martin if I'm not back in time. I don't want him left unguarded at any time."

Rose tied a shawl around her shoulders, for the spring wind blowing off of the Ohio had a chill. She found Harry on the deck fishing, but he anchored his poles and went inside the shanty boat with Rose. Lottie sat in her chair piecing a quilt top.

"Hi, honey," she said. "What's troubling you?"

"Seems like I'm always coming to you with my troubles. But it's Edward Moody again." She explained in detail the things that had occurred with Edward in the past several days. "Do you think he can take Martin away from me?"

"Nah!" Harry said indignantly. "No court in Kentucky will allow that."

"If Mr. Moody has a lot of money, it could happen. I've known courts to be bought off before," Lottie countered sagely. "But I wouldn't worry, Rose. For one thing, Martin won't go with him, and God is on your side. You may have a lot of heartache before this is over, but right will win out."

"I've tried to tell myself that over and over, Granny, but I get down every once in a while, and I needed to talk to you about it. Do I smell gingerbread cookies?"

"Yeah," Lottie said, smiling. "I baked them this mornin'. I just had a feelin' you or Martin would stop by today."

Lottie lifted herself out of her rocker. She poured a cup of coffee and handed it to Rose. She sipped it gratefully. Gramps always said that Granny's coffee was stronger than a mule. Rose agreed, but today she needed a little extra power. She nibbled on one of the large cookies and drank the coffee and asked for more.

When she was ready to leave, Lottie gave her a plate of the cookies to take to Martin. "Sallie will have a fit for me sendin' vittles up there." She cackled. "But I like to bake cookies for my boy."

"I still wish you and Gramps would come live with me. You could help Sallie with the cooking, and Gramps, you would be a help with Martin. I miss seeing you every day. Besides, he *does* need a man in his life."

"Now, honey," Lottie said. "We've been over this before. We'd be out of place in that fancy house. We've lived on the river too long to leave it now. Besides, we're going to spend the summer with you on the showboat, so that will be like old times."

Rose had known the answer before she asked, and she didn't blame her grandparents. She missed the river, too.

৵

Edward's anger soon dissipated, but he was still hurt by Rose's reaction. Why would marriage to him be such a terrible thing? Up until he had returned to Louisville, Edward had never considered marrying again, but he had plenty of women who had given him the opportunity. He must not be totally repulsive to women.

He and Martha had only been married a year when Martin was born. She had been ill during most of her pregnancy, so they had not been able to spend a lot of time getting to know each other, as most newlyweds do in creating a truly rewarding marriage. But once his craze for making a successful business life had been accomplished, he started realizing that he not only needed love but companionship as well. During the few days he had contemplated proposing to Rose, he had actually started anticipating having a home.

When a few days passed and Rose hadn't contacted him, Edward's anger surfaced. He visited Duncan McKee again and asked him to start proceedings to gain custody of Martin. More than once, he asked himself what he would do with the child if he did get him. He was an only child and had never lived in a house with another child. He supposed he could hire a nanny to raise the boy. But was that fair to Martin?

Edward conceded that he wasn't spiritually competent to raise the child and turned to God for wisdom.

God, I'm at my wit's end. I have no one else to turn to. What is the right thing to do?

Edward had packed a Bible when he started to Colorado, but in the hectic days he had spent in that state, he didn't know what had happened to it. At a retail store near the hotel, he bought a Bible. When he started reading it, Edward felt as if he were being reunited with an old friend.

As he found Bible passages that had been special to him when he was a youth, it was as if he were reading them for the first time. Many of the scriptures comforted Edward.

> *For I am persuaded, that neither death, nor life, nor angels, nor principalities, nor powers, nor things present, nor things to come, nor height, nor depth, nor any other creature, shall be able to separate us from the love of God, which is in Christ Jesus our Lord.*

But other Bible passages condemned him—especially his lifestyle for so many years.

> *Lay not up for yourselves treasures upon earth. . .but lay up for yourselves treasures in heaven. . . . For where your treasure is, there will your heart be also.*

He had failed to heed those words. He hadn't sent any treasures to heaven. All of his treasure had been stored in earthly banks. His father had left Edward financially sound. Why hadn't he been content to stay in Pittsburgh and carry on the foundry business that had prospered his father? Why had the lure of greater riches pulled him toward the West? He knew that Rose's accusation had been just. It was doubtful that Martha would have died if he hadn't been determined to invest in a get-rich-quick scheme.

Knowing it was too late to change the past, Edward prayed for God to give him the strength to make the right decisions now.

When she didn't hear anything from Edward for several days, Rose began to breathe easier. She had finally mastered playing "Old Folks at Home" on the piano, and she and Martin enjoyed singing together. She had a strong soprano voice, and when Martin joined his childish tones to hers, the result was harmonious. They were in the parlor practicing on a new song when the door knocker sounded. Rose's hands hovered momentarily over the keys as a strange sense of foreboding threatened her peace.

"I'll get it, Mama."

Martin ran to the front door, but he soon reappeared in the parlor door. "The man wouldn't give the letter to me. He said you had to sign for it."

With a sigh of resignation, Rose went to the door. The letter delivered by a deputy sheriff was from the office of Duncan McKee. She signed for the letter, thanked the deputy, and closed the door.

"What is it, Mama?" Martin asked.

If he hadn't been present when the message came, she would have tried to conceal it from him; but whatever it was, he should know. With her fingernail, she opened the seal and read aloud. "This is to notify you to be present in the court of Judge Roy Canterbury, Tuesday, April 20, for a hearing concerning the custody of Martin Moody. Plaintiff in the case, Edward Moody; the defendant, Rose Thurston."

She sat heavily on the sofa, and Martin leaned against her knees. "What does it mean, Mama? Is that man trying to take me away from you?"

She put her arm around him and drew him close. "Yes, that's what it means. But trying to do something and actually doing it are two different things. Don't worry about it. I'm glad he's doing this. If the judge decides in our favor, then we won't have any concern about him any longer."

"I'm afraid, Mama."

"Don't be. But let's go tell Granny and Gramps about this. They will need to know as soon as possible."

"Will Gramps go beat up on Mr. Moody?"

Despite the agony in her heart, Rose laughed at the thought of wizened Harry Thurston doing physical battle with Edward Moody, who appeared as solid as the Rocky Mountains. "Of course not. Christians don't fight their battles that way. We're going to pray for God's will to be done."

"I would like to have a father, Mama, like the other boys, but I don't want Mr. Moody."

His comment saddened Rose. What could she have done to give her son a better attitude toward his father? She had tried everything possible to make him remember his parents with love. Could it be that her resentment of Edward Moody had come through to his son? And she knew she had resented Edward.

Did she still resent him? She wished she could be unconcerned about the man now. In the past week Rose had wondered if her anger at Edward's proposal stemmed from her own thoughts of marrying him to provide a family for Martin. But she didn't want it to be a business arrangement.

If she hadn't been so preoccupied with her own emotions, Rose would have noticed that Martin was quieter than usual during their visit with Harry and Lottie. But it came as a total surprise the next morning when Sallie went to Martin's room to get him ready for school and found an empty room. Martin hadn't slept in his bed.

Rose had just arisen when Sallie knocked and entered the room.

"Now I don't want to scare you, Miss Rose, but do you know where Martin is? Did he sleep in here last night?"

"What do you mean?"

"He's not in his room, and the bed is just like it was when I turned it down last night. Usually his bed looks like a tornado has struck when he gets up in the morning."

"I'll look for him as soon as I dress. He seemed extra quiet last night, and I knew he was worrying about this lawsuit. Maybe he slept in the barn so he could be close to Tibbets."

"I'll send Isaiah to find out, and I'll be back in a minute to help you," Sallie said.

When Isaiah didn't find Martin in the barn, Rose rushed to the waterfront, praying that Martin had spent the night with her grandparents. Surely if he had gone to them in the middle of the night, Gramps would have come to tell her. But she had to make sure.

Lottie saw Rose running down the riverbank, and she was on deck to meet her.

"Granny, is Martin here?"

"I ain't seen him since you left last night."

"He isn't at the house, and Sallie says he hasn't slept in his bed. I'm afraid he's run away."

"Maybe his father took him. The *Mary Ann* headed downriver this morning. Captain Parsons blew the whistle just as we got out of bed. Maybe Martin and his father were passengers."

Determined not to think the worst about Edward, she answered, "Martin wouldn't go with his father without a fuss. And I don't think Edward would take him without at least telling me. But I suppose I'd better check with him."

As worried as she was about Martin, Rose's steps lagged as she approached the hotel. What if Edward was gone? When she inquired about Edward, the clerk said, "He just came through the lobby from the dining room. He's up in his room."

"Was he alone?"

Looking at her strangely, the clerk said, "Yes, ma'am."

He looked at her even more strangely when she asked the number of Edward's room.

Rose ran up the stairs, really scared now. She pounded on Edward's door, and her tension was unbearable until she heard him unlatch the door.

"Why, Rose," he said, when she rushed past him and looked around the room.

"Do you have Martin?"

"No. What's wrong?" His voice was harsh with anxiety, and she knew he was telling the truth.

"He's gone! I think he's run away."

She told him quickly what had happened and where she had looked. "I didn't think you would steal him, but in a way, I hoped you had."

"What a thing to say!"

"But I knew you wouldn't harm him. I'm imagining all kinds of things."

Her shoulders slumped, and she started toward the door.

"Wait a minute until I put on my coat," he said, "and I'll go with you. Surely we can find him."

"Do you suppose he's been kidnapped?" Edward asked. "I'm sure there are people who know we each have money."

Rose shook her head. "I think he's run away. A bucket is gone from the kitchen, as well as some bread and cookies that Martin especially likes."

"Has he ever done anything like this before?"

"Never."

"Does he know about the lawsuit? Would he go to such lengths to keep from coming to me?"

"He was at the house when the notice came from Mr. McKee's office, and he was upset. Don't hold it against him, Edward. He's just a child. And he's been hurt. As he grows older, he'll be different."

She looked so helpless leaning against the doorjamb that Edward put his arm around her and hugged her slightly. "We'll find him. Do you have any idea where he might have gone?"

"I've already been to the *Vagabond*, and he isn't there," she murmured into the lapel of his coat. "You might go to the cemetery—he may have gone to his mother's grave, although he has never gone by himself. While you do that, I'll check on our showboat, the *Silver Queen*. He likes to play there sometimes."

"I'll meet you at the *Vagabond* after I've been to the cemetery." He released her. "Don't worry."

But no one had seen Martin around the waterfront, and when Edward came to the shanty an hour later, he hadn't found the child either.

"Should I report his disappearance to the police, Gramps?" Rose asked.

"I'll do that," he said. "You go to school and find out if any of the kids know where he is."

Rose and Edward left the waterfront together and walked uptown. When they parted in front of Rose's house, Edward said, "It's all my fault. I'm sorry I came back, and even more sorry that I've caused you this trouble."

Now it was Rose's turn to comfort him, and she laid her hand on his arm. "Don't feel that way. I've been having my moments of self-incrimination, too—thinking that I've failed him, or he would have talked to me about how he felt. And Martin is at fault, too. I've taught him that Christians must forgive, and even a child can make the wrong decisions. He has always been hesitant to talk about the things that worry him."

With a wry grin, Edward said, "I'm afraid that's a trait he got from his father. It's probably best for me to leave the decisions up to you and your grandfather. I'll be at the hotel. Send for me if you need me."

But in spite of a thorough search of the city, the morning passed and Martin wasn't found. Rose went to the *Vagabond* to be with her grandparents, for she knew they, too, were concerned about Martin. She ate supper with them, and after they washed the dishes, Lottie and Rose joined Harry on the deck where he was fishing. No matter what might be amiss, Harry kept busy.

Rose felt so helpless just sitting, waiting. But what else could she do? Volunteers were combing the town and the countryside looking for Martin. How could a ten-year-old boy have disappeared so completely?

A steamboat whistle sounded repeatedly downriver, and the three Thurstons exchanged puzzled glances. "That sounds like the *Mary Ann*," Harry said. "Cap Parsons just left out of here this morning, headin' for Cairo."

The familiar steamboat came into view, whistle sounding, black smoke pouring from the stack. Lottie shaded her eyes and peered into the gathering dusk. "It's the *Mary Ann*, all right. What's the matter with Captain Parsons? He's got full steam on that boat and keeps blowing the whistle. Reckon he's got a sick man on board?"

With a quickening of her pulse, Rose had a happy thought, suspecting the reason for the captain's quick return. She hurried to the aft deck of the shanty when the *Mary Ann's* speed slackened perceptibly, angling toward the *Vagabond*. Captain Parsons stood in the pilothouse, a small figure beside him.

"That's Martin!" Rose said, and she waved her hand.

The *Mary Ann* drew to within a few yards of the shanty boat. Captain Parsons turned the wheel over to his mate and came out on the top deck, pulling the small boy.

"Hey!" he shouted. "I found a stowaway on my boat. Do you think I ought to throw him overboard?"

Laughing, Rose said, "If you do, be sure he lands on the deck of the shanty. I'm sorry he caused you so much trouble, Captain."

"I'll take some of Lottie's pies for my trouble next time I stop in Louisville."

"You've got yourself a deal, Captain!" Lottie shouted.

"And I'll even pitch in a mess of catfish," Harry added.

The giant paddle wheel slowed and lazily splashed a spray of water as it turned. One of the deckhands lowered a gangplank toward the deck of the *Vagabond*. Harry secured it. Head down, Martin plodded across the makeshift bridge. Lottie grabbed him and hugged him hard. Rose waved to the captain as he returned to the pilothouse, turned the *Mary Ann*, and headed downstream once again.

Peering from the safety of Lottie's arms, Martin asked, "Are you mad at me, Mama?"

"I've been too worried to get mad, son. But now that you're back safely, I probably will get mad. Why did you do such a thing?"

"I didn't want to leave you, Mama—I didn't want to go with Mr. Moody."

"You're too young to make decisions like that. Besides, when you hid on the *Mary Ann*, you were running away from *me*. How do you think that made me feel?" She discovered that her knees were trembling, either from relief or anger. "Let's go home. Isaiah and Sallie will be worried. And I'll have to notify the police that you're safe."

"I'll take care of that," Harry said. "You look after the boy."

"Will you get word to Edward that Martin is all right, Gramps? He's very concerned, and he blames himself."

"Yes, I'll go to the hotel first."

✆

Edward hurried downstairs with a heavy heart when he was summoned by the front desk. Rose's grandfather was here to see him. If it was good news, he believed Rose would have come to tell him herself.

"Martin is all right," Harry hastened to tell him. "He hid away on Captain Parsons' boat, and the captain didn't find him until they were a far piece down the river. He turned around and brought the boy back. Rose took him home, but she wanted me to let you know."

"Thank you. I'm happy he's all right. I told Rose I was sorry, but I owe you and your wife an apology, too."

Harry negated his apology with a wave of his hand. "You were a boy yourself once, Mr. Moody. You know how notional a kid can be. I reckon most of us have run away at one time or another. I've got to tell the police now."

Remembering the time when he had run away from Martin, Edward returned to his room. What should he do? He wanted to see Rose, but he wouldn't go to her house and further antagonize his son. Should he just forget about him and leave Louisville? But where would he go? He had sold his property in Colorado, so he had nothing to go back for. And after ten years away from Pittsburgh, he had no ties there.

He didn't want to leave the area. Even if he couldn't get custody of Martin, he would like to see the child occasionally. But Edward needed to keep busy.

Edward decided to pass time by looking around Louisville for business investments. The river crest had come and gone, and the water was at its normal level. He often walked along the river in late evenings, experiencing a penetrating loneliness he had never known before.

One night he wandered toward the *Vagabond*. Martin sat on the deck with Harry, and they both had fishing lines in the water. Edward leaned against a tree, partly hidden by the foliage so they couldn't see him. It was obvious they enjoyed being together because he could hear them talking. Occasionally, he also heard Martin's childish laughter. So interested was he in the scene below him that he didn't hear Rose's approach.

Rose was walking to the *Vagabond* to pick up Martin after a visit with her grand-parents when she saw Edward watching Martin and Harry. She stopped in her tracks and watched him as intently as he was watching them. The sadness on his face dismayed her.

Perhaps sensing her presence, Edward turned quickly, starting guiltily that she had caught him spying. He turned away from her.

"Good evening, Edward," Rose said quietly, coming closer to him. "I came to walk home with Martin."

"Do you hate me, Rose?"

"No, of course not," she said, thinking that she liked him better now than she ever had. No longer was he the self-confident man she had known. The humility on his face brought tears to the surface of her eyes. She looked away, blinking, not wanting him to see her vulnerability to his presence.

She motioned to a wooden bench her grandfather had built in the shade of a tree. Granny often came here to rest when the heat in the shanty was unbearable.

"Shall we sit down?"

He joined her on the bench. "I wouldn't blame you if you did hate me. I've caused you nothing but trouble. I should never have come back."

His self-deprecating attitude was more than she could handle, and she prayed for wisdom in dealing with him.

"Is Martin all right now?"

"He's not very happy with me," she said. "I've taken away several of his privi-leges. He's not allowed to ride his pony for two weeks. He goes to school and comes right home and then stays in the house. Tonight is the first time I've let him visit Gramps and Granny."

"I've decided to drop the custody suit," Edward interjected suddenly.

She looked at him in surprise. "Why?"

"What if I win? Martin hates me so much that he ran away at the thought of belonging to me. What would I do with the child? In the best interest of my son, I think I should leave. You were getting along fine until I showed up. Ten years ago I forfeited any right to call him my son."

Rose looked across the river, trying to find the right words. She longed for wisdom to know how to deal with the situation. "No. I want the judge to hear your side of the case. I'm not in a position to make an unbiased judgment. I'll make any sacrifice to do what's best for Martin. I will never voluntarily agree to give him up, but Judge Canterbury is not biased. He'll be fair. If he thinks you should have Martin, I'll accept it."

Edward was shocked at Rose's words. He knew he would never take the child away from Rose, no matter what the decision was. The more he was around her, the more he decided that his proposal to Rose was not as absurd as she had considered.

He wasn't sure he was in love with Rose yet, but given an opportunity, he believed he could become very fond of her. But after he had been rejected once, he felt that Rose would have to indicate that she was interested in his proposal before he spoke again. And as long as Martin refused to accept him, Rose wouldn't do anything to upset the boy.

"I'll be honest with you. Mr. McKee told me from the outset that he didn't think I had much of a case."

"We'll see," Rose said. "I'd better go get Martin," she added, rising to her feet. "He has a curfew to keep."

"How much longer will his punishment go on?" Edward asked, knowing that Rose was a good mother.

"Another week."

"I'd like to have dinner with you again, Rose."

She shook her head. "It isn't wise for you to fraternize with the enemy. Thanks for the invitation, though."

Edward watched the graceful movements of her body as she walked to the shanty boat. Sighing wistfully, he turned toward town. He found it difficult to think of Rose Thurston as an enemy.

Chapter 6

S ince it was a private hearing, only six people were in the courtroom when Judge Canterbury entered and took his seat behind the bench. Lottie and Harry had come with Rose and Martin. Edward and Duncan McKee sat at a desk on the opposite side of the aisle.

The judge read the papers on his desk; then he looked over his glasses at Rose. "You don't have an attorney, Miss Thurston?"

"No, Your Honor."

"Does that mean you are not contesting this claim?"

She stood, her knees shaking, a slight tremor in her voice. "Yes, I do contest it, but Martin's life with me is well-known to anyone who's interested in finding out. It's my opinion that I don't need any defense other than my record as a mother to Martin. However, if Your Honor has any questions, I believe I can answer them satisfactorily."

Judge Canterbury nodded.

"Mr. McKee, you represent the plaintiff in this case?"

Mr. McKee stood. "Yes, Your Honor. Edward Moody is the father of the child known as Martin Moody Thurston."

The judge raised his hand. "Just a minute." He turned to Rose. "Do you agree to that?"

"Yes, Your Honor. I saw Mr. Moody the night Martin was born on the *Vagabond*. I recognized him as soon as he returned to Louisville."

"Go ahead, Mr. McKee."

"Your Honor, Mr. Moody is suing to have the adoption of his son by Rose Thurston overturned. Since he didn't give his approval to this adoption, he contends that the action is illegal."

Martin scooted closer to Rose, and she put her arm around him.

"Is your client bringing any charges of neglect against the defendant?"

"No, Your Honor. He simply wants to be acknowledged as the child's father and rightful guardian. We've submitted a folder of Mr. Moody's assets to prove that he is able to provide for his son."

"I've already deliberated several hours about this case. But before I give my judgment, I want to hear from the one most affected by my decision. Martin Moody Thurston, will you stand, please?"

Martin cringed even closer to Rose. She smiled and encouraged him to stand. He looked small and vulnerable; but he stood straight, a determined look on his face.

"Martin," the judge inquired, "are you aware of what these proceedings mean? If I decide in favor of Mr. Moody, he will assume the role of your father. If I decide against Mr. Moody's appeal, you will continue to live with your mother as you've been doing. Do you understand?"

Martin nodded, whispering, "Yes, sir."

"I will make a decision based on what I feel is best for everyone, but I think it's only fair to give you the opportunity to make your wishes known. What is your opinion?"

God, Rose prayed, *don't let him say anything to hurt Edward. I know what my son wants, but I don't want him to embarrass his father.*

In a barely audible voice, Martin said, "Mr. Moody may be a very nice man, but I don't know him. He's a stranger to me. But I love my mama—I want to stay with her."

"Thank you, Martin," the judge said. "You may sit down."

Sniffing, Martin sat close to Rose, and she smoothed his hair and caressed his shoulders.

"All of you may stay seated while I state my decision. Mr. Moody," he said. "I'm a father myself, and I can sympathize with your desire to have your son. I don't doubt that, somewhere in the multitude of adoption cases on the books in this country, there's a law that would substantiate your claim. But here in Kentucky, we're a little behind the big courts in the eastern cities. I don't know any such law, and I'm not going to look for one."

He paused, and Rose sensed a tense and expectant silence throughout the room.

"I was the judge of this court and made the decision for Miss Thurston to adopt this boy. At that time, she indicated that you had been gone for three years, and that she had no knowledge of whether you were dead or alive. She also testified that you had given the child to her. Is that correct?"

Shamefaced, Edward said, "Yes, Your Honor."

The judge nodded. "I've watched your son grow strong, and he's been happy under Miss Thurston's care. Her character is above reproach. She has the financial means to provide for the boy. And I personally feel that it would be a travesty of justice to annul Martin's adoption. So I'm deciding against you, Mr. Moody. It is possible that if you appeal to a higher court, you may receive a different decision."

"Mama, does that mean I can stay with you?" Martin asked with excitement.

Rose put a finger to her lips to silence him, but she nodded slightly. Martin's mouth spread into a wide grin.

Mr. McKee stood. "Your Honor, I will discuss an appeal with my client, but in the meantime, could he be awarded visiting privileges with his son?"

"Mr. McKee, the defendant has legal custody of the child. It's up to Martin and Miss Thurston to decide if your client has any contact with the boy. It will violate the order of this court if your client forces a relationship with the child."

Edward touched Mr. McKee's arm. "I will not appeal this decision," he said quietly.

"Your Honor, Mr. Moody has indicated that he will not continue his suit further."

"Very well," Judge Canterbury said. He pounded his desk with a gavel. "This court is adjourned."

The judge stepped down from the bench and shook hands with Rose and her parents. He patted Martin's head.

"Thank you, Judge Canterbury," Rose said. When the judge left the room, Martin laughed happily and hugged Harry and Lottie. Rose found it difficult to join in their merrymaking when she saw Edward leaving the courtroom alone. She felt sorry for him, for she knew the agony she had experienced in the past few weeks when she thought there was a possibility she would lose her son. If Martin weren't so biased against his father, would she accept Edward's proposal of marriage?

The next morning, Edward sent a message asking Rose to have dinner with him that night at the hotel. Knowing that matters had not been settled between them, Rose didn't hesitate to accept the invitation.

～

Rose found Edward waiting for her in the lobby. "Thanks for coming," he said. "I wouldn't have blamed you if you had refused."

He took her arm and escorted her into the dining room, and he asked for a secluded table. They spoke of trivialities while the waiter brought their beverages. Edward's eyes seemed desolate, and Rose missed the self-confidence always so evident in his speech and manner.

"I wanted to see you once more before I left town. I thought it was wiser not to come to your home."

Rose felt an immediate pang of disappointment, and her voice broke slightly when she replied. "You're leaving? So soon?"

"There isn't any reason for me to stay. It will make things easier for you and Martin if I'm not here."

Rose wasn't prepared for the sense of loss she experienced, knowing that she wouldn't see Edward again. She wasn't sure she was successful in concealing her consternation from him. "Where are you going?"

He shook his head. "I don't have any close relatives in Pittsburgh, except my wife's sister and her family. And I sold out my businesses in Colorado. I haven't decided yet where I will go. Maybe to California."

Choosing her words carefully, Rose said, "Then why don't you stay in Louisville a little longer? I still have much to learn about children, but I know that they change their minds often. Given time, I believe Martin will soften toward you. Did you notice at the trial he didn't say he hated you, but that you were a stranger to him?"

"I don't want to leave," Edward admitted. "But I don't want my presence to be an embarrassment to you."

"And I appreciate that. My conscience hurts because you were denied the right to see Martin. If he ever decides to pursue a relationship with you, I won't oppose it."

"Then you don't mind if I stay?"

She reached her left hand across the table, and Edward clasped it tightly. "I don't mind at all," she said.

Edward leaned forward and kissed her fingertips. "Then I will stay for the time being."

The waiter came with their food, and Edward released her hand reluctantly. "I also had another reason for seeing you tonight. I was in the lobby this morning when a man arrived from New York. He introduced himself to the clerk as Walt Boardman and stated that he had come to settle the estate of his uncle, John Boardman. Isn't that your benefactor?"

"Why, yes," Rose said, surprised. "I was the only beneficiary in John's will. I didn't know he had any close relatives. He lived here for years and didn't mention any family at all. I suppose everyone assumed he didn't have anyone."

"Could this man cause you any trouble?"

"I hardly think so," Rose said slowly. "It's been over a year since John died. The showboat was in dock all last summer because the estate wasn't settled. The will has been probated, and it's on record in the courthouse. But if John did have relatives and didn't mention them in the will, could that cause a problem? I've heard that close relatives can make a claim unless they are given at least a dollar."

"I don't know anything about Kentucky laws, but if Boardman was in sound mind and body when he made his will, it won't be easy to break."

"He had made the will two years prior to his death," Rose said.

"You might want to discuss the matter with an attorney."

Rose nodded. "I'll do that."

"May I walk you home?"

"No, thank you. Isaiah should be waiting with the phaeton."

When Rose arrived home from church the next day, a carriage was in front of the house, and a man sat on the porch. He wore impeccable clothing, and Rose suspected immediately who he was. In fact, he had the same large head and piercing black eyes that had characterized John Boardman's appearance.

He stood when she and Martin approached the house.

"Are you Miss Thurston?"

She nodded.

"Then let me introduce myself. I'm Walter Boardman. I've come to town to settle my uncle's affairs. My father is his closest relative, but he was unable to travel so far. As I understand, you've been looking after the house since my uncle's death.

I've brought my trunk from the hotel—if you'll call one of the servants to haul it inside."

Convinced that the man knew the state of affairs exactly, she immediately mistrusted his amiable attitude.

"I beg your pardon, Mr. Boardman, but I'm not 'taking care of the place.' It belongs to me. John willed his whole estate to me, and the proper legal procedures have been concluded. I have two helpers only, and they already have all the work they can do. We're not equipped to take in overnight guests."

"You're making a big mistake, ma'am. My father bankrolled John when he moved to Kentucky, and he never paid back a red cent. It won't take long for me to prove that the property is mine. I might as well look the place over."

"No," Rose said, wishing Gramps or Isaiah was here.

As if in answer to her wish, Isaiah strolled around the corner of the house. Having just returned from church, he was dressed in his Sunday clothes. He flashed a belligerent glance toward Boardman. "Do you need somethin', Miss Rose?"

Glancing at Isaiah, Boardman said, "Is this your man? He can carry in my trunk."

Shaking her head at Isaiah, Rose said, "He is *not* my man. He works here as he did for John before me. And I told you that I'm not equipped for overnight guests."

Favoring Rose with a withering gaze, he said, "Very well. I'll leave, but I'll be back."

"As a matter of curiosity, why have you waited so long? John died over a year ago."

"We only recently learned of his death." He spat out the words angrily. Rose felt suddenly weak and scared in the face of his anger. She sank weakly into a white wooden chair on the porch as he stalked toward his carriage.

Martin, who had been a silent spectator to the whole episode, said, "Does that mean we can move back to the *Vagabond*, Mama?"

Rose laughed and ruffled his fair head. Her efforts to turn him into a gentleman weren't progressing much better than her attempts to become a lady. But it pleased Rose that he hadn't lost the down-to-earth values that she had taught him.

From the bottom of the steps, Isaiah stared after Boardman. "Who is that, Miss Rose?"

"John Boardman's nephew. He came prepared to move in here and prove that his father was John's heir."

"Can he do it?"

"He can try, I suppose. I know John thought he was doing me a favor by making me an heiress. But I don't know why anybody wants to be rich. If you're poor, nobody is trying to take anything away from you. I've just proved my right to have Martin, and now it looks as if I'll have to get a lawyer to prove John's will is valid. I can't wait to get on the *Silver Queen* and leave Louisville for a few months."

~∘

Even though Rose had appeared unconcerned about Walter Boardman, Edward had dealt with men of his caliber many times, and he made it a point to watch the man.

Monday evening when he went for dinner in the hotel's dining room, Edward tipped the waiter to give him a table close to Boardman, who was having dinner with three other men. Edward hadn't seen them before, but the men were burly, uncouth characters whom he immediately mistrusted. While ostensibly interested only in his food, Edward took in every word from the nearby table. He was furious when he learned that Boardman had hired these men to go with him to Rose's house in the middle of the night and evict her. With an effort, he controlled his temper.

Moving leisurely so Boardman wouldn't suspect that his plans had been overheard, Edward ate most of the food on his plate. But as soon as he returned to the lobby, he rushed upstairs to his room and put a gun in his pocket. To protect Rose and her household, he needed the advice of someone older and wiser than he was. He borrowed a lantern from the hotel clerk and hurried toward the waterfront. He figured the Thurstons would already be in bed, but Harry was still on the deck, setting trotlines for his nightly catch of fish.

"Mr. Thurston," he called from the bank. "It's Edward Moody. There's an emergency, and I must talk to you. May I come aboard?"

"Yeah, son. Watch your step on that plank. It gets slippery when the dew settles at night."

Edward held the lantern so Harry could see his face as he crossed the narrow board. "Rose has told you, I suppose, about John Boardman's nephew being in town."

"Yep. Sounds like he's gonna make trouble for my girl."

Edward nodded his head. "And right away, too. I sat close to Boardman in the restaurant tonight. He's hired some men, and they're intending to break into Rose's house tonight and put her out."

"Are they now?" Harry said, hitching up his pants, his nostrils twitching like a warhorse heading into battle. "That's easier said than done."

"Will you go to Rose's house and tell her while I try to round up some help? We'll give Boardman a warm reception when he gets there."

Harry scratched his head. "Just a minute. I've got a better idee. You don't know people here like I do. I'll rouse Lottie out of bed, and the two of you can go warn Rose. I'll pick up two or three men who know how to fight, and we'll be there right away. Do you know what time they're planning to attack?"

"He didn't say exactly, but I'd judge it will be after the town settles for the night. Probably after midnight."

"That will give us plenty of time to get ready," Harry said as he disappeared inside the shanty, calling, "Lottie, get up—we've got trouble."

Ten minutes later, Lottie and Edward headed uptown toward Rose's home.

"You've done your part now, Mr. Moody," Lottie said, "by warning us. Don't feel you have to make any more trouble for yourself."

"It isn't any trouble, Mrs. Thurston. Besides, the attack may come before Harry gets there with his men. I might be needed."

"We may need your help—that's a fact. Rose's handyman, Isaiah Taylor, will be good if it comes to a fight. The two of you can hold them off until Harry comes."

Edward was relieved that the Thurstons had accepted his help so readily. The thought of Rose and Martin being in danger distressed him, and he wanted to do all he could to keep them safe.

"Rose and Martin sleep upstairs, and they might be hard to rouse," Lottie said. "Isaiah and Sallie live in a one-story house in the back, and they'll have a key to the mansion. We'll wake them, and Sallie can let us in the big house."

Edward was relieved when they reached Third Street and saw that Rose's house was dark. They had arrived in time.

Lottie motioned him around to the back, and she stopped at the door of a small cottage. She knocked twice, then said, "Don't shoot, Isaiah. It's me, Lottie." She chuckled quietly. "Isaiah sleeps with a shotgun under the bed. Didn't want to take no chances."

Edward heard footsteps approaching the door. "Who is it?" Isaiah said in his deep voice.

"It's Lottie, Rose's grandma. Mr. Moody is with me."

Isaiah opened the door. "What's goin' on to bring you out this late of a night?" he asked.

"Let us come in and close the door," Lottie said. Sallie entered the living room, wrapped in a long robe, carrying a lighted lamp. Nodding toward Edward, Lottie said, "Mr. Moody overheard that Boardman feller planning to break in on Rose tonight and kick her out of the house."

Sallie put her hand over her mouth to stifle a scream. She set the lamp on a table and turned the flame low.

"Don't surprise me," Isaiah said, his black eyes gleaming angrily. "Meanest-acting man I've seen in many a day."

"Can you let us inside the house to warn Rose and Martin?" Edward said. "Harry is bringing more men. We're planning a surprise for Mr. Boardman and his friends."

"Count me in on that welcome party," Isaiah said. "Let me get my gun."

"I hope they don't come until Harry gets here so he can tell us what to do," Edward said. "But I doubt we will have to shoot anybody."

"A little buckshot aimed in the right direction might scare them away."

"I've got a gun in my pocket, too, if we need it," Edward admitted. "But I'm hoping they'll run when they find out they aren't dealing with only a woman and a child. But Harry will tell us what to do when he gets here. Right now, Sallie, you and Lottie should warn Rose. I'll go inside the house and be on guard there, Isaiah, if you'll watch from the yard."

Sallie stepped into a pair of shoes and lifted a large key off a hook beside the door.

"Isaiah, blow out that lamp," she said. "We can see to get to the house with the light from Mr. Moody's lantern. It's better if we don't have any lights—make 'em think we're all asleep."

The last few days Edward had fretted about Rose and Martin living alone, but after seeing the loyalty and efficiency of Sallie and Isaiah, his fears lessened. He walked behind Sallie and Lottie, carrying the lantern so that it lighted their path. The scent of spring flowers filled his nostrils, and he wondered why evil should be afoot on such a beautiful night. A night like this was meant for love and praise to God, not violence.

They entered the house through the kitchen, and Lottie plodded quietly toward the central hall. "Sallie, you go tell Martin," she said, "and I'll get Rose up."

༄

Rose always slept with her door open in case Martin called her during the night, and she kept a lamp burning in the upper hallway. She roused quickly when she heard voices murmuring in the central hall downstairs. She recognized Sallie's voice, which didn't startle her, thinking the housekeeper had forgotten some task that needed to be done.

When she identified Lottie's voice, she *was* disturbed. She got out of bed, pulled on her robe, and rushed into the hallway. She picked up the lamp and started downstairs.

Halfway down, she paused, saying, "Granny, what's wrong? Has something happened to Gramps?"

Lottie moved up the steps toward her. "No, honey—nothing like that, but there is some trouble."

Sallie passed them on the steps. "I'm gonna wake Martin."

"What *is* wrong?" Rose demanded.

"Boardman is planning to kick you out of the house tonight and move in himself." Pointing over her shoulder, she said, "Mr. Moody heard him planning the attack and came to warn us."

Rose lifted her head and looked toward the lower hall. She hadn't realized anyone had come with Rose and Sallie. Her eyes connected with Edward's, and she was speechless.

Rose had been thinking about Edward when she had gone to bed, and it seemed that he had stepped out of her dreams. She felt her cheeks warm when she looked at her grandmother and saw the smug expression on Granny's face as she glanced from Rose to Edward.

From the first day he had seen her, Edward had wanted to see Rose's hair hanging around her shoulders. The lamp she held illuminated her face, which was framed with her golden hair. She wore a white, long-sleeved, floor-length robe over her nightgown.

He had once seen a painting of an angel descending from heaven on a gilded stairway. Rose could have posed for that artist. Her disheveled hair hung halfway to her waist. Her face was shadowed, and he couldn't make out the expression in her eyes. If he hadn't felt anything special for Rose before, Edward knew at this moment that he was beginning to care deeply for her. He refused to consider the barriers preventing any mutual happiness for them. Tonight he was only thankful that God had given him this opportunity to protect her—a task he would like to take on for a lifetime.

Chapter 7

The special moment Rose felt between Edward and her was shattered when Martin ran down the hallway. "Mama," he shouted excitedly. "Sallie says there's going to be a fight. Really?"

"I don't know. Mr. Moody brought the word. Let's see what he can tell us."

Martin looked down and saw Edward. "Oh, him!" he said disgustedly and slumped down on the stairs.

Rose saw pain spread across Edward's face, and a sharp reprimand hovered on her tongue. But she stifled it and left the boy to Sallie. She went downstairs and stopped beside Edward and gave him her hand. "Thank you. Will you tell me what you know?"

He explained what he had overheard and that he had gone to Harry for advice. "He's bringing some men to help scare Boardman and his men away. He sent your grandmother and me to warn you. Hopefully, he'll get here before Boardman arrives, but Isaiah is on guard outdoors. I think the two of us can keep them out of the house until Harry gets here."

Sallie now stood on the bottom step. "I ain't too bad in a fight, either, Mr. Moody."

"I'll go upstairs and dress," Rose said. "I'll be right down." She patted the dejected Martin on the head as she passed him, but that was all the time she had for him now. They had to get ready for what was coming.

Edward watched as, working by candlelight, Sallie prepared some coffee. It was ready when Harry arrived with three wiry-looking men, who appeared as if they would be able to take care of themselves in a fight.

"All was quiet on the street when we passed through town," Harry reported.

"I hope I haven't gotten you out on a wild goose chase," Edward said. "But I'm sure Boardman said he would strike tonight."

Rose had changed her robe and nightgown for a plain dress when she came downstairs. She had thrust a couple of combs in her hair to hold it away from her face, but it still fell from the crown of her head like a waterfall.

Martin had sneaked down the stairs, and he sat sullenly on the bottom step.

Ignoring him, Edward asked, "Harry, what plans do you have? Give us some orders."

Harry shook his head. "You're more a man of the world than I am, Mr.

Moody. Since you've been in Colorado for years, you've probably seen your share of fighting. You take charge."

Without argument, Edward said, "Don't do any shooting unless we have to. We can't take the chance of killing someone and get into trouble with the law. However, it will be all right for Isaiah to shoot his shotgun in the air to scare them." He parted the curtains in the parlor and peered toward the silent street.

"There are six of us men. Four of us will go outside to intercept the would-be intruders and hopefully drive them away before they get inside the house. Two of you will stay inside, in case they break through our lines."

"You say not to shoot, mister," one of Harry's friends said. "But this ain't goin' be no picnic. Can we rough 'em up some?"

"We may have to for self-protection. And we have the right to do that. I can't give you a lot of orders when I don't know what to expect. Just use your best judgment."

He walked into the parlor and looked out the front window. "I'll go outside," he said. But glancing toward the women, he added, "Maybe you'd better stay here, Harry. Do you have any better suggestions?"

"No," Harry said, apparently content with Edward's handling of the situation.

"All right. Choose the men to go with me. Put out all of the lights so Boardman will think Rose and Martin are sleeping. Once your eyes are adjusted to the darkness, you can probably feel your way around. I'd suggest that the women and Martin go upstairs."

"No," Rose objected immediately. "This is my property they're trying to take."

Lottie and Sallie also stated their refusal to hide in the bedrooms. Edward glanced at Martin, who looked like he was glued to the first stair. He had his chin cupped in his hands and his elbows on his knees. His stubborn expression reminded Edward of himself, and smiling, his eyes met Rose's.

"I'll watch him," she said softly.

Harry named off the men who would go with Edward. "Let's take time to pray," he said, and he knelt stiffly on the floor.

Surprised at himself, Edward soon found himself on his knees beside Harry.

"Lord God, You protected Daniel in the lions' den. You looked out for Joseph in Egypt. You led Moses across a far stretch of desert. We believe You've got the same power today, and that You can reach out and touch us tonight. This trouble ain't of our own makin'. We're holdin' You to Your promise from the book of Psalms—'Let all those that put their trust in thee rejoice: let them ever shout for joy, because thou defendest them.' We're praisin' You tonight, God, and lookin' to You for deliverance. And all God's people said, amen."

Edward found himself joining the chorus of "amens" shouted around him, and it felt good. Yes, it felt good to be praising God after so many years. He had sensed that Rose had knelt beside him, and he turned toward her and took her hand to help her to her feet.

"Be careful," she whispered.

Edward stationed Isaiah and one of the men in the backyard, in case the attackers came that way. There was no covered porch on Rose's house, just a narrow area with a few chairs. He sat in a chair, hidden by a blooming bush. His companion knelt on the ground a few yards away. The gas-burning streetlight dimly illuminated the front lawn where a piece of marble statuary gleamed in the faint light.

A clock in the belfry of a nearby church struck the midnight hour, and Edward started worrying. Had he been mistaken in what Boardman planned to do? Had he reacted too quickly because of his concern for Rose? He had been heaping all kinds of incrimination on himself until his companion cleared his throat in warning.

A lone man walked up the street. He paused before the house, looked around carefully, walked into the yard, and circled the house. Edward and his companion sat as statues, and apparently Isaiah and his buddy also stayed hidden. After a few minutes the man reappeared. He hurried to the street, whistled, and gave a beckoning summons with his arm.

The *clip-clop* of a horse's hooves sounded in the quietness of the night. Edward hunkered down beside the man hidden in the bush. "What do you make of it?" he asked.

"They're bein' cagey. That man wanted to be sure no one was on guard before the whole gang came. The fellers in the back must have stayed out of sight, too."

"That's the way I figured it," Edward said. "That wasn't Boardman. I want to catch him in the act."

Edward crawled across the porch and knelt behind another shrub. He spread the branches to give him a view of the street. A wagon drew up. Two men sat on the seat, and the wagon was filled with two trunks and several satchels. Another man sat in the wagon bed, so that meant they had at least four men to deal with. Edward recognized Boardman by the black Homburg hat he was wearing.

Anger surged through Edward. How dare this man plan an attack on Rose and her son! He always thought of Martin as *her* child now. He knew it was only fair that he would have to patiently earn the right to call the boy *his* son.

The four men walked in a close-knit group on the paving stones until they almost reached the porch. Boardman gestured with his arms, and two of the men started around opposite sides of the house. After waiting a minute or two, Boardman approached the house. When he put his feet on the first step, Edward rose from his hiding place.

"A little late for a social call, isn't it?" he said.

Boardman gasped and stepped backward.

"Who are you? What are you doing here?" he demanded.

"I might ask you the same thing. But to ease your mind, I'll tell you I'm

Edward Moody. I'm a guest in the hotel where you're staying. I overheard your scheme to put Miss Thurston out of her home, and I decided to deal myself a hand in the game."

Looking wildly around him, Boardman said to his companion, "Rush him!"

When the rogue started toward Edward, Harry's friend, hidden by the bush, jumped up, turned the man around, and slugged him. He crumpled in a heap on the grass.

Apparently enraged over his thwarted plans, Boardman stepped close to Edward and planted a solid fist on his jaw. The move surprised Edward, and he staggered backward. When Boardman tried to take advantage of his successful punch, Edward was ready for him. He hit Boardman on the chin with a powerful whack that lifted him off his feet. Edward followed up his advantage with another blow to the stomach that immobilized Boardman, who spread-eagled at the foot of the steps.

In the silence that followed, Edward heard the blast of Isaiah's shotgun. He quickly tied the hands of Boardman's accomplice and motioned for his companion to watch Boardman. Within two minutes the other two attackers walked around the house with their hands lifted over their heads. Isaiah plodded behind them, holding his shotgun menacingly. His companion carried a lighted lantern.

"Harry!" Edward shouted. "Come on out. We've got things under control."

Harry still held his rifle when he stepped out on the porch, and he, too, brought a lantern. Rose came behind him, with Martin clutching her robe.

"What are we going to do with them?" Edward asked.

"Send for the police to haul 'em off to jail," Harry said. "They'll probably try to lie their way out of it and say we attacked them, but they didn't have no business on this property."

"You take care of that, and the rest of us will guard them until the police get here."

"Isaiah, how about hitchin' up the phaeton to drive me to the central station? I hope Lieutenant Bell is on duty."

"Yes, sir, Mr. Harry. Back in a minute."

The other man, who had been guarding inside the house, stepped out on the narrow porch. He took Isaiah's shotgun and held it ready.

When Edward turned his head, Rose touched his cheek. "You're hurt," she said anxiously.

"Not much," Edward said, rubbing his burning jaw. He was embarrassed that he was the only one of the men who had a wound of any kind. "I didn't dodge in time, and Boardman hit me."

"Come inside. Sallie has some liniment that will help."

"Maybe after the police come. I'm all right now."

"Thank you," she said softly, so softly, he wasn't sure anyone else heard. She reached for his hand and squeezed it gently.

Edward's gaze held Rose's for a long moment, sending a private message; but conscious of Martin trembling beside her, Rose turned away.

"Come inside, Martin. Mr. Moody and Gramps's friends will keep watch. We'll be safe now."

They found Lottie and Sallie in the kitchen. Lottie was stirring the coals in the stove and adding fuel for a quick blaze.

"We're fixin' some coffee for the men, Miss Rose."

"I'm sure they will like that," Rose agreed, her voice shaking. "I could use a cup myself."

Lottie was spreading thick slices of bread with butter and jam. She looked at Martin's frightened face and said, "Come help me, Martin."

"Wash your hands first," Rose said.

Now that Martin was occupied, Rose returned to the porch. Boardman had regained consciousness, but he was still lying on the ground. When he saw her, he snarled, "You're going to be in big trouble having these rowdies beat me up."

He started swearing at her, and Edward hopped off the porch and planted one of his feet on Boardman's stomach.

"Stop it," he said, applying pressure to Boardman's midsection. "You got what you deserved—sneaking here in the middle of the night expecting to find a woman and a child alone."

"This house is mine," Boardman said.

"If you can prove you have a legal right to Boardman's estate, I'm sure Miss Thurston will move out. But you know that you have no claim to it. And I'll personally see that you don't steal it from her."

"She won't get away with this," Boardman said unrepentantly. "She's in trouble."

"I told you I'm the one who's responsible for upsetting your plans, Boardman. If you want to blame anyone, I'm the one."

"I don't know why you'd champion her. Way I hear it, she stole your boy just like she stole Uncle John's. . ."

Again Edward applied some pressure to Boardman's abdomen, cutting off his words.

"Then you heard wrong. I gave my boy to her ten years ago."

Rose realized that Martin and Lottie had joined them on the porch with a tray of sandwiches. No doubt Martin had heard everything. Would this admission make him hate his father even more?

A paddy wagon soon arrived, with Isaiah and Harry following in the phaeton. Lieutenant Bell and his deputy handcuffed the four men. While his deputy took them to the wagon, the lieutenant, whom Rose had known all of her life, said, "I'll hold them overnight, Rose, but I don't know how much of a case I can build against them. Because you were forewarned, and they didn't have the opportunity to do any damage, I don't know exactly what I can charge them with—probably no more than trespassing."

"Do what you can," she answered.

After the police left, Rose asked everyone to come inside for some coffee.

"If you can make a bed for Lottie and me," Harry said, "we'll spend the rest of the night here."

"Of course, you can stay. You can sleep in that small bedroom across from the kitchen where John slept most of the time."

"I'll fix the bed, Miss Rose," Sallie said.

"I'll do that while you and Granny serve some food to our helpers." When the others turned toward the dining room, Rose said, "Do you want to help me, Martin? Let's go upstairs and get some sheets and pillowcases. And you can bring a quilt from the linen closet."

Edward watched Rose and Martin climb the stairs, but before he went to the dining room, he drew Harry aside.

"Boardman doesn't strike me as the kind of man to give up easily. Don't tell Rose about this, but if you can find a couple of men who'll guard the house at night, I'll pay them."

Looking keenly at him, Harry nodded. "I had the same notion. I think Lottie and me will have to move in for a spell. At least till Boardman leaves town or until Rose takes the showboat out in a few weeks. Course if Boardman is still around, there will have to be a guard posted during that time, too. But you won't have to pay for it—Rose has lots of money."

"I want to help," Edward insisted. "For the time being I intend to stay in Louisville. You take any steps you think are necessary to protect Rose and her property, and I'll help foot the bill."

Harry favored Edward with a sly grin, as if he would like to comment on Edward's attitude, but he only said, "I'll keep in touch with you. You gonna be at the hotel?"

"I'm not sure. I've been talking to Mr. Duncan about buying some property in Louisville. I'll let you know if I move."

Edward had no intention of leaving Louisville as long as there was an opportunity to pursue a closer relationship with Rose. Their future depended on Martin, and he wanted to be reconciled to his son, too. He had to win the boy's confidence before he could approach Rose, and that would take time. But Edward was a worker, and he had to have something to do while he bided his time to repair the breach with his son.

Since Edward knew Rose wanted him to stay in Louisville, he started looking for a place to live. He had soon grown weary of the hotel's restaurant, and he ate most of his meals at the Kentucky Diner, a large eating place near the waterfront.

WHERE THE RIVER FLOWS

He had noticed a FOR SALE sign in the window of the diner on his first visit. When he asked questions, he learned that the owner had died and that his daughter, who lived in another state, wanted to sell the restaurant, lock, stock, and barrel, which included a furnished apartment on the second floor.

Edward looked over the restaurant's books and decided that the business was a good investment. He had owned a restaurant in Colorado, but he hadn't been directly responsible for operating it. A man had owed him money he couldn't pay, and when the man skipped out without paying his debt, Edward took over the business.

He approached Duncan McKee to help with the purchase, which was completed quickly, because Edward had already transferred some of his assets to the First National Bank of Louisville. Since he had no knowledge about operating a restaurant, he chose to put a great deal of the responsibility in the hands of the employees who had worked for the former owner.

The three-room apartment was adequate for his personal lodging for the time being. Edward asked Lottie to suggest a housekeeper for him, and he hired Mrs. McClary, a staid Irish woman, who came in three days a week to see to his needs.

Boardman and his three hired men had stayed in jail overnight, paid their fine, and been released. He had not left town as Edward had hoped, and he was convinced that Boardman wouldn't easily give up his scheme to take Rose's property.

∽

One night when she couldn't sleep, Rose peered out her bedroom window to look at the stars. Her heart skipped a beat when she noticed a man standing in the shadows along the street. Frightened, she woke Harry, who explained that the man was part of the protection Edward had insisted on providing. He also told her that at Edward's expense, he had hired a man to stay on the *Vagabond* at night to keep it from being destroyed while he and Lottie lived in Rose's house. Two of the men who had helped forestall Boardman's takeover of Rose's home alternated guarding her home during the night hours.

This information pleased Rose, who was a bit annoyed at Edward, whom she hadn't seen since the night he had come to her rescue. The court order had stipulated that Edward wasn't to seek Martin's company without Rose's permission, and apparently Edward didn't intend to force his company upon them. She had learned that he had bought the restaurant and settled in town. She decided to talk to Martin about seeing his father.

On Saturday afternoon, Rose had Isaiah saddle her mare and Martin's pony, and they rode out to the cemetery. After they had pulled the weeds from his mother's burial plot, they walked to the point where they could see Louisville's harbor.

"Martin," Rose began. "I know you don't like Mr. Moody, and I can understand why you feel hard toward him. However, I *do* like him. He's been very fair about your adoption, and certainly he was a big help when Walt Boardman tried to drive us from our home. As a thank-you gesture, I want to invite him to dinner some evening. I'm not forcing you to talk to Mr. Moody. And you won't have to eat with us—you can eat with Isaiah and Sallie. However, I won't invite him if you object."

"Will Gramps and Granny eat with you?"

"Gramps likes Mr. Moody and provides fish for his restaurant. Granny appreciates what he did for us. I'm certain they'll be glad to entertain him."

"And you won't invite him if I say no?"

"That's right. I'm leaving the decision up to you," Rose said. She crossed the fingers of her mind, thinking, *At least for the time being.* Edward was constantly in her thoughts, and she knew she couldn't deny her heart much longer. Hopefully, she could have her heart's desire with Martin's blessing, but she had to move slowly.

"Well, I guess it's all right. But I want to eat in the kitchen with Sallie and Isaiah."

Thank God from whom all blessings flow, Rose thought, joy flooding her heart. But she retained a nonchalant attitude with Martin.

"Then I'll send an invitation to him."

They were almost back to the horses when Martin said, "He sure took care of those mean men, didn't he?"

"Yes."

"Will he feel bad if I don't eat with you?"

"Why, I don't think so. He understands why you don't like him."

"Oh," Martin said, and he remained thoughtful and silent during the rest of their ride.

~

With trembling fingers and many false starts, Rose composed the invitation without giving much information. She didn't know how much Edward would read between the lines.

> Dear Edward:
> Will you come for supper tomorrow evening at six o'clock? Granny, Gramps, and I will look forward to your company. Although Martin approved the invitation, he's chosen to eat in the kitchen. Don't be hurt by that. I really believe his attitude is softening.

She signed the message and asked Isaiah to deliver it to Edward's restaurant.

~

Edward had been interviewing a prospective manager for the restaurant when the message came. He stopped to send an immediate acceptance of her invitation. As soon as he concluded the interview, he went to his apartment. He sank to his knees beside his favorite chair.

"God, I'm not worthy to even call on Your name, but I thank You for giving me an opportunity to make amends for my mistakes of the past. Some men are not so fortunate. My child could have died, and I would never have seen him. If he never accepts me, I can't blame him. But I do want a relationship with him, if it's in Your will. As for Rose, when I'm with her I have a feeling of contentment I have never known. God, give me wisdom and patience. Amen."

When he rose from his knees, Edward reached for the Bible, which he had laid on the table when he moved into the apartment. He turned the pages, looking for a message to strengthen his faith.

He had always been interested in the plight of the Hebrews after they turned away from God and He had allowed them to be captives in Babylon for seventy years. Edward felt as if he had been in bondage for ten years, since the time he had turned his back on God, blaming Him, as well as the Thurstons, for Martha's death and for the loss of his son. He searched for the promise that God had made to the Hebrews to restore them to their homeland.

> *Then shall ye call upon me, and ye shall go and pray unto me, and I will hearken unto you. And ye shall seek me, and find me, when ye shall search for me with all your heart.*

Edward felt blessed. He had turned his back on the bondage of sin, and he was on the homeward journey. His observation of the deep faith of the Thurstons had encouraged him to leave his past behind him.

Chapter 8

Harry and Lottie still found it difficult to eat in the luxury of Boardman's dining room, but they were slowly adjusting. However, Harry refused to dress up when Edward came to dinner. "I can't do it, child," he said to Rose, when she offered to buy him some dress clothes. "I don't want you to be ashamed of me, but that just ain't my style of livin'."

She kissed his whiskery cheek. "I could never be ashamed of you," she said. "I only wanted to give you the opportunity to have some new clothes. Whatever you wear at my table is acceptable."

"And promise me that when my time comes to die, you won't put no suit on me."

Laughing, Rose said, "I promise, Gramps."

Lottie, however, seemed to anticipate wearing the new dress that Rose had bought for the occasion. She refused to wear a bustle and would put on only one petticoat, but she liked the iridescent silk dress, which was striped rose pink, green, and brown. White lace bordered the long sleeves. She entered the parlor tentatively, waiting for Harry's opinion.

"Well, I say, wife!" Harry said in wonder. "Those new duds sure suit you. I ain't seen you look so good since the day I married you."

Lottie actually blushed, and Rose was still laughing at her grandmother's discomfiture when Edward knocked. Sallie hustled from the kitchen to open the door.

Martin had stood in the entrance hall and applauded Lottie's regal appearance. But when the door knocker sounded, announcing Edward's arrival, he scuttled toward the kitchen. Perhaps noticing the look of dismay on Rose's face, Lottie whispered, "I bet he sits behind the door and listens to every word we say."

Since Edward and Harry had become friendly during their joint effort to protect Rose, conversation flowed easily around the table as they enjoyed Sallie's roast beef, served with new potatoes boiled in their jackets and a variety of vegetables canned the previous summer. Sweet potato pie topped with fresh cream finished their meal.

As they lingered over cups of coffee, Rose led Edward to talk about his mining experiences in Colorado, but Edward was equally interested in Kentucky history, which Harry could supply. While they talked, Rose felt a nudge on her foot. She looked up, and Lottie nodded toward the kitchen. Rose glanced surreptitiously over her shoulder, and she saw Martin's knees in the doorway. He was obviously unaware that he wasn't totally hidden behind the wall.

"That's a small step forward," she whispered to her grandmother under cover of Harry's laughter over one of Edward's stories.

When the meal was over, the four of them went outside. The day had been hot, and they moved chairs to the grassy lawn, where they experienced night falling around them. A slight fog drifted in from the Ohio, barely discernible in the dim light. A steamboat whistle sounded in the distance. While Harry answered Edward's questions about Louisville's history, Rose noticed that Martin sat inside an open window, listening to their conversation.

Edward was clearly enjoying himself, but after an hour he stood and told them he hated to leave, but it was time to go.

"Watch your back," Harry cautioned Edward as he prepared to leave. "Boardman may be having you shadowed—trying to get you alone."

Her grandfather's comment alarmed Rose. She rose and walked down the sidewalk with Edward. "Be careful, and please visit again soon."

"I will. I made several enemies in Colorado through the years, so I've learned to defend myself."

"In a fair fight, maybe, but we know Boardman doesn't play fair. I wish he would leave town. Why is he still hanging around? We leave in two weeks on the showboat's summer tour. I won't rest easy if Boardman is still here."

Edward took her hand. "Thanks for the invitation."

"Consider it an open invitation. The judge gave us a loophole that you could visit upon my say-so. We're going to be busy preparing the *Silver Queen* for sailing for the next several days, so I won't be planning another dinner, but stop in when you want to. Martin was listening most of the evening in the background. He will eventually come around."

"Then you're willing to share him with me?"

"Yes," she answered simply.

"I'd hoped so. That's one of the reasons I've put down roots in Louisville, and I'm trying to be patient."

Noting the sweet tenderness of his gaze, Rose didn't have to ask what his other reason was, and her heart turned over in response. He lifted the hand he held and kissed her long fingers, one by one. "Good night," he said softly and walked away.

૮૭

The closing day of school was always marked by a program at which awards were given and students demonstrated some of the things they had learned during the year.

"I've thought of inviting Mr. Moody to the closing exercises," Rose said when Martin brought the announcement from his teacher. "He would probably enjoy it."

Martin was silent for several minutes, and Rose didn't press him for an answer.

"I reckon that would be all right," he said firmly. "As long as I don't have to talk to him."

"That won't be necessary. But he might like it if you just said hello."

"Oh."

"Mr. Moody doesn't know many people here except our family, and I'm sure he must get lonesome. It would be neighborly to invite him."

Martin slanted a skeptical glance in her direction, and Rose wondered how much Martin really understood about her efforts to include Edward in their lives. She gave a silent prayer for wisdom. As each day passed, she realized how little she knew about rearing a child, especially a boy. God knew what He was doing when He provided *two* parents.

As she knew he would, Edward welcomed the opportunity to attend the program. When they were being seated in the school's auditorium, Rose arranged for Lottie to sit beside her, and for Edward to sit on Harry's right. She didn't want any speculation among Louisville citizens about what was going on in her life. She had been the brunt of gossip before, for some people had speculated that Martin was her illegitimate child. Perhaps Edward had helped put that particular gossip to rest when he returned and tried to claim the boy.

Rose had bought tailor-made clothes for Martin to wear to the program, and she was gratified to note that he looked as fashionable as the other boys. He wore a dark blue broadcloth waistcoat and jacket, and a white shirt. His black tweed knickerbockers were gathered just below his knees. He wore long black socks and buttoned boots with cloth tops.

Almost two hundred children attended the school, grades one through eight. The program opened with the entire student body singing a few patriotic songs. Each grade was responsible for a short oral presentation, and Martin's teacher had chosen to use a segment from Longfellow's narrative poem, "The Song of Hiawatha," focusing on the young native's childhood. All nineteen boys in Martin's class had been assigned a portion of the poem to memorize.

Rose was so proud as Martin stepped forward from the group and spoke his part.

"Then the little Hiawatha
Learned of every bird its language,
Learned their names and all their secrets—
How they built their nests in summer,
Where they hid themselves in winter—
Talked with them whene'er he met them,
Called them 'Hiawatha's Chickens.'

"Of all beasts he learned the language,
Learned their names and all their secrets—

"How the beavers built their lodges,
Where the squirrels hid their acorns,
How the reindeer ran so swiftly,
Why the rabbit was so timid,
Talked with them whene'er he met them,
Called them 'Hiawatha's Brothers.'"

As soon as the program ended, Edward approached Rose with a huge grin on his face. "Thank you for inviting me to come tonight. I will treasure the memory of this evening. I owe you so much for giving him a secure childhood."

Rose smiled. "Thank you again. Why don't you tell Martin you enjoyed it?"

"I would like to, but I don't want to cause him discomfort on this night. Thanks for allowing me to share a small part of Martin's life." He clasped Rose's hand briefly, then left.

Rose watched him go, and when she looked to the stage where the teachers were congratulating the children, she noticed that Martin was watching his father's departure. Was there disappointment on his face? Had he expected Edward to speak to him?

Although Martin still liked to be caressed in private, he was afraid his friends would call him a sissy if he was hugged and kissed in public, so Rose simply put her hand on his shoulders as she congratulated him and the other students.

Rose knew Harry and Lottie were uncomfortable in crowds, and they, too, left after telling Martin how proud they were of him. Once more, Rose assumed the sole responsibility of Martin's upbringing as she mingled with the other parents and children at the reception.

～

John Boardman always started the showboat tour on the first of May, but Rose delayed the departure for a month until Martin was out of school. The two years she and Martin had sailed on the *Silver Queen*, they had caught the boat after its downriver trip. After mooring overnight at Louisville, the boat had traveled the northern Ohio.

Although Rose was eager to take the *Silver Queen* out for the summer, she had some reservations. First of all, she wasn't going on a pleasure trip, as it had been when she had traveled with her grandparents on the *Vagabond*. And the two summers she had worked on the showboat, she had had no responsibility except to obey orders. As the owner and manager of the *Silver Queen*, all of the responsibility was now hers. She doubted that she was equal to the occasion.

She also did not want to be away from Edward for three months. Since Boardman was still hanging around Louisville, she hesitated to leave. He might be waiting for the chance to take over when she was gone. She supposed Edward would continue to keep his eye on her home, but she couldn't expect someone else to accept all of the responsibility.

All day she had been moping around the house, thinking about the carefree days she had enjoyed when she was a girl. After supper, leaving Martin in the care of her grandparents, she walked to the *Vagabond*. Even this brought sadness to her when she reached the vacant boat. It didn't seem the same when her grandparents weren't there to greet her. And she knew that they missed living on the shanty, too. They were sacrificing their pleasure for her, just as she had changed her lifestyle for Martin's benefit.

She sat on the deck of the shanty, took off her shoes and stockings, and splashed her feet in the cool water of the Ohio. She had thought being on the *Vagabond* would make her feel better, but it didn't. She was close to tears when she sensed that someone was watching her. She turned quickly. She wouldn't put it past Boardman to do her bodily harm, and she had been careful not to let him catch her alone. Although she had taken the precaution of lifting the gangplank when she boarded the boat, she was momentarily startled.

Her heart skipped a beat, and happiness overwhelmed her when she saw Edward watching her from the bank.

She smiled, and he asked, "Are you feeling lonely?"

"Morbid is a better word." She stood up and lowered the gangplank to the bank. "Come on over if you like. But I warn you, I'm feeling grouchy."

She motioned him to Harry's rocking chair; and she sat on the deck, her knees flexed, leaning against a bench, her bare feet hidden by her long skirt. "I thought a visit to the *Vagabond* might bring back the days of my childhood when my grandparents and I spent the spring and summer traveling along the river."

"Tell me what those summers were like."

"Our life wasn't much different than it was when we were moored in Louisville, except we were in new settings. We accepted tows from friendly steamboat captains to move around. We stopped at various towns along the river and stayed for a week or two."

"What did you do for money?"

"We didn't need much money. Grandpa caught fish by putting out trotlines at night. He would take the fish to the stores in town, or sell them from house to house. Sometimes he got fresh vegetables or store items, like sugar, matches, and flour, by barter. The steamboats depended on Gramps to provide fish for them. Granny carried herbs with her, and lots of people bought those. At night we hung lighted lanterns on each end of the shanty so the big boats would know where we were. We might stay in a town for two or three weeks when there was a protracted meeting going on at a nearby church. I know it must seem like wasted time to you, but we were happy." Laughing in remembrance, she said, "People called us 'water gypsies.'"

"Did Martin like the river?"

Smiling, Rose said, "He loved it. He learned to swim before he was two years old. But I knew that life was changing, even on the river, and that Martin couldn't live as I had. I worked to pay for his education. I'm thankful to God that I've had the chance to offer him more opportunities than I had. But I'm still happy he spent his childhood on the river. That way, no matter what profession he decides to follow, he will have had the best of both worlds."

"Is this the first summer you haven't traveled along the river on the *Vagabond*?"

"We went last year, because John had died, and there was no one to take out the showboat. The two summers before that, Martin and I sailed on the *Silver Queen*. I worked for John in the summer and made enough money to keep Martin in school for another year."

"Aren't you taking the *Silver Queen* out soon?"

"Yes, next week, but it won't be the same. I know John thought he was doing me a favor by willing his estate to me, but it's more responsibility than I think I can handle. To jump overnight from a shanty boat to a mansion on Third Street was quite a change in my social status. If it weren't for Sallie, who has worked in the homes of several rich women, I'd be making more blunders than I do now. And I'm terribly worried about managing the *Silver Queen*. We've been cleaning the theater and the staterooms on the showboat getting ready for the actors and actresses who'll show up over the next few days." She laughed. "See, I told you I was feeling morbid."

~

Edward ached to say that he would help Rose with her responsibilities if she would let him, but he couldn't push himself into her business. They had progressed a long way in their relationship over the past month, but he didn't want to add to Rose's frustrations.

"You aren't being morbid—you're just discussing your problems with me. I hope by now you consider me a friend, and that you feel free to talk with me about anything that bothers you."

Without looking at him, she said, "Yes, I do count you as my friend. I don't have many, so I value the ones I have."

"Then as a friend, let me advise you to take one day at a time. That's what I learned to do when I was trying to succeed in Colorado. It seems to me that you've already succeeded at being a 'lady' and a mother. And you will do the same as proprietor of the showboat. If there's anything I can do, please ask me."

"There is something you might do for me. I still employ the same investment firm where John had his money, but I wouldn't know if they're cheating me or not. I've gathered that you have experience in that type of business. Would you mind looking over my records sometime and giving me your opinion? I don't want anyone in Louisville to know the extent of my inheritance, but I would like to know if I have my money in the right place."

Edward breathed a silent prayer of thanks that she trusted him to such an extent. "I'm not without experience along that line, and I'll look at your files when you want me to."

"If you'll walk home with me, I'll give you a copy of my investments. The original documents are in the vault at the bank, but I have copies."

Rose reached for her stockings, put them on, and rolled them around her ankles. Then she put on her shoes and tied them securely. Out of the corner of his eyes, Edward saw her suddenly stop and blush a bright crimson. He surmised she had realized her societal faux pas at dressing in front of him. He quickly fixed his eyes across the river, hoping she was unaware he'd witnessed her actions.

Rose rushed on. "I must go home. Gramps might start worrying. I didn't tell anyone where I was going—in fact, I didn't know where I'd end up when I started out."

Edward extended his hand, and she grasped it and accepted his help as she stood. He held her hand a moment longer than necessary, but she didn't seem to mind. Rose showed him where to store the gangplank in the small outbuilding. They walked along the waterfront, and she waved to the guard on the *Silver Queen*.

"Have you ever been on a showboat?" she asked.

"No. I know very little about boats."

"We'll be working on the boat all day tomorrow. If you want to come by, I'll give you a tour."

"I'll do that. I've finally chosen a manager for the restaurant, so I'm free most of the time. I didn't know anything about restaurants either, but there aren't any gold mines in Kentucky, so I thought I'd try my hand as a business owner."

"Did you choose the man who has worked there for several years as your manager?"

"Yes, and I trust him to do what is right."

He walked with her to the house. "I'll see you tomorrow." As she went inside, he realized he was already looking for tomorrow to come so he could see Rose again.

❧

The next day, Rose practiced playing "Camptown Races" on the calliope on the top deck of the tugboat, *Rosewood*. She had stopped playing and was crossing a catwalk to the showboat when she saw Edward approaching from a distance. She looked with pride at her "queen." A fresh coat of white paint made the boat appear new, and the large letters of BOARDMAN'S SILVER QUEEN were emblazoned across both sides of the majestic three-deck boat.

Unlike most people, Rose knew showboats like the *Silver Queen* were actually floating barges and did not travel on their own power. A tugboat moved a showboat along the rivers.

All of the Thurstons had been involved in preparing for the boat's departure. At breakfast, Rose had told Martin and her grandparents that she had invited Edward to tour the boat. None of them had made any comment, but Lottie had favored her with a significant glance. Rose realized that her grandparents were well aware of her interest in Edward. Rose asked Gramps to meet Edward and bring him to the ship's theater.

Rose was onstage when Gramps found her, bringing Edward with him through the French doors. Martin followed them at a distance.

Gramps said, "If you'll show Edward around, I'll go back to swabbin' the deck."

Rose hurried to Edward's side, amused at the shock of discovery on his face as he surveyed the floor-to-ceiling wall hangings featuring scenes of Kentucky's history. His eyes drifted next to the backdrop—a huge painting of the *Silver Queen*, midstream on the Ohio River.

"I'm amazed," he said. "I didn't realize you would have such an elegant theater. This rivals theaters I've seen in New York City."

"Remember, Mr. Boardman came from New York, so he knew how a theater should look. Let's go onstage and start our tour," she said.

The boat rocked under his feet, and Rose saw that Edward found it difficult to keep his balance for a few minutes. She was able to walk as sure-footed as a mountain goat on a high peak.

Edward laughed at his own awkwardness. "The river is definitely in your blood."

Rose and Edward then exchanged significant glances when Martin followed them.

"John had the *Silver Queen* built eight years ago," Rose explained as they climbed the steps to the stage. She sat on a stool and motioned him to an upholstered chair that would be one of the props for the dramas. Martin hunkered down on the steps not far from them.

"You can get an overall view of the theater from here," she said. "We provide seating for two hundred fifty people—two hundred on the main floor and fifty in the balcony."

"Will you have such a large audience in the smaller towns?"

"The theater is full the majority of the time, and sometimes people pay for standing room only."

"Apparently this is a profitable business," he said.

Rose smiled slightly, knowing that it was Edward's nature to judge every venture in dollars and cents. "I'm not sure—maybe you can tell me that after you've finished looking over my business accounts. John made his money in the steamboat business, but he sold all except two of them before he died. The showboat was a toy for him in his old age. He really didn't care whether he made any profit on the *Silver Queen*, just so he didn't *lose* money. So I don't expect to make much profit, for it's expensive to operate a showboat. We provide room and board for the actors besides paying them a salary. We have a pilot and four deckhands for the tugboat, which burns a lot of fuel. We take on coal several times as we travel."

"Aren't any showboats self-propelled?"

She shook her head. "I don't think so."

"What's your route?"

"Since we won't be showing as long as John did, we'll go north along the Ohio until we come to the Kentucky River. We'll follow it as far as it's navigable and stop at most every town along the way. Depending on how much time is left before Martin starts back to school, we may go south of Louisville for a performance or two. I plan to tie up the boat soon after the first of September."

Although most of the theater's seating was general admission, there were a few box seats close to the stage. The stage was four feet wide by fourteen feet long. Several small dressing rooms were backstage. The staterooms and Rose's private apartment were on the second deck. The kitchen and dining area were located behind the staterooms. The pilot and deckhands lived on the *Rosewood*.

Rose explained that the *Rosewood*'s original name was *Tiger Lily*, which she hadn't liked. "I'll never change the showboat's name, but I decided I would put my stamp of ownership on this outfit by changing the tugboat's name."

At the end of the hour-long tour, Rose felt that Edward had a good notion of the showboat's interior, as well as the work involved to put on a show. They climbed the inside stairway to the top deck and entered the pilothouse. Martin had trailed them silently, always in hearing distance, but not close enough that Rose felt inclined to include him in the conversation. When they entered the pilothouse, he joined them and put his hands on the huge wheel, which was locked in place now. He wasn't tall enough to see out the window, but Rose knew the pilothouse had always fascinated him.

Putting her hand on his shoulder, Rose said, "You'll have to grow another foot or two before you can be our pilot."

He climbed up on a bench and looked upriver. "Do you think I can be a boat pilot like Cap Parsons, Mama?"

"I'm sure you can be anything you want to be," she answered. "There's plenty of time for you to decide." Turning to Edward, she said, "The *Silver Queen* can be steered from this pilothouse or from the tugboat. John had his pilot's license, and he steered from the *Silver Queen*. He sometimes let Martin stand on a box and hold the wheel when we were out in the open river."

"That must have been a treat for you, Martin," Edward said. Martin didn't answer. Hearing a sigh and noting the unspoken pain in Edward's eyes, Rose regarded him with sympathy. Perhaps it was right that he should suffer for his actions ten years ago, but she prayed Martin would soon let go of his hurt.

"Cap Parsons has leased his boat to another company for the summer, and he's going to be our pilot. He wants to steer from the *Rosewood*, which suits me. This can be a retreat for the showboat residents when we have a break from our duties. The days do get tedious when we're confined to such a small area."

"This looks like a good place to relax after the day's work is finished."

"Yes, but I learned during the two summers I worked on the boat that there

190

wasn't much time for resting. Everybody had to work. When we weren't rehearsing or presenting the shows, we were studying our lines, helping in the kitchen, or cleaning the boat. I'm hoping to provide more leisure time for the performers this summer."

As they walked down the two flights of narrow stairs to the lower deck, Rose said, "I dread tomorrow when I meet with the cast. I've followed John's example. He didn't hire single women—thinking it led to problems. He took man-and-wife teams and single men. I've hired two couples and two single men, and they arrive tomorrow. That doesn't sound like many, but with rapid costume changes, the performers can play more than one role in each play. I hope they will accept me as their boss."

"You don't know any of them?"

"No. Sometimes John had performers return year to year, but he thought it led to more interest if he changed some of the cast."

"Remember, I'll help any way I can. I'm going to miss you and your family while you're gone this summer. Thanks for the tour."

Rose watched Edward as he walked away from the showboat. She had been anticipating the opportunity to leave Louisville and spend a few months on the river. But her pleasure had dimmed considerably. She didn't look forward to the empty weeks when she couldn't see Edward.

Chapter 9

Rose worked two more hours after Edward left. She and Martin stocked the ticket office shelves with snacks and gifts to be sold when they started on tour.

Lottie and Harry had already gone when Rose and Martin finished for the day. As they walked toward home, Martin seemed unusually quiet. When they passed the Kentucky Diner, he said slowly, "Mr. Moody seemed to like the *Silver Queen*, didn't he?"

"Yes, I thought so."

"Maybe you ought to invite him to go along and help this summer."

Rose's hands clenched, and in her heart she shouted, *Thank You, God, for Your many blessings!*

Nonchalantly she said, "I imagine he's too busy to spend much time away from the restaurant, especially since he just bought it. But I will mention it to him. I could use his help."

As soon as the evening meal was over, Martin and Isaiah went to the stable. Lottie helped Sallie wash and dry the dishes, and Harry and Rose went to the porch. Harry rocked serenely in a large, cushioned chair.

Rose was amused that her grandfather seemed to be adjusting to town living quite rapidly. He went each morning to check the trotlines for fish, and he still delivered his catch to his best customers, but she believed he found a more leisurely life pleasant. This made her happy. After all her grandparents had done for her and Martin, she hoped that she could use Boardman's legacy to make their waning years easier.

Rose sat on the floor near her grandfather so she could look up into his face. "When Edward came for a tour of the *Silver Queen* today, Martin followed us everyplace we went. When we were walking home, he suggested that I invite Edward to sail with us on the showboat."

Gramps wagged his head wisely. "I figgered the boy would come around. Are you going to ask him?"

"I don't know. I wanted to talk to you about it first."

"You like Edward, don't you?"

"More than I should," Rose admitted.

"I don't agree with that. Edward has changed a lot in the past month. He's a good man."

"I hesitate to ask him to go with us. I don't want him to feel obligated. Do you think he would be interested?"

"Does a dog bark?" Gramps said, followed by his cackling laughter.

Slightly annoyed because Gramps was treating a situation so lightly that mattered a great deal to her, Rose scowled at him. "What is that supposed to mean?"

"It means that it's high time you open your eyes, girl. Do you think Edward has been hanging around here just because of Martin? He likes the boy, but you ought to see how he watches *you* when you ain't lookin'. I don't know if he even knows it himself, but it 'pears to me that the man is in love with you."

"Gramps!" Rose said, although her grandfather's words caressed a spot in her heart that had been lonely for a long time.

Cackling again, Harry rocked back and forth in his chair.

"And that would please you?" Rose asked.

"Yes, child, it would please me. My time on earth can't be much longer, and when me and Lottie are gone, I'd be glad to know that you have a man to share your life. Edward ain't without faults, but he *is* a good man. He's shown that in a dozen ways since he's been here."

"I know that. I appreciate his attitude about Martin and the many things he has done for me."

"But don't you take no man out of gratitude! That ain't the way to have a good marriage. Lottie and me have had a good life—lovin' each other through thick and thin. And there's been more thin than thick; I can tell you that. But them things don't matter when there's love in the home. I don't want you to settle for nothin' less."

Wiping her eyes, Rose said, "Now you've made me cry."

"Cryin' is good for a body onct in a while," Harry said. "Washes out some of our doubts. But about askin' Edward to sail with you on the showboat, I'd say do it. Matter of fact, I've been worryin' some about all of us leavin' for the summer, with that Boardman feller still hangin' around here. If Edward will go with you, I think Lottie and me had better stay in Louisville and keep our eye on your property and ours. I won't fret about you if Edward is on board—he strikes me as the kind of feller who would stay calm in a cyclone."

"Very well," Rose said, standing. "I'll go talk to him now. You can explain to Granny."

Looking at the western sky, Harry said, "It's gonna be dark before long, and you'd better not be out by yourself."

"If Edward doesn't walk home with me, I'll hire a carriage. I'll go upstairs and get my bag so I'll have some money."

"Well, keep your eyes open."

❧

Rose had eaten in the Kentucky Diner many times, but she hadn't been inside since Edward had bought it. The manager recognized her and offered to show her to a seat.

"No, I'm looking for Mr. Moody. Is he here?"

"He's been upstairs in his apartment for about an hour." Pointing to the rear of the restaurant, he said, "You can use the inside stairway if you like."

"Would you mind asking him to come down and talk to me?" Although she had no qualms about seeing Edward alone in his apartment, Rose tried to avoid anything that would reflect adversely on her reputation.

"Not at all," the manager agreed.

He signaled for one of the waitresses to take his place behind the reception desk and turned toward the steps. He soon returned, followed by Edward, who looked somewhat alarmed.

"Is something wrong?" he asked immediately.

"No, but I have some business to discuss with you."

He motioned toward the dining room. "Would you like to have something to eat?"

She shook her head, refusing his offer. "I've already eaten. Could we walk instead?"

He opened the door for her. He must have sensed that she wanted privacy, because he said, "There's a courtyard behind the restaurant. Shall we go there?"

"That will be fine."

When they were seated, shoulders touching, on a bench in a small white gazebo in the courtyard, Edward said, "What has happened?"

"I hesitate to mention this, and please don't agree if you aren't interested. Martin suggested that we invite you to go with us on the showboat tour."

A happy, eager look flashed in his brown eyes. "I accept," he said.

With a happy heart, Rose smiled. "Just like that? No details about how long we'll be gone? No questions?"

He took her right hand and squeezed it gently. "Just one question—do *you* want me to go?"

She looked away from him—fearing what he might read in her eyes. "Yes, I do," she said quietly.

"That's all that matters. I've been feeling very sorry for myself that I wouldn't have any of the Thurstons around this summer. Louisville would have been empty without you."

"I discussed this with Gramps, and he says if you go with us on the boat, he will stay in Louisville to keep an eye on the *Vagabond* and my home. I suppose he thought if you were in Louisville, you would watch over things."

"Which I intended to do, and I agree that either Harry or I should stay in town while the other one goes on tour."

"He's still worried about Boardman."

"And so am I. He's hanging around town for no good reason."

"What about your restaurant?" she asked, motioning toward the building.

"I have full confidence in my staff, but I can return to check on them occasionally, or have Harry do it."

"It's always possible to come home for a brief visit on another boat. And there's train service from Frankfort to Louisville."

Rose realized that Edward was still holding her hand, and she started to remove it from his grasp, but he tightened his hold.

"Do you know what this means?" Edward asked softly.

"That Martin is starting to accept you?"

He tenderly squeezed her hand. "That and other things, but we'll have the whole summer to discuss them."

Because her heart was flopping in her chest like a headless chicken, Rose freed her hand, saying pertly, "There won't be as much time as you anticipate. Don't think you're going on a pleasure cruise—everybody works on a showboat."

They stood, and he said, "It's getting dark. I'll walk home with you, and you can tell me what I'll have to do to earn my keep."

As they strolled through the gathering dusk, Rose said, "While I walked here to see you, I tried to think what your duties could be. I knew well enough that you wouldn't be content to spend the summer without some responsibilities."

He laughed. "You know me too well," he admitted. "But what can I do?"

"I'm too inexperienced to manage everything like John did, so I intend to delegate some of the responsibility. Since you're in the restaurant business, would you be in charge of feeding the showboat's workers? That would mean buying food when we dock, and although it's customary for all the women on board to take their turn preparing food, I believe it would be an advantage if you would hire a cook and two other men or women to work in the kitchen, who would also be available as stand-in performers. Your duties would include supervising these workers, too."

"I had more people applying for work in the restaurant than I needed. I'll contact them and find three workers for you."

When Edward and Rose reached the house, she asked, "Do you want to talk to Gramps about anything? He may still be on the porch."

But the porch was empty.

"I won't come in now," Edward said. Without asking permission, Edward leaned forward and kissed her forehead. She smiled at him and went inside. He walked slowly toward his apartment with a light heart.

Although it appeared that a closer relationship with Rose was a possibility now, he wondered what might have happened if he had stayed in Louisville when his wife died. From what Rose had said, it must have been several months before they knew if Martin would live. If he had waited until the boy was well enough to travel, would he have taken him and gone to Colorado? Or would he have fallen in love with Rose then and been content to remain in Kentucky? Remembering his love for Martha at that time, he doubted he would have had room in his heart for any other woman. But had he missed ten years of Martin's life, as well as almost that many years of being happily married to Rose?

Edward knew it was pointless to wonder what might have been, but he realized now how dreary his life had been without the love of a woman. Since this summer might bring him the things he wanted most in life, he could be patient a little longer.

⁓

When Rose was ready to leave the house the next morning, she realized she must have looked frightened when Granny took her into the parlor and motioned for Rose to sit on a chair. Rose suppressed a grin, remembering the few times during her childhood when Granny had found it necessary to reprimand her.

Favoring Rose with a stern look, Lottie put her hands on her waist. "Rose, I want you to march down to that boat and let those actors know right away that you're the boss. In the Bible, Paul the apostle did some plain speakin' when he was advising Timothy, his young son in the Lord. He said, 'For God hath not given us the spirit of fear; but of power, and of love, and of a sound mind.' As Paul said to Timothy, I'm telling you today—*don't be afraid*."

"I don't know that it's fear, Granny. It just isn't my nature to be giving orders."

"Then you will have to let God change your nature. I don't mean for you to bully the people on board the *Silver Queen*, but don't let them put anything over on you, either. God, through John Boardman, has given you this opportunity, and you've got the strength to handle it."

"Thanks for the prodding," Rose said as she stood up, and in a whining, childish voice, added, "Kin I go now, Granny?"

Lottie swatted Rose on the slight bustle she was wearing. "Don't get sassy with me, missy," she said. "You're still not too big for me to bend you over my checkered apron and paddle you."

Laughing, Rose said, "I don't believe you know how to do that. You've threatened me before and didn't carry through on your threats. It's too late now."

Lottie followed her out on the porch. "Mind what I say, now."

"Look after Martin," Rose said. "He's eager to leave on the showboat, but he's worrying about being away from Tibbets all summer. He's persuaded Isaiah to take him riding this afternoon. See you tonight."

When Rose reached the *Silver Queen*, she saw that Edward hadn't wasted any time. He was already at the wharf supervising the unloading of several cartons of food items that would last until they arrived at another large city. He had bought all of the staple items, such as flour, sugar, lard, and canned goods. Fresh vegetables, fruits, meat, and milk would have to be purchased at towns along the way.

"I'll give you a check to pay for everything," Rose called, waving to him as she went on board and walked to the small room near the ticket window that John Boardman had used for his office. None of the performers had arrived yet, and that gave her time to rally her defenses.

She had hired these people sight unseen, and she hoped that their résumés had been correct. Since she hadn't considered anyone who had traveled on the *Silver Queen* when she worked as a kitchen helper, she probably wouldn't have much trouble. She would have less resentment from people who had never known her before her social and financial rise in the world.

The morning went better than she had expected, and Rose attributed the success to her conviction that Sallie and Granny had spent much time on their knees praying for her. As she discussed their duties with the entertainers, Rose often heard Edward's voice as he instructed the workers about unloading the foodstuffs and where he wanted them stored. He obviously wasn't any novice at giving orders. She was heartened by knowing he would be available to help her. All she had to do was call him, and he would be with her immediately.

His nearness furnished the strength she needed to tell the newcomers what she expected of them. She showed them to their staterooms, and since Edward was bringing the cook and her helpers on board today, she told the performers that their supper would be served on the boat. She gave them copies of the two plays they would be presenting during the summer, asking them to study the scripts and be ready for rehearsals on the first full day of traveling.

Since showboat audiences loved plays that included a villain trying to woo the heroine, she had chosen *Becky Goes to the City*. The drama featured a country girl who leaves her betrothed behind on the farm to go to the city to make enough money to help them get started in life. She takes a job in the villain's factory, and at first she succumbs to his smooth talk and almost forgets her beloved. When the villain kidnaps her and takes her to a lonely cabin, where he intends to keep her until she agrees to marry him, the hero comes to the rescue.

The second play, *'Til We Meet Again*, was a Civil War play. Although Kentucky had not left the Union during the war, there were many Southern sympathizers in the area. The heroine's boyfriend goes to fight with the Confederacy. While the Union army is in Kentucky, a Union soldier courts her. Three years pass, and the heroine hears nothing from her beloved. She's almost on the point of marrying the Union soldier and moving north when the hero returns. She immediately knows that her heart lies with the Confederate soldier.

When she finished for the day, Edward waited for her on the lower foredeck. "I rented a wagon to haul the groceries to the boat. Do you want to ride home with me?"

"I probably need the walk, but I am tired, so thanks for the offer."

"You've done a lot of walking up and down stairs today. That's all the exercise you need."

"Yes, sir," she said, her eyes twinkling.

A slight blush spread across Edward's face. "Sorry, I didn't mean to be giving you orders."

"Oh, I don't mind. I need somebody to tell me what to do. Granny sat me down and told me how to behave before I left home this morning."

"Harry stopped by today and gave me orders, too. If anything happens to you this summer, I get the idea that they will hold me personally responsible."

"He shouldn't have done that," she said, frowning. "I've already given you enough responsibility. What did you tell him?"

"I asked him if he thought I had to be ordered to look out for you."

Slanting a glance toward him, she said, "I'm afraid to ask what he answered."

"He didn't even answer me. He laughed knowingly and went on his way."

Rose allowed Edward to hold her arm and help her into the wagon. He then untied the horse, took his seat, and flicked the reins. The mare turned her head and looked at him. He touched her back with the tip of a whip. She didn't move.

"Giddup," he shouted, and the mare plodded away from the wharf.

"Apparently the stable man is trying my patience by always renting this animal to me. Surely there are better horses available for hire."

Because the day had gone well, Rose was in a roguish mood, and she asked mischievously, "She won't take orders from you either?"

"No," Edward said. He touched the horse's flank with the switch again, but it didn't change the animal's gait. "When we get back from this tour, I'm going to buy a horse. I did a lot of riding in Colorado."

As the horse plodded slowly away from the river, Rose sighed deeply. "Maybe the mare is as tired as I am," she said. "But as far as I can tell, we're ready to set out two days from now."

"At what time?"

"Around noon. That will give us time for any last-minute preparations or to take care of things we've forgotten."

"How did the interviews go?"

"All right, I guess, but I won't know how good the performers are until we've put on a show or two. They all came with good recommendations, so I pray everything will turn out for the best."

"How many performers do you need?"

"I hired six adults. Stephen and Naomi Buckley and their twelve-year-old daughter, Becky, who will do children's parts. The other couple is Ranson and Hannah McCall. They not only act, but sing as well, and he can play the calliope. They've had experience on showboats in the New Orleans area. There are two single men, Anthony Persinger and Luke Melrose. For some reason I don't feel satisfied with Luke. He doesn't seem as open about his past as the others, but I'll not judge him until he gives me some reason to."

"I won't interfere with your work, but remember I'll be available to help you."

"Thanks. I'll count on that. I've put the performers in the three staterooms on the right side of the boat. Your quarters will be on the same side as the stateroom

Mr. Boardman always used. Martin and I will stay there. The cook and kitchen helpers' rooms will be between ours."

When they arrived at Rose's home, Edward helped her out of the wagon. She was sad when he refused her offer to have supper with them. Martin stood at the front door waiting for her, so she told herself she was glad Edward had not kissed her again, but in her heart she knew that was not the truth.

Since Louisville was the *Silver Queen*'s home port, a large crowd gathered on the riverfront to watch the boat's departure. Red, white, and blue pennants waved from the top railing of the showboat. Captain Parsons had steam up on the *Rosewood*, and black smoke poured from its smokestack. Ranson McCall was playing the calliope as loud as he could. Edward recognized "Oh, Susanna," which was a popular song in Colorado. Ranson soon swung into "Old Folks at Home," and "Beautiful Dreamer," two other Stephen Foster songs.

Lottie and Harry had come aboard with Rose and Martin, helping to carry their satchels. Now they had gone ashore and stood watching the activity. To Rose, they looked rather lonely and forlorn, and she knew they would have liked to go on the journey. Martin was running around the walkways, too excited to stay in one place very long.

When Captain Parsons blew the whistle for departure, Edward came to Rose's side.

"All of Louisville's residents must be here to watch us leave," he said.

"Not all of them, but it's nice to have such a send-off. And the performers are excited, too. I hope we're this happy when we return at the end of the season."

"Why wouldn't we be?"

She shrugged her shoulders. "Lots of things can happen during a trip like this. Thirteen of us will be confined on this boat, besides Captain Parsons and the deckhands on the *Rosewood*. We might get on each other's nerves. Two years ago, one actor quit right in the middle of the season and walked out—leaving Mr. Boardman in the lurch."

"Don't worry," he said, placing his hand lightly on her shoulder.

"I'm not much. I'm sure you noticed that there's one onlooker I'd rather not have seen." She motioned toward Walt Boardman, who leaned against a wharf building, close enough for Rose to detect the sneer on his face. "I'm worried that he's remained in Louisville. I'm not concerned for my property as much as I am about what he might do to Granny and Gramps."

"When Boardman didn't leave town, I hired a man to shadow him. So far, he hasn't done anything. And Harry and I have arranged for several men to keep an eye on my restaurant, your home, and the shanty boat. Besides, Harry knows how to look after himself. He won't be caught napping. And if Boardman follows the boat, I'll be around."

"You'll never know how much comfort that gives me," she said softly, touching his arm lovingly. He pulled her close for a moment.

The showboat moved slowly away from the dock as the *Rosewood* gave it a gentle nudge. A shout erupted from the shore.

"We're on our way," Rose said. Martin loped toward them and snuggled close to Rose. She put her arm around his shoulder.

"It's so much fun, Mama. A summer out on the river. This is almost as good as being on the *Vagabond*."

Rose exchanged glances with Edward. The shanty compared poorly to the *Silver Queen*, but the riches she had inherited hadn't changed Martin. His early years had molded his character.

Too excited to stand still, Martin raced away from them.

"After all," Edward said quietly, "he was born on the *Vagabond*."

"And since he may inherit two steamboats, as well as a showboat someday, perhaps it is good that he loves the river."

As they headed downstairs, he said, "I've been looking over your investment portfolio, and I'm impressed not only with John Boardman's business acumen, but also with your brokers. I noticed that when Boardman sold several of his steamboats, he invested in railroad stock."

"And you believe that is wise?"

"Absolutely. Just as I think it was wise for him to keep a couple of steamboats. There will always be boats traveling these rivers, but railroads will be vastly important in the development of this country, especially the West. I've invested in railroad stock, too."

"Thanks for checking this for me."

"When we have more time, I'll sit down with you and explain facts and figures. I'll help anytime you want me to, but you should understand what you have. Also, when we return to Louisville, I'll go with you to the investment company if you like."

"Thanks. That's one less worry on my mind. During the summer, I hope running the showboat is all the responsibility I have."

Chapter 10

As soon as the boat was out of sight of Louisville, Anthony Persinger, whom Rose had chosen as their director, called the cast together, and they started rehearsing. Their first scheduled stop was at Madison, Indiana, and they had to be ready to perform. He had chosen *Becky Goes to the City* as the play they would present first.

Since in emergencies every person on the boat might be needed for backup performances, Rose invited Edward to go with her and Martin into the theater for the first rehearsal.

"After a week or two, when the cast members know all of their parts, we won't have to do much practicing," Rose explained to Edward. "But at first everyone is tense. Anthony has had some experience in directing. He's single and has never worked with any of the other performers, so he won't be likely to play favorites with the roles he assigns. But we need backup performers for each role, which involves all of us who have other duties. You can listen and decide which role you want to play," she said with a smirk on her face.

Edward stared at her. "Me? Stand up in front of two hundred people and act?"

"Everyone pitches in to help in an emergency," she insisted. It was pleasant to see that some things could discomfit Edward. "Even the cook and the waitresses pull extra duties occasionally."

She could tell that he knew she was enjoying his discomfiture when Edward said sternly, "If I remember right, acting wasn't mentioned in my job description."

Anthony Persinger came by their seats, and Rose asked, "Anthony, do you have any standby parts where Edward could fill in?"

Anthony looked Edward up and down. "Why, I'm sure we can use someone like you. You will be an excellent standby for the hero in both dramas."

He rifled through the papers he held and handed Edward a couple of scripts. "Study these in your spare time, and I'll have you read some of the portions to me privately to see how you fit in."

Still amused at the consternation exhibited on Edward's face, Rose teased, "If he doesn't work out for the hero, he might make a good villain."

Edward groaned. "This is going to be a long summer."

⌒

Advance notices had been sent ahead, and the Madison townspeople were expecting the showboat. Several miles downstream, Ranson started playing the calliope, and when the showboat rounded the curve in the river and the town came into view, the hills echoed with the sounds of "My Old Kentucky Home."

The *Rosewood* edged the showboat toward land, and the deckhands jumped across the water to secure both the tugboat and the *Silver Queen*. At least a hundred cheering, excited people waited on the bank.

Standing beside Rose on the top deck, Edward said, "I'm surprised there are so many people in this town."

"There will be more here tonight when we put on the show—they'll come in from the country when they hear the calliope. The sound travels for several miles. Are you going uptown with us this afternoon for the parade announcing the performance?"

"If you want me to."

"Are you always this docile?"

"No. Enjoy it while it lasts. But after all, you are the owner of this boat."

"I keep forgetting that."

His eyes conveyed a message that Rose couldn't interpret. "So do I," he replied. "I'm going onshore now to buy a supply of fresh meat and ice. We'll need it before we cast off in the morning. What time is the parade?"

"Midafternoon."

"I'll be back by then."

~

Captain Parsons had volunteered to go with Edward and introduce him to the local merchants. They passed a long line of people waiting to board the *Silver Queen*.

"Why are they waiting now?" Edward asked the captain.

"Some of them will buy tickets for tonight's show. Others are just curious to see if any changes have been made since last year. The coming of the showboat is the most exciting thing that happens to some of these people all year."

Glancing over his shoulder, Edward noticed that Rose stood near the gangplank, greeting people as they boarded the boat.

"I hope all of this responsibility isn't too much for Rose."

With a short laugh, Cap Parsons said, "Don't worry none about that gal. You've not seen her grow up like I have. She'll still be goin' strong when the rest of us have had enough."

"Her grandparents gave me orders to look out for her."

"They told me the same thing. Nothin's gonna happen to her."

When Edward and Parsons returned, the sightseers were all gone, and the performers were ready to go into town to advertise their show.

Edward and Luke Melrose walked in front of the others, carrying a large banner advertising the event. Rose played her banjo. Ranson McCall played a trumpet. Stephen Buckley pounded on a drum. Becky Buckley and Martin gave pieces of wrapped candy to the children. The other performers shook hands with the spectators who lined the streets, and the actors handed out show bills. They gave twenty free tickets to children.

The show was scheduled to start at seven thirty, and the ticket office opened an hour earlier. The gangplank had been lifted to keep the guests off the boat until they were ready.

By curtain time, all of the seats were filled, and for half-price tickets, some stood on the deck and peered in through the windows. Rose stood on the main deck, with Martin beside her, welcoming her guests until the theater was almost filled. Then she went backstage to chaos.

Acting the part of a big-time producer, Anthony Persinger was tearing his hair, haranguing the cast, and wandering up and down the walkway between the stage and dressing rooms, his eyes wild and his voice strained.

"We'll never pull this off," he said. "We're not ready for opening night. No talent at all in this group. Why did I ever agree to be the director?"

Even though the Buckleys had not worked with Anthony before, with a grimace Naomi said in an aside to Rose, "This is usual opening night behavior for a director—think nothing of it. The show will be wonderful, and then he'll strut around the showboat as if he pulled off the whole thing single-handedly."

Rose shared the woman's laughter, for during her two years of working with John Boardman, she had learned that actors were generally a volatile group. But opening night was always tense until the performers got the audience's reaction to their presentation.

Only a few minutes were left before opening time when Rose peered through a small opening in the curtain, and a flicker of apprehension spread through her. Walt Boardman and another man were walking down the aisle into the box-seat area, close to the stage. Was he following the *Silver Queen*? Would he try to harm the performers?

Rose hurried backstage. "Do any of you know where Edward is?" she asked the assembled group.

"I saw him in the back of the theater a few minutes ago," Hannah McCall said.

"Delay opening the curtain for a few minutes until I get back," she said to Anthony.

"Oh, no," he cried, threading his fingers through his thick mop of black hair. "We can't be late on opening night."

"Most of these people have no idea what time it is. I'll be back soon and welcome everybody." Anthony's agonized pleas to start the show immediately followed Rose as she hurried offstage.

Martin and Becky were perched on the stairs that led from backstage to the theater floor. They wanted to see all the backstage action.

"Have you seen Mr. Moody?" Rose asked.

Martin pointed to the rear of the theater where Edward stood like a sentinel guarding the room. As she hurried toward him, she marveled that Martin always seemed to know where Edward was. He saw her coming and hurried toward her.

"Boardman is in the theater," she said.

She knew her face was clouded with uneasiness, and he smiled reassuringly. He put his arm around her shoulders, gave her a gentle squeeze, and held her close for a moment. She melted into his embrace, gaining courage from his strength.

"I saw him. I'll keep my eye on him. Go on with the show." He motioned to the opposite side of the theater where one of the deckhands stood. "He's on guard, too. Don't worry."

"Why do you think he's here?"

"Probably to intimidate you. Don't let him do it."

Thankful for the quiet assurance Edward gave her, her confidence was restored. Rose lifted her hand and caressed his cheek. Smiling her thanks, she hurried back to the stage. She signaled to Stephen and Ranson in the orchestra pit. Stephen played a Viennese waltz on the violin, and when he finished, Ranson presented a drumroll to indicate the program was beginning. The two musicians hurried backstage.

Rose breathed a prayer for help as she parted the curtains and stepped out. The audience grew silent, except for a trill of excitement among the spectators eager for the show to get under way.

Although she had done some bit parts during her two years on the showboat, Rose had never in her life given a speech. The silence of the audience frightened her. She was determined not to look toward Boardman, so she glanced in Edward's direction. He saluted and threw her a kiss.

Encouraged, she spoke earnestly to the crowd. "Welcome to the premiere presentation of the *Silver Queen*'s 1886 summer tour. Tonight's performance is dedicated to the memory of John Boardman and his contributions to the showboat industry.

"Let's bow our head in a moment of silent prayer as a tribute to our friend, who died a little more than a year ago." In the silence that followed, Rose detected a hissing sound from the box seats where Boardman was seated. Knowing that Edward was on guard gave her the courage to keep her eyes closed through the prayer.

"God, we thank You for the life of John Boardman, who provided several years of meaningful entertainment to the residents of Kentucky. This opening night's performance is dedicated to him. We also pray Your blessings on this audience as well as the performers. Amen."

Rose raised her head, and with a genuine smile of welcome, she said, "It's a pleasure to be your hostess tonight." With a sweeping gesture of her arm, she said, "Let the show begin!"

The performance went well. When the cast appeared onstage for the grand finale, an a cappella rendition of "My Old Kentucky Home," the audience collectively rose to its feet and sang with them. A deafening applause came simultaneously with the closing words of the popular song.

When the last guest left the boat, the cast gathered in the kitchen to celebrate with coffee and ate heartily of the fruit pies the cook had made for the occasion. After an interval, Rose went to the top deck, taking Martin with her. Edward followed them, asking, "Do you mind? Or would you rather be alone?"

"No, sit down," she said as she sank wearily to a bench. Edward sat on a bench opposite hers. Martin leaned over the rail and peered into the water. A cold breeze blew across the boat, and Rose asked, "Martin, would you mind going to our stateroom and bringing my black shawl?"

"No, Mama, I'll get it," he said, clambering down the steps.

"What about Boardman?" Rose asked when Martin was out of hearing. She didn't want the child alarmed unnecessarily.

"I kept my eyes on him, expecting him to throw something at the actors. You probably heard a few boos coming from his section, but he didn't do anything else. I followed him when he left the boat. He had horses stabled in town, and he and his buddy rode away. I don't know anything more than that."

"He's up to some devilment."

"I think so, too. But we're on guard."

"Should I warn the cast?"

"Not yet. We'll see if he comes back. It may be that he was curious about a showboat performance and this was a onetime visit."

"You don't believe that, do you?"

He grinned. "No, but I wanted to ease your mind if I could."

Martin returned with her shawl, and she wrapped it around her shoulders. They were silent, listening to the gentle lapping of the river on the boat. A cacophony of croaking frogs surrounded them. An occasional splash in the water indicated the presence of fish. Insects droned quietly in the background. Martin leaned over the railing, watching the shimmer of the showboat's lights across the water.

Edward looked upward. "We have quite a display of stars tonight. Do you see the Big Dipper?"

"I know very little about the stars," Rose said. "Although I've loved a starlit night since I was a child. Gramps showed me where the North Star was, but not much more."

"If you can find the North Star, it's not difficult to locate the Big Dipper." He stepped behind Rose and pointed upward as he talked. "The Big Dipper has seven stars in it. The two stars in the front of the cup point to the North Star. The Little Dipper is part of a group of stars, and it's very important as an indicator of the north, because the North Star is in the end of the Little Dipper's handle."

Rose was conscious that Martin had left the railing and was standing beside Edward, hanging on to his words. He had never been this close to his father before.

"Apparently you've studied this," Rose said.

"I spent four years at Harvard. I majored in history and business subjects, but I took some classes in astronomy for pleasure. People have been intrigued by the mystery of the heavens since the beginning of time."

"One of the earliest Bible verses I learned was, 'When I consider thy heavens, the work of thy fingers, the moon and the stars, which thou hast ordained; what is man, that thou art mindful of him?' I always think of those words when I'm out on a night like this," Rose replied.

"Mama, wonder what the big white group of stars means?"

Edward put his hand on Rose's shoulder and squeezed it gently. Rose sensed that he was pleased that Martin was joining in their conversation.

"I don't know," Rose answered. "Perhaps Mr. Moody can tell us."

"That's called the Milky Way, Martin. I've looked at that group of stars through a telescope, and there are many more stars than we can see. There are clouds of dust particles and gases that lie throughout this galaxy. On clear, dark nights like this one, it appears as a milky-looking band of starlight stretching across the sky. The longer I study the universe, the more I realize how much is yet to be discovered."

"You'll have to talk to us about this again, Edward," Rose said. "But it's time for bed now."

They walked silently downstairs and along the walkway to their rooms. They spoke quietly so as not to awaken any of their shipmates who were already sleeping. At Edward's door, Rose said, "Good night."

A long-held look with Edward spoke volumes about their feelings for each other and about the slight indication that Martin was slowly accepting his father.

Martin was sleepily removing his clothes by the time Rose entered the stateroom. He knelt beside the cot for his prayers. "God bless Mama, Gramps, Granny, and. . ." He paused. Rose wondered if he was going to include Edward in the prayer, but Martin continued, "And Tibbets. Help me to be a good boy. Amen."

In the darkness, Rose undressed, donned a night shift, and crawled into her bunk. She supposed that Martin was sleeping until he said, "Mr. Moody knows a lot, doesn't he?"

"Yes. He's a very smart man."

Martin said no more, and soon his even breathing indicated that he had gone to sleep.

～

As they continued showing on the Ohio River, all went well on the *Silver Queen*. Boardman didn't return to the showboat, and Rose became optimistic that he had left Kentucky.

Then irritating things started. They arrived at Carrollton to find only a few people on shore waiting for them. The man Rose had hired to tack up advance notices hadn't been seen.

Three rowdy spectators showed up when they stopped at Worthville, threw eggs at the performers, and started a fight in the balcony. The culprits escaped before the men on the boat or the police could apprehend them.

The next morning when Captain Parsons couldn't start the engine on the *Rosewood*, he discovered that sand had been poured into the engine. It was obvious that someone was trying to hamper their performances. Rose became concerned for the safety of the crew members and performers.

Captain Parsons and Edward discussed the situation with Rose, both convinced that Boardman was responsible for the vandalism, although they hadn't seen him since opening night. The three also considered the possibility that some of the employees could be responsible, for the damage to the *Rosewood* must have been done at night after the gangplank had been lifted. Luke Melrose, one of the actors, was a loner; and although he did his acting well, Edward proposed that he might have been hired by Boardman to disrupt the performances. But Parsons was more inclined to suspect one of his deckhands, a man he hadn't worked with before.

When the *Rosewood* was ready to sail again, Rose called the crew and performers together. She explained Boardman's enmity toward her and that she blamed him for the harassment. She didn't want to endanger their lives, and she gave them the opportunity to vote whether or not to continue the tour.

"I've been in danger before," Stephen Buckley said. "If we stop now, we'll be out of work, for it's too late to sign on with any other troupe this late in the summer. All of us can be on guard now that we know there's a problem."

Edward noted to Rose that Luke Melrose was the only one to vote for discontinuing the tour. He protested that they were making a mistake and that they might be in danger.

"That's well enough for you to say," Ranson McCall countered. "You don't have a family to support. My mother is keeping our two daughters for the summer, and I need some money to provide for them."

"I still think it's a mistake," Melrose said.

"Does that mean you want to leave?" Rose asked with a mixture of relief and misgiving. She should have hired an extra performer to step into the breach if someone quit the tour.

"Not yet," Melrose retracted. "But I value my life, and if we have any more trouble, I may leave."

"Then we'll plan to go on as usual," Rose said.

The next day, Stephen and Naomi Buckley became sick with vomiting and diarrhea. Both were too weak to leave their beds. Anthony paced the theater floor.

"Why did this have to happen?" he cried, tearing at his hair until it hung in strings over his forehead. "Never again will I agree to be a director. I can't bear the loss to my prestige when we have inferior acting."

Edward and Rose walked in on him, and he peered at them between the strands of hair.

"What are we going to do?" he shouted. "*What* are we going to do?"

Stifling a smile, Rose said, "We can use the standby performers. We're fortunate that we haven't had to do so before this. Two years ago a couple walked out on Mr. Boardman, and the stand-in actors performed the rest of the season."

Anthony slumped into a seat and lifted his hands upward. In an agonized voice he said, "Don't even mention such a thing. If this tour is a disaster, my reputation will be ruined. I might as well jump in the Ohio to spare myself the embarrassment."

"Perhaps we should cancel the show until the Buckleys get better," Rose suggested mischievously.

"No! No!" Anthony said. "We will cope." He headed toward the stage.

"While he's coping," Edward said, "I should tell you that someone may have put a large portion of castor oil in the Buckleys' food. They were late coming into the dining room last night, and they served themselves from a pot of stew that had been left on the stove. There was a little left in the pot this morning. The cook took a taste, and she thinks somebody had added something to the food."

"But why wouldn't they have noticed the taste in the food?"

"Perhaps because it was hot when they ate it—I don't know."

"That would have been done by someone on these boats," Rose said.

Before they could discuss it further, Anthony came back. "My decision has been made. The show must go on. Rose, you will play the heroine in *'Til We Meet Again*. Edward, you can be the hero. Your lines are not long, but you will have to pretend to be in love with Rose."

Lowering his left eyelid at Rose, Edward said, "That will take a lot of acting."

Rose felt her face flushing, and she frowned at him. But Anthony took Edward seriously. He wrung his hands and took a turn around the theater, gesticulating wildly.

"Oh, I know. You don't strike me as being very romantic, but I don't have any other choice."

"I'll do my best," Edward said meekly, and Rose pinched his arm.

"Oh, I forgot!" Anthony shouted in agony. "Can you sing? That closing scene requires a duet."

"Get your banjo, Rose," Edward said. "I've listened to Stephen and Naomi sing 'Beautiful Dreamer' several times. Let's give Anthony an audition."

Rose picked up the banjo and strummed a few chords. "Since you have such a low voice," she said, "I'll sing the melody, and you take the harmony part."

They sang a few lines, and Rose was surprised at the skill in Edward's voice.

He had a natural, pleasant speaking voice, but that didn't necessarily mean he could sing. Rose strummed a final chord and looked at Anthony.

"Well, if you can act as well as you sing, we'll be all right," he said grudgingly. "I only hope you don't mess up the production and ruin my reputation."

"I'm sure your reputation will still be intact after the show," Rose said dryly.

Anthony was a good director, and Rose had learned to live with his pessimistic attitude. She knew that Edward's and her voices blended well, and would be a hit with the audience, but Anthony was meager with his praise.

Rose and Edward spent the rest of the morning studying their parts, and the afternoon rehearsal went well. During the evening presentation, they performed well. Edward seemed to find it difficult to forget himself and put himself wholeheartedly into the hero's role, but he spoke distinctly.

Fortunately, he didn't appear to develop stage fright. In the first act, when the hero was leaving to serve in the Confederate army, they received spontaneous applause, and Rose heard some sniffles from the audience. Edward didn't appear onstage again until the closing scene. Three years passed, the war was over, and when nothing had been heard from the hero, the heroine believed that he had died. On the eve of the day she was to give the Union soldier an answer, she sat on the porch, her head in her hands, mourning her dead love.

Edward, portraying the hero, stepped onstage and watched Rose for a few minutes. He snagged her attention by singing, "Beautiful dreamer, wake unto me."

Rose jumped up from the chair, hand at her breast, and ran toward him.

"Oh, my love!" she cried. "I thought you were lost to me. I have missed you so much."

"The years have been long, my dearest one. Every night I prayed that I would live to see you once more. God has answered my prayer. I will never leave you again."

"Thank God, you've returned. I thought you had died and that my heart had been buried with you."

Edward bent over her. During the rehearsal, he had not kissed her but had drawn her into a close embrace as the curtains had closed.

Rose forgot that she was in view of two hundred people playing a role, and she sensed that Edward, too, had forgotten they weren't alone. She stood on tiptoe to touch her lips to his. His lips pressed against hers, then gently covered her mouth. The moment was electrifying, and when Rose gasped, Edward backed away from her quickly.

Apparently in a daze, Edward forgot his closing line.

"You're supposed to say you love me," Rose whispered.

Holding her eyes with his, he said loudly and sincerely, "I love you. I love you."

The audience roared their approval, but Rose wasn't ready for the emotions his caress had roused. She picked up her banjo, strummed a few chords, and forced herself to forget what had just happened. She blended her voice to his in the timeless words of Stephen Foster.

"Beautiful dreamer, queen of my song,
List while I woo thee with soft melody,
Gone are the cares of life's busy throng,
Beautiful dreamer, awake unto me."

After the play was over, Rose went through the motions of bidding good-bye to her guests with a smile on her face; but she was confused, and her mind rioted at the implication of Edward's gesture. She was convinced that the caress had surprised Edward as much as it had her.

Unwilling to deal with her rioting emotions, she avoided Edward the rest of the evening and went to her room as soon as the last guest left the showboat. Long after midnight, Rose still lay wide awake on her cot. The boat was quiet. Finally, tying a full-length robe over her nightgown and leaving the door of her stateroom open in case Martin awakened and called for her, Rose wandered to the front of the walkway. She leaned on the banister overlooking the water, hoping for peace from the conflict within her heart. The gentle lapping of the waves against the hull didn't calm her tonight.

Edward couldn't sleep but lay on his bunk, fully dressed. He had left his door ajar, hoping he might have an opportunity to see Rose. He hadn't intended to kiss her, but he had actually forgotten he was acting a part. It had seemed right to tell Rose that he loved her, and the caress was automatic—something he had wanted to do for days.

When he heard her door open and Rose's steps on the walkway, doubting his welcome, Edward walked quietly in the direction she had gone.

Seemingly deep in thought, Rose didn't turn around until Edward was directly behind her. She started to move away, but he gently gripped her arm.

"Are you trying to avoid me?"

"Yes, I guess I am."

"Rose, we have to deal with what happened. Why put it off?" When she didn't answer, he added, "I suppose I should say I'm sorry."

"Are you?"

"No."

She shivered, and he led her toward a nearby bench that offered some protection from the cool breeze. "Let's sit for a while. I saw your door is open, so we can hear Martin if he calls. I didn't intend to kiss you. I simply forgot for a moment that it wasn't real."

She put her hand on his arm. "It's all right. I'm not sorry either."

"I automatically did what I've wanted to do for a month. Did I embarrass you?"

She shook her head, and he sensed that she was crying. He took a handkerchief from his pocket and wiped away the tears.

"I've wondered a few times what it would be like to have you kiss me. But it stirred feelings I can't deal with now. We have several more weeks on this showboat, together every day. It might have been better if we could have remained just friends, without any disturbing, hidden emotions."

"Maybe. I promise to exert more self-control from now on. I don't want to add to your worries."

"Do you think Martin is warming to you?"

"He seems to be."

"If he senses anything between us, it might upset him very much. I don't know how I can handle a sulky child with everything else confronting me. Even though I wanted to carry on this showboat tradition to repay John for having faith in me and giving me his estate, I don't think I'll ever take this responsibility again."

"Couldn't you lease it to another person? You could still own the boat and let it carry the Boardman name."

"I'll consider that before another season. I know my limitations, and I'm not authoritarian enough to manage this boat, the actors, and the crew. I'm constantly fretting whether I'm making the right decisions."

She didn't resist when he dropped his hand over her shoulder and drew her closer. If he got his heart's desire, Edward had an answer for her problems. He had no difficulty handling authority, but he didn't want her to agree to marry him because she needed a business manager. He wanted more—much more—from Rose. He wanted her heart.

She turned to him and grinned. "Since we're going to be circumspect during the rest of the voyage, will you kiss me again before we go back to our rooms?"

"Happy to oblige," he said, affection in his voice. He kissed her forehead, the tip of her nose, and her closed eyelids before he lingeringly kissed her soft lips.

"I'll have this to remember when I'm overwhelmed with decisions," she said. "But now we must get some sleep. Captain Parsons intends to weigh anchor early tomorrow morning."

Chapter 11

The next morning, Edward suggested to Rose that they should hire a night watchman. "I'm worried about all of us sleeping without anyone on guard."

"This is so frustrating to me," she said. "All the years we traveled the river in the *Vagabond* we never locked a door, day or night. And nothing was ever bothered. Same way with the *Silver Queen*. All John did was pull in the gangplank when the crowd left after the show."

"It's just a suggestion. But if you do decide to hire a guard, he can share my stateroom and sleep during the daytime."

"I've been checking the books, and we're barely breaking even on expenses and ticket sales now. Delays like we had when the *Rosewood* was vandalized were costly. You said you had looked over my investment portfolio. Am I making enough money so I can afford to take a loss on the showboat tour?"

He couldn't control his burst of laughter. "You'll never miss it. John Boardman was obviously a shrewd businessman. But I'll pay for the night watchman. It will be worth it for my own peace of mind."

"I'd rather pay for it myself, but whom shall we hire?"

"I'll talk to the sheriff when we come to the next county and let him suggest someone. In the meantime, I'll patrol at night. I'm used to going without sleep. I can manage."

But when Luke Melrose learned that Edward was standing guard, he insisted on spelling him every other night. Edward still suspected Melrose, and he stayed on guard even when the other man was on duty. His vigilance paid off one night when he heard whispering on the lower deck. He removed his shoes and eased down the stairs.

"Melrose," a man's voice muttered, "see to it that you're on guard two nights from now when you're docked at Frankfort."

Edward had only heard Walt Boardman's voice a few times, but he felt sure Boardman was the man speaking.

"I'm sorry I ever got involved in this mess," Melrose said. "Miss Thurston is a fine woman."

"Do what I tell you, or I'll see that you're sent back to New York to face that robbery charge."

The two men moved out of hearing, and Boardman soon left. Edward hurried back to his stateroom and spent the rest of the night wondering what they should do. It was obvious that Boardman had known Melrose in New York where he was a wanted man. Edward was tempted to confront Melrose and force him to implicate Boardman. Or was it best to post a watch and catch Boardman in whatever scheme he was hatching against the showboat? Was it risky to wait? Although he wanted to spare Rose the worry, it was her right to make the decision about this new problem.

After breakfast the following morning, Edward asked Rose to accompany him to the top deck. He looked carefully in the pilothouse and checked behind every pile of rope or equipment where someone could be hiding. Then he invited her to sit beside him on a bench facing the stairway.

Quietly he told her what he had seen and heard the previous night. As he talked, Rose's shoulders slumped in despair. Edward was tempted to propose to her on the spot. If she accepted him, he would be more inclined to offer his advice.

"Oh, Edward!" she said finally. "If Boardman would promise to leave Kentucky and never come back, I'd gladly give him everything I inherited and be done with it. I didn't want John's legacy in the first place. I learned through the years with my grandparents that it didn't take riches to be happy and to live a worthwhile life. I guess it's impossible to change a shanty boat mentality."

"Rose," Edward said sternly. "Don't give up. We grow through adversity. There is nothing wrong with a shanty boat mentality. Your background with Harry and Lottie turned you into the wonderful woman you are today. I'm willing to take the responsibility for dealing with Boardman, but you *are* capable of doing what has to be done."

"I know," Rose said. She paused for a few minutes. "I'm acquainted with the sheriff of Franklin County. He and John were friends, and he hung around the showboat during the time we were docked at Frankfort. If we go to his office to enlist his help, Boardman might become suspicious. But I expect the sheriff to be at the dock to welcome us when we arrive in Frankfort. I'll talk to him privately, and he'll help us. If we can catch Boardman in the act of sabotaging the boat, or whatever he means to do, maybe that will take care of the problem."

"That's my girl," Edward said approvingly, gently rubbing the tense spot between her shoulder blades. "What do you want me to do?"

"One of us should keep Martin in sight all of the time. Boardman might try to do something to him. You didn't overhear what they're planning to do?"

"No. They moved out of hearing, and I didn't dare go any closer, for I didn't want them to know I had overheard their plans. I'll also watch Melrose. If Boardman is holding his knowledge of Melrose's crime over his head, he's probably the one who sabotaged the *Rosewood*. He might do something else to one of the boats."

"Perhaps I should have checked the background of the performers more thoroughly. If there is a next time, I'll be more careful. But that won't help me now. I can't dwell on my past mistakes."

Edward took her hand. "That's something I've had to come to terms with, too, Rose. When I think of how I acted and what I said to you and Lottie the night my wife died, I feel lower than a snake. What I did then ruined ten years of my life. But for weeks now, since I've started reading the Bible again, I keep turning to Paul's words in the book of Philippians. Although the apostle's situation differed from mine, I keep thinking of his words, 'This one thing I do, forgetting those things which are behind, and reaching forth unto those things which are before, I press toward the mark for the prize of the high calling of God in Christ Jesus.'" His eyes darkened with misery, and his brow moistened.

"Don't, Edward. You don't have to explain anything to me."

He shook his head. "I have to speak. I'm trying to put the past behind me because I've asked God to forgive me. I believe He has, so I want to ask your forgiveness for the long years you had to struggle to raise Martin alone. Also for the worry I caused you when I returned to Louisville."

Rose put her hand over his mouth. "Since God has forgiven you, do you think I can do any less? I don't regret one minute I've spent with Martin. I should thank *you* for giving me the opportunity to have ten years of his life. He's been a joy to me and my grandparents. I'm only sorry that you missed his early years. I forgive you, and I don't want you to ever mention it again. You must eventually have a talk with Martin, but the slate is wiped clean between you and me."

"But the only way I can put the past behind me is to look toward the future. I believe the highest calling I can strive for is to be a good husband and father. I can't see any future without you and Martin in it, and when the time is right, I hope all three of us will know it."

"We will," Rose said, and lifted her face for his kiss. He didn't touch her, but leaned forward and pressed a light caress on her lips.

~

When they arrived at Frankfort, as Rose had expected, Sheriff Collins was on hand to meet the *Silver Queen*. He was among the crowd who hurried onto the showboat to see if any changes had been made since the year before and to meet the new performers.

Watching carefully to be sure that Melrose didn't hear her, Rose stood close to the sheriff, a rugged man in his midfifties. Quietly she said, "I'm expecting some trouble here. See me privately."

The sheriff was as shrewd as he was competent, and he walked on without acknowledging Rose's comment. He circulated in the dining room where the cook was serving coffee and cookies to the crowd, chatting with the actors.

Soon Collins stopped beside Rose, and in a moderate voice he said, "Miss Rose, we're thinking about starting new regulations next year regarding reserved space along the waterfront so we can be sure to accommodate everyone. Can you spare me some time?"

"Sure, come into the office."

They walked to the office, and Rose closed the door. "What's up?" the sheriff asked.

Quickly Rose sketched Boardman's arrival in Louisville and his claim on John Boardman's estate.

"We've had some trouble with harassment in a few towns," she said. "And Mr. Moody, my associate, overheard Boardman plotting with one of our actors about something to happen here in Frankfort. We're going to be on guard, but if the police can catch Boardman in this plot, I might get rid of him once and for all."

"We aim to keep the law in this county, and I'll have some of my men watching day and night." He motioned to a grove of trees on the bank. "That's a good place to keep out of sight."

"Mr. Moody will volunteer to work both nights, and if Melrose insists on guarding one of those nights, we'll guess that is the night to expect trouble."

"I'll come to the show tonight, and you can say either 'tonight' or 'tomorrow night' when I pass by. But I'll probably post a guard both nights, just to be sure."

When Melrose insisted on guarding the second night, Edward agreed. And when the first night passed without incident, Rose and Edward were convinced that Boardman and Melrose would strike the next night.

After the show, while the actors greeted guests, Edward moved from the showboat to the *Rosewood*. He told Captain Parsons that he wanted to spend the night on the tugboat, but he didn't want anyone to know about it. Parsons favored Edward with a shrewd look, and Edward had the feeling that the captain would also be on guard.

While the performers were still in the dining area, Edward went to the second deck and placed a roll of blankets in his bunk to resemble a body. He didn't know that this precaution was necessary, but it was possible that Melrose might be suspicious and check on him. Walking in the shadows as much as possible, he crossed from the showboat to the tugboat on the catwalk. He eased into a supply room that had a tiny porthole facing the front of the showboat and quietly closed the door.

After an hour of waiting, quiet settled over the two boats. Edward walked out on the deck of the *Rosewood*. Fortunately, it was a moonless night, and in his dark clothes, he didn't think he could be seen. He sat on the deck with his legs flexed and peered through the railing.

In the faint glow from one of the lighted lamps, he saw Melrose sitting on a coil of rope on the foredeck of the *Silver Queen*. The gangplank had been pulled in for the night, but Luke could quickly lower it into place across the six feet of water separating the boat from the bank.

Edward didn't dare strike a match to look at his watch, but he knew when several hours had passed. Had he been wrong? Had he misunderstood what Melrose and his companion had said? His legs were numb from holding them in one position for hours. He moved backward to stretch his legs, and fighting the desire for sleep, he yawned.

He became alert at once when Melrose stood, picked up the gangplank, and quietly lowered it toward shore. Two figures moved stealthily down the bank. Edward crawled toward the showboat and eased his way to the larger craft. In his need for quietness, it took longer than he had anticipated to reach the main deck of the *Silver Queen*.

When he smelled kerosene, he launched his body into a run and sped toward the front of the showboat. A slow blaze burned near the ticket office, and he recognized Melrose as the figure pouring kerosene on the blaze. Edward tackled him, and Melrose fell backward into the fire he had just started.

Melrose screamed as the can of kerosene exploded in his hands and ignited his clothing. Edward jumped away from him to avoid being burned. Melrose's screams increased, and pandemonium broke loose. Sheriff Collins and a deputy ran across the gangplank, cutting off the escape of Boardman and his ally.

"Fire! Fire!"

⁓

Rose, who hadn't undressed and had spent the long hours sitting on her cot, ran from her stateroom and down the steep steps. She witnessed Edward pick up the screaming Melrose and pitch him into the shallow water near the bank to extinguish the flames. Within minutes, the *Rosewood*'s crew and the residents of the showboat formed a bucket brigade.

Momentarily, Rose stared at the spreading flames, knowing how quickly the boat could be destroyed, but she was more concerned about Edward than the boat. She saw that trapped between the sheriff and Edward, Boardman snarled like an animal at bay. Edward rushed toward him. Boardman fired a gun at close range, and Edward collapsed. The sheriff clouted Boardman on the head, and while he was staggering from the blow, the sheriff handcuffed him. The deputy captured his accomplice.

"Edward!" Rose shouted and rushed to him. Exerting all of her strength, she turned him over, and the last embers of the fire illuminated a bloody hole in his chest.

"God," she whispered. "I can't lose him now."

Stephen Buckley knelt beside them and searched for a pulse in Edward's wrist. "He's still alive."

"Let's get him to a doctor right away," Rose said. "Sheriff Collins will tell us where to go."

Wildly she turned to Stephen. "Will you stay with the other performers and be sure the fire is out? Captain Parsons, have your deckhands bring a cot, and we'll carry Edward to the doctor. I'll tell Martin where we're going."

Ranson McCall and Anthony Persinger knelt on the deck trying to get Luke Melrose's attention. The water was shallow, and the flames were out now, but Melrose still floundered in the water. They threw a float board to him, but he ignored it. Ranson jumped in the water and lifted Melrose's body to the deck of the showboat. The fire must have burned him badly, for Melrose writhed on the deck of the boat, groans accompanying each move he made.

"He'll need a doctor, too," Captain Parsons said.

"Take care of it then. I'll go see about Martin," Rose said.

Martin had slept through all of the commotion, but he sat up in bed rubbing his eyes when Rose rushed into the stateroom. She explained what had happened and said, "I'm going to the doctor with Edward, but Naomi and Becky will stay with you."

Martin jumped off the cot and reached for his clothes. "I want to go with you, Mama," he said.

"Hurry and dress then." Although she couldn't bear the thought of Edward dying, she knew if he did die, he would want to see Martin.

The next hours passed in a daze for Rose, and she only focused on the important details. She and Martin followed as the men carried Edward and Melrose up the bank and into town. The sheriff arranged for two wagons to haul them to the nearest doctor. Since the doctor's home was less than a mile away, they took the injured men there instead of to a hospital. Rose and Martin rode on the wagon bearing Edward's body, and for reassurance, she kept her hand on his pulse.

After they carried Edward to a bedroom, she and Martin waited in the living room of Dr. Shively's home. His wife brought coffee for her and a glass of milk for Martin. He finally went back to sleep, leaning heavily against Rose.

Rose monitored the passage of time by listening to a striking clock on the mantel. Two hours passed before Dr. Shively entered the room and motioned for her to follow him. He set Rose's mind at ease immediately. "As far as I can tell, the bullet missed any vital areas, but it lodged inside his right shoulder, and I had to remove it. That caused him to lose more blood and will delay his recovery. But he has a strong body, and I can't see any reason why he won't recover after being laid up for a few weeks."

"Thank You, God," she said, her lips trembling. Taking the doctor's hand, she said, "And thank you, too, Doctor."

Mrs. Shively had worked with Melrose while her husband operated on Edward, so the doctor left Rose to sit beside Edward while he checked on the burned man.

Rose pulled a chair to the bed and took Edward's hand. Since Edward always seemed full of vitality, it was heart wrenching to see his immobile body. But in his unconscious state, he seemed younger, more vulnerable, more like he had looked the first time she had seen him.

Martin knelt beside the bed for a long while, but finally fatigue overcame him and he curled up on a blanket Mrs. Shively had placed on the floor. Daylight filtered into the room, and with the sun shining, Mrs. Shively came to extinguish the lamp. She invited Rose to come to the kitchen for some food. When Rose refused to leave Edward, the doctor's wife brought her a cup of coffee and a hot biscuit.

"I'll feed the little tyke when he wakes up," she said. "But I'm afraid your mister won't feel like eating for a while."

"Mr. Moody is a friend," Rose said, hastening to correct the assumption that Edward was her husband.

The doctor's wife blushed, and she stammered, "I'm sorry. I just supposed. . ."

"Don't be distressed. It's only natural you would assume that." Smoothing back Edward's hair, Rose added, "He's a very *dear* friend, however."

Mrs. Shively looked from the patient to Martin, lying asleep on the pallet. Rose noticed that in sleep Martin resembled his father more than at any other time. Mrs. Shively must have been curious, but she asked no questions.

"Yes," Rose explained. "They are father and son but were separated at Martin's birth. I adopted Martin when he was three years old. His father only came into our lives in April, and Martin hasn't accepted him yet. We need your prayers," she added.

Embracing Rose's shoulders, the motherly woman said, "You will have them."

Edward's even breathing and the return of color to his face encouraged Rose. In midmorning he stirred restlessly and moaned in his sleep. Believing he was regaining consciousness, Rose whispered to Martin, "Wake up, son." Martin yawned and wiped his eyes, but he scurried off the floor and crawled up on the bed at Edward's feet. Rose knelt beside the bed and wiped Edward's face with the damp cloth Mrs. Shively had provided. Her arm rested lightly on his bandaged shoulder when Edward opened his eyes. When he shifted his shoulders, he visibly winced. Rose knew his wound was painful even if it wasn't fatal.

He blinked his eyes and focused on her face. She leaned over and kissed his cheek. Martin moved forward, and Edward looked toward him.

"Have I died and gone to heaven?" he asked in a weak voice, so unlike his usual vibrant tone that Rose's eyes filled with tears.

"Not this time," she answered, squeezing his hand. "You won't get away from me that easily."

"Are you feeling better, Mr. Moody?" Martin asked.

"Yes, thank you, Martin." His eyes were unusually bright when he turned to Rose. "What happened?"

"Boardman shot you. The bullet missed your lungs and your heart, but it was embedded in your shoulder. Dr. Shively had to remove it. You'll be laid up for a few weeks, but you're going to get well."

"Did the *Silver Queen* burn?"

"No. The men put out the fire. I've been here with you, so I don't know how much damage there is. Now that I know you will be all right, I'll go to the showboat and find out what has to be done."

"What happened to Boardman and his crew?"

"Melrose is in the next room with a sheriff's deputy guarding him. Sheriff Collins stopped in an hour ago and told me that Boardman broke away from him and jumped in the river, trying to escape. He was in handcuffs and apparently wasn't much of a swimmer, for he drowned. They did recover his body. They questioned the man who was working with Boardman, and he's implicated Boardman in all of our trouble this summer. As soon as Melrose is well enough, he'll be sent back east to face the charges against him."

"Why did he team up with Boardman?"

"Walt knew him in New York. There's a warrant for Luke's arrest in the East, and Walt told him that if he didn't help destroy the *Silver Queen*, he would report him to the authorities."

"I pitched him in the water to put out the flames."

"Yes, I know. He will go to jail as soon as the doctor releases him."

"Mama told me how you fought those mean men," Martin said. "You were very brave, Mr. Moody."

Before Edward could reply, Dr. Shively came into the room. "So," he said. "You're awake and able to talk."

"Yes," Edward said. "Thanks to you."

"Partly due to my skill, but mostly because you are strong and healthy." The doctor looked sternly at Martin and Rose. "Now you two need some rest. My wife will fix beds for you."

"Thank you," Rose said. "But I want to go to the showboat and see how things are there." She leaned over and kissed Edward's forehead. "We'll be back this afternoon."

Martin reached out his right hand, and with a slight grin, Edward grasped the tiny hand with his left one and shook it gently. "Mama and I will pray for you, Mr. Moody."

⁓

After Rose and Martin left the room, Edward reflected on what had just occurred. He couldn't believe what Martin had said to him. *It's a beginning.*

Edward silently thanked God that He had seen fit to entrust Martin into Rose's care. He had always thought it was chance that he had found a midwife when Martha went into premature labor. But had God ordained his meeting with the Thurstons? Had He been orchestrating his life and theirs during the past ten years to eventually bring them together again? It was a humbling thought, but Edward knew it was true. Surely the day was soon approaching when Martin would accept him and the three of them could become a family. *God, grant me patience,* he prayed.

Chapter 12

Until she crossed the gangplank and stepped on the deck, Rose didn't notice any damage to the showboat, but the impairment was soon evident. A sizeable hole had burned in the floor beside the ticket window. The fire had crept up the stairway to the balcony, and several of the steps were charred beyond use. The door to the office was blackened, but a quick look inside indicated that the safe and other files hadn't been damaged.

She had to make some immediate decisions, and she wished her grandparents were here to tell her what to do. She couldn't ask Edward for advice when he was so ill. It was up to her, and she prayed for guidance.

Holding Martin's hand, she moved toward the dining area, where she found the performers. They were eating breakfast, but she glimpsed despair on their faces. They rushed toward them when they saw Martin and her in the doorway.

"How is Edward?" Anthony asked.

"Recovering, thanks be to God," Rose said.

"We're sorry for your misfortune. None of us had any idea that Luke was working against you," Ranson said.

"I realize that." To the cook Rose said, "Please bring a cup of tea for me and some breakfast for Martin." She sat down and motioned for all of them to gather around her.

"I did a lot of thinking during the night," she said. "Without knowing the extent of the damage to the boat, I was sure that we couldn't continue the show this season."

They nodded forlornly, and she added, "But you will all receive your full pay."

"Oh, no, Miss Rose," Persinger protested. "We don't expect that. This tragedy isn't your fault."

"Anthony, by now all of you have heard about my youth. I spent twenty-seven years of my life without much money. My grandparents and I lived from season to season. And I know that's the same way with you. I don't even have to consider between losing some money and helping you and your families make it through the next few months. I'm sure John Boardman would have made this same decision."

Naomi Buckley sobbed and sat down in a nearby chair, pulling her daughter to her side.

"We won't start back to Louisville until Edward is ready to travel, and I don't know how long that will be," Rose continued. "So all of you performers must make arrangements to leave when you can. There will be other boats along, or it might be quicker if you take a train into Louisville. It's possible you can still find some employment for the rest of the summer. I don't know what will happen during the next year, but if we do take the *Silver Queen* out again, I'll keep you in mind."

She turned to the cooks and the deckhands. "I want you to stay with the boat and travel back to Louisville with us. You'll also get full pay."

"Do you want us to go ahead and clean up the mess, Rose?" Captain Parsons said. "We might as well do something while we wait."

"The boat is insured, and the insurance adjusters will want to look over the damage. Do we need to make repairs now?"

"We'll have to fix that hole in the deck before we go back out on the river," he insisted.

"Then do what you think is necessary," Rose said.

The performers left the next day on the train, but it was a week before Edward was brought to the showboat in a wagon. Putting him on a mattress, Captain Parsons and the three deckhands carried him on board.

Rather than taking him to the second deck, Rose had made a bed for him near the stage in the theater. Soon Captain Parsons gave the departure whistle, and the *Rosewood* nudged the showboat out into the river. From the top deck of the *Silver Queen*, Rose played "God Be with You 'Til We Meet Again" on the calliope, as Frankfort citizens waved from the bank. She made a few mistakes, but no one seemed to notice.

Still weak from his wound, Edward slept often during the first two days. Martin volunteered to read to him one morning, and he accepted with gratitude, pleased with how well the child read. But though Martin was friendly, there was a wall of reserve that Edward couldn't break through.

After Martin left to pester Captain Parsons into letting him steer the tugboat, Edward complained to Rose, "Will he ever accept me as his father? Do we have to wait forever? I love you, and every day that passes, I think it's another day we could be happy together. I want to be your husband, even if I can't be Martin's father."

"I love you, too, and I won't let Martin's attitude keep us apart any longer. He has to learn to forgive. As soon as you are well, I want to get married. I don't know how, but God will work out the details."

"Sorry I can't seal our promise with a kiss."

"There isn't anything wrong with me," she whispered. Rose leaned over him and lowered her lips to his. With his left arm, Edward pulled her tightly against him and deepened the caress.

On the last night before they reached Louisville, after Edward was asleep, Martin and Rose stood on the top deck, listening to the drone of the insects and looking at the stars.

"Mama, are we going to take Mr. Moody home with us so Granny can look after him? He might get lonesome in his apartment."

Rose moved to a bench and pulled him down beside her. "Martin, I need to talk to you about this. There's only one way we can bring Edward into our home to live—and that's as my husband."

His shoulders tensed, and she didn't press the point for a few minutes. She had carefully avoided saying that Edward would be his father. "Do you like him enough to agree to that?"

After a minute passed, he slowly nodded his head.

"No," she said firmly. "A nod isn't enough. I don't want any misunderstandings between us. Edward and I love each other. If we're married, that means Edward will be sharing my life—my bedroom, my business decisions, and all that I do. My love for him will not alter how much I love you, but he *will* be as important to me as you are. You look me in the eye and tell me how you feel about it."

He swallowed, and he sniffed a little. She knew it was a difficult decision for the child to make, but finally he lifted his head and looked at her. His lips trembled a little when he said, "It's all right, Mama. I'll share you with Mr. Moody."

Thank You, Lord, Rose prayed silently. She kissed Martin tenderly. "You've made me very happy, son."

Rose went immediately to tell Edward. She knew they had won a major battle, but the war wasn't over yet.

Edward disagreed with the plan to take him to her home until he could go there as her husband.

"I'll be perfectly comfortable at the apartment," he said. "Mrs. McClary will come in every day. The Bible teaches that we should shun all appearance of evil, and we don't want any gossip attached to our marriage. I can be patient now that I know we will soon be together. Let's plan a honeymoon. Where would you like to go?"

"Somewhere on the river," she said.

"How does New Orleans sound?"

"Good, but we would be gone a long time."

"We'll talk it over with Harry and Lottie as soon as we get settled at home and see if they'll watch out for Martin."

❧

"It's an excellent plan," Lottie said at once. "We can take Martin with us on the *Vagabond*. Now that Boardman ain't a threat, Harry has been chomping at the bits to take off in the shanty. We can spend a month out on the river. Harry will keep Martin so busy, he won't miss you. We can be back before his school starts, and that will give you and Edward time for a weddin' trip."

"Granny, my life has been like the flow of the river—sometimes peaceful, other times a bumpy ride. And I've been tossed on the waves. But in God's own timing, He brought Edward and me together."

"I pray that you and Edward will find the happiness you deserve."

"We will, Granny. We will."

The wedding took place in Rose's home with only the Thurstons and Sallie and Isaiah present. Instead of a formal wedding dress, Rose chose a blue silk garment that would be suitable as a traveling dress when they boarded the packet boat for the trip to New Orleans. Dr. T. T. Eaton, pastor of the Walnut Street Church where Rose and Martin attended, came to the house to perform the ceremony.

Martin had been quieter than usual at the wedding, but he didn't shed any tears, and as Edward and Rose stood on the deck of the boat waiting for departure, he waved to them. It was the first time Rose had been separated from Martin, and she felt a tug at her own heart when the boat left the wharf. She knew the separation was necessary, not only for Edward and her to bond in the special meaning of marriage, but it also would be good for Martin to understand right away what sharing her with Edward meant.

The days on the boat and the week in New Orleans strengthened the love that Rose and Edward had for each other. They spent hours strolling around the streets of the old town, marveling at the mixture of Spanish and French architecture. They tried out all of the famous restaurants. They spent one day at a nearby plantation purchasing an Arabian gelding for Edward.

Rose sent word when they expected to return. The day of their arrival, her grandparents, Martin, Sallie and Isaiah, and many other acquaintances waited for them. As they walked down the gangplank, Martin ran to Rose, threw himself into her arms, and kissed her, something he hadn't done in public for a year or more. Her arms tightened around him because she had missed him, too.

When she released Martin, he turned to Edward and held out his hand. "Welcome home, Mr. Moody."

With a resigned look at Rose, Edward shook his outstretched hand. "Thank you, Martin."

The Arabian hadn't been happy about the boat trip, and the trainer Edward had hired to make the journey had had a difficult time controlling the animal during the unloading.

Martin was delighted with the spirited horse. "I want to ride him, too," he shouted.

"You'll have to be content with Tibbets for a while," Rose said.

The trainer led the horse away from the landing, and they had quite a following before they reached Third Street. Martin was more excited over the new horse than he was over the gifts they had bought for him.

"Probably Tibbets is going to seem pretty tame to him now," she told Edward after they had gone to their room and were preparing for bed. She expected trouble keeping Martin away from the animal, but she didn't expect trouble to come as soon as it did.

∽

Rose and Edward awakened to a frantic pounding on their bedroom door.

"Mr. Edward. Miss Rose!" Isaiah shouted. "Martin is riding the new horse."

Edward yanked on his clothes quickly, but Rose simply tied a robe around her nightgown and hurried to the paddock. Martin sat bareback on the Arabian, which looked around at the child as if he wondered what the small object was doing on his back.

When Edward and Rose arrived at the paddock, the trainer came running from the stable. "I turned the horse out to let him get over his frisky ways before I rode him," he cried. "I didn't know the boy was even around here. He must have mounted him from the fence."

"Martin, get off that horse right now!" Rose shouted.

The horse moved away from the fence, and the child looked terrified as he monitored the long distance to the ground. The horse switched his tail and shook his shoulders as if to rid his back of the foreign object. Martin's face turned white, but Edward opened the paddock gate and stepped inside.

"Careful, Martin," he cautioned. "I'll come closer to help you."

"You'd better let me do that, Mr. Moody," the trainer said. "That horse is skittish."

Edward shook his head. As he neared the animal, the Arabian started a fast walk around the paddock. As the horse's pace increased to a lope, Edward moved closer.

"Daddy," Martin cried, terror-stricken, "I'm afraid. Help me."

Rose was quick to catch the significance of Martin's call, as if the child had been thinking of Edward as his father for a long time.

When the horse made another circle and neared him, Edward shouted, "Jump, son! Jump! I'll catch you."

Martin had been holding to the Arabian's mane, but when the horse circled again, he let go and leaped toward the ground. Edward grabbed him and took a rolling plunge away from the horse. The trainer ran into the paddock and grabbed the Arabian by the mane.

"Daddy! You saved me!"

Rose ran toward Edward and Martin, tears in her eyes and laughter in her heart.

Two little arms encircled Edward's neck and a moist kiss was planted on his cheek. Hugging Martin tightly in his arms, he started crying.

Kneeling beside them, Rose spread her arms around the two people she loved most in the world. They were a family at last.

IRENE B. BRAND
Irene has been publishing books since 1984. Her forty-fifth book will be published in June 2008. She has published in three inspirational genres—historical fiction, romantic suspense, and contemporary romance. A retired public school teacher, Irene also has many years of teaching experience in her local Baptist church. She and her husband, Rod, live in Southside, West Virginia.

Moving the Mountain

Dedication

A special thanks to Jeanette Cloud
for her expertise on Harlan County, Kentucky,
and my writers' group (Ann, Debbie, Lisa, Lori, and Michelle)
for their helpful comments.

Chapter 1

"Life's not hard," Jonas McLean said to his horse. "It's impossible."

Unable to concentrate on the May 24, 1912, *Weekly Enterprise* he'd just purchased at the Poplar Grove Depot, he tossed it into the back of the wagon.

Thoughts of Molly Pierpont clouded his mind. She would arrive any moment, and he could do nothing to prevent it.

He hadn't known how to deal with Sarah's dying wish. His wife had made him promise to ask her sister, Molly, to help take care of Dawn and Caleb if anything happened to her.

Sarah must have had a premonition because she died in childbirth nine months ago, along with their baby. Molly had offered to stay after the funeral, but Jonas insisted he could take care of his own daughter and son just fine. After all, Dawn had just turned nine and could handle two-year-old Caleb while Jonas plowed his fields, planted his crops, and cared for his farm animals.

Three months ago, Jonas received a telegram from Molly. Her husband, Percival Pierpont, had met with an untimely death. By the time he retrieved the telegram from town, the funeral would have been over. He'd telegrammed his condolences.

Although he and Percival hadn't related well on the one occasion he'd visited along with Sarah, Jonas was sorry to hear of anyone's untimely death. But he hadn't had to worry about Molly showing up to help where she wasn't needed.

During the winter months and spring rains, he was pretty much confined to the cabin with the children. A neighbor came by to take Dawn to school since Jonas had taken a leave of absence from teaching history at Pine Hollow and Coalville schools. He didn't see how he could return until Caleb reached school age. Those were hard months without Sarah, but he felt with time, they'd adjust.

They would have if Dawn hadn't attempted to roll an iron pot up a hill. She lost her grip, slid, tried to catch it, and the weight of it broke a bone near her elbow. The doctor said the bone having protruded through the skin put her at risk for infection.

Neighbors would help if he asked, but they had their own lives to live. Also, this was planting season. Trying to be positive, Jonas reminded himself that at least school was out for the summer. But for the past week, Dawn was either in pain or so drowsy from the laudanum she could do nothing but lie around.

Reluctantly, Jonas had made a visit to the impressive house in the city to express his sympathy and ask Molly to help out for a couple of weeks, just until he could get additional planting done and look for someone to handle Caleb.

He didn't expect that a twenty-four-year-old city woman like Molly could adjust to life back in the cove of Kentucky's Appalachian Mountains—not even for a couple of weeks. But Sarah had made him promise to ask.

When Sarah and the baby died, he'd thought things couldn't get worse. But they had.

Dawn had enough trouble handling Caleb when he was only two. After he turned three, he gained experience and delighted in getting into everything. Jonas had faith in God, but not in having to take in a city woman who knew nothing of hunting for supper in the forest, fishing from the creeks, or the rearing of children.

At least Molly had two good arms. He knew what his children needed most was someone to help them stop crying themselves to sleep every night. He had his doubts about that since he didn't expect anyone or anything to ease the ache of loss he felt deep within his heart.

He knew nothing about how to treat a city woman. Not one who wore silly hats, frilly clothes, and carried a parasol.

If only Sarah hadn't made him promise to ask. . .

His anxiety grew when the whistle blew and the train came protesting, chugging and huffing around the mountain with black smoke curling from its stack. Jonas took a deep breath, feeling like a weight was on his chest. He wouldn't be surprised to see a puff of black smoke come out of his lungs.

∼

Molly attempted to look as morose as the black mourning clothes she wore. Many of her acquaintances would be mortified to think she'd dress otherwise for less than a year. However, upon glimpsing her reflection in the train window, she warned herself to get that happy expression off her face.

She must indeed be an ingrate, being so eager to leave behind the kind of life for which she'd often been told she should be grateful. Her sights were set on the challenge ahead.

No one had ever understood her—except Sarah. And she hadn't been allowed to see her until the past few years, and then only once or twice a year. That thought wiped the smile from her lips. She should wear black for Sarah, if not for her deceased husband.

She'd been told through the years, "Look on the bright side. Count your blessings."

Molly decided to do that now. Her excitement heightened as did the scenery. She'd watched the change from valleys of bluegrass to high hills and then the craggy mountain peaks of Harlan County.

She thought of the times when she'd stepped from the train at Poplar Grove depot, which was surrounded by Kentucky's forested mountains. Sarah would come running to give Molly the kind of hug and welcome she longed for.

The last time she came was nine months ago for Sarah's funeral. Aunt Mae accompanied her, without Percy, who said he couldn't get away from business. A few of Jonas's relatives had arrived on the same train. They made a somber appearance, all dressed in black, riding up the mountain in rented black carriages.

This time, Molly told herself not to think of Sarah's absence, but of the presence of Jonas and his children.

The train pulled around the last bend. The whistle blew as if in celebration. Molly thought she couldn't get any happier, but when the train's rhythmic movement slowed until it stopped at the depot, she felt her heart might burst with anticipation.

As soon as she stepped from the train and her pointed-toe shoes touched the hard-packed earth, a pine-scented wind whipped her long skirt to the side, and she touched her hat to keep it from blowing away.

She laughed, gripping her gift-bearing bag.

Her laughter caught in her throat when she saw no children. Jonas, looking like the life had gone out of him, ambled toward her. His broad shoulders slumped, as they had at Sarah's funeral.

A stab of regret washed over her. For a moment she allowed her own loss to linger. Just when she'd found her sister, she'd lost her. She did not want to lose Sarah's children, too.

She'd learned through the years that outward appearance didn't necessarily reflect a person's inner qualities, or lack of them. She was wearing mourning clothes, but Jonas was the one grieving.

Maybe, just maybe, she could take away some of his burden. His smile did not reach his eyes—eyes that she remembered as being a soft brown now looked like they were troubled by a dark rain cloud.

His smile now gone, he nodded. "Molly." He reached for her bag. "Thank you for coming."

She didn't want to show her disappointment that the children weren't with him.

She relinquished the bag and walked beside him toward the wagon. "Jonas, I—I have trunks."

"Trunks?"

The way he said it, it sounded as if he'd never heard the word before. "Yes. My clothes. . .and things."

His rugged face reddened. "Of—of course." He set the bag in the wagon. "Here." He held out his hand. Molly laid her shoulder bag on the seat and placed her gloved hand in his strong one. She hoisted her skirt to her ankles and stepped up.

Jonas hurried around to the other side, jumped up beside her, and picked up the reins. "I'll drive closer," he said. "Your trunks may be heavy."

He turned the wagon, and the horse trotted down to the luggage cart. Molly tried to reason why he seemed so somber.

She chided herself. Of course he was somber. He was grieving for his wife. He was a proud man who had to ask for help. She was dressed in black. He would expect her to be grieving and likely thought it wouldn't be proper to seem happy at such a distressing time.

She would swallow her excitement and act the proper mourning lady. At least until she could get out of these dismal clothes.

During her brief visits, she had never conversed with Jonas very much. When Percy came, he stayed in town at the hotel in Poplar Grove and Jonas slept in the lean-to. That way, Molly shared Sarah's bed, and the two of them talked until the wee hours of the morning. Trying to sleep would have been a nuisance when they had so much to talk about. Sleep was for when they were no longer together.

Jonas had always been polite but reticent. Molly understood that. She'd learned to be exactly that with Percy. She observed Jonas being kind to Sarah and the children. But it was from Sarah that she'd gotten the impression that Jonas was a remarkable man.

Sarah hadn't explained in what way he was remarkable.

"I thought the children might be with you," she said as they pulled away from the depot.

She watched his chest rise slightly, but maybe that was from flicking the reins and giving the horse a command to pick up speed. "No," he said. "I, um, didn't think it fitting."

"Oh." Molly supposed he meant because they were grieving. His next words seemed to confirm her thoughts.

"I'm sorry I couldn't get away for Mr. Pierpont's funeral."

"Oh, I understand." She did exactly. He had children to take care of. He might have felt out of place, too, the funeral being a rather extraordinary event, unlike Sarah's simple one. "I'm just so glad you asked me to come and help."

He nodded. "I hope I wasn't imposing by asking. I just had nowhere else to turn."

His words sounded like he considered her not a loving aunt to his children, but a last resort. His next comment surprised her even more.

"You may not be here long enough to wear all those clothes." His head jerked toward the trunks, then back at the winding dirt road ahead of them. "Dawn's arm should heal within a few weeks."

Molly opened her mouth to respond, but her glance at his concerned face caused her to close it. Was he hoping she wouldn't stay? She knew he and Percy hadn't cared much for each other, but she hadn't thought that extended to her.

For a long moment, she gazed at his set face. She knew how to act and remain silent. However, no one could stop the thoughts she allowed to roam about in her head.

MOVING THE MOUNTAIN

For years, she'd wanted to do something useful, and now was her chance. No one else but Sarah had recognized the longing in her heart to be part of a real family.

She longed to give love to a young girl and little boy who had lost their mama. Molly knew how that felt because she'd lost her mama when she was eight years old. In a sense, soon after that, she'd lost her dad and sister, too.

Now Jonas, Dawn, and Caleb needed her. As much as she regretted that Dawn had broken her arm, she thought Jonas would otherwise never have consented to her coming to his home in Pine Hollow.

She would like to stay in this mountain cove permanently.

Her sister's children needed her and liked her.

She resolved right then and there that Jonas McLean, too, would learn to like her.

Chapter 2

Molly's "Oops" brought his glance around to her. With one hand, she braced herself on the wooden seat, and with the other she secured her hat on her head. Try as he might, Jonas was unable to avoid the wagon wheels dropping right down into the wide mud hole in the dirt road.

She swayed when the front wheels found level ground and the back wheels dipped into the hole.

"Sorry. Spring rains do this to dirt roads." His body rose a couple of inches into the air before settling back onto the seat.

The force of her laughter near his ear so startled him, he almost dropped the reins.

There had been none in his life since Sarah died. He and Sarah would have laughed about this, but it didn't seem fitting with someone else.

Molly's glance swept past his face and she gestured behind her. "At least the trunks are still there."

Jonas barely concentrated on her story of when she and Sarah were little girls in the back of her papa's wagon. The roads weren't even this good, and they'd bounce up and down like rubber balls.

He couldn't manage more than a forced turn of his lips. He and Sarah had had many happy times in their marriage. But he couldn't remember any of them without that insatiable longing rising up within him. Now, hearing Molly's laughter, he felt her loss of a sister didn't come close to his loss of a wife, or his children's loss of a mother.

She faced the front again. "I remember those mud holes. I've even played in a few."

Watching the road ahead for more holes to try to avoid, he spoke honestly. "Everything's different, being an adult. When you're responsible for a family."

"Oh, I know how hard it must be for you, Jonas, without. . ." He heard the catch in her voice. "Without Sarah."

He could only nod. Did she really know? Had she loved Percival Pierpont the way he loved Sarah? "I have to think about the children, Molly. This is hard on them."

From the corner of his eye, he saw her turn slightly toward him. "Jonas, you can't imagine what it means to me that you asked me to come here."

He swallowed hard. "Sarah made me promise to ask you for help if anything ever happened to her."

MOVING THE MOUNTAIN

Molly turned toward the front again. He glimpsed the movement of her gloves against each other as if she didn't know what to do with her hands. Maybe she thought he didn't appreciate her willingness to help. He did. He had asked her because he had nowhere else to turn. He could at least be kind.

"I do thank you for coming, Molly. But life here is different than in the. . ." They both lifted from their seats again as a wheel bumped through another hole. He said, "city," while she emitted a small sound of glee.

Sarah had been quick to laugh, too. She'd packed joy into every day's living, as if—as if she knew her life would be short. Somehow, Molly's laughter seemed out of place, considering the situation. She'd lost her husband only three months ago. She was wearing black. And yet she was behaving as if she were about to see Sarah again and experience those happy times when she'd visited.

He and the children didn't need someone to pretend everything was all right. Molly had lived a pampered city life. Maybe she didn't realize what she was getting into. He took in a deep breath. "Visits aren't the same as daily living, Molly."

Without looking around, he knew her head had turned sharply toward him. His mere glance to the side revealed her smile had vanished and her chin had lifted, reminding him of how Dawn often looked when things didn't go her way. Sarah said their daughter got her hardheadedness from him, but he suspected it ran in Sarah's family.

A wave of remorse swept over him. He forced it away. He didn't have the luxury of spending time thinking about what couldn't be. He had two children to raise and didn't know how he could do it without their mother.

If he didn't know, how could she?

At least, he should warn her about his daughter.

"About Dawn—"

"Oh, that adorable child. I can't wait to see her. Jonas, this is just what I need." She gasped then whispered, "Listen."

He listened but heard nothing other than the *clop-clop* of the horse's hooves and churning of wagon wheels on a rough road. Had she heard a wild animal? Wouldn't surprise him to see a bear with her cubs, a deer, or even a bobcat.

He shrugged a shoulder.

"The birds." She pointed toward the trees where a flock of birds flew and twittered. "You're so right, Jonas. This is different from the city. We don't see that many birds. Our spring is pretty, of course. But here there is so much more abundance. I mean, look at the colors."

He hadn't noticed. His world was a cold, gray one. He looked at the delight on her face—the face that held a resemblance to Sarah and yet was so different—as different as the city from the mountains. He marveled, almost resented, her describing the colors of red maple buds; pink, purple, and white rhododendron; delicate mountain laurel; new leaves on tall oaks; and the yellow-green poplar flowers that resembled tulips. She laughed lightly and turned her face toward him. "And. . . springy-green growth on towering pines."

Jonas looked, but the colors of spring didn't seem to register. His heart felt cold like winter and black as the coal the miners took from Black Mountain.

He'd heard people say that winter seemed endless back in the hollows. Now he knew what that meant—and it had nothing to do with weather or a season.

Molly was wearing black, but he was the one feeling the blackness. Maybe she looked upon this as a long visit. He was the one who had a lifelong responsibility.

He decided not to say that Dawn was not the same little girl she'd been when Molly had visited. Dawn had more than a broken arm. She had a broken heart and a broken spirit.

~

Molly reveled in the changing sights as the wagon made its circuitous route around the Pine Mountains. Craggy peaks and forested slopes rose to over four thousand feet above sea level. Cascading waterfalls rushed over smooth boulders, splashing and rippling along creeks, and the fresh smell of water mingled with rich soil.

Orange lilies along the roadsides waved in welcome. Red-crested songbirds greeted. The wagon moved past men building a dirt road off the main road. Yellow daffodils and delicate pastel narcissus grew beside a fence.

Rather than continue talking to this man, whose grief seemed so heavy he couldn't respond with more than a few words, she breathed in the fragrance of mountain-fresh air, spring flowers, and spicy pine.

After a few more miles up and along the winding road, Jonas turned onto his wooded land in Pine Hollow. Soon, they rode out of the trees, and ahead was a sight that made her heart leap with joy. The small valley stretched out ahead—land she'd seen in the past that had corn as high as a man's head, beans that formed a blanket of green, wildflowers that grew freely, grassy stretches of pasture where cattle fed—then the forested mountains reaching into the sky.

Oh, how she preferred that to a trolley car running on rails down the middle of a cobbled city street. She loved the natural beauty here, away from any man-made contraptions.

Molly began to feel like Jonas looked when the log cabin came into view. A churning in her stomach made her feel sick, and a tightness in her throat kept her from speaking. Her determination to think only of the good, of coming home again, left her. She fought against moisture in her eyes and breathed deeply.

No Sarah ran out to meet her.

In front of the cabin, no spring flowers bloomed in the bed, except a few jonquils struggling to survive in the weeds.

A dread hammered in her chest as it had when they'd lowered Sarah's coffin into the ground. Dawn had begged them not to cover her mother with dirt. When they did it anyway, she'd run back to the cabin and wouldn't come out of her room.

Molly's gaze moved up and away, to the distant hills, beyond which Sarah lay beneath the earth in a pine coffin. For the first time since Jonas asked her to help, she had her doubts. Could she do this?

Hearing the creak of a door, the name "Sarah" sounded from her throat in a whisper. She looked quickly at Jonas. He appeared not to hear but stared at the cabin.

When the cabin door swung open, Molly expected Dawn would run out, followed by a toddling Caleb. Instead, a stocky woman with her shirtwaist sleeves rolled to above her elbows rushed into the yard, brushing back some of the hair that had come loose from the roll at the back of her neck.

Jonas walked up, looking concerned. "The children?"

"They'll be right out," she said. "I'm sure." She didn't sound sure.

Jonas nodded, although he didn't look too sure of anything either. "Molly, you may remember Birdie Evers, the pastor's wife."

Molly had met her nine months before at Sarah's funeral. She recognized her mainly as the woman who had one completely gray streak along the right side of her black hair.

Molly extended her gloved hand. "Nice to see you again, Mrs. Evers."

The woman wiped her hands on the apron covering her long, gray skirt, ignored Molly's hand, then opened her arms and gathered Molly against her ample chest. "Oh, my dear." She began expressing her sorrow for all Molly's losses. "I'm glad you're here."

She moved back. "Now, you call me by my front name. It's Birdie. Everybody does."

Molly wondered if that was her name, or a nickname because of the movement of her hands when she talked, and equally darting black eyes that gave her the appearance of being all aflutter.

Molly smiled. She sent a quick glance toward the house while Jonas set her bag next to her, then returned to the wagon.

Birdie clasped her hands then unclasped them and yelled at Jonas. "Let me help you with that, Jonas. You'll break your back."

She rushed to the wagon and seemed to have less trouble than Jonas with the heavy trunks.

Birdie brushed her hands together like someone playing the cymbals. "There. Now let me help you inside with them."

"The porch will be fine," Jonas said.

Molly felt planted in the yard. Why did he unload her trunks here? Where were the children? Napping? Maybe someone else was coming to load her trunks. "Why didn't you leave the trunks in the wagon?"

Jonas stared back. "What do you mean? You've already decided not to stay?"

Molly's thoughts were all a-jumble. Jonas and Birdie wore expressions of confusion. Molly thought he would have arranged for her to stay with someone who had an extra room, and she'd come to the cabin during the day.

"Of course I'm planning to stay," she stammered.

He looked over his shoulder at the trunks, then back at her. "I don't understand why you're asking about the trunks. This is my home."

Figuring she'd just make things worse by trying to explain, she shook her head. "Never mind." She touched the side of her head. "Must be the mountain air."

Birdie looked from one to another with raised eyebrows and a quirk of her lips that seemed to say she was enjoying this. Her nose squeezed together and she inhaled deeply, then spread her hands. "Well, I should be leaving."

"Thank you, Birdie," Jonas said. "I appreciate your help."

Her hand lifted in a wave. "Bye-bye, Molly. Call on me if you need anything. I'm just across yonder creek and up a few miles."

Molly didn't see a yonder creek but watched Birdie stride across the yard to a horse tied to a tree limb. The woman, now obviously wearing a divided skirt, mounted the horse and disappeared around the side of the cabin.

Molly turned back.

Jonas still stared at her. "Did you forget I live here?"

"No, no." She knew he had only two bedrooms. "I just didn't think we'd be—I'd be—staying in the same house with—you."

If she didn't know better, she would think he'd been working out in the sun all day, the way color flooded his cheeks. "It wouldn't be proper for us to stay in the same house together."

She felt reprimanded, as if she had suggested such. Now she felt like the one who'd worked all day in the sun.

He explained further. "You'll have my room. I will be in the lean-to at the barn."

She opened her mouth to say she didn't want to put him out of his house, but that might sound even less proper, and he'd probably send her back to the city before her trunks could get through the front door of his cabin.

About the time she again remembered the children, she heard their voices.

"You stay right here!"

"Wanna go."

"No. She's not your mama. We don't have no mama no more."

Molly stared. Dawn, with her arm in a splint and sling, tried to hold a squirming little boy with one hand. He broke loose and ran straight to Molly.

With his little arms around her legs, he looked up into her eyes with a hopeful face. "Mama?"

Jonas took hold of the boy's shoulder. "Caleb," he said in a reprimanding tone.

Molly looked over at him. "It's all right."

Caleb was so young when his mama died. But old enough to know he had one. Molly knelt down to the little boy's level. "I'm your aunt Molly, Caleb. I'm here for a visit until Dawn's arm is healed."

His little lips quivered and he looked disappointed. Molly patted her bag. "I have something in here you might like."

Caleb took in a deep breath and let it out in a rush, as if he'd been told to be brave and not cry. He nodded and she stood, picking up her bag. Caleb reached for her hand. The two of them walked to the screen door.

Dawn slammed the wooden one in her face.

Chapter 3

Jonas opened the door Dawn had slammed. Although his heart hurt for his little girl, he'd have to reprimand her for such bad behavior. Caleb and Molly held the screen door open while Jonas dragged the trunks across the hardwood floor of the front room.

"Oh," Molly said, coming into the room. "You've divided the rooms."

He'd done that during the winter. It's something Sarah had wanted so she could entertain visitors without always taking them into the kitchen. He didn't know if that was something Molly had put into Sarah's head or if he'd done it to Sarah himself by describing city homes that had large living rooms, dining rooms, and kitchens, all separate.

He dragged one of the trunks toward the bedroom. "Sarah wanted the rooms separate after we got the new cookstove." He felt a pang of regret that Sarah never got to see the finished room. So many things they discussed never came to fruition. He'd thought they had all the time in the world.

He looked up from his bent-over position when Caleb pulled on Molly's skirt and asked if she brought "canny."

Molly smiled down at Caleb. "You remember Aunt Molly bringing you candy?"

A dimple dented his cheek. His cotton-top head bobbed up and down.

"Well, I've heard your mama say that you can't have candy until after supper. Remember that?"

He clamped his lips tightly together, looked from side to side, and shook his head. Molly laughed and rubbed her hand across the top of his hair that was already rumpled and falling down over his forehead. "I'll bet you'll be ready for supper before long. Want to show me the kitchen?"

"Uh-huh." He reached for her hand.

"Yes, ma'am," Jonas corrected.

Caleb looked up at Molly with big, soulful blue eyes, the color of Sarah's, the color of Molly's.

Jonas knew Molly was trying to relate, but Dawn should be the one showing Molly the kitchen and where to find things.

He dragged the trunk into his bedroom, then came out and walked down to the closed door of the children's room. He thumped on it with the side of his fist. "Dawn, come out."

He waited.

She didn't.

He opened the door. Dawn sat on the floor at her window, looking out. "Dawn."

She glanced over her shoulder with a defiant look then turned away.

"You come out right now and behave yourself. We have a guest. You know how to act."

Her only movement was a shrug.

"You mind me now, Dawn. Come out and show your aunt Molly the kitchen."

"She's seen it before."

Jonas had never had to deal with this kind of behavior from her. He tried to keep his voice calm. "She hasn't seen it from the viewpoint of a cook."

Dawn stood and walked past him with downcast eyes. She walked ahead of Molly as she and Caleb followed. His daughter, who seemed like a stranger now, stopped at the doorway and gestured. "There it is." She returned to her room and shut the door.

Jonas tried to apologize. "I've never seen her act this way."

"I understand," Molly said and glanced at Caleb as if she didn't want to say too much in front of him. "I'm sure it's hard for a child to deal with a broken arm. Maybe later she will feel more like showing me the kitchen, along with Caleb. I could go ahead and unpack a few things."

He dragged the other trunk into the bedroom. Caleb followed Molly, looking her over with a mixture of curiosity and admiration.

Jonas apologized again when he took his few work clothes from the chest and realized Sarah's clothes were still in the closet and stacked in drawers. Molly said she would take care of them.

Dawn might be the one who was right in this situation. Molly was not her mama. Jonas was moving out. Sarah's things would be stored away. Molly would sleep in the bed where he and Sarah had slept. Was this right?

Should he have sent Dawn and Caleb to the city until Dawn's arm healed? But that wouldn't have been reasonable with Dawn's having a broken arm and being on medication. He had to stop thinking about what might have been and concentrate on what was. "I'll take my Sunday clothes to the children's closet. Wouldn't seem right being in church smelling like a cow or a horse." Soon as he said it, he realized some did smell like their animals.

"That's fine. Now, Jonas, would you like to see the presents I brought for the children?"

They left the bedroom. He started to set his stack of clothes on the sofa, then thought better of it. "I'll see them after I carry these out and take care of the horse."

Molly nodded. "Maybe Dawn will join us then."

"She will come out now," he said, pretending he had control of this situation. He thumped on Dawn's door with the side of his fist. "Young lady. Come out of there right now."

He held his breath for a couple of seconds. Suppose she didn't come out? She didn't need a spanking or harsh words. But she didn't need to be holed up in her room, either. They had to get through this somehow.

In the past, Dawn had been as eager for Molly to visit as Sarah had been. They had looked forward to Molly's laughter, presents, and talk about city life. Surely Dawn had not forgotten that.

He opened the door, and almost immediately Dawn came up to him. She stood like a sad little statue, staring at the floor. He wanted to take her in his arms and cry and say he knew—he knew. Her comfort had been in taking care of him after Sarah died. Sarah had taught her to cook many things. She swept and dusted and even had Caleb help with some chores until she broke her arm.

She stifled her emotions, like he had to do. "You were rude to your aunt Molly who has come to help out. I want you to apologize and behave yourself."

She obeyed, but it was obvious her heart wasn't in it. She spoke to the floor. "Sorry."

"It's all right," Molly said. "Now, maybe you and Caleb can show me where everything is in the kitchen. After your papa comes back, you can have your presents."

Jonas took a deep breath when he walked out onto the back porch. Caleb took to Molly. That was good. But set against Dawn's hostility, was that good enough? And was it good for Caleb?

"What's done is done, Jonas," he told himself while walking to the lean-to. He'd added this room for hired hands who sometimes needed to stay overnight during harvest season.

Now he'd be living like a hired hand.

He sat on the bunk and, with elbows on his thighs, put his hands over his face and bent forward. "Lord, I'm at a loss here. I don't know what's right anymore. Sometimes I feel like I'm two people being pulled in opposite directions. Most times I feel like half a person without my Sarah."

He raised his head and looked at the wooden-beamed ceiling, seeking answers. What he saw were dusty cobwebs.

He went out to bring his wagon into the barn and unhitch Mac. When Dawn was a toddler she had inadvertently named the horse after hearing the lyrics in "Yankee Doodle" about a man who went to town on a pony, stuck a feather in his hat, then called it macaroni. She'd gleefully called their foal "Mac-a-pony." Jonas and Sarah had laughed until they cried. "Mac the pony" was fitting for the McLeans' youngest horse.

At least in the barn he had something alive to talk to. "Okay, Mac. This is not forever. It's only for a few weeks—if she stays that long. I'll find someone from the mission house or an older woman who doesn't remind the children of Sarah. But it's good to have someone to take care of Caleb and do the cooking."

Mac snorted, and Jonas didn't know if that was agreement or not.

MOVING THE MOUNTAIN

After a few weeks Jonas could return to his house. Molly could return to the city, and he would appreciate her help of occasionally sending a dress for his daughter or some other feminine things. That's probably what Sarah had in mind anyway. Isn't that what aunts did for their nieces?

In the meantime, he needed to see what gifts their aunt had brought. Maybe that would bring a smile to the face of his young daughter who hadn't smiled in a long time.

∽

Molly pretended she didn't notice that Dawn sat in a chair at the table, unresponsive to what was going on. At least the young girl was going through the motions. Sometimes that's all a person could do. She knew.

Caleb opened a cabinet door. "A pot for corn.

"A pot for. . .um. . .beans."

Caleb pointed to a pan. "A pot for. . .eggs." He looked up. "And chicken." He made a chewing motion with his lips. "Mmmmm."

Delight bubbled up inside Molly. Caleb was trying so hard to please her. Yes, he needed her. So did Dawn, although she didn't know it. "Maybe we could have chicken for supper."

He nodded. "An' canny."

"Yes, you little scamp." She rumpled his hair again and his blue eyes shone. She knew he was more hungry for a woman's touch than for food. Molly wanted to shower him with affection, but she'd have to be careful. She needed his love and acceptance, too. How to give and accept that without driving a deep wedge between the boy and his sister, she didn't know.

Caleb opened a drawer. "A-p'ons," he explained.

"I'll wear one of those while I cook supper."

For an instant she let her hand rest on the soft fabric. Sarah had worn this. She unfolded it and was about to slip it on.

Dawn's voice stopped her. "That's my mama's apron."

Caleb gave his sister a mean look, then touched the apron. "You can have it."

"No, she can't. It's Mama's."

Molly's gaze shifted to Dawn, and her heart went out to the sad-faced little girl. "You're right, Dawn. This is a beautiful apron. Did your mama make it?"

Dawn's nostrils flared slightly. She averted her gaze. "Yes."

Molly pretended not to notice Dawn's distant attitude. She refolded the apron and returned it to the drawer. "I'm sure your mama would want you to wear it someday in your own kitchen."

Dawn said, "This *is* my own kitchen."

"Dawn!"

Molly breathed a sigh of relief to see Jonas standing in the doorway. She didn't know how long she could keep from taking the little girl by the shoulders, looking her in the eye, and telling her she knew exactly how she felt. But this was not the time, and that was not the way. Molly wanted to love her—did love her—and it hurt not to have that love accepted.

Caleb yelled, "Pwesents! Pwesents!" easing the tension.

He ran into the front room, took hold of the handle of the bag, and tugged, scooting it a little closer to Molly.

Molly picked it up, went over to the couch and sat down, then opened it. She took out a package wrapped in paper and held it out to Dawn, who stood against the door casing.

When Jonas cleared his throat loudly, Dawn walked over and took it. She sat in a chair and unwrapped it. She stared at the porcelain doll.

Jonas prompted, "What do you say, Dawn?"

She responded blandly. "Thank you."

"You're welcome." Molly had planned to tell Dawn she chose that doll because it reminded her of Dawn with its brown hair with golden highlights and light brown eyes. The doll reminded Molly of a Victorian princess in silk, adorned with lace and seed pearls, and she carried her own little parasol.

Molly decided not to mention the dress for Dawn and outfit for Caleb that were in her trunk. She knew from experience that toys and dresses didn't mean much when your heart was breaking.

"My pwesent now," Caleb said.

"Oh, you want a doll, too?"

He screwed up his nose and shook his head.

Molly laughed and took out three small boxes. Caleb jerked off the top of one. "Ohhhh." He took out a train car.

Jonas leaned forward. This interested him more than the doll. Dawn stared at the boxes. Maybe she would have preferred a train.

Caleb jerked off the other lids. Jonas explained that one was an engine and the one painted red was a caboose.

"Ca-booze," Caleb repeated and laughed.

Jonas sat on the floor and hooked them together, then Caleb took off with them across the floor. Molly thought that small turn of Jonas's lips might be a smile.

She had a present for him, but this wasn't the time.

"Well," she said. "Caleb wants chicken for supper. What about you two?"

Dawn remained silent.

Jonas spoke. "Sounds good to me."

Molly cleared her throat. "Um. Jonas, do you want to do the honors? I mean"—she winced—"chop off the head?"

She heard a groan from Dawn, but Jonas said, "Sure thing."

"And where do you keep your milk?"

This time Molly preferred that Dawn remain silent. But the girl spoke up. "The milk is in the cow."

Chapter 4

Jonas wasn't sure how to pray. He hadn't been sure for a long time. It wasn't that he blamed God for Sarah's death. He knew life was hard and people died. But during the past nine months he just didn't know how to face it all with a positive attitude.

He sat at the head of the table, trying to ignore the odor left over from the pan of grease catching fire. "Let us pray."

Caleb folded his hands beneath his chin. They all bowed their heads.

Jonas began. "Lord, we come to You needing Your help. You've blessed us real good and put a meal on our table. Especially, we want to thank You for Molly coming to help us out for a while. Bless this food, and may it help us be strong. Amen."

Molly looked over at Caleb, who'd insisted he sit beside her.

He smiled at her. "I want a 'eg, pwease."

Seeing Molly's surprise, Jonas quickly explained. "His favorite piece of chicken is the leg."

Apparently realizing Caleb wasn't too articulate with his *L*s, Molly's expression relaxed. She forked a chicken leg and laid it on Caleb's plate.

"Thank you."

He was being particularly polite, obviously wanting to please Molly. He needed a mother figure, but he'd lose it again when Molly left. For now, however, Jonas would accept about anything to distract his children from their loss.

Molly forked her chicken and held the plate out to Dawn.

Dawn took hers and curled her lip. "It's burnt."

Jonas didn't know how his sweet little girl could have become so vindictive. On second thought, he did. Although he knew better, he'd done his share of taking his frustration and loss out on a bale of hay he'd pitchforked into the barn. He'd given his cow and horse an earful while shoveling out the waste.

Caleb had openly cried for his mama. Jonas had been able to hold him and soothe his grief while his own tears wet his cheeks. Dawn had withdrawn and remained quiet, except at night when he heard her cry into her pillow.

But that didn't mean she could be disrespectful to Molly, no matter how burnt the supper might be. "It's just a little brown. I. . ." He cleared his throat. "I like it that way." It wasn't exactly a lie. He'd had no lunch, was hungry, and a raw chicken might taste good at this point. Since the grease caught fire, there was no gravy, but the mashed potatoes were good. Lumps were still potatoes. He was thankful there wasn't much one could do to ruin green beans taken from a jar.

Dawn's eyes said plain as day she knew that wasn't the most truthful thing he'd ever said.

"I've done better," Molly admitted. "I just have to get used to the woodstove."

Caleb confirmed that Molly could do no wrong. "I wike it aww," he said. But after a few minutes he said he was full. "Can I pway with my twain?"

"After you clean up your plate," Jonas said. He decided to steer the conversation to city life just to have Molly talk and the children listen. He should make an effort to involve her, act interested, and make her feel a part of things. "Um, Molly, you went to the city to live with your aunt and uncle when you were around Dawn's age, right?"

"A year younger." She picked at the dark crust on her piece of chicken that looked rather dry. Apparently, casual conversation wasn't going to be easy.

"Dawn," he said, "wouldn't you like to know what the schools are like in the city?"

She shook her head. "No. I don't like the city."

"You've never been there."

"I've heard about it. I don't like it. I like right here."

He felt apologetic and addressed Molly. "After your visits, Dawn would ask all sorts of questions about city life." He took a bite of chicken. The inside was fine, and he didn't want to insult Molly by peeling off the burnt crust.

Molly took a sip of milk, lifted her chin, and smiled. She began talking about the city as if nothing were amiss. "The schools have several classrooms and many teachers. Most people have small gardens, but they don't have to. They can choose to grow their own food or go to a store and buy it. There's the butcher shop where you can buy all kinds of meat. And there are grocery stores that sell vegetables and fruit. We can even have ice for our drinks and eat ice cream."

Dawn spoke up. "We don't have to go to the city for ice cream. I had some in town."

Molly's eyes brightened. "Oh, don't you just love it?"

Dawn shrugged. "It's okay."

Jonas studied his daughter. She had been excited about eating an ice cream sundae at the store in Poplar Grove. She had told her friends and discussed many times that she had vanilla ice cream with chocolate syrup, nuts, and a cherry on top.

Glancing at Molly, he saw the look of defeat in her eyes before she turned her attention to the one she could count on for a positive response. "Did you have ice cream, Caleb?"

His lower lip poked out and he shook his head, giving her that poor-little-hound-dog look.

Molly laughed. "We'll just have to do something about that."

Dawn piped up. "Don't take him to the city for that. He can get it in town."

Jonas both admired and sympathized with Molly's trying to draw Dawn into the conversation. She asked about school, friends, and interests; and Dawn's replies consisted of "Yes, ma'am; No, ma'am; Don't remember," or a shrug.

Finally, Molly gave up and addressed her questions to Jonas. "Could you teach me to milk a cow?" She laughed. "I'm not sure I'm ready for. . ." Her gaze settled on the chicken plate. "For. . .some things."

He figured she meant chopping off a chicken's head.

At least she wasn't overly sensitive about her ineptness as to their way of life. He wasn't exactly the greatest in the kitchen himself. "Sure," he said. "Dawn and I will clean up after supper while you get unpacked. Then we can have a milking lesson."

After supper, he delighted in watching Caleb, not listlessly playing at something, but enjoying the train and even making *choo-choo*, *chug-chug*, and whistle sounds.

Jonas had wanted to talk with Dawn. He washed a plate with the dishrag and laid it in the rinse water. "Are you trying to hurt your aunt's feelings, Dawn?"

"No." She swished the plate around in the water, shook it, and laid it on a towel. Her face turned toward him with a sincere expression. "I liked her visiting us, Pa. But she don't belong here now. Mama said I was s'pose to take care of you and Caleb."

"She didn't mean you were supposed to do all that she did. You're still a child, Dawn. You need to. . ."

What did she need to do? Have fun? Not do adult things?

She shook another plate and laid it aside. "Nothing's fun anymore. And Caleb's acting like she's his mama. That's not right. He shouldn't forget Mama."

Forget. If only Jonas could for one waking moment, maybe life would be easier. "Caleb needs Molly right now."

Her voice quivered. "If I hadn't broke my arm, he wouldn't."

If.

A lot of things would be different, if. . .

"We can't change what is, Dawn. We just have to do the best we can. The good Lord will get us through this. Can you be the sweet little girl I know you are to your aunt Molly?"

Dawn's hand stilled in the water. She didn't seem to be a child when she raised her head and looked through the window over the sink. Her words echoed what he so often felt deep inside. "I don't know."

~

Surely not!

Was she really supposed to do *that*?

Molly felt more aversion to touching a cow's underside than at the thought of chopping off a chicken's head.

Was she good for nothing, as Dawn's every look implied?

Jonas likely thought so, too.

At least Caleb, accompanied by a couple of hounds, was having fun finding rocks to put in his train car. Was there nothing else positive about her being here? Would there ever be?

While Jonas and Dawn cleaned up the kitchen, she had unpacked a few more things and laid out some dresses that needed ironing. Then it was time for her milking lesson.

Dawn called the cow into the barn, and Jonas set a pail under the animal. With her foot, Dawn scooted a stool up to the pail.

Jonas gave his first instruction. "Just don't get too close to the hind legs. Cows can kick."

Having no idea in how many directions the cow could kick, Molly moved the stool to midway of the cow, wondering if she had to crawl under there. Observing the knee joints of the cow, she figured the front legs kicked backward.

Dawn huffed. "You need to be close to the udder."

With open mouth, Molly stared at Jonas. Would he allow his young daughter to say such a word? He didn't react except to move the stool closer to it and sat down. "Here's how you do it."

She watched and heard the *squirt, squirt, squirt* of milk streaming into the pail. A big gray cat appeared, obviously accustomed to the stream of milk Jonas directed its way. Then the cat obeyed his, "Scat."

He stood. "Just squeeze and pull."

Rather than let him stare at her burning face, she sat. She reached out a hand, almost touched it but drew back.

Dawn snickered.

Jonas's eyes warned Dawn, but his dimple, like Caleb's, indicated he was stifling a laugh.

"Go outside and tend to Caleb," Jonas said to Dawn.

Molly wanted to tell Dawn her eyes might get stuck if she kept rolling them up toward the sky like that. Instead she faced the cow's side. Determined, she reached one hand out and grabbed.

"Both hands," he said.

She did, but groaned. "This is much too personal."

"It's just a cow who's going to get mighty grumpy if she's not milked. Now pump."

Pump!

Angry with him and herself, and the stinky cow in a musty barn smelling of odors she didn't want to think about, she tightened her grip and jerked. The cow protested, and she screamed.

She got a face-full and a dress-dousing at the same time. Coming from Jonas was the strangest-sounding throat clearing she'd ever heard. About ready to tackle a man instead of a cow, she jumped up and faced him, swiping her face with her hand and drying it on the side of her dress.

The look on his face was strange, too; but something about the way his brow furrowed and his gentle tone when he said, "You're supposed to aim at the bucket" eased her frustration somewhat. She felt like running out, but facing Dawn would be an added humiliation.

He sat on the stool and started pumping. Milk flowed freely into the pail. Molly marveled at that. Maybe the cow didn't like her either.

"That was fine for a first lesson," he said. "You need strong hands for this. That will come with practice."

What she needed more was a strong stomach and an iron will. She wasn't sure that would come. She watched until he finished the milking; then they walked outside.

"I see we got milk," Dawn said.

"Of course," Molly retorted as if she had done it, even though she suspected Dawn had peeked into the barn and knew who did the milking.

"I'll put the children to bed," Jonas said.

"Do you want me to bathe Caleb?"

"No, I'll wash him off."

"Tell your aunt Molly good night."

Molly knelt down, and Caleb hugged her.

She kissed his cheek and told him good night. In a fast getaway, Dawn had already reached the cabin.

~

Molly felt close to tears. She walked across the backyard, past the wooden swing hanging from a long rope tied to a branch of the big oak. She'd just had her first lesson in milking, and it was as big a disaster as the grease fire. At least she'd known to throw flour on the fire—the flour she'd planned to use for gravy.

Now she looked like she'd made gravy on her clothes after the milk combined with the dusting of flour on her black dress. She'd seen plenty of cows in her childhood but had never milked one. Her papa had done that chore.

Something seemed to catch in her throat at the thought of him. She'd never quite forgiven him for what he did. But she missed him. And Sarah.

Her gaze moved to the fields—some showing evidence of early planting, others waiting to be plowed—and to the grazing field for the horse and cow. The occasional mooing of cattle and the horse's whinny were replaced by insects coming out and having a party of their own, accompanied by the baying of a distant hound.

A silvery moon made an arc in the graying sky. A few twinkling stars appeared. Gray twilight began settling over the landscape.

Looking at the approaching darkness was like looking at her life. How quickly her concept of it had changed. She was to come here, be loved and accepted, then, like in a fairy tale, live happily ever after.

She should have known better. She'd believed in fairy tales when she was a child, and they never came true. She was a mature woman of twenty-four now and needed to face facts. Jonas asked her here only because he had nowhere else to turn. Dawn resented her. Caleb wanted her to be his mama, which meant he had another heartache in store.

But she couldn't leave her sister's family when they needed someone. She crossed her arms and hugged them when a sudden gust of cool air swept over her.

"There you are," she heard from behind.

She blinked away any moisture that the wind must have brought to her eyes and turned her face toward Jonas as he walked up. "The children asleep?"

"Caleb can hardly keep his eyes open. He doesn't want the lamp out before he goes to sleep. He wasn't that way before. . . ."

Molly realized Jonas had a hard time talking about Sarah. He looked into the distance. "Dawn's reading to him. She's allowed to stay awake longer, so she reads."

A slight hope surfaced that she might be able to reach Dawn through the books she'd brought from the city.

Her thoughts returned to Jonas when he said, "Sorry about the dress." His lips tightened, and his brow wrinkled. Apparently, Jonas wasn't about to laugh about anything, even if he thought it funny.

"I'll just throw it away. I don't like wearing black. I did it for appearance."

His surprised look made her realize he didn't understand. He couldn't, and this wasn't the time to explain it. Wearing black for her deceased husband seemed a mockery, like living a lie. Much of her life had been like living a lie. She'd hoped to escape that.

Maybe it wasn't possible.

"Oh, Jonas. I don't mean to make light of anyone's death. But, no matter what I wore, I mourned for Sarah over the past fifteen years."

After an extended thoughtful gaze, he nodded and glanced at the mess on her dress. "If you can't make anything out of the dress, you might tear it up for rags. We can always use cleaning cloths."

"Oh, I didn't think of that."

His voice was distant, sort of like the baying hound. "Well, you didn't need to in the city."

No, but her aunt's hired hands would have worn anything she discarded. But she didn't think it would sound right to ask if he knew any mountain woman who would want her milk- and flour-spattered, grease-stained mourning dress.

She should learn to be silent, like Dawn.

Only Sarah had seemed to enjoy whatever she had to say, no matter how foolish. And she'd been with Sarah so seldom. So seldom.

That reminded her of what she wanted to do. She reached into her pocket and drew out an item wrapped in a lacy handkerchief. She held it out. "I have a gift for you, Jonas."

His arm came up, bent at the wrist to ward her off as if she were a disease.

Chapter 5

You don't need to give me any presents, Molly. Really, I—"
Many times, Molly had been admonished to be grateful for what she was given and to appreciate gifts.

Now she recalled that Sarah had said Jonas was afraid her presents would spoil her and the children. But Sarah had seemed to love the presents. Molly hadn't taken the remark seriously. She'd heard mothers say their children were spoiled, but they'd smiled like that was an attribute. Had Jonas not liked her giving presents? In the past, that had been all she had to offer.

She felt a tremor in her hand and hoped her voice wouldn't reveal such. "Just. . .take a look."

She placed the item in his open palm. He tentatively opened the folds of the white handkerchief. He turned the small picture frame over. He stared, as if seeing a ghost. His face paled. "You—you did this?"

"No. I'm not an artist. You remember the photographer who was here, taking pictures after that mining accident and how the crowds gathered? Percy didn't like the man taking a picture of me and Sarah. The photographer promised to send the photograph to Percy. I've had it ever since."

"But. . .this is colored. . . ."

Looking fondly at the picture, Molly nodded. "After Sarah's death, I took the photograph to an artist. I had him paint Sarah's portrait and helped him choose the right colors for her face, hair, and eyes."

Jonas held the picture out to her. "It's. . .yours."

"No, Jonas. I did it for you. I have the black and white." He closed his eyes and swayed. The only thing she could think to say was, "It's oil."

He nodded. Night had come with a bright moonlight shining down upon them, making a silvery halo on his dark hair. He replaced the folds of the handkerchief over the frame.

His lips trembled. So did his voice when he whispered, "I don't have an image of her. Thank you." He choked out, "Good night, Molly."

The last thing Molly saw before looking away were the moon-silvered streaks of wetness running down his cheeks.

∽

The last thing he looked at before going to sleep was the little oil painting of Sarah in that pewter frame sitting on the crate beside the bunk. He whispered, "Good night, Sarah, my love," and turned the knob on the lamp. The flame went out, a thin trail of smoke disappeared in the darkness, leaving behind the faint odor of a burnt oil wick.

"That's my life now, Sarah." The slats creaked with the weight of his turning on his back. With open eyes, he felt the darkness, despite the moonlight shining through the windows. He closed his eyes against it and reminisced. His grandpa built that cabin, raised their son in it, and passed it down to Jonas. He and Sarah built a life there. That's where she birthed their children, the ones who'd lived and the ones who'd died. That's where she breathed her last.

So what was he doing in the barn while a city woman slept in their bed?

He reckoned he really couldn't have stood it if Molly hadn't given him the painting of Sarah. He would have marched up there and said he and his children would find some way to make it without his leaving them with a citified aunt.

But that gift touched something deep in his heart and made him think maybe—maybe Molly could do some good here.

Maybe she did understand grieving more than he gave her credit for. What she said about black clothes made sense. He just wished he could remove the black covering that had wrapped its way around his heart and tear it up for rags. But it just lay there, without producing any warmth at all.

~

The first thing Jonas said after hearing the rooster crow was, "Good morning, Sarah." He picked up the picture but didn't need to turn it toward the early morning light to see it better. He saw Sarah. "I know you loved your sister. She's given me this gift. I have nothing to give her but my acceptance. I'm really going to try."

Later, Jonas reminded himself of his resolve to try when he came home for lunch. When plowing on a clear day like this, he usually took his lunch with him and didn't come home till dark. The situation being what it was, he thought it best to look in on things.

With all the ruckus going on, nobody noticed him riding up. Something terrible must have happened. Birdie Evers was there and they all were gathered around something. He heard Molly wailing, "Oh, I broke it. I broke it."

"Don't worry, child," Birdie said. "There's more than one way to kill a chicken." Birdie picked up the staggering chicken with its head hanging to one side. After one terrific swing of her arm in a circle, the chicken's head was in Birdie's hand, dripping blood, while the body flopped all over the yard.

Molly wailed, "It's hurt. It's hurt."

"That's reflex," Birdie said. She held up its bloody head. "You don't hear it cackling, do you?"

Molly's hand went to her heart and she paled, moaning.

Birdie chuckled while Caleb, with his arms outstretched in front of him, ran around chasing the flopping chicken body.

Molly moaned. "I don't know if I'll ever eat another chicken."

"That's what the good Lord made them for."

Jonas tied his horse and walked closer. Dawn saw him first. She had that disgusted look on her face, shook her head, and rolled her eyes toward heaven. She walked over to him and spoke loudly enough for all to hear this time. "We had chicken last night."

Molly looked helpless. "Well. . .there's nothing else."

"Sure, there is," Jonas said. "Didn't Dawn show you the canned meat? We also have cured meat in the cellar."

Dawn turned and ran off across the yard, past where the cow was grazing and up to the top of a hill. Jonas didn't try to stop her.

Birdie seemed to size up the situation. He figured Dawn had likely told her how she felt about Molly's coming even before she arrived. The woman smiled. "There's more than one way to cook a chicken. Just clean out the innards and throw the chicken in the pot. You make dumplings, don't you?"

Molly's face brightened. "Yes, yes, I do."

By suppertime, Jonas was ready for a good meal, and he didn't mind having chicken two nights in a row. There were some folks who'd be pleased to have chicken once a week. He was blessed. He needed to remember that.

It was hard when he sat at the table and realized his son's shirt was streaked with blood and mud. Apparently he'd wrestled with the chicken after he caught it. Dawn's hair looked like it hadn't been combed since yesterday when Birdie had cleaned the children up for Molly's arrival. He tried to keep his eyes averted from the blood spatters and smudges on Molly's apron.

He'd rarely seen his children so unkempt. And he'd certainly never seen Molly with hair loose from her roll and hanging alongside her face. Nor had he seen her brow damp with perspiration.

Think something positive, Jonas.

After the prayer, Molly dished out the chicken and dumplings from the pot on the stove. She set each bowlful on the table. She looked on while Jonas took a big spoonful, blew on it, then poked it into his mouth. "Mmmm." He chewed and swallowed. "Good."

He realized he kept nodding too long. The chicken was fine. The dumplings done and tender. The taste was a little weak. He was trying to figure it out when Dawn offered the information. "The milk's still in the cow."

At least Molly could draw water out of the well.

Molly filled her own bowl and brought it to the table. After one taste, she laid her spoon down and put her hands on her lap. "Oh, I should have used milk instead of water. Can't I do anything right?"

"Well, yes," Jonas said. "You did pull the feathers out of the chicken."

Molly laughed, despite the flush that had rushed to her cheeks.

Dawn giggled. Jonas felt it was better to laugh than cry. Thinking better of either, he asked, "What are your plans for tomorrow?"

Molly seemed pleased that he asked. "Well, I mentioned to Birdie that I needed to get some plants or seeds for the flower beds out front, and she said she would bring some by in the morning, the Lord willing."

"That's one of her favorite phrases," Jonas said. "Never know what might come up to call a preacher or his wife away."

Molly smiled. "Yes, she was just passing by this afternoon on her way to see a woman who recently had a new baby. Birdie told me she has a flower business."

"Birdie's done that as long as I've known her," Jonas said. "She gets many of her plants from the forest, and she's ordered some from catalogs. Her business is on her porches and in her gardens. You can trade her a chicken for the plants."

"Oh, I can pay her."

"No, ma'am." He felt he'd said it too shortly. But a man had to take care of his own family. Helping out was one thing. But he couldn't take money from a woman. "I mean, anything that is needed here is my responsibility. I appreciate your help, Molly. But I can't take your money."

"Jonas, I still have a lot to learn in the 'helping out' area. I could at least make things. . ."

She focused on her bowl of thin-souped chicken and dumplings when he shook his head and said, "No, thank you." He regretted the look of defeat on her face and the look of victory on Dawn's. He attempted to ease the tension. "I know our life here can't compare with that in the city. But we have all we need. Dawn's school fees have been taken out of what I made teaching history and mathematics. And I have substituted a few times at the school in the mining camp."

After a sip of sweet tea, she put her hand to her throat. "I didn't know you taught school."

"I'm not the full-time teacher," he hastened to explain. "But there have been times when the cove has been without one; I've helped out. So have the pastor and Birdie. Now I'm called upon for a few special classes or lectures at Pine Hollow School, the one in Coalville, and sometimes down at Poplar Grove."

He suddenly felt like a chicken without its feathers, the way she looked at him. What did she think? That he was just an ignorant country bumpkin? He forced away the thought, realizing he had lumped her into one not-too-savory category of city women.

Changing the subject, he said, "Sometime tomorrow you might think on making sure the children get their baths and seeing their clothes are clean for church on Sunday."

⌒

Molly got the point and continued eating her supper. Jonas didn't consider her enough of a relative or friend to allow her to help out with money. Strange, money didn't seem to mean much to Jonas. It had meant everything to Percy.

She would just have to learn what she didn't know about taking care of his house and children. Dawn offered no information.

Caleb willingly helped with anything and everything, but a three-year-old's knowledge was limited.

That morning she'd cooked eggs and pancakes, cleaned up, and breathed a sigh of relief when Birdie had stopped by. She offered to teach Molly how to kill a chicken. That's when Jonas had ridden up and saw the fiasco of the poor chicken with its neck broken.

She'd spent the afternoon wondering where Dawn had run off to and keeping her eye on Caleb. At least he was content to play as long as she was in his sight. She spent a couple of hours fixing supper. It wasn't that she didn't know how to do things. She just didn't know how to do them without modern conveniences like she'd had in the city.

Then she tasted her chicken and dumplings. A feeling of inadequacy struck her. At least she realized what she'd done wrong. She'd used water instead of milk. But milk came from the cow, and the cow was in the pasture grazing. Was she supposed to take the stool and pail into the pasture?

Before Molly could ask, Caleb picked up his bowl and drank the remaining juice.

"Caleb, the polite thing to do is try to get all the juice with your spoon. Like this."

He picked up his spoon and slurped the air. He and Molly laughed.

With enthusiasm, he laid down his spoon. "Cookie, cookie."

Molly's laughter halted. She had not seen any cookies in the pantry. She hadn't thought to make any. Even if she had thought, there hadn't been time.

"We're all out of cookies," she said. "Tell you what. Let's make cookies in the morning."

"What kind?" Dawn asked, with a challenge in her eyes.

Molly had no idea. "What kind would you like?"

The girl shrugged. "I like muffins."

Besides glistening with dried chicken soup, Caleb's face glowed with a happy smile. "I wike everything." He spread his arms wide. "And canny."

Thank the Lord for that. Otherwise she'd be a total failure.

$\backsim$

After supper, Dawn said she needed to study her Bible verses.

"Fine," Jonas said. "Right after you gather the eggs."

He turned to Molly. "I'll clean the kitchen."

She protested. "I came here to help, Jonas. You must let me."

"You are, Molly. You haven't stopped since you got here, and you worry about not being able to do anything. If I were in the city, I'd be having trouble adjusting, too. You deserve a break." He spread his hands. "Sit on the porch or take a walk."

"But I have so much to learn."

He nodded. "You will. You only arrived yesterday."

Strange, she felt like she'd been here a very long time.

"And," Jonas said, "there's still your milking lesson tonight."

Molly relented. At least the kitchen was neat as a pin compared with last evening. She took a cup of coffee to the front porch and sat in a rocking chair to enjoy the cool evening before grappling with that cow.

Caleb played at her feet. The hounds came up, gave her soulful stares, then flopped on their bellies near the steps.

Molly thought about the high hopes she'd had when she arrived here. Now she wondered if she had come here with some mistaken idea of recapturing her own childhood or having her sister's children fill her own need to have children in her life. She did want to help, but she wondered if she was making more trouble for Jonas by her ignorance of life here. And Dawn wasn't warming up to her.

But Jonas had asked her to come here. If he didn't run her off, she would stay long enough to know if she was a help or a hindrance.

Her thoughts turned to Jonas's teaching history and mathematics. He said he'd taught last year. Did that mean he hadn't since Sarah died? He probably couldn't, having to look after Caleb. Maybe, if she could learn mountain ways, he would ask her to stay on after Dawn's arm healed. But she had a lot to learn. And fast.

A little later, while sitting on the stool and daring to watch her hands, she determined to point the other way, hoping the milk would then squirt into the bucket instead of on her.

She shouted for joy. "Miracle of miracles! It worked, Jonas."

He grinned, and the cow mooed.

Jonas gestured toward the cow. "She's pleased."

"Hallejulah!" Molly said. "I've learned to please a cow."

Chapter 6

On Saturday morning, Jonas arose early, fixed his own breakfast, and was ready to go into the fields by sunup. He didn't want to begin his day with a prayer that God give them wisdom and strength to face the day, then have it followed by a tension-filled meal with Molly and Dawn. And, too, there'd been no rain since last week's downpour. It would come soon, and he'd like to get the plowing done in the far fields on the other side of the creek. Already, bean plants and tomato vines made an impressive sight, and the cornstalks were at least six inches high.

Dawn came in, rubbing her eyes just as he gulped down the last of his coffee. "I'm getting an early start, Dawn. Molly should be up shortly to fix your breakfast."

"What about my clothes?"

Since she broke her arm, Jonas had helped her with her clothes that needed to be buttoned. "Molly can help you."

"I don't want her help."

"Then do the best you can, daughter." Turning from the defiance in her eyes and the tremble of her chin, he hastened out the back door.

For several hours he and his horse plowed, stopping only for a few water breaks. Dawn running toward him caught his attention. He wiped his sweat-covered brow with his sleeve. The location of the sun indicated it was midmorning.

His heart leaped with concern that something dire had happened. At least she was fully clothed, so maybe she allowed Molly to help her with the buttons on her dress.

"Pa. Pa."

With a prayer for patience, he waited.

"Miz Birdie brought Preacher Evers with her to visit."

"I'll be there directly." He and the horse both needed a break. A look at the plowed field and the smell of freshly turned rich earth brought a sense of pleasure that this had been a morning well spent. He crossed the creek, washed his hands and face in the cool liquid, and shook off the water.

Clothes hung on the line, swaying in the gentle breeze.

Jonas entered through the back door and realized everyone had gathered out front. He walked out onto the porch. Caleb was showing the pastor his train.

The women were taking plants from the wagon and laying them near the flower beds. Jonas shook the pastor's hand.

When the women approached, he saw that Molly held a plate covered with a napkin.

"Like I told Molly yesterday," Birdie said, hiking up her skirt a few inches to ascend the three steps to the porch. "Ira had a funeral up in the Black Mountains and needed to visit the sick. Otherwise, he'd have been here sooner."

"I understand," Molly said. "Come inside. We'll need something to go with these cookies. I just brought in the tea pitcher from the creek. It's nice and cold."

"Oh, I remember," Birdie said, following her inside. "You always brought tea for Sarah, didn't you?"

"She loved it."

Jonas wished he'd been more attentive to the things Sarah had loved. Some remarks she'd made had rolled off him like a leaf being carried off down the creek and disappeared.

They all followed Molly into the kitchen and sat at the table. Dawn obeyed when Molly asked her to get glasses from the cabinet. Molly poured tea for each of them. She handed Caleb a cookie; then the others took one.

Pastor Evers did the proper thing of expressing condolence over Molly's loss of her husband and praised her for coming to help Jonas and the children. Jonas watched Dawn's mouth open for a deeper breath; then she looked toward a window as if she'd rather be elsewhere.

That concluded, Birdie's eyes brightened and her tone of voice lifted as it did when she began talking about her upbringing in the city. She met Ira Evers at church when he was attending seminary.

"It's been hard," she said. "I was so much in love it didn't matter at first when he felt called to preach back in this mountain hollow."

Ira set his glass down rather hard. "Well, if it's so hard, why are you still with me, woman?"

Birdie gave him a sassy look. "Well, Ira. I reckon it's because I still love you. You know what the Bible says. It's better to live in an attic with a good man than a mansion with a quarrelsome one."

"I think you got the gender wrong there, Birdie."

She shrugged. "The meaning's the same, whether it says man or woman."

"Yes," he agreed. "I know exactly what that verse means."

She hit at his forearm. "Why, Ira. You behave yourself now."

Molly laughed with them. Jonas picked up his glass and drank from it. He and Sarah used to insult each other like that. It meant their love was so strong they could joke and laugh. Maybe they did it so they could then say they were just joshing, and they'd hold each other and. . .

He shook away the thoughts, determined to listen to the conversation the two women were enjoying, talking about the city.

Miz Evers said that cove life was so demanding, particularly for a preacher's wife who is expected to be available to everyone, she hadn't returned to the city over a dozen times in the past forty years. She leaned toward Molly with an expectant look. "What does the church look like that you attended?"

Caleb listened to anything Molly said. Even Dawn's eyes were riveted on her aunt who told about the big brick church with its stained glass windows that reached from the floor to the high ceiling. There was a pipe organ, a choir loft, carpet down the aisles, and cushions on the seats. There were classrooms for children in Sunday school.

Dawn spoke up. "I thought it was a sin to go to school on Sunday."

"It's not like regular school," Molly said. Dawn sipped from her glass, but Jonas knew she was interested. She liked school. She liked learning.

Molly talked about Sunday school being a place where they talked about the stories in the Bible. In the summertime, when school was out, they even had a week of Bible school. "If you do that here in the cove, I'd love to help."

Birdie became eager. "We could plan something like that. Most of the parents would spare their children for a few mornings."

Molly said, "Oh, I'd love it."

"I didn't think you'd be here that long," Dawn said, reaching for another cookie.

At about the same time, Pastor Evers said, "Are you biting off more than you can chew now, Birdie?"

They all pretended not to hear the impertinence in Dawn's voice.

"Would it hurt to try, Ira?"

"Where would you do it?"

Birdie grinned and gave Molly an "I won" look. "At the school." She turned to Molly. "Church services are held in the school." She poked Molly's arm. "Oh, that reminds me. Let me tell you about the preacher who was here before Ira. He was a circuit rider. Came through every two weeks or so."

Ira was already chuckling, although he'd probably heard it more times than Jonas had.

Birdie enjoyed being listened to. "This circuit rider would hold church wherever he could. Well, he came to the school. He would bring paper with the words of a hymn written on it. He would read a few lines of a hymn; then the people would sing them. He was reciting 'Amazing Grace' and got to the third verse. He squinted at the paper and said, 'I left my glasses at home and can't see the words.' The people started singing that; then they all burst out laughing."

Molly laughed, not as exuberantly as Ira, though. Ira amazed him, always laughing at Birdie's stories no matter how many times he heard them. After a hearty chuckle, Ira stood. "Let's give the womenfolk time to talk."

"Come on, Caleb," Jonas said. "Let's get a chicken for the pastor. There's extra eggs in the creek, too."

The pastor grinned. "Just what I hoped you'd say."

"We have plenty of canned peaches, Birdie," Molly said. "Let me trade you some for all those flowers."

Birdie slapped a hand to her chest. "Ira's been after me to make him a cobbler. We'd appreciate that. Sarah put up the best peaches."

"Dawn," Jonas called. "You want to come with us?"

"No, sir. I want to go look at the flowers."

He didn't hear Dawn make a reply when Molly said, "Figure out where you want them, Dawn. We'll plant them later."

Jonas told himself the distance between Molly and Dawn wasn't serious enough to talk to the preacher about. Dawn would come around soon.

"Okay, Caleb, let's go chase a big fat hen."

Caleb began a singsong chant. "Big fat hen. Big fat hen."

"You're doing a mighty fine job there, Dawn," Birdie said. "And with only one good hand, too."

"Thank you." Dawn continued moving the plants around.

Molly picked up a potted plant. "This is so unique."

"My trademark," Birdie said proudly. "Being a preacher's wife, I have to grow jack-in-the-pulpits."

Molly marveled at the green curved leaf making a protective covering for the "jack" in the center of the plant, resembling someone standing in the pulpit. "It's gorgeous."

"You'll have to come and see the rest of my plants." Birdie climbed into the wagon, set the glass jar of peaches beside her, and took the reins since Pastor Evers was holding on to the protesting chicken for dear life. They all said their good-byes.

Molly turned to comment on the plants Dawn had laid out on the grass. "Is that how you want them in the bed?"

"Mama did it this way."

"I'm glad you remember, Dawn. Your mama's beds looked beautiful. I hope I can do half as well."

"Me, too," the little girl said matter-of-factly. "You'll have to dig that up." She pointed at the weeds.

Molly had planted flowers and vegetables in garden plots, but she'd never dug up beds like these that were about three feet wide and eight or ten feet long on each side of the steps. She hoped her voice sounded braver than she felt. "I'll need. . .a hoe."

Jonas pulled a long green growth, then tossed it aside. "Most of these can be pulled out. I'll get the tools and dig it up." He addressed Molly. "You can rake the weeds out; then the planting can begin."

While Jonas went to get the tools from the barn, Molly took her stained black dress off the clothesline and went inside to change.

When she came out, Jonas approached from around the cabin, pushing a wheelbarrow loaded with a mattock, hoe, rake, and a small shovel. Caleb was examining a plant rather roughly. "Be careful with those, Caleb."

Dawn turned toward him. "Leave them alone," Dawn demanded. His lower lip poked out, and he looked at Molly for an ally, but she didn't want to say or do anything to cause Dawn to run off and sit on that hill beyond the pasture where the cow grazed.

"Caleb, while Dawn and I plant these, you can pick up the weeds and these papers and put them in the wheelbarrow."

Dawn carefully removed the newspaper from the root of a fern, not an easy feat with only one hand. Caleb eagerly picked up the paper and proudly deposited it into the wheelbarrow.

Molly told Dawn she could loosen the dirt around the edges of pots with the little hand tool so the blooming flowers would come out easily.

Jonas dug and tossed aside some big roots.

"I know these are ferns." Molly pointed at the small plants that had shiny round leaves. "And these are galax. Those tall yellow ones with dark centers are black-eyed Susans." She shook her head. "I'm not sure of the others."

Dawn named them all. The yellow-centered ones with white petals were oxeye daisies. She seemed proud to be sharing her knowledge of wild geraniums, sweet white violets, purple and lavender larkspur, bluebells, and bluets.

Caleb picked up a ball of roots. He began tearing apart the matted root structure. But his getting filthy was better than her and Dawn reprimanding him. Dirt would wash off.

Molly thought maybe she'd made a breakthrough with Dawn as they worked together. Maybe that was the answer. Letting Dawn know that she wasn't here to tell her what to do or try to take her mother's place. They could work together to make life a little easier.

Not until Caleb said, "I'm hungry," did she realize lunchtime had long passed. "One more plant and we can stop."

After planting the last bluet, Molly and Dawn stood back to appraise the work. "Unbelievable," Molly said. "In a few hours we have this colorful, blooming flower bed as if it had been growing for weeks." She smiled. "Dawn, we did well."

Dawn looked pleased.

"You know," Molly said thoughtfully. "Maybe we could do something with that old iron pot out back—set it by the back porch and plant flowers in it. What do you think?"

One look at Dawn's face and Molly knew she'd said the wrong thing, but she couldn't imagine what.

"You can't do that," Dawn said, her eyes pleading.

Molly stared. Then she remembered Jonas said an iron pot rolled back on Dawn's arm, breaking it. "Is it because the pot broke your arm?"

Dawn shook her head.

"Then. . .why. . . ?"

Dawn backed away as if fearful Molly might strike her. "When my arm is healed, I'm going to roll it up that hill. That was a special place for me and my mama. She was going to take the pot up there so we could build a fire in it when the weather was cold. We could be warm, and even cook."

Dawn's words had come fast, as if they'd been bottled up inside her for nine months. At least she was talking about her feelings. That might be good. Molly watched Dawn run around the cabin and knew the girl was going to her and Sarah's special place.

Caleb looked at Molly for a reaction. He never seemed too upset about what took place; he just observed. Molly asked for a hug, which he readily gave. How she wished she could envelop Dawn in her arms.

Dawn needed so much more than someone to cook meals, clean the house, and plant flower beds. But each time she thought they were taking a step forward, it seemed they took several backward.

I don't know how to help her.

~

Other than the undercurrent of tension from Dawn that evening, supper passed without incident. Molly brought a ham from the cellar in the hillside and served it, along with baked potatoes. She'd opened a jar of tomatoes, cooked fresh spinach, and made biscuits that were only a little too dark on the bottom. Dessert was a jar of peaches.

At bathtime, Dawn asked Jonas to wash her hair. He refused, saying if she didn't allow Molly to help her, then she would have to go to church dirty.

He knew she hadn't had a tub bath since Birdie helped her on Thursday. "You know you can't get the sling and splint wet," he warned.

With a towel, Jonas took hold of the hot water tank that heated on the side of the cookstove and poured it into the tub in the corner behind the stove for Caleb's bath. He added buckets of cold water and refilled the stove tank. Jonas sat in a chair to watch. He'd warned Molly that the boy liked to duck under the water and hold his breath.

Molly washed his hair with her shampoo that conjured up memories for Jonas.

Caleb went under to rinse his hair and came up so forcefully his hands went down and splashed water on Molly. They both laughed, although she gently chided him. Jonas reveled in the aroma. Dawn came up and stood beside him. Her voice sounded as wistful as he felt. "That smells like Mama. Like—like roses."

After Caleb was clean as a whistle and dressed in a nightshirt, Jonas stood. "We can tuck him in while water heats for Dawn. Then I'll say good night. I'm sure you'll want to bathe."

Molly agreed. "Oh, yes. I don't remember ever being so dirty in my life.

After I bathe, I can go to the bedroom, and you can take your bath."

"No, it will be way too late by the time more water heats."

"You aren't. . .going to bathe?"

"There's a place out there in the creek where clean springwater cascades down the rocks. Great place for bathing."

She rubbed her arms. "Gives me the chilblains to think about it."

"Me, too," he said. "So I'm not going to think. Just plunge right in. Anyway, the water here's not going to heat up for quite a while."

He didn't need to be thinking of Molly, letting her hair down and bathing in the tub. He missed the times he'd wash Sarah's back and she his. He would rinse Sarah's hair for her. Most times her hair smelled like lavender soap. Sometimes she used the special shampoo Molly brought from the city—that smelled like roses.

Jonas left the cabin for the night. He wanted to get his dousing in a waist-deep part of the creek before dark. He'd been in and out of that creek for much of his life. Cold water was a way of life much of the time in these mountains. One got used to that.

Was he ever going to get used to being without Sarah?

Chapter 7

Molly and the children smelled like roses.

Jonas wondered if he smelled like mountain trout. At least that would be better than wearing the odor of a barn that hadn't been shoveled out.

Dawn's brown hair, pulled back from her face and plaited in a fancy braid with a ribbon on the end, looked better than it had since Sarah died.

So far, Caleb's hair was still in place, parted on the side and swept up in a wave over his forehead. Jonas didn't expect that to last long. "You wearing new clothes, son?"

"New clothes," he repeated, patting the waistband of the navy blue short pants, held up by suspenders over a white short-sleeved shirt.

"You look mighty fine."

Caleb nodded, smiling broadly. Apparently, he'd been told that already.

"He's about to outgrow his other clothes," Molly said, as if she needed to explain why he was wearing the outfit she brought from the city.

Jonas felt remiss. "I've noticed that on Sunday; then it slips my mind during the week." Molly had mentioned that she brought clothes for both children, but Dawn was wearing one of her usual Sunday dresses. "Your hair is pretty that way, Dawn," he said, and she smiled. He doubted she could braid her own hair like that, even with two good hands.

Dawn studied him. "Pa, you're dressed up more than usual."

"Not really, Dawn. It's only a tie."

"You don't always wear a tie."

Surely Molly wouldn't think he wore a tie for her. But in a way, he did. He'd seen her fancy clothes before and knew she wouldn't be wearing that now-atrocious black dress that was a reminder of death. In fact, he'd rarely seen a person look so alive.

He mustn't stare.

She came right out and said, "Maybe that's what cold creek water does to a person. Makes him act different. You do look nice, Jonas. Almost like a city fellow."

Whether that was a compliment, he wasn't sure, but he said, "Thank you."

He'd never commented to Molly on her looks or attire when she visited, so he felt any compliments now might not be fitting. He acknowledged her with a brief nod. What could he say anyway? That she was going to be the talk of the cove in that purple dress with white frills in front and a cameo brooch at the high neck, and a purple hat with a cluster of multicolored flowers on one side. Her honey-colored hair was rolled into a neat, thick roll at the nape of her neck. A few curly strands hung down in front of her ears.

She rode the three miles in the buggy without raising her parasol, but after he held out his hand as a courtesy when she alighted from the wagon at the school, she raised the parasol. He soon realized any compliment he might have paid would surely mean nothing compared to what she received in the churchyard.

Birdie exclaimed loudly that she was the prettiest thing she'd ever seen, just a walking angel, and called others over to meet her. Many had seen her at the funeral, but that had been somber.

Women welcomed her. Men tried to keep their eyes off her, and children stared, wide-eyed and with their mouths open. They whispered to each other and stared more.

She smiled, said thank you, and that she was glad to meet them on a happier occasion. He heard Bessie Cameron tell her she was sorry to hear that her husband died.

"I'm just trying to make the best of it," Molly said.

"That's all we can do," Bessie said. "I know. I lost my Jim a few years back in one of them mine accidents. I moved away from the camp. Just couldn't stand it no more. So I can see why you'd want to come here. A change of pace is what we need sometimes."

Molly agreed. Pastor Evers rang the bell. Women and children moved together and went inside.

Jonas was aware of the difference in having Molly sit with him and the children as a family. During the past nine months, he'd felt lonely in church without Sarah. His wasn't like other families anymore. He felt different, like half of him was missing.

Caleb sat between him and Molly. Dawn sat on the other side of Jonas. Caleb kept looking at Molly while she sang. His son had accepted Molly. Jonas wished Dawn had taken to her. He could raise his son to be a man. But he couldn't give his daughter the woman's touch she needed.

When they stood to sing, he couldn't. His throat hadn't been able to handle the words after Sarah died. He listened to the words and tried to make them part of his beliefs, like rejoicing when they all got to heaven.

Men and women wore their finest to church. Women who had them wore hats. But Molly dressed nicer than all of them.

He remembered when Molly visited and brought a city dress that Sarah had worn to church and had been so pleased with. Had Sarah envied Molly? Is that why she had made him promise to let Molly help if anything happened to her? He'd never doubted Sarah's love, but now he wondered if she'd liked to have had a different way of life. Had she been like Birdie, who indicated she preferred the city, but stayed in the cove because she loved Ira?

The pastor's sermon was about having faith the size of a grain of mustard seed and one could move a mountain.

He read that scripture, and Jonas didn't hear much else after the pastor asked, "What's the mountain in your life?"

Jonas began thinking about his mountains. He knew a mustard seed was a tiny thing.

He reckoned his faith wasn't as big as he'd supposed before Sarah died. When things were going well, one could think he had a lot of faith and loved the Lord.

When one lost someone like Sarah, he knew he shouldn't, but he questioned why the Lord let it happen. He knew better, and if it was a test of his faith, he reckoned he had failed.

Mountains were all around him all his life. The only moving ones he knew about were landslides and mine cave-ins.

Contrition for such adverse thoughts brought him to a deeper level. He knew mountains that really needed moving were the burdens of life, and that required a spiritual remedy along with one's own efforts.

What were the mountains in his life? There were the ones that required his work such as plowing, planting, tending and harvesting crops while caring for a family. But that was workable. He didn't worry that his children wouldn't have what they needed.

His mountains had to do with acceptance of Sarah's death in a way that brought peace. Finding a way to help his daughter adjust to a life without her mother.

How was faith going to work those things out?

He'd always thought his faith was sufficient. But it had never been tested like this.

When they stood for the final song, Jonas wished he'd listened more carefully. Maybe the pastor had said something that would help. How could he get that faith? He'd always known—when he had Sarah.

What had his faith been in?

God?

Or Sarah?

⁓

There were no stained glass windows. Open shutters allowed the smell of fresh pine, rich earth, and fragrant flowers to waft in on the cool breeze.

The singing wasn't like in the city church, where everyone sang the right notes and all together. Here, each one had his own rhythm and sang from the heart. The voices weren't trained, but they sang to the Lord. The setting took Molly back to her childhood and made her happy. She sang out, too, louder than she would have in the city. There, she had to blend. Here, one could sing as she wished and not worry about holding a note too long or singing too loudly.

Before the preacher started preaching, he introduced Molly to the congregation, although she'd met some of them in the yard. He said she was Sarah's sister who had come to help the family. He made a point of saying that Jonas was happy about that, even if he did have to sleep with the animals in the barn.

He also told that she was trained in piano and voice and maybe would honor them with a song some fine Sunday.

After church the people were kind and complimentary, but Molly felt she didn't really fit in. She wondered if she should not have worn her fine clothes. But she didn't have any other kind.

Wearing a plain skirt and shirtwaist would be hypocrisy since she would not feel right in church without her finest. And clothes shouldn't matter. Some of these people were nicely dressed, like Jonas, Birdie, and Pastor Evers, for instance. A few men wore overalls, and a few women wore scarves instead of hats. She did not think less of them, so they should not think less of her.

Molly told herself it didn't matter. But joy leaped into her heart when a couple of women approached her and said they'd met her at Sarah's funeral. One was BethAnn Mason, who lived near Birdie. Her husband worked at a store in town.

Earlene Haynes lived a couple of miles up the mountains from there, and her husband worked as a clerk in the miners' commissary in Coalville.

The two women were direct opposite in looks. BethAnn was pretty, blonder than Molly, fair and petite; while Earlene was several inches taller than Molly, had a wholesome look, and hair dark as a raven's wing.

They each had children, a reminder to Molly that they were no older than she, but she was childless. Caleb and William, BethAnn's young son, sat nearby playing with twigs and making train sounds. Molly surmised that Caleb had told William about his new train.

Dawn stood several feet from Jonas, talking to a girl about her age. When Molly looked, they both turned their faces away. Molly suspected Dawn would be telling the girl about her.

She concentrated on BethAnn and Earlene, however. Both apologized for not being able to help Jonas more.

"Sarah was our friend," BethAnn said, her eyes becoming moist as she glanced at Earlene, who nodded. "We feel so bad," she said, speaking for them both. "We've offered to make up a schedule for different ones of us to watch the children if he'd bring them to our cabins."

"But you know men," Earlene put in. "They're so proud and not about to be beholden."

BethAnn's bare hands caught hold of Molly's gloved ones. "We're so glad you came to help Jonas."

"Is there anything we can do to help?" Earlene asked. "Tom wouldn't mind my coming there with a woman in the house. Otherwise, he thinks it wouldn't look fitting."

BethAnn was nodding. "We really want to help."

Molly related some of her mishaps in trying to conquer that cooking stove and the cow.

They laughed and Molly joined in. "It wasn't funny when Jonas and the children had to eat burnt chicken."

Earlene shooed away any concern with a movement of her hand. "I declare, hon, we can help you get the hang of any ol' woodstove. Anyway, Sarah got one of those newfangled ones. Jonas managed to have it brought in last year on the Coalville train, then brought down the mountain in a wagon. It's not often that the coal train brings anything from the city. But Jonas got it."

Molly wondered how he managed that. "Oh, you two are so kind—"

BethAnn groaned and her fair face reddened. "Not really." She sent a sly glance toward Earlene, who grimaced. "We were whispering in church—"

"As if that wasn't bad enough," Earlene said and rolled her eyes, much like Dawn had a habit of doing.

BethAnn nodded. "We wondered what we could do to make ourselves an outfit like you're wearing. Oh, not exactly the same, but grand like that."

"I didn't make this."

BethAnn waved her hand. "We didn't think so. But I have a treadle machine, and the store down in Poplar Grove where Tom works gets in some mighty fine bolts of cloth. Earlene and I trade off things. We both know how to use that machine."

Earlene was nodding. "If we could look at some of your outfits, we could come up with ideas that look. . ." She searched for a word.

"Citified?" Molly grinned, feeling a closeness to these two women.

Both women nodded, returning her grin.

Molly stuck out her gloved hand. "A deal."

BethAnn's expression looked like a child's with her favorite candy. "What day should we come?"

Molly had no idea. Before she could answer, Birdie joined them. "I have a bone to pick with you, Molly," she said. "Oh, you girls stay. It's something anybody can hear."

Chapter 8

That night, instead of going outside after supper, Molly washed Caleb and dressed him in his nightshirt. Afterward, Jonas said, "What's your Bible verse, Caleb?"

His eyes widened and his chest poked out with his deep breath. He looked at Molly when he answered, "Jesus swept."

Jonas chuckled and said, "Very good."

Molly laughed and hugged Caleb. "Oh, you precious boy."

His little face lit up like a candle on a Christmas tree, having pleased her.

"Okay, buddy. Time for bed."

"I'm not Buddy." His lip came out, and his eyebrows drooped. "I'm Caleb."

"Bedtime anyway."

Molly felt such joy at Caleb's every word and action. Even when he was displeased or tired, there was so much wonder in the child.

Each night since she'd arrived, Jonas had suggested she take a break and walk outside while he did the dishes, then put Caleb to bed. She couldn't imagine that Sarah would ever do such a thing. And didn't Jonas ask her here to do the things Sarah had done? But she wasn't really close family. Maybe bedtime was too intimate to include her. At least he had let her get the boy ready for bed.

As if reading her mind, Caleb reached for Molly's hand. "Mama come, too." Jonas must have detected the hope in her eyes. He nodded.

Jonas got on his knees beside the bed, so Molly knelt on the other side of Caleb, who placed his little hands beneath his chin, bowed his head, and began thanking God, then got into "God bless" everyone and everything he could think of.

Molly marveled at the love in the faces of father and son as they hugged tightly. She couldn't imagine more beautiful words than "I love you, son" followed by "I wuv you, Papa."

Caleb lifted his arms for her, and Molly eagerly embraced him, conscious of the warm little body and tousled hair that still bore the faint aroma of her shampoo. Caleb had his own sweet little-boy smell.

Caleb didn't want to let go, and Molly felt she would love to cuddle up with him on her lap. In that hug was a world of love where troubles tended to vanish.

Jonas insisted Caleb let go.

Molly looked over at Jonas. "Do he and Dawn hug?"

A troubled look clouded Jonas's face. "They haven't in a while."

Molly had the feeling that "while" was since she'd arrived.

"I don't know if I should force such," he said.

"Could it hurt?"

The way Jonas looked at her with such tenderness in his eyes touched her heart. Softly, he said, "Thank you."

Those two little words, said so sincerely, seemed to say he thought she might be of some value here after all. He went to the doorway. "Dawn, come tell your brother good night."

Molly stood aside, hoping Dawn would concentrate only on her brother. Dawn came stiffly into the room, reminding Molly of the years in the city when she'd felt stiff, but went through the motions of doing the expected things, learning to say the right words, and pretending all was well. She hadn't thought anyone cared that things weren't right.

Maybe they, like she now, just didn't know what to do to make it all right.

Molly breathed a prayer. *Oh, Father, please help Dawn revel in the love her little brother so freely gives.* She watched Dawn's face soften in the embrace. Molly barely heard Dawn whisper, "I love you," after Caleb said the words to her. Her eyes closed, and her chin trembled. Someday, somehow, that dam inside her would have to burst. She needed love so much.

Could she ever accept it from her aunt Molly?

The thought staggered Molly.

Did I accept it from Aunt Mae?

～

As soon as Dawn backed away, Caleb said, "Mowwy sing muh-bwee."

Molly's glance at Jonas revealed neither of them knew what he was saying. Was he trying to say "Molly" instead of "Mama"? She didn't remember how she thought when she was barely into her third year of life, but felt it could be confusing for a young child to hear a woman called by her name and "Mama." She understood the "Mowwy" but not the "muh-bwee."

Jonas's glance questioned Dawn, who shrugged and took on that defiant lift of her chin. She turned, saying, "I'm going to my place," as she left the room. Molly knew she meant the hill beyond the pasture.

Jonas tucked Caleb in. Molly sat on the side of the bed, gently stroked his forehead with her fingertips, and sang one of the hymns she'd sung in church. Soon, his smile relaxed and his eyelids drooped.

Molly walked into the kitchen where Jonas stood looking out the window, toward the hilltop that Dawn said was her place. He faced Molly when she said, "I love that little boy so."

"I know." His brow furrowed. "He's transferred the love he had for his mama to you."

"I keep telling him—"

Jonas's raised hand halted her words. "I'm not condemning you. I'm just concerned about his heart being broken again."

So was Molly. Caleb's heart and her own. She sat on the bench. "Maybe it's true, Jonas, that it's better to have loved and lost than not to have loved at all."

"Maybe?" He stepped over to the table. "Surely you can answer that."

Molly turned away quickly from his questioning stare. She looked away and headed for the cabinet door and opened it, hoping it would hide the flush she felt on her face. She thought of her love for several people, particularly Sarah. In spite of the hurt that loss brought, she was glad they had renewed their relationship and loved each other, however briefly. "Of course I know." She set the cup down a little too hard. "Would you like coffee? I...need to talk with you about something."

He pulled out a chair and sat at the table.

Molly poured the coffee and set the cups on the table, then sat opposite him.

She didn't know how he would react to what Birdie asked of her after church. Since she was here to help with the children, she needed his permission. She plunged right in. "Birdie asked if I would go with her to the mining camp school. She said the missionaries are coming this Wednesday."

Jonas nodded. "They come every two weeks if the weather is good."

"That's what she said. And she goes in case they can't be there. She said you could explain about the Bible verses."

After taking a swallow of coffee, he set the cup down. "Missionaries come from Virginia every two weeks, weather permitting. They make their rounds of the schools where there are no churches and teach Bible verses to children of all grades. Birdie does that at Pine Hollow School. The children recite their verses and get prizes. When they recite two hundred fifty verses by memory, they win a Bible. Fewer verses get them a book, a toy, or candy."

Molly huffed. "How can a child remember two hundred fifty verses?"

"Not so hard. The Twenty-third Psalm has six verses. I'm sure you must have learned that at an early age."

Molly nodded. "Oh, and the one about making a joyful noise unto the Lord. I had a teacher who sang it."

He brightened. "Dawn was trying for the Bible, but she...lost interest awhile back." He looked down at his cup.

"If I can remember, I can sing it while I..." She stopped and laughed. "While I burn dinner."

Jonas's cheek dimpled. Would that man never laugh? "If I sing it, I'll bet both Dawn and Caleb could learn it."

Jonas agreed. "Likely."

"And the Beatitudes," she said.

He added, "The Lord's Prayer."

Molly lifted both hands above her head. "And the Ten Commandments. Well, of course they can learn two hundred fifty verses. One a day or a whole psalm in a week."

Jonas looked almost happy. "And they don't have to recite all two hundred fifty at one time. They recite what they've learned during the two weeks."

Molly was so excited. "And you know, Jonas, it wouldn't hurt me to brush up on what I learned years ago. If I'm going to teach a. . ." She stopped at seeing his surprised look. Then she remembered—like Dawn said, she wasn't going to be here that long.

That must be why Jonas suddenly looked puzzled.

"Never mind," she said. "I'm getting way ahead of myself. Is it all right if I take the children to the mining school on Wednesday? Birdie said she might even turn that job in Coalville over to me every two weeks."

"I think that would be a wonderful thing, Molly. Dawn became acquainted with some of the children there when she and Sarah sometimes went with Birdie. Dawn was afraid she would forget her verses before Birdie had time to listen at Pine Hollow."

"Oh, thank you," she said. He rose from the chair. When she said, "Another thing," he sat again. "BethAnn and Earlene want us to exchange visits. Is that all right?" She didn't care to reveal their reasons. That might sound like foolishness to him.

"Good," he said. "It's good you're making acquaintances. Being a part of the community."

"Yes, I would love to have friends. Oh, but I won't neglect the children. Both women have children, and BethAnn has a boy Caleb's age."

"Yes, I know. They used to visit." He took a deep breath. "Anything else?"

"Well, just one. Is there a pencil and paper around? I'd like to make a few notes."

"There's some in the bedroom closet in a box." He stood. "I'll get it."

He returned with a box and rummaged through it. "These are some of my papers that I use in teaching the history class. Some of Dawn's school papers are in here, too. Someday she may want to see what a good student she was."

He found a pad of paper and a pencil, then returned the box to the bedroom. She got up to pour herself a cup of coffee. "Would you like another cup?" she asked when he returned.

"I'll pour myself another cup and take it to the lean-to. It's almost dark, so I may have to yell for Dawn to come home."

Molly walked to the window and saw the young girl walking toward the cabin, her head bowed. She kicked a small stone. "She's coming."

Upon leaving, Dawn had run from the cabin, across the pasture, and up the hill. When returning, she meandered.

"Jonas," Molly said thoughtfully. "How do you have enough faith to move a mountain?"

She wondered if he thought she'd asked a foolish question. He didn't answer readily. Finally he said, "That's something I want to study on tonight."

Jonas thought on it. The brightness of Molly's eyes. Her resemblance to Sarah, yet so different. Sitting at the table, talking over things was like what he and Sarah used to do. Sarah's talents were taking care of the home, wanting many children. She had finished high school but wouldn't have considered teaching, other than teaching the children at home. She'd helped Dawn with Bible verses when she'd first started learning them.

But he needed to think on Molly's question. It involved belief in Jesus as God's Son who died for the sins of mankind, who was resurrected and alive. Faith was believing God's Spirit dwelt within those who believed. It involved repentance, obedience, hope.

He'd thought he had it. But now that God hadn't let life go the way he wanted, how much faith did he really have?

He turned to the concordance of his Bible. Faith. He read that faith was the substance of things hoped for, the evidence of things not seen.

How could he return to a childlike faith?

He couldn't. He needed an adult faith, based on the Word of God, not earthly circumstances. He'd believed God gave Sarah to him, and his children. He was supposed to believe God had a purpose and plan in all that He did.

Lord, I've not given my hurt and anger to You. I've seen men and women change their way of life when they come to You. I've seen healings beyond what a doctor can do. I haven't blamed You when I've known of a man thrown from his horse and he died out in the woods before anybody could get to him. I didn't blame You when there was that mud slide and the Hankins' cabin went down the side of the mountain. I didn't blame You for that barn burning. Or when Jeb got drunk and shot a man over a horse deal that wasn't fair. Not even when my pa died in the mine accident. But I've blamed You that Sarah and our little baby died.

Your Word says we live in a fallen world. One in which Satan rules. But You're always with us. You don't give us more than we can bear. How Molly can be an answer to our family's needs, I don't know. I don't understand. And I've fought that from the time Sarah asked for it.

A lot of that was based on my dislike of Mr. Pierpont and knowing how some city folk look down on some people just because we prefer life in the mountains. Lord, I don't always understand Your ways. But I know You have a plan and purpose for those of us who believe in You and try to live right. Help me accept what You bring my way. And if I make mistakes in my decisions, like bringing Molly here, work it out for us. Give me understanding to know what to do and what to say.

Chapter 9

The next morning, Jonas still wondered. Where was the line between keeping one's distance and acceptance? He might try conversation, like he and Molly had last night. Since Dawn wasn't offering any help, he might try that instead of running off to plow by daybreak.

Molly came in from the creek with eggs for pancakes when Dawn rushed up to the kitchen door, all excited. "Pa, baby chickens have hatched. I counted eight."

Caleb got up from the kitchen floor where he was playing with rocks representing coal he would haul in his choo-choo train. "Chickies," he said, heading for the back door.

"Just a minute, son. That hen might flog you if you get too close to her little ones. Here, let me take you." Jonas picked him up. Before he could ask if Molly wanted to go, she dropped the big spoon into the bowl and rushed to the door, excitement all over her face.

Dawn opened the door of the chicken house. The hen and little ones went out into the wire pen. Molly gushed. "Oh, look at those adorable fuzzy little balls peeping like that. Aren't they beautiful, Caleb?"

He began saying he wanted a chickie. He wiggled, and Jonas put him down. Upon seeing Caleb approach, the hen squawked and spread her wings. The little ones ran underneath. The hen's wings came down and covered them protectively. She sat as she had on the eggs before they hatched.

Caleb kept pulling on his papa's pants, saying he wanted to hold a chickie.

"The mama hen doesn't trust us yet. We'll just walk on by. When she sees we're not going to hurt them or take her babies away, I can pick one up and let you hold it."

"Oh, I want to hold one," Molly said, looking as eager as Caleb.

"Have you never seen baby chickens before?" he asked in wonderment.

"Oh, yes. My aunt and uncle took me to fairs and I've held them. They're so soft and sweet. But, Jonas, how did this happen? I mean, every evening Dawn brings in the eggs for you to take to the creek. How do you know which ones have yolks in them and which ones have chickens?"

Jonas had tried so hard not to laugh at her. But this one started low in his belly, rolled around, reached his throat, and there was no controlling it. If one must laugh, it might as well be a big one. He'd had only shallow laughs for such a long time, this one felt odd in his stomach, like pulling a muscle.

The way Molly lifted her chin, tolerating his laughter, made him laugh even more. He looked at Dawn, who had her hand over her mouth, and her shoulders were shaking.

"Sorry." He issued a couple more quick sounds still left inside him. "That just struck me so funny."

"Good," she said saucily. "It's about time you laughed, even if you have to make fun of me to do it." She hurried over to Caleb, who was trying to open the door to the henhouse. She helped him.

The rooster went out, strutting like a proud papa.

They all went in. "I don't mean to make fun, Molly."

"Laughter's good, Jonas. I've wanted to laugh and cry about my inept-ness. I mean, if it's funny, it's funny. Why run around all solemn with a mule's face?"

Was that how he looked to her?

But she wasn't looking at him just now. Her gaze swept around the chicken house as she tried to avoid the droppings on the floor and looked up at those roosting. "So that's where they lay their eggs."

"Sure is," Jonas said while Caleb ran around chasing chickens and Dawn stepped inside. "Each one usually lays one a day."

She looked around, puzzled. "Where are all the roosters?"

"He went outside when you opened the door."

"You have only one?"

"That's all we need."

"Well. . ." She looked around again, and finally spoke in a low tone. "There are a lot of chickens in here. Doesn't he get—you know—tired?"

Jonas felt it coming again. Why try not to? He laughed heartily. He wiped the moisture from his eyes. The Good Book said there was a time to weep and a time to laugh. He felt like doing both. Weeping because he hadn't laughed in so long. Somehow it felt like a release, as if he'd like to follow it with weeping. Like there were things stuck deep inside him that needed to be let loose.

"I'm sorry. It's not that funny."

She stood with her hands on her hips, but he got the impression she en-joyed seeing him laugh. He supposed that was better than the mule's face. She shrugged. "I'd like to see you in the city trying to use a telephone."

He leaned back, pretending to be insulted. "Beg your pardon, ma'am. I know about city ways. I did go to the university." He grimaced. "But to be honest, the first time I talked into a telephone, I yelled as if trying to force my voice into the next county. Believe me, the laughter of my peers was torture to a young moun-tain man trying to fit in."

"Well, when you're finished, I'd like to know about the poor rooster. How often do you have to get a new one?"

He emitted a few spurts of laughter between explaining. "A hen doesn't have to have a rooster around to lay an egg. She does it all on her own."

He knew she didn't believe him. "Then why have a rooster?"

He lifted a finger. "Ah. The rooster is only needed to fertilize an egg. That's where the baby chickens come from."

"Well," she said. "Get ready to laugh again because that brings this discussion back to my first question. How do you know which eggs are fertilized?"

"I don't," he said. "But the hen does."

She looked skeptical.

He explained. "I don't know how the hens know, but they do. They make a nest for themselves, lay the fertilized eggs in it, and sit on them to keep them warm until they hatch."

"Isn't that amazing?"

He'd taken such things for granted as far back as he could remember. For an instant, however, he was seeing this through her eyes. "Yes," he said. "I suppose it is amazing."

"So, if I gather eggs, I would take the ones which a hen is not sitting on?"

"Yes and no. I let the hens sit on the fertilized eggs so we can have new chickens in the spring to grow up and lay more eggs, and of course grow them for trading and eating. Little chickens might not survive the winter, so we can take even the fertilized eggs then."

"Okay," she said. "You can tell me when you have enough new chickens; then I can gather the other eggs."

"I think you're beginning to understand."

She smiled, and he smiled back.

It's all right, he told himself. *She's my wife's sister.* He turned toward the doorway. "My stomach is yelling for some of those eggs and pancakes."

The tension had lessened for Jonas. If his daughter was ever going to accept Molly, he needed to set the example. He had no business avoiding her when all she wanted to do was help.

He stuck around the kitchen and even turned the pancakes. "Just helping," he said.

"Oh," Molly said in her sassy way. "Are you trying to say you're tired of that charred flavor?"

"It really hasn't been so bad."

"I will learn," she said.

That was a lot like Sarah. When she put her mind to something, she did it. "I'm sure you will."

While they ate, Dawn gave Caleb a verbal lesson on how to handle baby chickens. She would take him out after he ate. That resulted in his having to be warned not to poke an entire pancake into his mouth.

"You two can water the flowers, too, after you see the chickens," Molly said. "Now, Caleb, you mind Dawn."

MOVING THE MOUNTAIN

Instead of rushing off to work, Jonas started clearing the table and putting the dirty dishes in the dishpan. "I think I've been remiss not to help you more, Molly. I'm sorry. You've had to find your way around, and Dawn hasn't been any help. I haven't really known how to approach this and didn't think it right to say you have to do things a certain way."

"It's all right, Jonas. We've all been feeling our way through."

"Is there anything I can do or you need me to explain anything to you?"

Molly laughed lightly. "I'm glad you asked." She tilted her head to the side. "You can tell me how to cook, clean, raise children, feed a pig, and get an egg from a chicken."

He began nodding. "I get your point."

She cleared away some of the dishes. "But like I told you last night, I have help coming this week, and I'll learn all those things. Like you've said, it takes time."

"In the meantime, I can help a little more around here. Believe it or not, I did help Sarah."

"I know," she said. "She told me."

That was remarkable.

A silence hung between them for a moment. He saw the look of sadness cross her face that matched the sudden sinking feeling he had in the pit of his stomach, talking about Sarah in the past tense.

"Jonas, I never had to cut wood, kill a chicken, or handle a woodstove. After marrying Percy, I planned parties, volunteered at the hospital, told others what to do. I did some needlework. I continued with voice and piano lessons. After a while, I began taking in piano students."

Something tightened in Jonas's stomach. A few days ago he hadn't wanted Molly here. Now he wondered if she decided the tension was too great between her and Dawn. That she needed to leave.

But for a few minutes, she had taken his mind off his loss. She made him laugh. Caleb loved her. Dawn needed her, even though she didn't know it yet. Sarah's friends took to Molly. Birdie liked her. He should get to know Molly. She was his Sarah's sister.

With an elbow on the table, he placed his forehead in his hand. "I'm sorry I couldn't tell you how Sarah managed the household chores, took care of the children, or got meals on the table at the right time."

"I know," she said. "I'd like your opinion of something. I'll be right back."

"Would you like more coffee?"

He poured the coffee. She returned with a piece of paper, so he sat.

"I made a schedule for the work to be done."

He stared. She wasn't talking about leaving. She was planning how to do more.

He looked at the schedule.

Wash clothes on Monday.
Iron on Tuesday.
Mend on Wednesday.
Sweep on Thursday.
Scrub on Friday.
Bake bread on Saturday.
Church on Sunday.

When he was silent for a moment, she asked tentatively, "Any. . .suggestions?"

"Just one that might make things easier. Sarah used to cook the big meal at noon, and leave leftovers on the table. We could come in and grab a biscuit or corn bread anytime, and have a light supper. That way the house wasn't so hot with the fire going all day."

She exhaled like a weight had just been lifted. "Oh, I like that. Cooking is not my long suit."

She tapped the schedule. "Of course those aren't the only things I will do. But that sort of organizes things. I'll listen to the children say their Bible verses on Wednesdays." He detected the uncertainty in her voice. "And I don't need to wash all the clothes this coming Monday since I did that Saturday morning. I can plan the Bible school when Birdie comes by today."

Jonas could see her interest lay not in housework, but in teaching. He complimented her on the schedule. "Well, one doesn't have to stick to a schedule avidly. I plan to plow but sometimes rain prevents it, so I change plans."

Her schedule looked good on paper. He told her so. "Sounds like a good idea."

"I can't really take the credit. It comes from a song." She began to hum the song.

Jonas knew it.

Her pretty blue eyes gazed at him tenderly. He smiled. He thought her face was more tanned than when she'd come a few days ago. Maybe that's what made her hair seem lighter and her eyes a clearer blue.

Realizing he must be staring, he took a last gulp of coffee and stood.

Dawn and Caleb came into the kitchen.

Jonas looked at his son. "Caleb, let's gather these ham bones for Lad and Lassie."

Molly's eyes questioned.

"The dogs," he said. "They're. . .twins."

He liked to hear her laugh. Now that laughter had returned to his household, he rather yearned for it.

Chapter 10

Almost all day on Monday, Molly and the children dug potatoes, pulled onions, and picked the biggest squash to put in the cellar for seeds and for supper.

Molly heard an "Ohhh" from Caleb.

He was holding a little green tomato. When they all looked, he tried to put it back on the vine. Molly held back any laughter since his little face clouded like he was about to cry. He'd been told not to pick little green ones.

"I just touched it," he said.

Molly nodded. "Sometimes they just fall off. But that looks like a really fine one for lunch." She smiled and he brightened, then put it in the basket with the other vegetables.

Dawn hadn't made any adverse remarks all day, and by evening Molly doubted anyone had the energy for negativism.

They all went to bed a little earlier than usual, and Molly felt she hadn't slept so soundly since arriving in Pine Hollow. She did recall hearing a steady rain during the night that had been soothing.

She tried to rid herself of that groggy feeling with a cup of coffee while looking out the kitchen window, thinking she'd wake up by going to the creek for breakfast food. Then she saw Jonas, with bent head covered by a wide-brimmed hat, sloshing his way up to the house.

He opened the back door, shook the water from his hat over the porch, took off his jacket, and hung them on a peg. She had to smile at the pleasure on his wet face as he held out a basket. "Breakfast," he said.

She laughed. "You must have known I had in mind to feed you biscuits only."

"Crossed my mind," he said and smiled.

He poured himself a cup of coffee while she made breakfast. He walked over to the table and looked at her sheet of paper.

"Ironing day," she said. "I'm glad the weather cooperated Saturday and dried all those clothes."

Jonas looked up. "I'll take the children to the barn. You probably need a break." Just as she opened her mouth to protest, he added, "Sarah used to say for me to take the children out and give her a breather. Especially on ironing day."

Molly appreciated his thoughtfulness. As soon as she began ironing, she was particularly grateful not to have Caleb underfoot when she needed to move the handle from one iron to the other on the stove.

As time passed, she relished the hours alone, thinking, absorbing her surroundings. She'd been so busy, so tense, so concerned about caring properly for the children, then having Dawn's resentment, Jonas's distance, and Caleb's possessiveness.

She could understand Sarah's needing a break. Sarah would have done many chores that Molly hadn't yet learned. Besides that, she had pregnancies and miscarriages. No, Molly knew she had no room for complaints.

As the day dragged on, she began to miss them. A loneliness settled around her. She'd come here, determined to immerse herself into this family's life and help ease the pain of losing Sarah.

Things hadn't happened quite as she wanted or expected. She'd come to know this family in so many ways. She couldn't live with people, sleep in their bed, have responsibility of their home, touch their animals, watch their chickens being born, or bring their milk with her own hands without becoming absorbed into that family.

She'd observed a man pine for his wife, struggle with his faith, care about his daughter's withdrawal, try to carry on in spite of all that, plow his fields, mend his fences, care for his cattle, encourage her, eat burnt food without complaining—seeming to think some of her ineptness was not a matter of ridicule but amusement—and ultimately ease tension by laughing. He kept hoping that he, she, or time would make a difference in the way they all felt about their loss. He was trying to go on with his life, even leaving his home and living in the same building as his animals in hopes of accomplishing something.

She supposed he was rather. . .remarkable.

He'd begun to mention that she did things like Sarah had. They both had been concerned about Caleb's attachment because he needed his mama so much. Was Jonas in danger of the same kind of attachment?

She thought of how long it takes to really get to know a person. When Percy worked as bookkeeper for her uncle, she would pass his office and see him working on books, sometimes even late at night.

After Uncle Bob brought his new bookkeeper, Percival Pierpont, to dinner, Molly thought she knew something about him. After that, he took her to restaurants for dinner, to the fair, to a horse race. During the three months they associated with each other, she supposed she spent the equivalent of forty-eight hours with him, including the couple of times he managed to sit with them in church.

Three months had seemed long enough to know a person. After all, her uncle had known him for several months before inviting him to dinner at their home. But when she counted the hours, they were fewer.

Here, spending all the hours of the day with a family was getting to know them—not eating out, having fun at a fair, rooting for a horse, or sitting in church.

No, getting to know a person wasn't what one observed in public, but what went on in their everyday lives.

She'd learned that the hard way.

She'd learned more about Jonas and his family in a few days than she had about Percy in a few months.

Around noon, when she called them in to eat the meal she'd had time to concentrate on, Jonas commented that it was quite tasty. She'd prepared mountain trout that swam into the trap Jonas rigged up in the creek. She'd baked bread, made a sweet potato pie, and fixed fresh spinach from the garden.

Dawn even made the comment, "It's not burnt."

Molly took that as a compliment and felt quite pleased with herself. "I discovered that less heat and more time makes for a better meal." Her pleasure turned to chagrin. "Oh, I don't mean that I need to be alone. Oh, my, no. I missed all of you today. I...oh, dear."

Jonas chuckled. "Around cooking time is when Sarah shooed us all out of the kitchen. That's one reason she wanted the partition separating these two rooms—to get us out from under her feet. Cooking and keeping a little one away from the stove's not easy. Believe me, I know. Especially during the winter months when we have the stove and fireplace going at the same time."

Molly looked at the fish on her plate. Good for her. She'd managed to remind him of Sarah again. Would someone ever like her for herself?

～

The rain let up for a while, and from the kitchen window Molly watched Jonas, Dawn, and Caleb shovel straw and waste into a wheelbarrow. Jonas rolled it to the newer compost pile near the older one that was fertilizer for the gardens and fields.

The rain had cooled the air somewhat, but she felt hot and sticky from the day of cooking and ironing. Dark clouds rolled in again and a downpour began. It looked to her like one that would fall hard and vanish quickly.

A little later, upon hearing laughter, she peered out the kitchen window again. With a gasp of surprise, she ran to her room to grab her rose shampoo and several towels. She dropped the towels near the back door, then rushed across the porch and down the steps. Not only would she get a bath, but she wouldn't have to scrub her shirtwaist and skirt as hard as on wash day. With a squeal of delight at the deluge, she joined her temporary family, exclaiming, "I've gotten wet plenty of times, but never had a rain bath before!"

"Not as cold as the creek," Jonas said.

She'd never bathed outside or fully clothed. But it was delightful. They all splashed around, washed their hair, lifted their faces and drank the rain. Laughter was the outstanding quality of the hour. Molly gave permission for Caleb and Dawn to make Lad and Lassie smell like roses.

After drying off on the thirsty towels, they changed and, having worked up an appetite, had a supper of their choice from beneath the tablecloth, which included freshly baked oatmeal-raisin cookies.

Jonas had smiled upon looking at the table covered with the cloth. "That's what Sarah used to do."

Jonas said the children couldn't go back outside and get into the mud. "You two can read or play games. How about checkers?"

Caleb shook his head. "Meow."

Even Dawn joined them in the front room. Molly listened to Jonas's explanation of "Poor Tom," although she remembered having played it years ago with Sarah and other children.

Caleb was first to be the cat. He got on all fours and meowed. First Dawn, then Jonas, patted him on the head and said "Poor Tom" three times without laughing. When he came to Molly, she'd already felt the laughter bubbling up at his antics of a cat chasing a rat. She laughed at him.

Dawn's acting like a cat getting milk squirted into its mouth was hilarious, particularly when she shook her head so vigorously her hair covered her face. Then it was Jonas's turn. The sun had lightened his hair that looked golden-brown against the darker roots. She quickly repeated "Poor Tom" three times and he moved on.

When she patted his head, she wasn't even thinking about his catlike antics. She'd never before touched his hair. Jonas was the only one who could make no one laugh, which meant he was the loser unless Molly made no one laugh.

Molly didn't expect Dawn to laugh at her and wondered if she'd even pat her head and say "Poor Tom" at the appropriate time. Before Molly could get on all fours, they were already in hysterics when her knees got caught in her dress. Dawn couldn't hold back her giggles when Molly had trouble moving from one person to the other on all fours. She didn't think her restrictive movements were catlike but had no doubt she looked funny—ridiculous, really.

Molly had not felt so happy and pleased since she arrived. She was being accepted.

She hoped Dawn might start a conversation after supper while the two of them cleaned up the kitchen. She felt as though she'd accomplished something today, put a good meal on the table, and was beginning to know how it felt to be part of a close, loving family.

She could even imagine having a man like Jonas for a husband, a loving child like Caleb who kept every moment filled with joy, energy, and challenge, and even a daughter like Dawn who would be fine. . .with time.

She lifted her face from the dishpan and looked beyond the window. She could almost see the corn growing. The gardens, pasture, fields, and hills looked fresh and clean after the rain. The bean fields glistened with silver droplets.

A good feeling of contentment welled up inside. Absently, she began to hum a tune from a faraway memory.

A plate crashed to the floor. Molly jerked around. The look on Dawn's face was as broken as the pieces of china scattered on the hardwood floor.

Dawn's chin quivered and her eyes sparked with misery. "Don't you dare hum that tune! That's my mama's song." She turned and ran into her room, slamming the door.

Jonas came from the front room. "What happened?"

"An—an accident."

Molly was thinking a more apt question might not be "What happened?" but "Why had it happened?"

She thought she knew. But she needed to be sure. If she was right, then she knew what Caleb had wanted her to sing last night, and why. Dawn had known, too.

Jonas's eyes were troubled. "We've all broken dishes or something, but it's never been a big issue. Every little thing upsets her now." He opened the pantry door and got the broom. "Were you talking about anything in particular?"

Talking. "No. We weren't talking at all."

"Maybe with time this will straighten out. Anymore, I just don't...understand." He began to sweep the broken pieces into a pile.

Molly thought she did understand.

Dawn's life and heart were as broken as that plate lying shattered on the floor. The plate would be thrown into the trash. What would happen to Dawn's brokenness?

Molly sighed. "If only I could find a way to get her to talk about her feelings."

He straightened and held on to the broom. "Today was good, kind of like how things used to be. Sarah loved playing games. I think Dawn enjoyed today."

Molly turned and gazed out the window and looked toward the clearing sky. Yes, today had been good. But far from ideal.

Jonas liked her better when she did things like Sarah.

But Dawn resented her more when she did things like Sarah.

She lifted her eyes toward the sky where several dark clouds lingered.

Lord, I don't know a lot about faith.

But I'm learning a lot about mountains.

Chapter 11

"Oh, my." Molly looked out the window early Wednesday morning upon hearing a wagon pull into the back. "I didn't expect Birdie this early." She hadn't finished breakfast.

Jonas opened the back door before Birdie had a chance to knock. Instead of the pleasant expression Molly expected, Birdie's face was flushed. "There's been an accident." She set a large basket on a clean section of the kitchen table.

While all eyes were on her, she clasped her hands in front of her ample chest, then spread them, making motions as she spoke rapidly. "A rider came to the cabin early this morning to get Ira. The missionaries were on their way up here when one of the wheels came off and the carriage turned over. Mr. Simpson is just bruised, but Miz Simpson is in the hospital in town. She's unconscious. I just stopped by on my way down there."

After stopping long enough to take a deep breath, she brushed at the gray streak in her hair. "Molly, I was so looking forward to taking you up to Coalville." She pointed to the basket. "Besides food, I have my Bible and records of what the children recited last week. Is there any way you could let them know what has happened?" Her dark eyes pleaded. "Could you listen to their verses?"

Molly had thought of a dozen reasons why she wanted to go to Coalville and take part in Birdie's project. Now, more than a dozen reasons loomed large in her mind why she couldn't. She glanced around at Dawn and Caleb. "I have the children, and I don't know how to get there."

"I thought of that." The flip of Birdie's wrist implied Molly's protests were futile. "Extra food is in the basket. And there's only one main road up to Coalville." She pointed at Jonas. "He can give you directions."

Molly sent Jonas a pleading look, hoping he would agree that she couldn't possibly go alone.

Instead he nodded. "I'm sure Molly will help you out, Birdie. Don't you worry."

Birdie clasped her hands and looked toward heaven, then grasped Molly's hands. "Oh, Molly, you're an answer to prayer. Thank you, dear. I'll return the favor somehow. Just you wait and see."

Before Molly could protest, Birdie was out the door and gone.

A long moment passed before she could face Jonas, trying to control her frustration. "Jonas, I can't do that."

"I know," he said. "I'll take you."

She had to take in a deep breath. "You know?" Her hands went to her hips. "You think I can't handle a horse and wagon?"

His eyebrows lifted. "Can you?"

"No, Jonas. I'm planning to drive into every mud hole so the wheels will fall off, we'll turn over, and all go to the hospital."

He lifted a hand. "Sorry."

Caleb looked from one to the other, wide-eyed. Molly glanced at the boy and apologized. "I was joking, Caleb." She addressed Jonas. "Sorry."

After a deep breath, she explained. "My uncle let me try my hand at it when we'd go to the market. I don't care for riding in those newfangled automobiles. They're smelly and break down all the time. I prefer to pass them up with a horse and buggy any day. Besides—" her voice rose with conviction—"I can even walk faster than those contraptions."

"That's something you won't have to worry about in these parts." Jonas got up to pour himself another cup of coffee. He lifted the pot with a questioning look; she nodded, and he refilled her cup. "From what I've seen of automobiles, they couldn't make it up these mountains." He put the pot back on the stove. "Hasn't been long since trains have been able to come up this far."

Oh dear, now she'd convinced him she could handle a horse and wagon. But she hadn't driven one in the mountains. How could she handle a horse, keep a young girl from running off, and control an energetic little boy who might decide to jump out and chase a squirrel or something? She didn't want to say that maybe mountain women could do anything, but she was a city girl. She'd been trying so hard to be a mountain woman.

She hurried over to her cup of black coffee.

Jonas must have read her mind. "Like I said, Molly, I'll take you."

"The rain has stopped. What about the planting?"

He grinned. "Well, if you can take time out from your schedule, I suppose I could break my routine."

"You pick a most inconvenient time for humor, Jonas."

That little-boyish look appeared on his face. "I'm really being conniving. If I take all of you up the mountain, then on a planting day, each of you can help plant."

"I would be glad to help plant, Jonas, anytime you need me."

He nodded. "I know that. But no matter how experienced you might become, I'd never approve of you and the children going up to Coalville alone."

Dawn spoke up. "Pa, I've been studying. Could I say my verses there?"

"Dawn, for a long time now you've been saying your verses at Pine Hollow."

Molly jumped in immediately. "Wait a minute. If I'm to be in charge today, then I make the rules." She watched his face carefully, not wanting to overstep. A gleam of approval was in his eyes. "So I think anyone who wants to say their verses may do so."

Dawn scooted off her chair. "I'll change my clothes."

That was the most enthusiasm Molly had seen in Dawn. Maybe something good would come from this after all.

After they headed up the mountain in the wagon, sloshing through some puddles but mainly rolling along on the hard-packed road, there wasn't much Molly could do but listen.

She turned in the seat to keep her eye on Caleb and to glimpse Dawn's expression. When they got in the wagon, Caleb had wanted to sit up front, but she told him to sit right behind her. He could reach up and touch her at any time. Dawn sat right behind her papa.

"Jonas, I wonder if you would do me a favor if we have time."

"If I can."

Molly decided her conversation should be for Dawn's benefit even if she had to say things Jonas already knew. "You know Sarah and I lived in the mining camp when we were children."

He nodded.

"One of my fondest memories is a big mulberry tree near a creek up there. I wasn't much older than Caleb, and I guess Sarah was close to Dawn's age. Our mama would take us down to the creek."

Molly turned her head farther back. "Dawn, you said that song I was humming last night was your mama's song. It was your grandmother's song before that. Mama would take me and Sarah down to the creek, and we'd sing and dance around that mulberry tree. There was one bush in the front yard at our house. We would dance and sing with other children in the mining camp and pretend that bush was the mulberry tree."

Dawn's head turned toward her. "My mama did that with us."

Molly's heart skipped a beat. Dawn's tone of voice did not sound resentful, but reminiscent.

Jonas smiled. "Sarah even had me doing it."

Caleb laughed. "Muh-bwee."

"Yes," Molly breathed. "The mulberry bush. I guess we could call that song an heirloom."

After a short silence, Dawn asked, "What's an heirloom?"

Dawn was actually conversing with her. "It's something that's passed down from one family member to another, like a piece of jewelry, or a man's watch, a special book, a painting, or even a lacy handkerchief."

"Mama had her mama's ring. Pa said I can have that and Mama's rings when I grow up. I guess that's an heirloom."

"That's about the most special kind."

After a thoughtful moment, Dawn looked at her. "You and Mama had the same mama, right?"

"Yes, your mama and I are sisters. Just like you and Caleb are sister and brother. You have the same mama."

"What heirloom do you have from your mama?"

Molly was about to say she didn't get anything. But there was one thing. "Well, Sarah was the oldest, so she was entitled to the ring. When Papa sent me away with my aunt and uncle, he gave me Mama's Bible. And it has some of her favorite recipes in it."

Dawn's glance met Molly's. "Can you cook them?"

Molly didn't know if that remark and the little gleam in Dawn's eyes meant she was being sarcastic, trying to joke, or just conversing. At the moment, it didn't matter. She felt that overwhelming sense of loss that she felt when all she had of her family was her mother's Bible and a few recipes. "No. I never tried."

"But I guess you read your mama's Bible."

"No." Molly felt the roles had been reversed. She felt like a grieving child and didn't want to be questioned about things so private—that still hurt. "But I keep it with me."

A solemnity settled on Molly as they neared the place where she spent her early childhood. The air was cooler the higher they went. She drew her shawl closer around her shoulders. The craggy peaks jutted straight up into the sky in some places. In others, she could look down on beautiful hollows where horses and cows grazed. There were small farms with fields of corn. Others appeared to be beans, some tobacco, all lush and green, likely having been nourished by frequent mountain rains.

For a moment she closed her eyes against an unwanted memory of another small farm. Forcing herself to think of other things, she thumbed through the papers, along with a list of instructions that Birdie had left with her. She began to read.

After a while, she looked around. "I keep hearing that same sound, like a bird is following us."

"It's not a bird," Caleb said. "It's a chickie."

Caleb lifted the corner of the tablecloth covering the basket. He took out a little peeping chicken.

"Oh, Jonas. Caleb brought his pet with him."

Jonas looked around and laughed. "Be easy with that baby chick, and I don't want you crawling all over the back of the wagon while we're going up the mountain. Dawn, you watch him."

"I already told him what he has to do," Dawn said. She took a few seeds from her dress pocket and laid them on her lap. "Now put the chickie in my hand."

Caleb passed the chicken to her hand. Dawn told him to pick up the seeds. He held them in the palm of his hand, and they giggled as the chick pecked at them.

Caleb giggled. "It tickles."

After a while Dawn told him to put the chick back in the basket because it was just a baby and needed to rest. Caleb obeyed, then picked up one of the books Molly had brought with them.

Molly had wanted to come home. Now, here she was, in Coalville. The houses looked the same. She, Sarah, and their papa had lived in a box house like these that had only two rooms. That was after the fire.

As they rode through the mining camp, Molly said, "I...think that's the one we—" Her voice broke. "—we lived in."

Jonas glanced at her. "What's wrong, Molly?"

She swiped at a tear. "I didn't know this would be so emotional. The memories are just flooding in. Coalville is where I spent the happiest and saddest days of my life."

Chapter 12

Jonas understood what Molly must mean. During his courtship of Sarah, she confided in him how the loss of her mama in a fire had been so heard to bear. She didn't go into detail, and he didn't press her for information. Her early life had been like Molly's. But like Molly, Sarah had seemed happy and outgoing.

He admired Molly's way of not wallowing in self-pity but turning her attention to other projects.

Jonas realized she wasn't as blasé as he'd thought at first. Her hurts went deep. She just put on a happy face, while his was—mulish. He'd have to do better.

He did, later, while standing around the wall of the long, one-room schoolhouse with other men and women. The male teacher expressed sympathy for the events of the morning, which prevented the missionaries and Birdie from coming, but welcomed Molly as the teacher who would listen to their verses.

If he didn't know her, he might not notice that lift of her chin, which didn't mean stubbornness as he had once supposed, but determination in the face of whatever challenge presented itself. He could admire that.

She took a moment to gaze around the room, smiling, trying to put the nervous pupils at ease. He knew they didn't often see a lady dressed so finely in pale yellow and wearing a multicolored shawl. Yet her outfit was plain compared with her frilly, fancy ones. She had been astute enough to dress down in a nice but simple skirt and shirtwaist.

Two older girls near the back whispered. Jonas heard one say, "She's purty."

The other spoke in an awe-filled voice. "She must be a queen."

When Molly smiled and spoke, however, she sounded more like a loving encourager. He wasn't sure Birdie would be as accommodating as Molly who said she wouldn't count off if they missed a word or two, as long as it was close and the meaning clear. She gave an example. It would be fine if one turned words around like "For God so loved the world" to "God loved the world so much."

"Now," she said. "We will start with the younger ones first. But before I call on the first graders, my nephew would like to say his verses. Caleb McLean."

Caleb left his place on the front row and toddled up to Molly. He faced the other children.

He took a deep breath and looked over at Molly. She smiled. "Caleb has two verses. Go ahead."

He kept looking at her. "God is wuv."

"Perfect," she said. "Now the other one."

289

His overload of confidence came quickly. He faced the front, leaned forward slightly, and spoke loudly and distinctly. "Jesus swept. . .the fwoor."

Molly gave a cue by beginning the applause to cover the giggles and one boy's hearty spontaneous laugh. Adults were laughing, too.

Why Caleb decided to nod as if bowing, Jonas had no idea. Maybe it just came natural, like his penchant for attention.

Jonas motioned, and Caleb ran up the aisle to him, like he'd been instructed.

Molly cleared her throat as the applause died down. "Any additions like that are not acceptable, unless you're a three-year-old."

Tension vanished as the children realized Molly wasn't going to bite them, and a mistake wouldn't be disastrous.

Using the alphabetical list Birdie had left, Molly called Billy Adams.

The boy raised his hand. "I don't have one."

"That's fine," she said. "Ellie Brooks."

Caleb leaned next to Jonas's ear and whispered loudly. "I wanna say my verses again."

The two girls at the back looked around. One giggled and the other put her hand over her mouth. Caleb was entertaining, but this was not the occasion. Jonas took him outside where an older woman watched small children sitting on a blanket beneath a tree, waiting their turn to be pushed on a swing.

"I can watch this one if you have other children to recite," the woman said.

He thanked her. "I would like to hear my daughter recite in a little while. She's an *M*, so it will be awhile."

One little boy got up and started to walk away. To the boy's delight, Jonas scooped him up and held him high. Then he set him back on the blanket. Wanting more, the boy started to get up again. "Hold on," Jonas said. "If you're real nice about waiting your turn and mind this nice lady, after my daughter says her verses, I have a surprise for you."

Caleb clapped his hands. "Surprise. Surprise."

"Now don't you be guessing, Caleb. This is to be a surprise for everyone." Jonas put his finger to his own lip.

A light began to dawn in Caleb's eyes, and he put his finger to his lips lest the secret spill out. He pulled on the woman's skirt. "I said my verses."

"Oh," she said, taking a little girl out of the swing. "My, you're a smart little boy."

Jonas urged. "What do you say, Caleb?"

Caleb looked up at the woman with his big blue eyes and said, "Yes, ma'am."

When Caleb's turn came to swing, Jonas hurried back to the school. A boy returned to his seat, amid applause; then Molly called on Becky Hill. There were two *J*s who recited, one *K*, and then Dawn.

She didn't look at Molly, who gazed at her fondly, but kept her head down until she turned and lifted her chin in that way characteristic of Sarah and Molly.

She began, " 'To every thing there is a season. . . .' "

Sarah would have been proud to see her little girl, looking so ladylike in a school dress and her hair brushed neatly to her shoulders. Her arm being in a sling didn't detract from her appearance at all.

Jonas had been blessed with bright children. He couldn't bear the thought of Dawn spending her growing-up years taking care of him, the way Sarah had with her pa.

He didn't think she missed a word in all those verses. Neither did she, apparently, from the pleased look on her face when the children and adults applauded.

Jonas returned to the yard and took the warm little chick from the picnic basket. None of the little ones got bored after that, and when the others were dismissed, adults and children alike enjoyed the running, pecking, and peeping of the little chick that seemed to like attention as much as Caleb.

The teacher, wearing a grin, came up and stood by Jonas. "Thank you for the entertainment." He laughed lightly. "For your boy and the chick."

Jonas glanced toward the school. "I trust all went well with the recitations."

"Perfect," the teacher said. "I like the way Miz Pierpont had applause after each child recited. That hasn't been done before, but I could see it helped everyone, particularly those who forgot their words and had to start over. I realized they need to be applauded for effort."

Jonas agreed.

The teacher grasped Jonas's arm. "Like I told Miz Pierpont, we'd be real proud to have her come and teach a special class like you've done with history and mathematics. Being from the city, and having graduated college, she could likely teach a lot of subjects."

Jonas grimaced. "Not too many, though. I need the job."

The two laughed lightly. But Jonas knew that a lot of teachers as educated as Molly didn't want to take a job back in these mountains. They'd want a city job.

Finally, when Jonas felt the chick could take no more, he scooped it up and returned it to the basket. Dawn and Caleb climbed into the back of the wagon.

At Molly's request Jonas drove out to the miners' camp where two-room box houses sat in rows on dirt yards. Obviously, life was meager. That wasn't what Molly mentioned. Instead she spoke of fond memories. "Sarah and I were so close in those days. She tried to be like a mama to me after. . ." She swallowed hard. "After Mama died."

"Nobody can be a mama except a mama," Dawn said.

"I know. And we hear that good comes from everything. Losing our mama may be what helped her be such a wonderful mama to you and Caleb."

Jonas heard the sadness in Molly's voice and glimpsed the starkness on her face. He longed to do something to help, particularly since Dawn was implying that Molly's efforts in their home were in vain.

"You're right about one thing, Dawn," he said. "We can have only one natural mother. But many people fill the role of parents. In some ways, my own grandfather was more like a papa to me than my own. I loved him as much."

"It's not the same," Dawn said with a pout.

Caleb reached around and caught Molly's sleeve and said, "Mama."

How long, Jonas wondered, could he or Molly overlook Dawn's remarks? He hardly knew which ones he should attempt to debate, or ignore, or agree with. He took his cue from Molly who changed the subject. "Dawn, you said all eight verses of chapter three of Ecclesiastes," she said. "And I'm so proud of you."

Jonas also complimented his daughter, who then began to talk about others who recited.

Following Molly's direction, Jonas drove to a spot where the mulberry tree stood majestically. "There it is!" she exclaimed, as excited as the children had been about the chick.

Her enthusiasm seemed contagious. Even Dawn was in reasonably good spirits. "You can take the chick out," Jonas said. "But don't make him run or play. He must be very tired after all that activity at the school."

Forcing any contemplations aside, Jonas felt rejuvenated. This outing reminded him of when he and Sarah took the children and enjoyed a ride, a visit to neighbors, or a picnic.

He helped Molly spread the cloth out on the grass and set out the lunch Birdie had prepared and Molly had added to that morning. In a clearing by a creek beneath craggy peaks reaching into the sky, how could anything not taste good? Birdie must have assumed he would accompany Molly and the children. The basket held fried chicken, biscuits, cheese, strawberries, cookies, and a container of water, complete with four glasses.

He realized what he'd been missing by not having taken the children on outings when the weather had begun to warm up.

They were well into their meal, watching the chick peck around in the grass when Molly pointed to the tree. "That's a mulberry tree, Caleb. The very one your mama ran around when she was almost Dawn's age."

Caleb's eyes widened and he began saying "Muh-bwee" over and over in a singsong voice.

Jonas said, "He remembers. I was afraid he'd forgotten everything about her."

"We can teach him not to forget," Molly said. "It's good to remember. . .the good times."

Jonas was beginning to realize that remembering and talking about the good times eased the pain of loss.

When Caleb finished eating, he took Molly's hand, singing over and over, "Muh-bwee."

Molly laughed. "We have to go around it. You two going to join us?"

Dawn shook her head. Jonas decided he'd best just watch. "You two go on and play while Dawn and I do all the cleaning up."

He and Dawn put everything back into the basket, then sat in the grass watching. Molly and Caleb couldn't reach each other's hands around the tree. Molly took one of his hands and they danced around it with Molly singing and Caleb doing his best to join in.

Even Dawn laughed when they stopped to make the motions of washing their hands and their clothes. Dawn said, "If he ever washed clothes like that, he'd drown himself."

Molly ran around the tree, hid, then peeked out at Caleb with a playful, "Boo!" Her hair was coming out of its roll, and she finally took the pins out and shook it free with her hands.

Her long blond hair, which reminded him of corn silk, hung down like Sarah's had. It was naturally straight but had the wave from being in a roll. When she stood still, it hung almost to her waist. It reminded him of times when he'd run his fingers through Sarah's wheat-colored hair. Yesterday, when her hair was wet, Molly's had looked more like Sarah's.

He missed his wife, but it was different now—less painful.

"Pa, you look like you went away." Dawn's words brought his eyes around to her.

He exhaled heavily and picked up a blade of grass. "I was thinking about corn and wheat."

"Like you said this morning, Pa. We can help you plant. I only plant with one hand anyway."

He chuckled and drew her close for a moment. "Okay, daughter, you get the chick and I'll get the basket. We need to head back down the mountain."

She looked up at him. "It was a good day, wasn't it, Pa?"

He smiled. "Yes. Better than staying home and planting."

She nodded.

He wondered. Were some mountains beginning to move?

Chapter 13

W   ait and see!"
          That's what Jonas had heard Birdie say on Wednesday when she
          needed to go down to Poplar Grove.

Not much time had passed. Early Thursday morning Birdie rode up and joined them for a cup of coffee at the breakfast table. She announced that the missionaries wouldn't be able to continue their journey into the mountains.

"The mister will be fine. His bruises will heal," Birdie reported. "The missus has a concussion and must remain in the hospital for a while, then they need to go back to Virginia and take it easy. So, I'll be going further into the Black Mountains since they can't." She peered over her cup at Molly then set it down. "How did things go at Coalville?"

"Nobody complained," Molly replied.

Jonas saw the pleasure in her eyes and the slight color in her cheeks. Modesty became her.

He couldn't let it pass with that. "She's a natural teacher. Believe me, I've seen plenty of them."

Birdie folded her hands beneath her chin and smiled with a triumphant look in her eyes.

"Parents and children alike responded well." He laughed and told about Caleb reciting his verses.

Birdie laughed, spread her hands, then clapped them once. "I knew all would go well. Just by the way you have come to these mountains in a time of need speaks well for your love of children."

"Oh, I do," Molly said. "Those children in Coalville stole my heart. They were so eager to show what they'd learned."

Birdie shook her finger at Molly. "Yes, and for days I've been thinking and praying about your ideas for a Bible school. The Lord won't let me forget. Didn't I hear BethAnn and Earlene say they're coming here today?"

"Yes," Molly said. "So I thought the children and I would help Jonas in the fields; then I can visit with them this afternoon."

That was the end of Birdie's "wait."

Next came "seeing" from Birdie Evers's organizational point of view. She planned out the days for Molly, with Molly's eager anticipation, offering her own suggestions, too.

Dawn began clearing the table and even enlisted Caleb to help her.

"My," Birdie said. "You're a helpful child and with only one good hand, too."

"I can do my part," Dawn said. "And it won't be long till I can use both hands."

Birdie smiled. She looked down at her cup and picked it up. Jonas knew Birdie realized Dawn was clearing the table to prove she was useful, and they wouldn't need Molly much longer.

Not need her?

That thought lingered in his mind.

The Lord knew what Jonas needed, and He had brought Molly here to teach him that.

He needed to see activity in his house again. After Sarah died, some of the men had come to offer help. Their womenfolk would bring a pie or a casserole, but that stopped after a while. A wife couldn't go to another man's house and take care of his children when there was no woman in the house. He only asked Birdie in times of emergency. She had a full life visiting the people in the cove, helping with their needs, having missionaries and circuit riders stay in their home when needed, taking care of her plants and her own household, and doing her volunteer work at Coalville and Pine Hollow schools.

He could understand why Molly seemed like a godsend to her.

Jonas took Caleb to the barn with him. The chickens were glad to get the seeds but clucked and scattered at Caleb's chasing the little chicks. After Dawn watered the plants in the flower bed, she joined him in the barn. She headed toward the ladder leading to the loft.

"Dawn," he called. She stopped and held on to the ladder. He had to try to find out what was on her mind. "Molly is becoming a big help to us and the community. You can see that, can't you?"

He didn't know his little girl's expressions anymore. What kind of emotion moistened her eyes? Was it anger, hurt, frustration?

She took a deep breath and lifted her chin. "Pa, she looks a lot like Mama. She has a pretty voice like Mama, though it's different. She loves Caleb kind of like Mama did. She likes to help people like Mama did. But, Pa, she's not Mama. She shouldn't be in our house."

"Where do you think she should be?"

She answered immediately. "In the city." Her frail shoulders rose with her rapid breaths. "I see you look at her sometimes the way you used to look at Mama. Are you thinking of letting her take Mama's place?"

I look at her like—what does that mean? How did he look? And when? Was Dawn making that up? Had Dawn sensed his longing for a woman of his own, the memory of his wife? It wasn't Molly he looked at. It was a memory.

Wasn't it?

He tried to dismiss Dawn's remark. After all, she was only a nine-year-old girl. What did such a young child know about looks? He'd been nine once upon a time. He thought back to what he knew. He knew when his parents were angry, when they were sad, playful, loving, disappointed, worried. Yes, he knew those things as far back as he could remember, without his parents saying a word.

He would have to be careful of his thoughts about Sarah when he looked Molly's way.

"No," he said finally. "You've said it yourself, Dawn. Nobody can replace your mama."

Dawn blinked, heaved another sigh, then hastened up the ladder and disappeared into the loft.

The day would come when Dawn's arm would be healed. Then they could go back to being the way they were before.

Is that what Dawn wanted?

Would she be happier?

Caleb would be sadder.

And Jonas. . .

How could he answer the questions in his mind when he wouldn't even allow them to form?

~

Molly's change of life for the better really began on Thursday. Birdie brought Earlene, BethAnn, and her son, William. A teenage girl named Rhoda came to watch the little boys and brought her sister Nettie, who was a friend of Dawn's.

The young girls joined the women when they struck off for the blackberry bushes and wild strawberry fields. Rhoda was helping the little boys build a train station. Jonas said he'd be within shouting range in case Rhoda needed him.

When they returned midmorning, Molly learned how these mountain women canned their fruit for the winter season. Molly brought out the empty jars she had washed after using their contents for a meal. Other jars were stored in the cellar. The other women had their jars in Birdie's wagon.

They put big rocks in a circle, built a fire in the center, put a big washtub over the fire, and poured water into it. After filling the jars with berries and sugar, they tightened the lids and boiled the jars for twenty minutes.

While the jars were cooling on the back porch, the women made pies with the fresh berries they hadn't canned.

"I've never seen days go so fast," Molly said the following day when they picked beans while the pot of water was heating.

"We'll save the biggest and best for Jonas to keep for planting next spring," Birdie instructed.

They filled twenty-four glass jars with green beans, water, and a half teaspoon of salt in each jar for seasoning.

After they put the lids on, Birdie clapped her hands. "Now, we let those boil for four hours."

"Four hours?" Molly could hardly believe they needed to cook so long.

Birdie explained. "It takes awhile to cook in those jars. And, too, the heat kills the bacteria, makes pressure, and as the jars cool they are vacuum sealed." She spread her hands. "Then when you open them this winter, you'll have green beans as fresh as if they've been picked today."

"I love it when we work together like this," BethAnn said. "Now, let's dig some potatoes, and then we'll spread out a great lunch."

Birdie agreed. "Ira said he'd come by if he could."

Earlene laid her hand on Molly's arm and smiled. "We women used to work together like this with Sarah, too."

Molly was so glad to be included with these mountain women working together. She'd never had such close fellowship with women like this. When she'd been married to Percy, she maintained an appearance, but never got to know other women personally. These women talked about their husbands, children, and daily living. They cared about each other, and Molly wanted to be that kind of person.

During the next days and weeks, the group of women went to each other's homes to pick berries, green beans, sugar peas, and to shell peas. Each day, they would divide up the jars, and each woman took her portion home to put in her cellar or pantry.

Sometimes the men got together and helped plow, plant, pick, and eat.

Molly realized this activity could go on all summer, and there would be other produce toward the end of the season. Tomatoes were coming on, and she began to fix fried green tomatoes for their big meal. Soon she'd be canning red, ripe tomatoes.

One afternoon, after the men had helped each other in the fields and were all eating together, the women were cleaning up while jars cooled.

"Tomorrow," Birdie said, "is candy-making time."

Molly learned that children could appear not to be listening and prove her wrong. From several feet away, the two little boys looked their way. Caleb clapped his hands like Birdie had a habit of doing. "I want canny."

Birdie ducked her head and gave him a long look. "Tomorrow."

"Tomowwow," he repeated and sighed. Will stuck out his lip.

BethAnn laughed. "Those boys act like tomorrow is forever."

Molly wiped her forehead with her sleeve. "Although I love this activity, I sometimes think all this work lasts forever."

Birdie lifted a finger. "You're right. Making sure there's enough to eat here in the mountains is a never-ending job. You'll be grateful for this when winter comes and you're holed up in that cabin."

Molly felt a jolt. "I won't be here this winter."

Birdie gave her a long look, then patted Molly's shoulder in a sympathetic gesture. She must have sensed that Molly would like to be here. Then she gestured toward the peas being shelled so they could can those. "We have to get most of this done before the Fourth," Birdie said.

"The fourth what?" Molly asked.

The other women laughed. "Oh, our big Fourth of July festival," Birdie said.

When "tomorrow" came, they gathered at Birdie's house, first admiring the gardens of beautiful plants and flowers imaginable and unimaginable. Her front and back porches were also full.

Birdie proudly talked about them all. "I don't believe in weeds," Birdie said. Their eyes followed the gesture of her hand toward a field of wildflowers that she had tamed into rows. "They're all God's creation," she said. "You just need to put them in the right location. He did leave some things for us humans to do."

They laughed and agreed. Soon, on Birdie's long wooden table, she laid out the ingredients for peanut butter roll ups. She mixed powdered sugar, butter, and vanilla flavoring in a large bowl and kneaded it.

"What's that festival you mentioned?" Molly asked.

"The Fourth is the biggest event of the year. We celebrate, dance, play music, sing, play games, and eat."

Earlene laughed. "And this is one time we try to outdo all the others." She stared at Birdie's hands, now patting her mixture out on waxed paper. "Birdie always wins blue ribbons with her plants."

Birdie lifted a white sugared hand. "That's because I'm the only one in the area who has a flower business."

"Yes," BethAnn put in. "But there are others who bring plants. Anyway," she said, looking at Molly as she continued. "People all over the mountains come, and we compete with everything from pigs to pies."

"Including Earlene's prize-winning peanut butter." Birdie scooped peanut butter out of a jar with a big spoon and spread it over the mixture she'd flattened on the table. "And right after the festival might be the best time to hold our Bible school."

Molly watched Birdie powder her hands with the sugar, then begin to roll up her handiwork.

As soon as Birdie cut the roll into half-inch slices, Molly delighted in the little white wheels with alternating spirals of white and brown inside. Earlene and BethAnn reached for a piece. Birdie laughed and stuck one into her mouth, so Molly did the same.

"Hmmm. Deli-thuth," Molly mumbled with peanut butter sticking to the roof of her mouth.

Despite the pleasant sweetness dissolving on her tongue, the wonder of these new friends, and excitement over the festival and Bible school, her mind went a step further.

Dawn's arm should be healed by mid-July.

Where would she be?

What would she do?

Chapter 14

Molly hardly had time to think about what she was doing. Her life was a jumble of activity that she dearly loved. There wasn't a moment's spare time, except for that last cup of coffee at the end of day before Jonas left the cabin and went to the barn. As the days grew warmer, the drink often became tea or lemonade.

Now she stood in the kitchen where she and Jonas had just come through the back door. It suddenly occurred to her that she had never been alone with Jonas—anywhere except that initial ride up the mountain. The children, or someone, had always been near. Now, the house seemed. . .different. Quiet—except for her heartbeat in her ears.

Dawn's visit with her friend had been planned during the week. After church, BethAnn asked if Caleb could come home with the family for the afternoon. Tom promised to take William fishing and invited Caleb.

When Molly asked Jonas, he got a thoughtful look in his eyes; then a little gleam she didn't understand appeared, and he said, "Yes, he certainly may."

They were all standing together, getting ready to put the boys in their wagon. Tom apologized. "Jonas, I should have asked if you want to come along. We'll be fishing up toward my parents' place and probably have supper with them. Beth-Ann wants to be alone today to do some women's work."

Women's work. Well, Molly figured she best get on with that herself, now that she and Jonas had returned to the cabin. She removed her hat and pushed at the roll of her hair although she felt it was in place. "I'd, um, better change and get lunch on the table."

"Change of clothes would be in order," he said. "Something less fancy and some good walking shoes. I'd like to show you something. We can take a picnic lunch."

Molly liked that idea. She never felt ill at ease around Jonas; but for some strange reason, the thought of just the two of them in the cabin alone having lunch made her feel a little awkward. "There's bread left from yesterday. And ham left over from breakfast. I put that in a jar and took it to the creek."

He smiled. "There's cheese out there, too. Any pickled cucumbers left?"

"Yes, a couple of jars. Oh, there's a jar of tea out there, too."

"Perfect," he said, turning to leave the kitchen.

"Oh." Her word stopped him. "I can take honey to put on the bread for dessert."

He lifted a hand. "Double perfect."

Molly didn't know what was wrong with her. She felt like she'd just been asked out on a date. That stopped her progress toward the bedroom. She felt rather like she had when Percy took her to a fancy restaurant, to the fair, or on a Sunday ride in the park when he was courting her.

A sadness washed over her. She was feeling more excited about this mystery outing with Jonas than she had with Percy. Oh, she was probably wrong about that. Her feelings were tied up with the difficulty of her marriage, and that colored her view of what the courting had been like. She'd been young, naive, flattered by an older man's attention, pleasing her aunt and uncle, being in love with the idea of being loved, and wanting a family of her own.

But there was no reason to compare Percy and Jonas. They were worlds apart and entirely different.

And she wasn't being courted!

~

When Jonas and Sarah had gone up on that craggy peak, she'd sat in front of him on the horse with his arms around her. He could not do that with Molly. It would be too intimate. He took the wagon.

As if knowing about his reminiscence, Molly broke his train of thought. "What was your courtship with Sarah like, Jonas?"

Jonas appreciated Molly's making him talk about Sarah. Others seemed to think the subject shouldn't be mentioned.

"At the funerals, after the mine accident that killed her. . .and your. . .pa along with mine, I noticed her. She was the prettiest girl I'd ever seen. I wanted to wipe her tears away. But my grandparents were doing that. She was a student at Poplar Grove, where my grandmother taught."

Jonas had already dissociated himself from the mining community. His grandpa had seen to it that he got his education in town instead of in the mining camp. "My grandfather sent me off to a college in Virginia. When I'd come home from college, I'd see Sarah working for my grandparents, helping with chores and the cooking. In return, they let her have their spare bedroom and provided her needs. Grandpa was a farmer and I'd help him in the fields. Sarah ate meals with us as if she were their daughter. I still thought she was the prettiest thing I'd ever seen, but she was only a high school student, while I was a big-city college fellow."

Molly laughed with him, knowing he was making fun of himself for being prideful.

"But none of the college girls impressed me like Sarah. She was smart. That's why my grandparents wanted her to live with them, to give her a chance. After your pa died, she had the opportunity to live with your aunt and uncle, but she refused."

"I didn't know that," Molly said, surprised.

He nodded. "She didn't want to tell you that. She thought you would think she didn't want to be with you. But she'd come to believe city life was best for you because that's what she'd been told when you were eight and she was thirteen. And, too," he added, "she had been taking care of her pa for three years when he died. She considered herself a grown woman."

He glanced at Molly, who shook her head and sighed.

"You see, up here in these mountains, some girls marry at fourteen. They grow up quickly. But I don't want that for my children. I want them to know something of the world before they settle down."

He smiled, returning his thoughts to Sarah. "My grandparents treated her like a daughter."

"But you didn't think of her as a sister."

"Oh, no," he said. The memory felt good. "There I was, a college graduate with offers to teach in Virginia and at a school in the city. But once I laid eyes on the grown-up Sarah, with her hair looking like corn silk in the sunshine and those big blue eyes. . ." He stopped and smiled. "Like yours and Caleb's. All of you have the same eyes."

Molly smiled and shielded hers by looking down at her hands.

"She had a lot of young men wanting to call on her, but she said she'd never marry a miner, and she didn't fancy the young men in school." Jonas smiled. "When she said that, she looked straight into my eyes, and I about swallowed my tongue." He chuckled. "Then she looked down at her hands like you just did."

He replaced his smile with a scowl. He had to stop comparing her with Sarah. When they'd played "Poor Tom," she had invoked his laughter before time for him to pat her head. But he'd intended to fake the laugh if necessary. He'd figured her hair would be soft like Sarah's. It wouldn't be fitting to touch it, even under the guise of a game.

Jonas had been impulsive when he thought of taking Molly up the mountain. This was part of his life, and he wanted to share it with someone. Of course, he would share it with his children when they were older. But that was a long time off.

He'd begun to realize life is short and unpredictable. He needed to learn to live life to the fullest, stop concentrating on his losses, and count his blessings.

Jonas continued to coax Mac up and around a forested mountain until he turned onto a narrow dirt road that ran alongside a wide creek until they rode out of the trees and into a hollow so typical of the eastern Kentucky mountains.

Molly jumped down from the wagon before he could walk around to hold up his hand to her. She ran to the ridge from which one could view mountain peaks and hollows below.

"Way down there to your left," he said, walking up, "is Pine Hollow. That long building that looks about the size of Caleb's train car is the school. A little farther, which you can't really see from here, are our cabin and fields."

Molly's shoulders rose with her intake of breath. She put her hand on her chest. "Jonas, this is breathtaking."

He laughed. "Could be the thin air, too."

She boxed him lightly on the arm and turned toward the wide clearing of about ten acres. He gestured toward the wide expanse. "This is where the Fourth of July Festival will be held."

She looked askance at him. "Suppose it rains."

He jested. "Wouldn't dare."

"Oh, Jonas." She shook her head. "I think you just invited God to send a thunderstorm."

He laughed. "If so, we'll postpone until the next day. Come on. I want to show you something."

They walked into the forest where Mac was tied at the edge. She followed as Jonas led her up a winding trail until they reached a clearing where they could look down upon the valley where the festival would take place.

They came upon a one-room hunting shelter. The fireplace hadn't been cleaned out. Bedding lay in a corner. An old coat hung on one of the hooks on the plank walls.

"I hear the creek," Molly said.

Jonas nodded. "There's a natural spring here that runs into the creek. This was my great-grandpa's hunting lodge."

Molly looked at him quickly. "So. . .this is all your family's."

Jonas nodded and sighed. "All two hundred fifty thousand acres of it. There was a lot of unclaimed land in these mountains after the Revolutionary War, and the government thought that was good payment for those serving their country. It's been in the family since then."

She followed along as he walked outside. "There wasn't anything that could be done with it for a long time. Some of it's been sold off for lumber, but getting the logs down the mountain on the river wasn't too practical. Now that the trains have been coming into Coalville and tracks being laid farther up, I've had offers from lumber companies to buy some of the acreage."

"You would sell it?" Molly asked.

"Maybe." He looked at the shelter, seeing more than that. "Sarah and I talked about building our house here for the big family we were going to have. She came up with the idea. She was innovative." He looked at Molly and smiled. "Like you."

Molly turned away from the shelter and looked beyond where blue, ridged mountains spread out. Jonas thought her innovative? She thought herself a perfect dodo, unable to do a lot of the things these mountain people could do in being so self-sufficient. The only innovative idea she knew of might be her plans for the Bible school. And that was not an original idea. But if he didn't know, she wouldn't tell.

"I've already sold some of the land," he said. "They're our neighbors."

Our?

Of course, he meant his and Sarah's, or his and the children's. Or both.

"Down there, where we will have the festival, is land I thought about donating for a church. I can visualize a community growing up there. More people living here in the mountains instead of having to go to the city for jobs. Now that the trains are coming this way, we can bring the needed conveniences and progress to this area and still enjoy the beauty of the land."

Jonas would donate those acres of land? Daily, Molly understood more and more why Sarah had labeled him "remarkable."

Walking back down the trail behind Jonas, Molly thought he and Dawn were accepting Sarah's death more easily than when she had first arrived at Pine Hollow.

"It's amazing how much Dawn can do with one hand," Molly said. "Having Nettie with her these past weeks has meant a lot. Keeping busy helps. I've not even had time to think of Dawn's resentment of me. Maybe she's beginning to see I'm not some kind of threat. If that were so, I would even. . .consider staying longer."

Jonas stopped and looked at her. He didn't mean to stare, but their eyes seemed to lock. Finally, he continued down the trail.

"I mean"—she said—"if you want me to. Even after Dawn's arm heals, there is a lot of work to do. As busy as I've been already, I'm sure it can hardly compare with harvesting corn."

She would stay longer?

"You're so right," he said, trying not to show his pleasure. Molly had made such a difference in their lives, even if Dawn didn't know how to appreciate it. "You think you've had fun already. A combined corn-shucking is almost as much fun as the Fourth of July Festival."

Fun? Yes, the women had fun. Like the men had fun helping build a cabin, clear land, or raise a barn. But it was work.

As soon as they came to the clearing, Molly said she would get the picnic basket. He walked past the wagon and to the lookout, unsure how to feel.

Gazing out at the valleys and mountains, Jonas realized that Molly was learning new things. Recapturing her childhood in a way. Feeling close to Sarah by doing what Sarah would be doing. Even going beyond with her teaching.

But this was temporary. A challenge. Something to take back to the city as a quaint experience. If she'd never known an easier way of life, it might be different. Most of the mountain people were unacquainted with city life, so they weren't accustomed to the modern conveniences like gaslights, automobiles, telephones, running water, and bathrooms inside the house.

Yes, in teaching history, he'd thought how interesting it might be to go back in time, to live in the Middle Ages, to be among the first settlers in America, to go to Europe and see the great cathedrals, to visit the Holy Land and walk where Jesus had walked.

That didn't mean he would want to live in those places permanently.

Molly's enjoying learning to work with her hands, preparing for winter months when they might be snowed in or there were no goods able to get up the mountain to purchase, didn't mean she'd want to live here permanently. Just a little longer.

The circuit-riding preacher and the missionaries came to do their service for the Lord, but then they went back to the city for their everyday living.

No, a city person caring about the mountain people, getting involved in their lives, helping out, didn't mean he or she wanted to live that way.

When she called his name, Jonas turned and walked toward her and the picnic set out on the ground.

Molly had never thought herself a shy person and could hardly understand this awkward feeling that swept over her when she'd watched Jonas looking out over the mountains and then turn toward her.

Maybe it was their being alone like this that did it. She saw him—not as Sarah's husband, not as Dawn and Caleb's papa—but as a man she was getting to know—and like. He sat on the ground across from her. The gold in his brown hair seemed lighter each day, being bleached by the sun. His eyes were soft brown with flecks of gold in the sun.

He reached for a ham biscuit. "You're very unselfish to give up the conveniences in the city to come here, Molly. I admire you for that."

She shook her head. "I'm afraid I don't deserve your admiration, Jonas. I do want to help out. But my main reason for coming was selfish. I wanted to recapture some of my childhood. I wanted to find out what it's like to have a life like Sarah had. She was happy, Jonas."

He nodded. "Yes, I think most of the time she was."

Molly nodded. "That's because she loved you. And she had children. Those are things I've longed for and never had. Wasn't. . .allowed to have."

"You can't bear children?"

"Oh, I think I can. But. . .Percy didn't want them. He really didn't want me, Jonas, except to show off in public. He liked me well enough, but after our marriage I realized he married me because I was. . .young. Or maybe because my uncle had a business and a fine house."

"Well, I can certainly understand why he would be taken with you, Molly."

She saw his face redden, and he tried to redeem himself. "I—I mean. . .well, I didn't mean to imply anything improper."

Molly couldn't help laughing. "Well, he didn't marry me because I could use a cookstove or wring a chicken's neck."

Realizing the implication of that, she tried to explain. "He liked to show me off, but he was jealous, too, and the jealousy took over more and more. He presented me as if delighted, but if another man seemed to think so, or showed me special attention, he would blame me for that when we got home."

Molly almost stopped the conversation there, but realized talking about their grief and problems is what she had wanted Jonas and Dawn to do. She should follow her own advice. Her aunt and uncle knew much of the story, but she'd never talked to anyone about it like this.

"It gets worse, Jonas. Percy was embezzling from my uncle—quite a bit. The house you saw in the city when you came and asked me to come here was not mine and Percy's. We lived with my aunt and uncle. All of us believed him when he said he was looking for a place to buy or build."

She saw that Jonas was chewing his ham and biscuit quite slowly, as if unaware it was in his mouth. "You'd better swallow before I tell the rest."

Jonas chewed, swallowed, and took a gulp of tea.

"My uncle discovered that Percy was wanted in Boston for having embezzled from a wealthy widow. He could be quite a. . .charmer."

She took a sip of tea before going on. "You don't know how he died, do you?"

"No. The telegram from you said he met with an untimely death."

"He was about to be arrested, Jonas. Public appearance meant everything to him. So much that he lied, cheated, and embezzled. He couldn't have faced arrest and imprisonment. The rumor was that on that cold winter night in February he was on some kind of errand in my uncle's automobile but got stalled on the icy bridge. Somehow, he'd walked to the edge to look at the river while waiting for help and lost his balance. Perhaps a sharp gale pushed him from the bridge into the icy river."

Jonas reached over and gently brushed away her tear with his thumb. "Molly, I'm sorry you had to go through that. I don't think Sarah knew you were unhappy."

She sniffed and blinked the moisture from her eyes. "Realization came slowly, Jonas. I was young and naive and didn't want to believe my marriage was a failure. Through the years I had to accept not having things the way I wanted them." She shook her head. "Looking back, I know Percy and I were not in love with each other."

～

Jonas wished he could say or do something to console her. Maybe all he could do is what she'd done for him. Just listen and encourage her to talk. He remained silent while she took a few deep breaths, then lifted her chin.

A small light came into her eyes again. Her voice was soft. "Being here takes me back to my childhood when I had the feeling of love and family. All during the years I was in the city, I longed for what I'd lost. I didn't know that when I lived here I was poor."

"Poverty is not just a lack of money," he said. "It's not having to work hard. Poverty is when you have no one to love."

He suddenly realized he hadn't felt that poverty of heart in the past weeks. His family worked together, played together, enjoyed other families together like when Sarah was alive. He'd felt the joy of activity again, of being alive for the first time since Sarah died. Whatever he thought had died inside him had not died, but was simply buried alive. Like a seed that had dried out was hard and withered.

It would spring to life again in another season, if given nourishment.

Molly was good to have around.

She said if Dawn could accept her, she might stay through the harvest.

Stay? Birdie Evers had been a city girl. She said her love for Ira turned her into a mountain woman.

Molly loved Caleb and Dawn enough.

Caleb returned that love. If only Dawn could accept her, then. . .

Molly had made a difference in his own life. He reached for a piece of cheese. Her sharing today, letting him know what lay deep in her heart made a difference, pleased him.

But, he reminded himself, she wasn't here for his pleasure.

She was here for the children.

Chapter 15

Molly couldn't be happier that Dawn was focusing on the work—or fun—of picking, cooking, and canning along with her friend and the women. If Dawn could get used to being civil to her when others were around, maybe she could begin to do so in private. Last week when Jonas again drove them to Coalville School, Nettie went along. The two girls practiced their verses in the back of the wagon, while Caleb worked at keeping his favorite chick from getting away. The chick now had the beginning of tiny wing feathers among its soft fuzz.

The women and children met at BethAnn's house today, canning tomatoes and talking about what each was taking to the festival.

"I was looking in my mother's Bible and found this recipe for mulberry pie," Molly told them. "I might try my hand at that."

They looked skeptical. She backed down. "Well, I know I'm a rotten cook. . . ."

BethAnn and Earlene shook their heads and laughed. Birdie patted Molly's arm. "It's not that. It's just that Mother Jane has won the pie contest for as long as there's been a pie contest." She shook her head. "If you come up with something to beat Mother Jane, you'll be queen of these hollows."

Molly took in a deep breath and looked toward heaven. "I'm already halfway there." They laughed as she added, "I've been pretty good at being hollow at times."

Nettie wasn't there today, and Dawn spent much of her time outside with Rhoda and the little boys, who had brought their wooden guns and rubber balls to play with. The girls were now throwing the balls over BethAnn's chicken house, and the boys were trying to catch them. So far, they'd been unable to, but loved running to get the balls.

While the jars of tomatoes were cooling and they put out the fire under the pot, Dawn came up. "I want to go see Mama."

Molly's breath caught in her throat. "What—what do you mean?"

Dawn got that expression of tightened lips and nostrils as if Molly knew nothing at all. The little girl's shoulders rose with her intake of a deep breath and her gaze moved away from the women.

BethAnn explained. "Her mama's buried out back."

"Oh. Then, of course, it's fine that you go."

Dawn sprinted away.

"You think she'll be all right?" Molly asked.

"Oh, yes. The graveyard's just beyond Birdie's house and the school." She pointed to the school on the other side of the creek.

Molly watched as Dawn ran across the backyard, across the footbridge over the creek, and through several trees. Then she spied some tombstones and a hill beyond. No, it wasn't far.

Molly put her share of the boxed tomatoes in the wagon, as did Birdie and Earlene. BethAnn took hers to the cellar. The women were laughing and talking as they packed a box for Rhoda, which was payment for watching the little ones.

Their laughter stopped when wailing and Rhoda's voice came from the kitchen. "Now, Caleb, I'm just going to wash this off and put some ointment on it, and you'll be fine."

Molly and BethAnn hastened into the kitchen. His knee was scraped and bleeding, but the wound was superficial.

"My 'eg is broke wike Dawn's arm. It hurts," Caleb said dramatically.

"I'm sorry," Rhoda said as she cleaned his knee. "He was headed for the creek in a place where the water's high. I yelled. He looked back, laughing, and tripped over a limb and fell on a rock."

"I know how that is," Molly said. "I'm not blaming you." She turned to Caleb. "Rhoda's got you all fixed up, Caleb. You can walk, can't you?"

He shook his head.

"Okay, you wait here with Rhoda for a bit, and I'll go get Dawn."

"I can get her," Rhoda offered as Caleb nodded.

"I'd actually like to see the graveyard," Molly said. "If you can keep your eyes on Caleb a little longer."

Caleb smiled at Rhoda, and Molly promised to be back soon.

When Molly reached the wooded area, she saw that Dawn had picked some wildflowers. She dropped to her knees at a headstone and laid her handful of flowers in front of it.

"I told you before, Mama. I'm sorry. But that don't do no good. I still feel bad about it. I didn't do the right thing. I'm just a—a bad person. I just keep being bad. But I'm so sorry. I know you can't love me anymore. But I love you, Mama. I miss you so much."

Molly put her hand to her mouth to stifle a cry when the little girl brought her fists down on the grave, then laid her forehead on them and sobbed.

Molly turned and leaned back against the tree, taking deep breaths. Her chest ached from the feeling, and she felt she couldn't get enough air.

"What are you doing here?"

Molly opened her eyes and saw Dawn through a blur of tears.

Molly reached out to her. "I—"

"Don't touch me," Dawn cried out. "You listened. This was my private time with my mama." Her breath was ragged. "I hate you. I hate you."

Molly couldn't speak. Finally, after Dawn was out of sight, she could whisper. "I know. I know how you feel."

But the horrible realization was, knowing didn't mean she could do a thing about it.

~

Seeing Molly hurry across the cornfield, now about two feet high, struck Jonas's heart with dread. What was wrong now? She wouldn't leave the children to come out there for small talk. He let go of the plow and strode toward her. "The children. Are they all right?"

"No. I mean yes. It depends, Jonas."

He squinted against the sun. "What is it?"

"Caleb skinned his knee. But it's fine."

He stared. "You came to tell me that?"

She shook her head. Tears formed in her eyes. "I was behind a tree near the graveyard and heard Dawn talking to her mama. She was apologizing for something she did, Jonas. I think she feels like she is responsible for Sarah's death."

Tears streaked Molly's face. She took a deep breath and blinked. Her eyelashes were wet. "She saw me, Jonas. That made her feel even worse. She said she hates me."

He shook his head and put his hands on her trembling shoulders. "She didn't mean it, Molly. She's just—"

"Jonas. She did mean it. She takes her frustration out on me. But she said she did something wrong."

Jonas thought back. "I remember after the doctor came and Sarah and the baby were dead, Dawn cried and said, 'I should have run faster.' I didn't know what to do. I think I just said it wasn't her fault."

He felt the sting of drying salty tears on his face. "I've never talked to her about it. I've been too busy blaming myself. She'd had two miscarriages before having Caleb. She always had a hard time. But we both wanted a big family. I've been thinking of me and my feelings and expecting time to take care of Dawn's."

"I need to get back," Molly said. "I don't want anything else to happen that I'll need to be sorry about."

He caught hold of her arm in a comforting gesture. "I'm glad you overheard Dawn talking to her mama. I'll talk to her later tonight. Sometimes I think we don't realize how deeply children feel things."

"I do, Jonas. That's why I'd like to ask a favor."

He nodded, hoping he could grant it.

"Before you talk to Dawn, let me tell her about my childhood and when I felt much like she is feeling right now."

"She hasn't been ready to listen to you, Molly. Don't you think she will be even more resistant now?"

"I'm sure that's what she's feeling. But if you demand she be at the supper table, I can talk then. It's not the most pleasant dinner conversation. But I think I'd like you to hear it, too. I just hope it won't make everyone sadder."

She looked at him a long moment, then turned and hurried back across the fields.

He doubted anything could make them any sadder. He'd hung on to his grief like it was a prized pig.

Dawn was hanging on to guilt.

Molly was always saying she knew and she understood.

He was beginning to believe she really did understand.

He knew how much Molly had counted on his taking her, Dawn, and Caleb to the mulberry tree so she could get fresh berries. As much as they all had looked forward to the festival, and Molly wanted to make a prize-winning pie, this problem with Dawn took precedence.

As he neared the cabin, he saw Dawn sitting on the hill. Her dress covered her legs that were drawn up, and her arm hugged them. Her forehead lay on her knees.

Soon after he followed Molly into the cabin, Birdie came riding up.

"I see Caleb has recovered enough to be wreaking havoc in the chicken pen." Her face clouded. "But how is Dawn?"

"I haven't talked to her yet," Jonas said. They went inside. Birdie's gaze followed his as he glanced at Molly standing at the sink, looking down into it.

Birdie pointed at Jonas. "You two go up there and get those mulberries. I'll stay here with the children."

Molly and Jonas remained silent until Birdie said, "Shoo! Scat! Go!" She reared back with her hands on her hips. "While I'm here I'll whip up something to eat and take back some chicken for Ira. That man never gets enough. I might even make up another batch of peanut butter fudge."

Jonas figured Dawn might need a little time alone to ponder the situation. Birdie might even be able to help. He hadn't seen Molly this distressed, not even when she talked about her disastrous marriage.

On the way up the mountain, they rode in near silence. Jonas stopped the wagon near a tree and tied Mac to a limb. Molly grabbed a basket, hopped down from the wagon, and walked fast toward the mulberry tree. She picked one and tasted it. "They're ripe," she said, but her voice held none of its usual exuberance. Had she given up on Dawn?

Jonas picked a mulberry and ate it. "You're right. Sweet and juicy."

"My mama found this tree. Oh, it wasn't this big then." She glanced at Jonas. "Well, neither was I. That's when she began to teach us the mulberry song. We had such. . ." She sniffed. "Fun." She moved to the side of the tree to pick from a low limb.

"Molly? You're—you're crying."

She leaned back against the tree and closed her eyes. "I'm sorry."

"I don't blame you. This situation with Dawn is exhausting. She seems unreachable."

"Oh, Jonas. It's not just Dawn. I'm being selfish, thinking of myself. Dawn's feeling guilty brings to the surface what I thought I had under control. But now, I'm feeling sorry for myself. My papa gave me away, my husband didn't love me, my sister's. . ." She choked on a sob. "D—dead. I can't comfort a little girl and. . . I'm feeling guilty about my own mother's—I'm sorry."

Jonas took the basket from her hand and set it on the ground. He propped his hand above her shoulder on the tree. "You don't need to be sorry, Molly. I have taken advantage of your kindness by asking you to come into this situation. You've given so generously. And what have we given you but problems? You've helped me by listening. Now. . ." He lifted her chin with his fingers.

She opened her wet eyes and gazed sorrowfully at him. His heart went out to her. "You need to talk about your feelings like the rest of us. Let me help."

"Jonas, I don't think anyone can. I'll get over this. This doesn't happen often. It's just. . .one of those times."

"Then tell me," he said.

She drew a deep breath and gazed beyond him. "I feel like I can't even help a little girl. I'm no good to anyone. Our house wasn't far from here before Papa moved to the mines. He couldn't stand the house anymore without Mama. He couldn't stand. . ." Her sob caught in her throat. "Me. He couldn't stand me anymore."

Jonas put his hands on her shoulders. "Molly, he thought he was doing what was best for you."

She shook her head. "It's my fault Mama died."

Jonas listened to the story that Sarah had never told him. They had a new calf. When Sarah thought Molly was asleep she got up and sneaked outside. Molly followed. When Sarah turned at the barn door to look back at the house, she saw Molly.

The two of them sneaked inside the barn. They were looking at the calf when they heard their mama and papa coming. They hurried up the ladder to the hayloft. After their parents left, the girls giggled together. The night had turned much darker. Sarah lit the lantern.

Molly began jumping around on the hay, playing and saying she didn't want to go to bed yet. Sarah pleaded with her. Molly swung around and knocked the lantern over. Oil spilled out. A fire started between the girls. Molly backed away into a corner, screaming.

Sarah couldn't get to her. Sarah started screaming for her parents. They came as Sarah tried to get down the ladder. Her papa told her to jump. She jumped into his arms. Her mama rushed up the ladder. In her haste, she lost her balance as she stepped into the loft. Her feet knocked the ladder down. She ran into the fire.

"Catch her at the window!" she yelled.

Her papa went outside, and her mama threw her down into his arms. Her clothes were already on fire. Her papa caught Molly, but the barn was already caving in. He couldn't get to the loft. The barn burned to the ground, and soon Mama was no longer screaming.

Jonas felt it, the pain, the loss, the grief, the guilt she was feeling. He enfolded her in his arms. Her head lay against his chest. He cried with her. He felt the rocking of her shoulders and heard her sobs. He soothed, "Cry it out, Molly. I think we both need to. For you, me, Sarah, Dawn—everything and everyone."

She nodded against his chest. He gently caressed her back.

After a while, he felt her body relax. His hands moved down her arms. She looked up at him. His hands came up and cupped her face. His head lowered, and his mouth touched her parted lips. They were stained with mulberry juice and tasted sweet. His eyes closed and his fingers were entwined in her soft, silky hair and his lips moved.

He breathed in her own breath then stepped away. He gazed past her but saw nothing—nothing but a man who had—what? Just betrayed his wife? Betrayed himself? Dishonored his sister-in-law? Sinned against God?

He then stared at Molly who stared back at him with wide blue eyes, bright as the summer sky. "Jonas," she said so low he had to listen closely to hear. "Thank you for. . .comforting me."

She turned then, smoothed her hair back, and began searching for more mulberries.

No, he didn't need to kick himself mentally. Maybe physically but, like she said, he was comforting her. He had needed that sharing of grief as much as she.

Should he ask forgiveness for comforting someone? She had given his children her unconditional love, and with it came a feeling of comfort Jonas couldn't yet define.

On the way back, the only reference either made to the event was when he said, "Molly, you need to forgive yourself."

Chapter 16

Birdie had supper on the table under the cloth when he and Molly returned from Coalville. Jonas gave her two chickens. "One for watching each child," he said.

She didn't refuse.

"Dawn stared at that old iron pot for a long time," Birdie told them. "Then she went up on the hill. When she came in, she said her arm was hurting. That had better be seen to, Jonas. You know how dangerous infection can be when there's been a broken bone."

He nodded, thanked her, and bade her good-bye.

Jonas found Dawn in her room. He asked about her arm, and she said it hurt some. "Maybe you've been working too hard lately."

"Pa, I can use my left hand better now than I could before. Pretty soon I'll be able to work better than ever."

There it was again. That implication they didn't need Molly.

He gently touched her arm. "Would you like to tell me what happened today?"

"Didn't she tell you?"

He nodded. "Yes, and she said she didn't mean to overhear."

"She spied on me."

"Did she apologize?"

Dawn looked down and nodded.

"Then you should forgive her."

"I'll try." She took a deep breath. "I don't want any supper. My arm hurts."

"I'll give you some laudanum."

He didn't know if that was just an excuse to keep from talking with Molly. His daughter's needs had to come first, and if her arm still bothered her in the morning, he'd take her to the doctor.

Surely Dawn wouldn't use her arm as a ploy to keep Molly from going to the festival. But judging by her prior behavior, that was a real possibility.

He decided to forgo the nightly cup of coffee with Molly. She was preparing the pie for tomorrow's fair after he'd raved about the one she made for supper. He told her it didn't need a thing as far as he was concerned.

Birdie and Ira were on the front porch with her plants when he arrived. "Which one goes to the fair?" he asked.

"One? Why, Jonas McLean, I'm taking three."

Pastor Evers snorted. "She wants to bring home all the ribbons."

She gave Ira that warning look of hers. "Ira, how many ribbons have you earned for your preaching?"

He grinned. "No ribbons, darlin'. Just stars and crowns."

She harrumphed. "If you don't wipe that smug look off your face, you're going to see a few stars, but they won't be the kind that come from the Lord."

"Whoowee. Jonas, we'd better get out of here," the pastor said with a chuckle.

"I just stopped by to say that Dawn said her arm is hurting. If it's not feeling better in the morning, I'll need to take her to the doctor. But I don't want Molly and Caleb missing the festival. You know how Molly's been planning."

Birdie set down the pot of red geraniums. "Don't you fret. If you don't stop by here, we'll go down and get her."

"Thanks. I appreciate that."

Jonas returned to the cabin. The moment he opened the back door and walked in, he closed his eyes briefly and inhaled. Molly had her hands in the dishpan. Her pie was in the oven, but the aroma permeated the kitchen. "That's the most heavenly aroma."

"Now what do you know about heaven, Jonas McLean?"

He leaned against the countertop. "Didn't I tell you? I went to visit the preacher and Birdie. Now what could be more heavenly?"

She laughed. "I have heard that God has a sense of humor."

He smiled. "Those two are a joy to be around. Couples couldn't tease each other like that if there wasn't a lot of love between them."

He moved away quickly. He realized he and Molly just teased each other, and had a few times. But that was different. They weren't married. Maybe he should clarify his statement. "Sarah and I kidded each other a lot."

Molly nodded. "She was free to laugh. I was never free to be myself until. . ." She stopped suddenly and dried her hands. "Oh, listen to us. Talking about laughter and humor but getting all serious."

What had she been about to say? She didn't feel free until what? Until her husband died? Until she came here?

A questioning look came into her eyes. He thought he might have been staring. Turning, he spied the pie container. "Any left?"

"Two pieces. But you need to save one for Dawn since she didn't have supper."

He took the cover off the pie. "You and I can share this one, although I did have two pieces for supper."

"I only want a bite," she said. "I have to watch my figure."

If Sarah had said that, he would have replied that he'd watch it for her. But he just smiled and set the pie on the table, then went for coffee cups.

❧

Molly awoke before the rooster crowed.

When Dawn came to breakfast, she had an expectant look and declared her arm didn't hurt.

Molly had been concerned. She didn't want the child to go to see a doctor instead of going to the Fourth of July Festival. From all she'd heard, the festival was the highlight of the year. Everyone got involved, wanting to show off their crafts or abilities, and wanting to see and taste those of others.

And she wanted to see her friends in the dresses they'd made for themselves. On the way, Jonas stopped by the Evers's place to let them know Dawn was fine.

Molly held on to her pie for dear life. If she could get even a third-place ribbon for her pie, then the people in the cove would be accepting of her as one of them. She was not just a city girl who knew nothing.

Jonas looked over at her. "You're looking smug this morning."

She smiled. "I'm afraid to say anything. It might jinx this pie."

"These womenfolk know how to cook, Molly. I've tasted their victuals. There's stiff competition, but I was speaking the truth when I said it's the best I've ever tasted."

Spread across Jonas's land were all sorts of activities taking place. People were arriving in wagons, on horseback, and in carriages. Many tables were set up, and men were putting doors on sawhorses to be covered with tablecloths.

A pig was roasting over a pit. Boys were throwing balls, and others played tag. Two little girls were yelling at the ridge to hear their echoes come back at them.

A couple of young girls came up to Dawn. They began talking about her arm. Others gathered as if that were some kind of prize. Dawn went off with them.

The sky was clear, and a cool breeze blew. Women were taking their baskets of food and prize entries to the tables. BethAnn rushed up to Molly.

"Your dress is beautiful," Molly said. "The blue makes your eyes look even bluer."

BethAnn smiled. "Thank you. That's what Tom said. Come on, I'll show you where to put your food and pie. Back here are the tables for the judging."

Rhoda came up to take Caleb and William to join the younger children being cared for by several young girls.

The tables were laden with every imaginable food. With care, Molly placed her pie with the others.

"It looks wonderful," BethAnn said and set down her jar of sourwood honey. She tucked her arm inside Molly's and introduced her to those she didn't know, including a young man named Harley, who was a teacher in the city.

There were crafts, quilts, and games including sack races, pig chasing, turtle races, and turkey shoots.

At the time she heard banjo picking, Tom came up and held out his hands to BethAnn. Off they went, swinging around on the grass. Other couples joined in. Molly enjoyed watching.

Several other players joined in with harmonicas and guitars. An older woman joined them, using two spoons to make her own rhythmic kind of music.

Jonas approached her and bowed. "May I have this dance?"

Molly laughed. "Jonas, I learned the waltz and the reel in the city, but I don't know how to do this."

"You don't have to know. Just stomp."

Everybody else was stomping, even the little children, whether or not they had a partner. Before long she felt like an old-timer, stomping, jumping, and laughing.

Molly was more certain than ever she would like to stay here in the cove and enjoy life with these people.

When the rousing music ended, the crowd began to clap in unison. Molly didn't know what it meant. Jonas looked down at the ground like something was wrong. Tom came up to Jonas. "This is when you always honor us with a song, Jonas."

Jonas crammed his hands into his pockets. "Tom, I haven't sung since. . ."

Molly knew what that meant. He hadn't sung since Sarah died. She tugged on his sleeve and lifted her chin. "If I can dance, you can sing."

"I don't know if I can." He walked over where the musicians were and took the guitar one man held out to him.

Molly heard the tremble and weakness of his voice after he strummed a chord. He closed his eyes and began singing "My Old Kentucky Home." His voice became stronger, and the baritone sound echoed around the mountains.

After the song, she saw that people who were sitting, stood. He struck another chord and began to lead "The Star-Spangled Banner." Molly joined in. When it ended, there were applause, whistles, and men throwing their hats into the air.

Jonas walked down to her.

"That was wonderful," she said.

He smiled. "Thank you. You weren't bad yourself. I don't think anybody else has ever reached those high notes around here before."

Someone rang a bell, and quiet fell over the crowd.

A big man yelled, "Folks, it's time to judge the contest entries!"

Molly nudged Jonas. "I hope the judges don't taste the pickles first, then the pies."

He grinned. "If I can sing, you can certainly win a pie contest. I'll go get Caleb. We'll eat after this."

BethAnn came and stood beside her. There were different judges at various sections of the tables. The desserts were last. She had high hopes for at least third place. When the judges tasted hers, however, they seemed to have trouble keeping a straight face.

The awards were called, the names read, and women walked forward to get their ribbons. Mother Jane's sweet potato pie won. Molly's didn't even place.

She couldn't understand why the judges didn't seem to even like her pie. Had she been so nervous that she left out something?

She couldn't put it on the serving tables if it was awful. After the others took their pies away, she asked BethAnn to taste it. BethAnn put a forkful in her mouth, turned, and spit it out.

Molly said, "At least the judges didn't do that."

Molly tasted it. She spit it out, too. "Salt!"

BethAnn nodded. "You must have used salt instead of sugar."

They both stared at the pie. After a thoughtful moment, Molly picked up the fork. She took a bite from beneath the lattice crust. Then she took a bite of the crust and spit it out. "The salt isn't in the ingredients. It's on the crust."

"Could you have sprinkled salt on the crust instead of sugar?"

Molly took a deep breath. The recipe didn't call for sugar to be sprinkled on the crust. She took the same sugar from the container for the crust as for the inside of the pie. Accusations wouldn't help anything. She laid down the fork and picked up the pie. "That seems like the obvious thing. I'll just find my basket and put this in it so nobody else tastes it."

She looked out over the crowd until she saw Dawn. The little girl stared at her triumphantly. Molly couldn't keep the moisture from her eyes.

BethAnn's gaze followed Molly's. Dawn spoke to Nettie. They turned and went to a food table.

"Don't worry about not winning, Molly. It may be a good thing. The cove women have the impression you're about perfect."

Molly swiped at her wet cheeks. "Me? Perfect? I can't even get a little girl to like me."

"They don't know all that. They take pride in the fact that you sing and play the piano like you're some angel or something. So they'll love it that you can't cook." She placed the pie in Molly's basket she found under the table.

Molly remembered hearing a sound during the night. She had peeked out from her bedroom door and saw Dawn in the kitchen. She figured the girl was hungry since she'd eaten no supper. Molly had left ham and biscuits on the table.

She wouldn't accuse Dawn, but salt didn't sprinkle itself on her pie.

BethAnn's words penetrated her senses. "Next year, you can win. It's really hard to compete with Mother Jane, anyway."

Molly nodded but felt defeated. Not about the pie, but because she'd failed to help the one she most wanted to help—a little girl who'd lost her mother.

How could she even begin to consider living in the hollow or in town at the settlement when she couldn't be a part of her own sister's family?

No, next year Molly wouldn't be there—maybe not even next week.

～

At lunchtime, Jonas noticed Dawn sitting with Nettie and another friend. Caleb ran over to sit beside Molly at the table with BethAnn. The preacher manned the beverage table. Jonas found a seat on a log beside Harley Sullivan, a younger man who stuck out like a sore thumb with his bright red curls. Harley had worked for

Jonas a couple of summers to help pay his way to school in the city.

He'd come home to visit his parents. "Don't get up this way much anymore," Harley said. "I've traded the hard physical work up here for the hard mental work in the city. Can't say it's an improvement, though."

Jonas laughed. "I think it's called progress. Becoming somebody. Making money. Get you a city woman and settle down."

"Speaking of city women." Harley gazed at the table some distance away. "I hear Sarah's sister is living with you now."

"Yep. That puts me out in the lean-to where you stayed when you worked for me."

Harley nodded. "My mama told me about her. I've already spoken to her briefly, and she was interested in talking to my parents after I told her they knew her dad. Um, I heard she's a widow."

Jonas didn't quite understand his interest. On second thought, maybe he did.

"She's mighty pretty, Jonas. And if she's anything like Sarah, she's one fine woman."

A quick answer sprang to Jonas's lips. "Molly's not like Sarah. She's lived in the city for the past fifteen years or so. Has city ways."

Jonas saw Harley's face turn toward him and felt his stare. The younger man spoke slowly. "There are a lot of fine women in the city, Jonas."

Jonas didn't know why he'd spoken that way. "I didn't mean it the way it sounds. She is a fine woman. But. . .not like Sarah."

They ate. Jonas hadn't seen the mulberry pie anywhere. They must have snapped it up quickly. He had a piece of Mother Jane's pie. "This is mighty fine pie, Harley. Want a bite?"

Harley forked a bite. After a long moment he spoke. "Jonas, I hope you won't be offended. But I was wondering. I'm going to be around awhile, helping the folks with some repairs and all. I wonder, would it be all right if I called—"

"Well, sure, Harley. You don't even have to ask."

Harley paled. "No, I don't mean on you. I mean. . ." He cleared his throat. "May I call on Miz Molly?"

Call on Molly?

Jonas's thoughts were jumbled. A part of him wanted to say that Molly wasn't there to be called on. She was there for him and the children, even if things didn't always work out too well. No, he couldn't call.

"Did you hear me, Jonas?"

Jonas finally swallowed his bite of sweet potato pie and felt it sticking in his throat. He cleared it. "Well, sure, Harley. She would probably like to talk with someone from the city. Of course, the final say-so is up to her."

He had no right to say if anybody called or didn't call on Molly.

Not a bit.

None whatsoever.

Chapter 17

I guess everybody's tuckered out," Jonas said on the way home. "Quite a different brood than when we left home this morning."

"Caleb ran all day long." Molly brushed her hand lightly over his head that rested on her lap. He had looked as if he were about ready to fall over, so Molly said she would sit in back with him. Dawn sat up front.

Molly hated her suspicions about the pie. She didn't want to think Dawn would do such a thing—disliking Molly was one thing, but taking such action against her was entirely another.

"You're tired, too, aren't you, Dawn?" Jonas said.

She nodded.

"Molly, I guess they snapped up your pie in a hurry. I didn't even get a piece."

Molly took a deep breath, not sure what she should say. "I had to put it back into the basket. The topping was. . .too salty."

"Salty?"

Molly looked from his to Dawn's profiles. His lips pursed in a thoughtful gesture. Dawn looked stiffly straight ahead.

"I didn't see you use any salt for the pie."

Molly didn't say anything.

No one else spoke all the way home.

◦

After arriving back at the cabin, Jonas carried Caleb inside. Dawn hurried and held the screen door open for him; then she went to her room.

Jonas returned to the kitchen to see Molly setting the basket on the table. He'd been in the kitchen last night when she took the pie from the oven. She'd set the pie on the sideboard, and this morning she'd taken it and put it in a pie dish and covered it with a lid.

He had picked up the basket this morning. Now, he saw traces of white granules on the table where the basket sat. He ran his finger across it and tasted.

Salt.

He got a fork, took a bite, then spit it out the back door.

Molly glanced at him and away, as if she didn't even need to taste it to know. He watched Molly take the empty dishes from the basket, then the pie.

"Wait," he said. "Let's put the pie here." He took it and placed it on the table and moved the basket away. "Dawn," he called.

Dawn came to the door.

Jonas gestured to the table. "Let's all sit down, have a piece of pie, and talk about the good times we had today."

Dawn looked at the pie and at him. "I'm not hungry."

"You always eat something before going to bed. Don't you want a few bites?"

"No, Pa. I'm tired."

He forked off a bite and put it into his mouth. He had to spit it out the door again.

"This is full of salt." He ran his fingers through the granules and held up his hand. "Wonder how this happened?"

Dawn looked scared. She shrugged.

"No idea?"

She shook her head.

"I wonder," Jonas said. "Caleb must have thought he was helping by spreading sugar on the pie but got the salt instead. I'll have to teach him a lesson. Take him out to the barn and use the strap."

Dawn began shaking her head. "Caleb wouldn't do that." She pointed at Molly. "Maybe she got the salt and sugar mixed up."

"No. Somebody had to get into the pantry and take out the salt. It's here on the table. If it wasn't you, it had to be Caleb, and he will have to be punished."

Dawn began to gasp and talk between breaths. Molly knew how that felt. She'd cried enough times from so deep inside it hurt to even breathe.

"It—was–n't Caleb. I d–did it. Maybe—maybe she—wants to w–whip me."

"No, Dawn." Molly took a step toward Dawn, but the little girl wrenched away.

Dawn began to cry. "I hurt."

"Your arm?"

She shook her head. "I hurt all over."

Jonas stepped forward. "I can't let this pass, Dawn. You're hurting yourself, too, when you try to hurt Molly."

Dawn ran to her room with a cry.

Molly stepped in front of Jonas as he started forward, his face flushed. His hands came up and caught her shoulders to keep from careening forward.

Her pleading eyes held his. "Please, Jonas. Let her be alone for a while. You spoke the truth when you said she's hurting herself. You need to be calm when you talk to her about this."

His hands lay on her shoulders. He took a deep breath, nodded, and stepped back "We can't let her take action against you like this. Where will it stop?"

"Yesterday you agreed I could talk to her. Let me try to help her understand that I know how she feels."

༺

The next morning, right after breakfast, Molly put on her black mourning dress. It was perfect for what she had to do. Jonas had gone into the fields. She told

Dawn to keep Caleb in the house.

Dawn's eyes swept over Molly's stained mourning dress. "Are you leaving us?"

Molly took a deep breath. "Not yet. I will be here until your arm heals. But right now, I have a job to do. You mind me, and I mean it. You keep Caleb next to you. He must not follow me."

Dawn nodded, her eyes fearful. Molly meant to put the fear in Dawn. Her attempts at being kind and patient had failed. She didn't know what else to try. Caleb was listening, his eyes as wide as Dawn's.

Molly marched out the back door, slammed it behind her, and went to the iron pot. She looked back and saw Dawn and Caleb staring out the window. Dawn's mouth flew open. She came to the door and cracked it enough to stick her head out. "Is that my punishment? You're going to take my mama's pot away?"

Molly put her hands on her hips and stomped her foot. "Dawn McLean. I could wash your mouth out with soap. I am not some kind of monster, and I'm tired of you making me out to be one. Now, get in that house."

The door slammed, and Dawn's face again appeared at the window.

Molly turned the pot onto its side and bent over to roll it with her hands. She'd surely pull the muscles in her back. How did Dawn get it across the yard, beyond the barn, through the pasture, and up the hill enough for it to roll back and break her arm?

Maybe determination was the answer. Knowing Dawn would be watching from the window was enough to increase Molly's determination accordingly.

She began alternating with her feet to roll the pot. Ah, the land was slanted enough that the pot rolled fairly easily, although it preferred a zigzag journey.

A few uphill spots in the pasture required her pushing with her hands. Getting through deep-set places, not to mention cow and horse droppings, required not only the hands, but getting on all fours doing some fancy maneuvers and getting the hips into it.

She stopped several times to wipe the sweat from her brow. Maybe Dawn hadn't tried to do this all in one day—nor in the summertime. She should have brought some water to drink.

She took several deep breaths and stooped down to begin rolling the pot up the hill. She got it up to arm's length and began to move her feet upward on the hill far enough to bend her arms and push again. However, her toes slipped. She lay facedown on the hill, feeling every rock beneath her. She could imagine this being precisely how the pot had rolled back and broken Dawn's arm.

How was she going to get out of this?

She heard Jonas's voice. "What, may I ask, are you doing?"

"Taking a nap," she snapped. "Can't you tell?"

"She's crazy."

That was Dawn's voice.

"I told you to stay. . ." She couldn't go on speaking. She had to reserve any energy she had, if there was any left.

"I locked Caleb in the chicken pen. And I had to go get Pa," Dawn wailed. "I thought you would break both your arms."

Dawn cared? No, she probably only cared that if Molly broke her arms she would have to stay here longer.

"Looks to me like you're trying to break your neck or your back," Jonas said. Unsquinching her eyes, she saw his booted feet next to her face. His strong arms reached down, and the weight of the pot was removed from her hands and out-stretched arms—from her entire body, in fact.

Jonas turned the pot so the rounded part was turned opposite the curve of the hill. He braced it with his booted foot against the level bottom of the pot. "Dawn, go take care of Caleb."

Molly managed to get to all fours, then looked over her shoulder to see Dawn running across the pasture, toward the house. Molly looked up at Jonas.

He shook his head. "Why didn't you ask for my help?"

"It didn't occur to me."

He chuckled.

Molly snickered.

He threw back his head and laughed, saying between breaths, "I've never seen anything look so funny. Not even the cat when it gets its back up."

Getting to her knees, although her dress seemed to make every effort to prevent it, she heaved a breath. "Why can't women wear pants for things like this?"

He laughed again. "Maybe because most women don't do things like this."

She managed to get to her feet, although shakily. "All right, mister. Let's see you roll the pot up the hill."

He shrugged. "No problem."

He bent, turned the pot, gave it a good arm's-length roll, moved his feet, and yelled, "Whoa!" As his foot slipped, he turned the pot to keep it from roll-ing down. Molly put her hands on her hips and laughed then, while he looked at her sheepishly.

"Maybe if the two of us do this."

They worked out a plan. He would push; then she would turn the pot and hold it while he moved up a few feet and began the process again. His final push over the top left him lying prone right below the pot. Molly tugged and set the pot on its bottom. "Don't want to chance it rolling anywhere," she said.

Jonas crawled up on top and sat, dirty and disheveled, as Molly looked. She pushed her hair out of her face. Then the laughter came.

Jonas looked at her, and it rumbled from him. They both laughed. He rolled onto his back. Molly got down and did the same. The two of them lay there, laughing until they almost cried.

Finally Molly sat up. "I'm rusty, scraped, dented, sore in spots, and numb in others."

Jonas sat up. His gaze swept over her dress. "I've never seen a mourning dress get so much wear."

"Yes, it has come in handy." She looked out to see what Dawn and Sarah had seen from this hilltop. Looking around, she gazed over Jonas's green fields, some with yellow squash visible, and beyond was corn with long leaves waving in the breeze. Beyond and above were the craggy peaks and forested mountains that belonged to Jonas.

"I can see why Dawn and Sarah wanted this as their special place," Molly said, all laughter gone from her.

"Thank you for attempting this."

Molly nodded. "I don't really deserve praise. I did it mainly out of frustration."

"Still," he said. "You're a remarkable woman for attempting it."

Remarkable? That's how Sarah had described Jonas. And she was right.

"Ah, well," Molly said, always having found it difficult to accept praise. "I figure, if you can't move a mountain, at least move a pot."

A smile spread across Jonas's face and into his eyes. "You're good for me." He stood, held out his hand, and helped her up. "Now let's see if we can get down from here without rolling."

She felt confident. He didn't let go until they reached the bottom.

❧

Since she was already filthy, Molly worked in the garden and cooked lunch in that black dress, which had become such an important item in her life. Good for dirty work. The house was extremely hot, not only from the temperature but the cookstove; so she spread out a tablecloth under a maple near the creek, and they ate there.

Dawn was quieter than usual, not even offering a snide remark or rolling her eyes. Molly decided not to try with her anymore, just take care of her as best she could, which didn't include much other than washing her clothes and cooking her meals.

During lunch, Jonas said, "Um, Molly, when is wash day?"

She looked at him quickly, and her mouth dropped open. She closed it when she saw his grin and the twinkle in his eyes. "I made a new schedule. It's do what needs to be done, when you can, if you can." She glanced down at her dress. "What I have in mind is to kill two birds with one stone."

"No," Caleb said, wide-eyed. "Papa said don't kill birds."

She reached over and patted his little hand. "No, sweetie. I don't kill birds. That's just a saying. It means I'm going to do two things at one time." She huffed. "Like you're doing right now. One, you're stuffing too much peanut butter and bread into your mouth. Two, you're about to squeeze the life out of that worm on your plate."

He gave her a *don't-you-know?* kind of look. "This is for the fish."

"Just make sure it doesn't end up down your throat." She laughed at the way he screwed up his face and emitted a peanut butter mumble of disgust.

"Anyway." Molly looked at Jonas again. "It's so hot today, I thought I'd borrow your bathtub."

He snorted. "I don't have a bathtub anymore."

"The spring," she said. "I can wash me and my dress at the same time."

"It's cold," he warned.

"The house is too hot."

"Fine. In case there are any bears or mountain lions around, I'll take Caleb and his worm up that way and go fishing."

"Oh, wonderful. You can protect us with the fishing pole."

He laughed with her, then turned to Dawn. "You want to go with us?"

She shrugged. "I don't know. When am I going to be punished?"

"Dawn," Molly said immediately. "I'm not going to punish you. I didn't come here for that. I came to love you. And I do."

Dawn leaned over on the tablecloth with her fists clenched. "I'm bad, bad, bad."

Molly looked into Jonas's troubled eyes.

Caleb moved over to Dawn and put his hand on her back. "You're not bad. I wuv you."

Dawn rose to her knees and hugged her little brother. He asked, "You feel better now?"

Dawn whispered, "Yes," and Caleb moved back to inspect the worm.

Jonas took a deep breath. "Dawn, we'll talk about it tonight."

She nodded. This time she didn't run up the hill, but back to the cabin.

Chapter 18

After supper, and once Caleb had been put to bed, Molly poured tea for her, Jonas, and Dawn to take out on the front porch. The air cooled quickly after the sun set. Jonas and Molly sat in rocking chairs. Dawn sat on the porch at the steps, leaning against the banister.

The hounds did their belly-plop next to the steps. Their big, soulful eyes reminded Molly of how she felt. What was going to happen?

Jonas took a gulp of his tea, then leaned forward and set the glass on the banister. "We could begin with an apology."

Dawn got that hardened look on her face that Molly had come to recognize as a defense against showing her emotions. She picked at a spot on the lap of her dress. "I'm sorry I put salt on your pie." She looked up at Molly with moist eyes. Her lips trembled. "I—really am."

Molly could tell by the sound of Dawn's voice and the tears forming in her eyes that she meant it. "I forgive you."

Dawn nodded. "And, thank you. . .for trying to roll the pot up the hill."

Molly realized Dawn was laughing, or trying not to, in spite of her tears.

At least Dawn was releasing some kind of emotion at last. "Well, I wasn't doing that with the right attitude. I was. . ." She started to say she was mad. But remembering Dawn's saying she was bad, Molly decided not to use those words. "I behaved badly, yelling at you like I did. Will you forgive me?"

Dawn nodded, blinking away the moisture in her eyes.

"I have bad attitudes sometimes, Dawn. Everybody does. But deep inside I wanted to get that pot on top of the hill for you, because that was special to you and your mama. I understand that. It's like the mulberry tree is special to me because of my mama. And I want you to know, I'm not trying to take your mama's place. I know that is impossible. Nobody can take another person's place. My aunt never took the place of my mama in my heart."

Dawn stared at her, something obviously on her mind. "But didn't you like the city better than the mountains?"

"Never," Molly said.

Dawn wasn't convinced. "But everybody talked about all the wonderful things you did in the city and the beautiful clothes you wore, like everything in the city is better."

"Things never replace people you love, Dawn. I wanted to be with my papa and my sister. I preferred that two-room box house to the big one in the city."

Dawn didn't seem able to fathom that. She looked at Jonas. "Did you know that, Papa?"

"Not exactly that way, no."

Dawn was trying to understand. "So you think your papa was wrong to send you to the city?"

Molly thought for a long moment. "I'm not sure, Dawn. Looking back on it, I understand why he did it. He thought it best. But I spent years feeling resentment toward my aunt and uncle. That was wrong. I thought my papa didn't love me because he sent me away. Now I believe he did it because he did love me."

"Then you know why I don't want to go and live in the city."

Jonas had promised to let Molly talk to Dawn, but that statement disturbed him. He stopped rocking and his feet came down with a *thud*. "Dawn, what do you mean by that?"

Dawn was hesitant. She seemed afraid. "I heard you tell Birdie that you thought about sending me and Caleb to the city to live with Molly. And everybody always talked like the city was the best place to be. Papa. . ." She began to take quick breaths. "I don't want to go live in the city. I know it's good, but. . ."

Jonas was flabbergasted. Apparently Molly was, too.

Molly got out of the rocking chair. She sat on the porch in front of Dawn. "No. I would not let you and Caleb come to the city to live. Not as long as you have your papa. You thought that's why I came?"

Dawn nodded.

Jonas watched Molly lift his little girl's chin with her fingers, then smooth her hair. Dawn didn't cringe or run away. "Is that why you. . . ?" Molly cleared her throat.

"Treated you so bad. You can say it." Dawn nodded. "Yes. I didn't want anybody to think I liked you. If I didn't like you, then Papa wouldn't send me away with you."

"He's not going to send you away. I don't want you to go to the city with me."

Dawn looked at Molly through her tears. "You don't like me now, do you?"

"I like you, Dawn," Molly said. "And I love you."

"I. . .like you, too."

Jonas felt his own tears wash his face when Molly reached for Dawn, and his daughter cried heartbreaking sobs. He looked at Molly with her sunny hair hanging far down her back, her arms around his little girl, her soothing words working wonders. He had held Molly not long ago, now she was holding his little girl. They all liked and needed each other.

When Dawn's sobs subsided, Molly moved back. "I'd like to ask you something. That day in the cemetery—"

Dawn looked across at her. "I really didn't like you listening."

Molly nodded. "I understand that, and I didn't mean to. But I think it would be good if you talked about why you feel you did something wrong. You were apologizing to your mama. Is that too private, or can you tell me why?"

Dawn remained quiet for a long time. Finally she said, "You already know that I'm bad."

Jonas noticed Molly didn't correct her on that but, wisely, just listened.

Finally Dawn spoke.

Jonas listened as his daughter poured out her guilt and remorse. He could see it as Dawn described it. Her mama was having pains. Dawn held her hand for a long time. "Go get your pa," Sarah had said.

Dawn knew her mama couldn't look after Caleb when she was hurting. He was crawling all over the place. He would burn himself on the stove or crawl into the fireplace. Dawn took him with her, although it slowed her down.

Dawn's words and his own memory seemed to mingle. By the time Jonas got home, he could tell things weren't right. He'd been there for miscarriages and the births of Dawn and Caleb. The nearest doctor was in Poplar Grove. Sarah wouldn't let him go try to find a midwife. "It's different, Jonas," she said. "Stay with me." She began to talk about how good life had been with him.

He couldn't bear to think of the rest. His baby, his wife—gone—and he felt the guilt. He'd known she had miscarriages and difficult pregnancies. Why hadn't he taken her to the city? He could have taken her to be with Molly until after having the baby. He could have taken her to Poplar Grove.

His vision blurred as he looked down at his nine-year-old daughter. She had felt the guilt all along, and he didn't even know it. He'd been too wrapped up in his own grief. Thank God for Molly.

Now Molly was telling Dawn about her own guilt of having disobeyed and gone to the barn late at night, which resulted in her mother losing her life in the fire.

"That's awful," Dawn whispered. She reached over and held Molly's hand.

"For a long time I thought my papa sent me away to punish me. I thought he blamed me for the fire. I was to blame, but I was a child and would never want to hurt my mama. I have felt so guilty for so long."

Jonas had the feeling Molly was still feeling guilty. He spoke up. "That's why we need to ask the Lord to forgive us when we do wrong, or think we're wrong."

Dawn sighed. "I have begged God and Mama to forgive me. Why don't I feel like He has?"

Children could ask very difficult questions. "Well, you also have to forgive yourself."

Molly looked at him quickly. "You said that before."

"It's true."

Her mouth opened, and her eyes questioned. But it was Dawn who spoke. "How do you forgive yourself?"

Jonas gazed at the night, wondering when the darkness had come and the moon had risen. Much of the tension in his household had been caused by a lack of communication. He didn't want that again. Dawn was nine years old—old enough to ask questions. She deserved good answers.

He would do his best.

"Dawn, you've heard about Jesus all your life. You know Bible verses that tell us about His being God's Son, dying for us, and being raised from the dead."

Dawn nodded like that was common knowledge.

"There comes the time in our lives where it has to go further than what we believe in our minds. We have to ask the Lord Jesus to come into our hearts. We have to admit we're sinful, or. . .bad. We ask the Lord to forgive us. That's called repentance."

She nodded again, like this was nothing new. He knew it wasn't. Pastor Evers proclaimed it from the pulpit almost every Sunday.

"It doesn't mean we'll always do everything right, but we will try to live the way Jesus wants us to. When we ask Him to forgive us, He does. So it's a sin not to forgive ourselves. That means we don't sit around feeling bad about ourselves, but we go forward and try to do better."

Dawn looked out into the darkness, and he wondered how much she understood of that. Pastor Evers could have done a much better job.

In a little while, Dawn stood. "I'm hungry. I didn't eat much supper."

Molly smiled at her. "There's food in the kitchen."

Dawn stood, then paused. "Aunt Molly," she said tentatively. "Could we. . . plant flowers in Mama's pot?" She grinned. "If your dress is not too torn up."

Jonas watched Molly's face almost glow with tenderness as she looked at Dawn. She took his daughter's hand. "Tomorrow we'll go to Birdie's, and you can pick out the kind you want."

After Dawn went into the house, Molly sat in the rocking chair. She took a sip of tea and returned the glass to the banister beside his. "Jonas," she said. "I've never heard that about forgiving yourself."

"That's something I tend to forget, Molly. As I talked about it, I was saying it to myself."

"I wonder," she said distantly into the night, where the sound of crickets became predominant. Wind whispered gently in the trees. "I wonder if I've ever forgiven my papa for sending me away. Or my aunt and uncle for taking me to the city. Have I even forgiven myself for feeling like I caused my mama's death?"

He drew in a deep breath. "Or I. It seems this is a time for all of us to let go of what we couldn't control."

"I've never discussed these things with anyone before. I was like Dawn in a way, except not as vocal. Since I've been here, being an aunt who was resented, I understand my aunt and uncle better. I would never consider taking Dawn to the city to live. I missed my family so."

His heart went out to her. "Sarah told me she missed you terribly. When she questioned her papa, he made her feel she was being selfish to want you here, instead of where you would have advantages of education and progress and not have to work so hard. Often I thought she might have wanted to be the one who went to the city instead of you, or with you. Life is not always easy here."

"Oh, Jonas. She had more in her few short years with you than I ever had in the city."

He reached for his tea glass. Did she mean she didn't want to leave?

She spoke quickly then. "Oh, I don't mean that the advantages of the city aren't worth it. They certainly are. Easy accessibility to religion, education, automobiles, gaslights, bathrooms, refrigeration, telephones..."

"We'll be getting those before long," he said. "Can't keep progress out. And they make life easier."

She agreed. "But I always wanted to come back here. Although I did want to help you out and I love your children, I had selfish motives, too."

He smiled, hoping to encourage her to continue with her honesty. This seemed a night for it.

"Jonas, I know I'm just their aunt. That's what Aunt Mae always was to me. I think it would have been different if I'd had the maturity to understand everything the way they and my papa did. But I was a child taken from everything I knew and everyone I loved. At the same time, I felt guilty because I didn't appreciate it more."

He set his glass back on the banister. "Maybe they didn't know how to help you, like you and I were at a loss for weeks."

She nodded. "Looking back, I think they might have tried. Just like I couldn't get through to Dawn until she was ready, maybe they couldn't get through to me. I shut them out."

"Then maybe it's time you forgive your aunt for not being your mother. Forgive your papa for not knowing what was best. Forgive yourself for—everything." He paused. "And forgive me for not always knowing what a wonderful woman you are."

He looked over. Her eyes were closed, but wetness was on her cheeks.

As if feeling his eyes on her, she faced him, opened her eyes, and smiled. He knew those were tears of joy.

His hand was on the arm of the rocker. She reached over and touched it. He clasped hers and held it for a long time.

He felt something stir deep within his heart.

"Did you feel that tremor?" he said. "I think a mountain moved tonight."

Chapter 19

I t's littler than the other one. It looks awful," Dawn wailed when Jonas took her to the doctor on Friday.

The doctor spoke kindly. "Now, Dawn. This is temporary. Your arm is weak because you haven't been using it. Take it easy for a while until the strength comes back, and soon it will be just like it used to be. You can even wear the sling if you think you've overworked it. But you have to start using it."

On the way back home, Jonas cautioned her. "I know you're in a hurry to use that arm, Dawn. But do as the doctor said. Sometimes we want the end results and hurt ourselves in the meantime."

He remembered his own advice about communicating and how effective that had been the night he and Molly had that talk with Dawn.

"It's like our sorrow over losing your mama. We had broken hearts, broken spirits. We have to go through a time of grieving. And I guess in a way, we'll always feel that loss. But we have to start reaching out to other people and other things. With your arm, if you overdo, you may hurt it. I think it's the same with our hearts. It takes time to heal, but if we go slowly, make the effort, in time healing will come."

On Sunday those words "Go slowly" came back to haunt him.

At church, Birdie made the announcement about the Bible school that would start on Monday morning. She had the workers stand. Among them were Molly, BethAnn, and Earlene dressed like they might be going to an Easter parade. A couple of other women stood with them.

And one man.

With her arms bent at the elbows, Birdie waved both hands and smiled broadly. "Harley Sullivan has volunteered to help with crafts, games, and teaching the boys." She crossed her arms against her chest and looked toward heaven. "What a blessing."

Blessing?

It then occurred to Jonas that he could have done that. He had more teaching experience than that young man who used to work for him.

That evening at twilight, Harley came calling.

On Molly.

"Let's walk down by the creek," she said.

They disappeared from Jonas's vision, from the kitchen window, after they walked into a clump of trees that shut out the evening light.

After dark, he was sitting alone at the kitchen table, staring into his cup of coffee when Molly came through the back door, all smiles.

"That was a short walk," he said.

"Yes, we both have to get up early in the morning." She didn't reach for the coffeepot, but walked through the kitchen to go to her room.

His coffee was cold. He stood. "Yes, I'd better bed down, too."

She stopped at the doorway. "Oh, Harley will pick me and the children up."

Jonas stared. "That's out of his way."

She smiled. "He doesn't mind."

"No, I'm—I'm sure he doesn't." Harley Sullivan certainly wasn't moving slowly.

On Friday afternoon, parents went for the final program to hear the children sing, recite, and show what they had learned during the week. Afterward, Pastor Evers had them all go down to the creek, where he baptized several children.

Dawn was one of them.

Later, when they ate what the women had brought to the schoolyard, Dawn came up to him and Molly while they were filling their plates. Dawn's face was glowing and her eyes shining. She put her arms around his and Molly's waists. "I'm forgiven, Pa, Molly."

"Yes," he whispered, and the three of them hugged. After Dawn ran off to be with her friends, Molly looked at him and smiled.

"Thank you," he said. "If you hadn't come here and helped plan that Bible school, this may not have happened. At least, not at this time."

"Oh, Jonas, seeing all those children learning this week and some of them taking Jesus into their hearts and being baptized makes me feel so good—like the Lord can use us, even in our inadequacies."

"You're far from that," he said.

She turned and spooned green beans onto her plate.

That night it rained.

He, Molly, and the children gathered in the front room. Caleb had learned he could play with his toys all over the room, instead of having to be right at Molly's feet, on her lap, or holding on to her as if she might go away. Molly was teaching Dawn embroidery.

Molly looked at Jonas. "This is one of the crafts the children were learning at Bible school."

Jonas smiled. He tried to concentrate on reading a book, but his thoughts focused on the pleasure this family-type group gave him, instead of the sense of loss he'd felt for so long.

After a while, Dawn laid down her embroidery. "My arm is tired."

"Rest your arm," Molly said. "The embroidery should help make your wrist and fingers stronger. Next time, you'll be able to go longer."

"Aunt Molly," Dawn said softly. "Now that I'm not being so bad, could you stay? I really like having you here."

Jonas held his breath, and Molly seemed to do the same. Her fingers stopped. Her mouth opened and no words came. Finally they did. "Your pa can't live out the rest of his life in the lean-to, Dawn."

"If you children are having a snack before you go to bed, you'd better get it," Jonas told them.

Dawn walked over and whispered in his ear. "You could marry her, Pa."

Marry? He stared at Molly, wondering if she'd heard. Her eyes were lowered to the embroidery, and her fingers were moving.

His mind shouted that he was already married—to Sarah.

No. Sarah was gone.

"Get your snack," he said to Dawn.

I can't.

Can I?

It was as if Molly answered for him. "Jonas," she said softly. "If it's all right, Harley would like to take me to dinner at the restaurant in Poplar Grove tomorrow night."

"That's up to you," he said.

She shook her head. "No. It's up to you."

He stood, tried to laugh lightly as he headed for the kitchen. Looking over his shoulder he tossed out the words, "I think I can handle the children for one evening."

～

The children were asleep, and Jonas sat in the front room again trying to concentrate on his reading when he heard voices at the door. When Molly opened it, Harley stuck his head in and spoke to Jonas, then left.

Bedtime had passed a long time ago. Jonas got up to leave. "Have a good time?"

Molly closed the door. "Yes and no."

"Is something wrong, Molly?"

"Yes, there is, Jonas. I'm—going to have to leave."

All sorts of possibilities hounded his mind. She was going to marry Harley? She couldn't take this cove life any longer? She'd fulfilled her purpose and now it was time to move on?

He said the words he'd heard her say so many times. Her reasons really weren't his business. He couldn't ask why, so he said, "I understand."

"No, I don't think you do. Jonas, could we sit down?"

He really didn't want to. He wanted to escape to that lean-to. He didn't want to hear that she was in love with Harley Sullivan.

She sat on the sofa. He sat in a chair near her.

"Jonas, there was a letter waiting for me in town. My uncle has had a stroke."

"A stroke," was all Jonas could manage. That was not one of the possibilities in his head.

"Aunt Mae says she needs me."

We need you, too, he could have said. Dawn was just beginning to accept the loss of her mama. And he. . .

No, he couldn't mention what he needed. He wasn't even sure. He could only nod. He had to put away selfish thoughts. This was another tragedy in Molly's life.

"Jonas, I know there are needs here. But I've never let my aunt and uncle know that I appreciate what they have done for me. I need to thank them before I can move on with my life."

What kind of moving on did she mean? Having a life with Harley?

"I suppose you need to go right away."

She nodded. "Harley had planned to leave sometime this week. So he and I will leave together on Monday. That will give me tomorrow to help Dawn and Caleb understand."

❧

The next day was difficult for Molly. Any decision about leaving or staying in Pine Hollow was no longer her decision to make. Dawn listened. "Can't your aunt take care of your uncle?"

"I suppose she could. But they took care of me since I was eight years old. I need to go and let them know that I appreciate that. I called Aunt Mae from Poplar Grove. The doctors say Uncle Bob may not live long."

Dawn was silent a long while. "I wish you could stay."

"So do I," Molly said.

Dawn's eyes brightened. "Will you come back after you tell your aunt and uncle you appreciate them?"

"I have to find out how ill he is, Dawn. My aunt says he is paralyzed on his left side. I can't say what will happen."

Telling Caleb wasn't easy. He clung to her and begged her not to go. She told him that her uncle was sick, and she had to go and help take care of him for a while. Jonas did his part helping the children understand she had to go.

She was hoping Jonas might talk with her later, ask her to come back. She had tried to make it clear she preferred the mountains to the city, was needed to teach if she wanted to, and loved mingling with the women of the hollow.

Would he hold her like he had beneath the mulberry tree and ask her to come back?

He didn't.

It was Dawn who said, "When your uncle gets well, you can come back."

While Jonas stood aside, Molly fell to her knees and drew Dawn and Caleb to her and hugged them. "Oh, I love you so."

❧

Harley and his pa drove up early Monday morning. They helped Jonas put Molly's trunks in the wagon, next to Harley's bag.

The only person on the premises who looked happy was Harley. Dawn behaved bravely, but Jonas knew well that reserve of hers and the kind of emotions she tried to hide. He felt it himself. He kept telling himself to stop being selfish and think about that poor man in the city who had a stroke and needed Molly—like he had.

Like he did.

The children and Molly again said tearful good-byes, and Caleb again told her to make Uncle Bob well and come back.

"If I can't come soon, you can visit me in the city." She looked at Dawn. "I said *visit*."

Dawn nodded. "I'd like that."

Jonas didn't know what to do. Harley watched with a grin on his face as if he knew something Jonas didn't. But Jonas figured he did know. This young man, who had been Jonas's hired hand for two summers, was now taking off with. . .

With what? The woman of his dreams? Leaving ol' Jonas there to fend for himself.

Well, he couldn't cling to Molly like Caleb had, and ask her to stay. He was a grown man. He held out his hand. Molly extended hers, and he shook it and couldn't find any words to say, except, "I can't thank you enough, Molly, for all you've done for this family."

Her eyes looked wet. "We have moved a few mountains together, Jonas."

He squinted as if the sun bothered his eyes and nodded.

They let go.

He and the children watched the departing wagon wheels stir up dust. They still stared long after the dust had settled.

His gaze moved beyond to the mountains. Yes, they'd moved some. But sometimes a person gets over one and another crops up. "Well," he said. "I'd better get my things and move back into the house."

"Want me to help you?" Dawn asked.

"If you'd like. But, Dawn, I don't want you thinking you have to take over what your mama used to do."

"I know," she said. "But I'll do what I can."

"That's all anybody can do," he said.

A little later, he stood in the bedroom. Sarah's and Molly's clothes were gone from the closet. They both had slept in that bed. He would turn the mattress.

When Caleb wanted to run around a bush and sing the mulberry song, could Jonas do it? How would it be to sit in church and not hear her voice? Would he stop singing again? He'd have to sit at the table alone and drink his coffee.

He'd have to rock on the porch with his glass alone. No, he couldn't do that. He didn't even know how to make sweet tea.

Chapter 20

M y, you look a lot different from when you came up last week to get the flowers for that iron pot." Birdie gave Jonas a long look.

"I'm sad," Caleb said. "Mowwy went away." He stuck out his lower lip.

"Her uncle's sick," Dawn added.

Birdie nodded. "Yes, I heard that. I'm so sorry, Jonas. Is she coming back when he's better?"

Jonas shrugged. "I don't know."

She gave him a long look. "You didn't ask?"

The only thing he could think of to say was, "She left with Harley."

Birdie reared back. "Ha. That whippersnapper."

Caleb began to flap his arms and say, "Wippuhsnappuh, wippuhsnappuh, wippuhsnappuh."

"Jonas," she said. "I know that Molly was thinking of staying in the hollow. But she's not going to come back unless she knows you want her to."

He looked at his children, who were staring at him like he was a villain. They were all trying, but since Molly left, Caleb asked about her every day, always at bedtime. Dawn wanted to know when Jesus was going to help her feel better about Molly's being gone. His daughter was beginning to question her faith.

Faith.

Hadn't he already seen a lot of mountains move? He'd even said it. Shouldn't he have faith that Molly would come back to them? Didn't he at least have to take a step of faith?

Birdie pointed her finger at him when he looked at her again. She must have seen a difference. "Jonas McLean, I'll be at your cabin early in the morning—in time for you to catch that train to the city."

Have faith. Have faith. Have faith.

That's what the train wheels sang while chugging down the mountain.

When Jonas arrived at Molly's house in a horse-drawn cab, he saw an automobile on the road by the sidewalk. Jonas stopped and stared as Molly came out of the house, so beautiful in her city clothes. She stepped down from the porch and opened a parasol that matched her dress.

He'd worn a suit for this—and a hat. He removed his hat.

Molly's gasp and open mouth as she hurried toward him was like a sweet

335

welcome. She held out her gloved hands. "Jonas." Concern touched her eyes. "Are the children all right?"

"Yes, in the way you mean," he said. "But they miss you."

"I miss them, too."

"I should pay my respects to your aunt and uncle."

She glanced toward the automobile. "The doctor is with Uncle Bob now."

He told himself he mustn't stall. "Molly, if we got married, you and I. . ." He looked down and saw that his knuckles were white from grasping the rim of his hat so tightly. Looking up again, it seemed a light had turned on inside her. "For the sake of the children. I know how you love them and. . ."

His voice trailed off. He followed her gaze and saw a horse-drawn carriage pull up. Harley alighted, rushed up, and slapped Jonas on the back, then shook his hand.

"Jonas. Good to see you." Then, looking like someone turned a light on inside his head, he glanced at Molly and back at Jonas. He smiled broadly. "Molly and I were going into town. She spends so much time helping out here, Aunt Mae insisted she take a breather since the doctor was coming. Join us?"

Jonas glanced at Molly, who didn't second Harley's proposal.

She wasn't commenting on Jonas's proposal—or saying anything to Harley that would indicate she would accept what Jonas had said.

He never should have come here.

He should have known Harley would be courting her. He'd come calling in the hollow. The comparison stuck out in Jonas's mind like a six-story hotel compared with a one-level, flat-roofed building.

Jonas could only offer a secondhand husband who had two children and lived the kind of life that depended on hard work and the weather.

Harley offered the comforts and conveniences of city life.

Jonas's fingers began traveling around the rim of the hat he held in front of him—a sad comparison to the top hat Harley held. "The pastor of the church I attended when I went to the university here made me promise to drop in on him whenever I was here. I need to do that, then leave on the first train in the morning to get back to the children."

Molly wasn't saying that he should join them. Nor was she saying they could talk later. Her silence was his answer.

Here was Harley, a direct comparison between a gentleman and a farmer/mountain teacher. How could Jonas have even considered offering Molly his children in exchange for a life of excitement in the city? He was a foolish man.

"I. . .must go," Jonas said.

Molly looked as if she might cry and whispered, "Good-bye, Jonas. Tell the children hello for me."

Harley popped his hat onto his head. "I plan to visit my parents as soon as I get a break from school. I'm hoping to have an announcement to make." His eyebrows rose, along with the corners of his mouth, and he flicked the brim of his hat.

"Would you like for me to call a cab?" Molly asked.

"No, no." Jonas lifted his hand as he hurried down the path to the sidewalk. With such a desire to leave this place and his humiliation, he'd likely be able to reach the depot long before a runaway horse could.

He'd rather walk.

He felt like running—from his foolishness and humiliation.

He rented a room in a hotel near the depot. Somehow in his fanciful thinking, he'd imagined she missed him and the children so much she would agree immediately. He would then take her to dinner at a fancy restaurant. They would return, and he would take her in his arms, like at the mulberry tree, but this time—

No! Such thoughts must not linger. She belonged to Harley now. They would come to the mountains and announce their engagement. Harley's parents would be so pleased. The hollow people would be pleased. His children would be glad to see her. She would bring gifts.

Jonas didn't think he could stand it. The heaviness in his chest was not from almost running down the many blocks to town. He felt like running all the way back to the cove where he belonged.

As soon as he got into his hotel room, he washed his face in cold water, trying to take away the burning humiliation on his skin and the stinging dryness in his eyes.

The water ran over his hands. He could hear her and the children singing, "This is the way we wash our hands."

There would be no more of that.

He had allowed seeds of love to grow in his heart and mind. He knew he and Molly had grown closer, had learned to be friends, had related better and better the longer she stayed.

She had made him laugh again, hope again.

Obviously, this was not God's will for his life or hers.

He must accept that. *Dear God, I didn't expect to love again. It grew on me. But now I must wash my hands of the entire matter. She can never be mine.*

He stared as the water flowed over his hands, fell into the basin, and disappeared down the drain.

Just like his hopes.

In less than a second, Molly went from feeling like a bird soaring high in the air to one that was suddenly shot by a rifle and dropped to the ground.

"If we got married," was only the beginning of Jonas's sentence. "For the sake of the children," he'd added.

Never had she been so grateful for an interruption when Harley arrived. Sarah had told her once she wished that Molly could know what it was like to live with a good man like Jonas.

Although Molly had slept in the cabin and Jonas in the barn for a couple of months, she did learn something about what it would be like living with a good man like Jonas. She could not bear to marry him and be like a servant in his cabin, loving him but not being loved.

When she returned from her outing with Harley, which had been filled with activity and excitement that kept her mind off herself for the most part, Aunt Mae said Uncle Bob wasn't improving, but they could keep him comfortable.

"I hope he can hear me, Aunt Mae," Molly said. "I never told him, because I didn't know how much I appreciate what the two of you did for me."

"You were the joy of his life, Molly. He didn't need to be told. Telling my parents they were appreciated never occurred to me either. Come, let's get some lemonade and sit on the front porch."

They went out on the porch. It reached across the entire front of the house and was bordered by a white banister. Molly realized she had spent many good times here. She'd held on to hurt and guilt for so long. But she really never doubted that her aunt and uncle loved her.

They sat on the brightly colored, flower-print cushions in the white rocking chairs. The hanging baskets of vines and pots of begonias reminded Molly of Birdie.

"Molly, Bob and I often wondered if we did the right thing. We knew you were so sad, but I thought we could make up for it and you would adjust. Then time passed. It seemed wrong to send you back then, and take you out of school and piano lessons, the church, your friends. And I was selfish. I couldn't bear to lose you after having you come here."

"Being with Jonas and his children has taught me that, Aunt Mae. But when I came here, I felt like I was being punished. I was just a foolish child."

"No." Aunt Mae reached over and patted her arm. "You were just a hurting child. I knew that but didn't know what to do about it."

"Aunt Mae, I don't know if it was right for Papa to send me to you. But it happened. I want to thank you for taking me in."

Aunt Mae was shaking her head. "It wasn't 'taking you in,' Molly. It was giving you a home and loving you."

Molly nodded. "I know that now. I guess I'm a slow learner."

"It's not always easy knowing the exact thing to do, Molly. Just as you've told me about Dawn and that you weren't sure how to handle her."

Molly nodded. "I don't know what my life would have been like if I had stayed in the cove with Papa and Sarah. Maybe I would have had a loving husband and children, like Sarah did."

Molly turned her face away from Aunt Mae. But when she soothed, "Oh, my dear, my dear," she exhaled heavily and turned again toward her aunt, knowing she could confide in her about anything. She was a very loving woman.

"But I wouldn't have had the opportunities that you and Uncle Bob gave me. I wouldn't have had the love you and Uncle Bob gave me. Without Mama, Papa wasn't the same. And Sarah couldn't give a mother's love. You did."

"There are advantages and disadvantages all around, Molly. We make a lot of our own choices, but some things in life just come to us that are not our doing. Like me and Bob never having children. And why did we live instead of your mama? Those things are out of our hands."

Aunt Mae nodded. "We didn't take you back there for a long time, thinking that would cause more heartache. After a few years, when I took you to visit—when the train tracks were finally laid to the town near Pine Hollow, Sarah was eighteen and in love with that strapping, good-looking young man who was getting his education, and she planned to marry him after he graduated. We knew you had never let go of your dream of living in the mountains again, but we didn't think it right to have you live with the newlyweds. Were we wrong, Molly? Was I wrong?"

"Until recently, I would have said yes. But looking back on it now, I think you were probably right. About separating me and Sarah, I'm not sure. But, no, I don't think it would have been right for me to go back to the mountains as a young girl, after having lived in the city for years."

Molly marveled that she could sit and talk this way with Aunt Mae. A couple of months ago, she never would have believed it. "Thank you," she said. "Aunt Mae?"

"Yes."

"I love you."

"Oh, honey. I have hoped and prayed for the day when we could sit and talk like this. I never had a daughter, so I don't know how to compare. But I have always loved you with my whole heart."

Molly nodded. "I know."

They sat and rocked and drank their lemonade. It reminded Molly of the night she and Jonas sat with their tea on his porch. They'd held hands and she felt so close to him that night.

She had learned so much in those two months with him. The blessings were so numerous, she must not pine for what could not be—just count her blessings.

So much was finally right in her heart and mind. By having that difficult time with Dawn, she had learned how to love and forgive—most of all, forgive herself.

She had so many blessings, she must not complain to God—just thank Him.

Chapter 21

Jonas had just entered the church when Harley came up behind him. "Let me shake your hand, Jonas."

Jonas turned to face the young man who looked like the sun itself was shining inside him. "Jonas, you've been an example of what a husband should be like, and I hope I can be that to the woman I will spend the rest of my life with."

Jonas shook his hand. Yes, he'd set the right example, all right. He'd fallen in love with Molly, and so had Harley.

Jonas led his children to his usual seat near the front. Before the sermon, the preacher announced that he was happy to have Harley back visiting with them and that he had brought along his fiancée. The people could greet her after the service.

So Molly had come, too. She must be staying at the hotel or with Harley's parents. She'd probably come by with gifts for the children later on.

Dawn and Caleb both looked back but didn't make a fuss. Caleb only said, "Wippuhsnappuh" twice.

Maybe they had accepted that Molly was gone for good.

That's what he needed to do, too.

Telling himself to guard his emotions, after church he gathered his children and walked up the aisle. When he reached the yard he saw a puzzling sight. People were greeting Harley and a woman who was obviously from the city by the way she was dressed.

That was not Molly. Harley's parents were nearby, receiving congratulations, too.

The young woman accepted hugs and kept on smiling. She and Harley often exchanged glances that appeared to be of more than friendship.

Jonas told himself not to believe what he was seeing. He walked up to them. Harley looked at the young woman. "Marylee, this is one of my best friends, Jonas McLean. Jonas, this is Marylee Walker, my fiancée. She just finished her last year at the university where we met."

Jonas shook her gloved hand, and for some strange reason felt jubilant to meet her.

On the way home, he warned himself that his joy was unfounded. Just because Harley and Molly weren't engaged to each other didn't make his situation any different.

Did it?

MOVING THE MOUNTAIN

One minute he wanted to go back to the city and talk to Molly. The next minute he was telling himself not to humiliate them both again.

After a couple of days, he took the children and rode up to see Pastor Evers. "I need some advice," he said.

"You two go out on the porch," Birdie said. "I just made some hot gingerbread. I'll take the children in the kitchen and give them some with milk. You want some?"

As good as that sounded, Jonas said maybe later, so Ira said no.

Jonas told him everything. From his initial resentment that he had to ask Molly for help. The change she'd made in him. Her own difficult growing-up years. The mountains they had overcome concerning her guilt, his grief, and Dawn's fears. "I tried to keep the faith, Pastor. But this situation seems to be a mountain I can't get over."

The front screen creaked, and Birdie came out. "Jonas McLean. You didn't say you told Molly you love her."

He should have known Birdie would be listening. "Not in so many words. But I... We..."

"Yes, I heard you say you kissed, and you held hands. Now does that tell a person you love them?"

"I guess not necessarily."

"And I heard you spouting that verse about faith moves mountains like that's the only verse in the Bible. Don't you know any other verses?"

He didn't know what he'd done to deserve this kind of reprimand. "I've heard a few."

"Well, try this one. Comes straight out of Corinthians. The verse says you can have the gift of faith so you could speak to the mountain and make it move, but without love you'd be no good to anybody."

Jonas looked at the pastor, who shook his head. "Now you know where I get the inspiration for many of my sermons. Birdie makes a good point, Jonas."

But Birdie wasn't finished preaching. "No woman is going to know you love her—no matter what you do—unless you tell her."

Pastor Evers spoke up then. "Birdie, that might be the way to a woman's heart, but we know the way to a man's is through his stomach. I'm ready for some of that gingerbread now."

She stared at him. He sighed and said, "I'll love you even more if you bring me some gingerbread. Please?"

Birdie looked triumphant. "See?"

ॐ

Jonas "saw."

But he couldn't believe he could go up to Molly, say "I love you," and she'd just fall into his arms. She might not even be in love with him.

Suddenly, something occurred to him. Molly had said, looking back, she

341

hadn't been in love with Percival Pierpont. Now how did she know that if she'd never been in love?

Was there a chance?

He wasn't sure he had faith that she loved him; but without finding out, at least letting her know, he was like what Birdie said, no good to anybody.

He needed to find a way to show Molly he loved her, not just stumble around on the words.

Harley was still in the hollow, so Jonas talked to him about his plan. Harley was eager to help. After Harley returned to the city, he sent word to Jonas that he found what Jonas wanted.

Jonas didn't tell the children where he was going, in case things didn't work out right. But Birdie was more than willing to keep them while he rode the train to the city and went to the place where Harley said the gift would be waiting.

Since the gift wouldn't fit in just any conveyance, Jonas hired a driver and wagon to take him to Molly's, then took it to her front door.

Molly came to the door and opened the screen. "Jonas? What—?"

"Molly, you gave me a gift, remember? I want to give you a gift that means something. So, here's a mulberry tree for you."

He'd rendered her speechless, but he mustn't be. "When I came here before, I asked if you'd marry me for the children. I thought if you did, you might learn to love me. But, Molly, I want to marry you because I love you."

He couldn't tell if she was about to laugh or cry or both. He supposed it was silly of him. She looked at him, at the tree, and back at him. "A mulberry tree," she said.

"If you think you can ever love me, let me know. If you can't, I still want you to know that I'm grateful for what you brought into my life and the lives of my children. I would like for you to be as much a part of our lives as you might want. They are remembering you as the beautiful, wonderful woman that you are. They love you, Molly. So do I. This is a symbol of my love. Can you accept it?"

Molly was totally shocked. That was the funniest, sweetest, weirdest thing she'd ever seen.

The mulberry song had been Caleb's connection with his mother and with her. The mulberry pie incident is what brought her and Dawn together in honesty.

Now she must be honest with Jonas and herself. "Jonas, is this because you see some of Sarah in me?"

He took a deep breath. "I kept telling myself that. I felt unfaithful when I saw you instead of Sarah. I tried so hard. But, Molly, it is you. Yes, I see Sarah in you. But I love Molly Pierpont—for herself."

Molly looked at him, the sincerity in his eyes, in his words—remembered his lips on hers when they both tasted of mulberries. Now Jonas was using the mulberry tree as a symbol of his love and his hope that she could love him.

She reached out and grasped the trunk of the small tree, trying to find the words to respond. Upon hearing wailing from the parlor and her aunt calling her name, she had to say, "Jonas, my uncle died today."

～

Jonas went inside and expressed his condolences to Aunt Mae and his obligation to return to his children. He bade them good-bye, saying, "God bless" to Aunt Mae and another sincere "thank you" to Molly.

"Thank you," she returned, while holding the hand of her aunt, who smiled despite her tears.

On the ride back up the mountain, he did not feel embarrassment or rejection. Even if she couldn't return his love the way he wanted, she knew she was loved. He felt good about that.

Leaving the flatlands and seeing mountain peaks coming into view, he thought how that train ride was like life. It was full of curves—up and down, around and around, and sometimes he felt like he was going in circles and couldn't see the destination.

Even if he could not have Molly, he learned that he could love again. Molly couldn't replace Sarah, just as Dawn and Caleb couldn't replace the children he and Sarah had lost.

It wasn't about replacement.

It was just another step in life.

I've learned, Lord, he prayed to the rhythm of the train puffing around the mountains, *that I can make it without my Sarah, without my babies, and now—even without Molly. Maybe You brought her into my life to thaw out my frozen heart, to teach my children what sacrificial love is, to have them realize they can be loved and can love again.*

I don't understand everything. In fact, I don't understand much at all. But I understand my attitude makes all the difference. I can look outward and see evil or good, ugliness or beauty. I can look inside for that, too. Thank You, Lord, that You can take away the bitterness and replace it with sweet.

What lies beyond life is better—and eternal.

But while I'm here, Lord, I'm now trusting You with all my heart and mind and soul. Here's my life. When I take it back, forgive me.

Help me not to pout. Just trust You.

Someday I'll be up there with You and I hope to hear, "Well done, thou good and faithful servant."

And, Lord, I'm not asking You for Molly. Maybe that's not Your plan. If it's not, I'm not going to like it, but I'm going to trust You anyway. The best I can.

After he returned home, Dawn and Caleb seemed to accept his answer; he couldn't say when Molly would return for a visit, but he knew she would not abandon them altogether. They prayed for her each night.

He prayed silently that she would find the love she deserved.

Chapter 22

L ook, Pa, look!"
Jonas stood from where he'd been bending over in the cabbage patch.
Caleb shouted, "Mama!" He looked at Jonas and stuck out his lip and changed it to, "Mowwy," for Molly.

Which is it? Jonas wondered.

The children ran toward the wagon where the driver was taking the mulberry tree out of the back. Molly knelt and they hugged, all talking at the same time.

When Jonas walked up, Molly stood and faced him. "The city's no place for a mulberry tree."

He dared to dream this beautiful creature, with her hair the color of corn silk shining in the afternoon sunlight and her eyes as blue as the sky, might be coming to him. Or was she returning the tree?

"Are you returning the tree?"

"I'm returning me. Jonas McLean, you asked me to marry you and don't you go backing out."

"Never," he said.

The driver called, "Sir, could you help me with the trunks?"

"Maybe you'd better get your wagon, Jonas. We can take them to Birdie's, and if it's not convenient for me to stay with them until the wedding, we can take them to town and I'll stay at the hotel."

Jonas glanced at the cabin. "I do have a place here."

"Why, Jonas McLean. Wash your mouth with soap. An aunt can stay in your house, but a fiancée cannot. I expect to be courted before the wedding."

"My pleasure, ma'am," he said and told the driver he'd be right there with his wagon.

After they put the trunks in Jonas's wagon, while the children were filling Molly in on what they'd been doing and all that was going on, Jonas went into the barn. He returned with a shovel.

"Maybe we'd better plant this near the creek," Molly said. "Mulberries drop to the ground easily and can be quite messy on shoes and bare feet. I don't want my house tracked up."

"Sassy as Birdie." He grinned, so full of joy and excitement he could hardly contain it. From the looks of Molly, he thought she felt the same. "By the creek," he said. "That will do until we have to dig it up and plant it near our new house up the mountain."

Molly blinked at the moisture he saw in her loving eyes, and she nodded.

They went to the creek; Jonas dug a hole and planted the tree. He held out his hands. They danced around the tree and sang the mulberry song.

"I've never heard a more romantic song," Molly said and laughed.

Jonas gazed into her eyes. "Neither have I. And it's coming straight from my heart."

He thought he could stand it no longer. "Children, go get a couple of buckets so we can water the tree. Hurry."

They took off.

"I was so afraid you might not love me."

"Oh, I do, Jonas. When I knew I was falling in love with you, I tried to be cautious, not wanting my childhood dreams of returning home and having a family to be mistaken for love. I knew I loved you that day when we kissed and you tasted like mulberries."

"So did you. I almost died from the sweetness."

She smiled. "I would have come sooner, but I had to make sure Aunt Mae would be all right. Her sister, Edna, came; and they insisted I leave and come here, where Aunt Mae said I belonged."

Yes, this is where she belonged. He embraced her. Their lips met while they stood by the mulberry tree. This time he was in no hurry to move away.

When they broke the embrace, she lay her head against his chest. She whispered, "I feel like I've come home, Jonas. I'm home."

Since neither Jonas nor Molly wanted to waste any time before getting married, Aunt Mae and Edna came to help with plans. Jonas moved back into the lean-to and gave Mae and Edna the bedroom. Edna's husband had been dead for years. Her children had married and moved away, and she missed her grandchildren.

The two women doted on Dawn and Caleb and found the mountain way of life quite challenging. Molly stayed with Birdie and Pastor Evers.

Jonas courted Molly. He took her for long walks along the creek, up the mountain to talk about the house they could plan for their present family and any children they might have later.

He took her to dinner at the hotel in Poplar Grove, and Molly proudly sported the ring the two of them picked out at a jewelry store when they'd gone to bring Mae and Edna to the mountains.

"I've already had a big wedding," Molly said to Jonas one evening when he returned her to the Evers's home. "This time, I'm not planning a wedding. I'm planning a marriage."

"Don't you want the ceremony to be in the church?" Jonas asked.

Molly thought. "Pastor Evers says a church isn't a building; it's the people. So I'd like it to be outdoors on the land you're donating to the church. Where we had the festival."

"Suppose it rains?"

She said what he had said about the festival. "Then we'll have it the next day."

The following day they shared their plans with Mae and Edna.

Aunt Mae said, "Someday I hope I'll be more like a grandmother to the children than their great-aunt."

"Aunt Mae, I know the children will love you as much as I do."

"Thank you, dear." She placed her hand on her heart and looked like she might be having a nervous attack. Excitement shone in her eyes. "Well, considering their ages, I'm way past spoiling them. We'll just have to make up for that. So while you and Jonas are on your honeymoon, the children can stay with me in the city. Edna and I can take care of them."

"I don't know what Jonas will say."

Aunt Mae straightened her shoulders. "I'm going to be a proper grandmother. I have something to say about this. Where are you going on your honeymoon and for how long? I need to start making plans."

Had Aunt Mae been that excited when she expected Molly to come and live with her and Uncle Bob? Oh, how Molly must have robbed her of that enthusiasm, much like Dawn had put a damper on Molly's excitement.

Aunt Mae looked at Dawn, then Caleb. "Just as soon as they say 'I do,' you can call me Grandmama."

"Gammama," Caleb said.

Mae hugged him. "Oh, you precious boy."

Dawn gave her a long look, then smiled. "I never had a grandmama before."

Molly went over and put her hand on Mae's shoulder. "I think it's time I called you Mama."

Tears sparkled in Mae's eyes. She put her hand on Molly's. "Oh, honey. You've made me the happiest woman in the world."

"I love you," Molly said, wishing the whole world could hear her. "I really love you."

⁓

Molly sat in a carriage with Harley seated as the driver, surprised at the big crowd that had gathered for her wedding. Birdie must have invited those from Coalville, Poplar Grove, Pine Hollow, and Black Mountain. There were at least a hundred people, if not more. They stood in rows, dressed in their finery, leaving a grassy aisle for Molly to walk down, toward the structure held up by a trellis Birdie had decorated with vines, pastel narcissus, and baby's breath.

Jonas and Pastor Evers took their places beneath the structure.

Birdie had put herself in charge of the music and there'd been no rehearsal, so Molly didn't know what to expect. She was pleased when two men who had played at the festival stood and played the hauntingly beautiful "Love Divine, All Loves Excelling" on harmonicas.

MOVING THE MOUNTAIN

Aunt Mae cued Caleb to begin his trek down the aisle. He was the most adorable ring bearer ever in his dark suit with short pants, his blond hair gleaming in the sunshine, and his eyes straight ahead. He walked slowly, holding the white cushion in front of him.

Dawn, looking beautiful in her new blue dress, scattered pink rose petals and took her place beside Caleb.

Molly exited the carriage. Aunt Edna straightened Molly's long veil and assured her that she looked beautiful. She had chosen an ivory gown with a high neck, long sleeves, and a bodice of seed pearls and lace. A blue sash adorned her waist. Aunt Edna handed her the bouquet of pink roses and baby's breath.

To Molly's delight, Marylee stood opposite Dawn and Caleb. She began to sing in a lovely soprano voice, "O Perfect Love."

Aunt Edna nodded, and Molly took a step. She almost laughed, realizing this was the spot where she hadn't won a prize for a pie. Now she walked on rose petals toward the most handsome man in the world, looking so grand in his dark blue suit, light blue shirt, with a white flower in his lapel.

He looked like she felt—about ready to burst with happiness. He held out his arm. She placed her hand on it and they faced Pastor Evers.

"Friends, we are gathered here today to join this man and this woman in holy matrimony. . . ."

❧

After Pastor Evers said, "You may kiss the bride," Jonas did. That initiated applause, shouts, harmonica playing, guitar picking; and men began singing, "Here We Go Round the Mulberry Bush." Everyone laughed.

With her hands on her hips, Molly shook her finger at Jonas. "You did that!"

He grinned. "Well, it's our song."

"So it is," she said. And he kissed the bride again.

Caleb tugged on their clothes. Jonas picked him up. "Caleb, Molly's going to live with us now. It's all right now if you call her Mama."

Molly touched his arm. "But you don't have to. I am your aunt Molly. Your mama is in heaven. She loved you very much."

He nodded and looked like he understood. After a thoughtful moment, his face broke into a smile. He boldly proclaimed, "Mama."

"Oh." That sweet embrace of his went straight to her heart. After a long moment, she opened her eyes. Dawn's gaze met hers. Molly let go of Caleb and stood.

Dawn took a step closer and smiled tentatively.

Molly reached for her hands and held them. "Dawn, you don't have to even try to call me Mama. Nobody can replace your mama. But I can try to do the things a mama does."

Dawn wrinkled her nose and got a mischievous look in her eyes. "Some not too well."

The playful duck of Dawn's head meant the world to Molly. "You're right. But we'll make do. And we will never forget your mama. My being your papa's wife doesn't mean that he loves your mama any less. You will understand this when you're older. You'll have a man in your life, and children, and you'll love them completely. You won't love your papa and Caleb any less. There's room in the heart for many loves, without having to let any of them go."

Dawn nodded. Molly knew the young girl was trying to understand. She knew, too, such a thing was not fully understandable until she experienced it. Molly hadn't really understood the wonder of being loved by a man until Jonas. Nor had she felt that indefinable, all-encompassing joy of love until Jonas.

Dawn sighed heavily. "This is what I'm going to do. I will call you the first part of your name. It's spelled different, but sounds like 'Ma.' Some of my friends call their mama's 'Ma.' How about that?"

That was a huge step for a girl like Dawn. "That would be fine. And if you slip and call me 'Aunt Molly,' that's fine, too. Just don't call me anything like. . ."

She couldn't think of what she didn't want to be called. Dawn said it. "Like. . .a scared cat."

"Ohhh," Molly quipped. "Now you're thinking cows and chickens."

Dawn laughed. "Exactly."

Molly's laughter joined hers. What a beautiful sound. Then just as quickly, Dawn grew serious again, looking uncertain. "I might forget to stop at 'Ma' and say 'Mama.'"

Molly could only whisper, "That's fine."

Dawn came into her outstretched arms and held her tightly around the waist.

Enfolding her, Molly said, "I love you, Dawn. With all my heart."

She felt Dawn's nod and heard her whisper. "I love you—Ma." She was almost certain that was followed by another "ma." That didn't matter so much. What mattered was the feeling of love they both shared in that embrace. She finally felt Dawn's full acceptance.

She looked over at Jonas and Caleb, who came to join in the embracing. With Jonas's hand on Dawn's shoulder and the other hand in Caleb's, his lips formed the words, "I love you."

∽

Aunt Mae came up and held out her hand to Caleb, who looked up at her with big blue eyes. Molly had a sneaky feeling Aunt Mae had won his heart.

Aunt Mae led him away to the food tables for the three-tiered cake Birdie had made. BethAnn and Earlene, looking like city women, served tea and lemonade.

Edna handed an envelope to Molly. She gasped. "Oh, Aunt Edna." She looked around. Jonas was holding out his plate for cake. "Jonas, come here."

"Can't you see I'm getting a piece of cake? Are you starting to nag already?"

he said with a wink.

"Well, I guess I can go on my honeymoon alone."

"Whoa!" He set his plate down in a hurry and ran toward her, causing others to laugh. "No, you definitely will not," he said, putting his arm around her waist.

"Jonas," she warned.

"You're my wife," he said possessively.

She almost couldn't look away from his loving eyes. Yes, she was his wife. She leaned toward him. "Look at this."

The playfulness left his face as he seriously regarded the train tickets in her hand. Two round-trip tickets to Charleston.

"That's my home," Edna said. "I can't leave Mae to take care of those two rambunctious young'uns by herself. I'm going to stay with her awhile anyway. So you two just go to my house—it's at the beach—and make yourself at home."

Molly feared he wouldn't accept such a generous gift. He let go of her waist and held out his arms to Edna.

"Thank you—Aunt Edna."

They embraced; then she stepped back. "*Now*, he claims relation."

He spoke seriously. "I'd be honored to have you as an aunt."

"Well, you've got me, like it or not. And I guess one of these days I'll just have to share my house with my—with Mae's grandchildren. It's a great vacation spot."

Aunt Mae gave them a generous monetary gift.

⁓

Later Jonas said, "I think I got the best of the deal here, Molly. I've married into a very fine, generous, loving family. You women are the best."

"I'm beginning to realize that, too, Jonas. A family shares what they have. Imagine if you had refused Edna's and Mae's gifts."

"It would have been wrong. And I could see Aunt Mae's need to shower love on my—our children. She wants to be a grandma."

His lips were very close to hers. She looked into his loving eyes. "For a while," she said, "I thought loving you was a mountain I couldn't move."

"Life is full of mountains, but we can move them." Right before his lips touched hers, he added, "With love."

MOLLY'S MULBERRY CRUMBLE

Filling
  6 cups mulberries (any species)
  ½ cup orange juice
  2 tablespoons arrowroot
  1 ½ tablespoons wild mint
  2 teaspoons vanilla extract
  ½ teaspoon almond extract
  2 tablespoons honey

Topping
  2 ½ cups fresh bread crumbs
  1 cup corn oil
  1 cup chopped nuts (any kind)
  ½ teaspoon salt
  1 teaspoon ground cinnamon

Pour filling into baking dish or pan.
Press topping on top of filling; sprinkle the cinnamon on top.
Bake at 350 degrees for about 40 minutes until topping is golden brown.
Serves 6—serve hot or cold.

*Do not *sprinkle with salt.*

YVONNE LEHMAN

Yvonne lives in the panoramic mountains of western North Carolina. She is a best-selling, award-winning author of forty-five novels including the recently published Heartsong novels *By Love Acquitted* and *A Bride Idea* and a novella in the collection *Carolina Carpenter Brides*. Three of her novels will be in a collection, *North Carolina Weddings*, to be released in the fall of 2008. She is director of the Blue Ridge Mountains Christian Writers' Conference held annually in May (www.lifeway.com/christianwriters) and the "Autumn in the Mountains" Novel Retreat held annually in October (www.lifeway.com/autumninthemountains or www.lifeway.com/advancedchristianwriters). Visit her Web site at www.yvonnelehman.com.

A Letter to Our Readers

Dear Readers:

In order that we might better contribute to your reading enjoyment, we would appreciate your taking a few minutes to respond to the following questions. When completed, please return to the following: Fiction Editor, Barbour Publishing, Inc., P.O. Box 719, Uhrichsville, OH 44683.

1. Did you enjoy reading *Kentucky Brides*?
   ❑ Very much—I would like to see more books like this.
   ❑ Moderately—I would have enjoyed it more if _____
   _____
   _____

2. What influenced your decision to purchase this book?
   (Check those that apply.)
   ❑ Cover   ❑ Back cover copy   ❑ Title   ❑ Price
   ❑ Friends   ❑ Publicity   ❑ Other

3. Which story was your favorite?
   ❑ *Into the Deep*   ❑ *Moving the Mountain*
   ❑ *Where the River Flows*

4. Please check your age range:
   ❑ Under 18   ❑ 18–24   ❑ 25–34
   ❑ 35–45   ❑ 46–55   ❑ Over 55

5. How many hours per week do you read? _____

Name _____

Occupation _____

Address _____

City_____ State _____ Zip _____

E-mail_____